W9-BLJ-263

SHE DIDN'T WANT TO LOVE HIM . . .

A shaft of sunlight piercing through the branches of a cypress landed directly on Adam's muscular figure. Throat tight, Catherine could do no more than stare at him.

"I would like to claim my winnings now," he said, approaching her.

She closed her eyes to try to avoid the gaze that had settled on her face. "Please leave. It would be unkind to take advantage of me after all that has happened."

Tenderly, he reached out and pulled the pins out of her hair, watching her long curls tumble down across her shoulders and back.

"But we have already established that I am not a kind man," he whispered.

His head bent closer. Catherine's heart pounded and the warmth inside her began to build. She understood why she had been so dreading this moment . . . not because she expected his touch to repulse her . . . not because he might claim far more than a kiss . . . she had feared her own return of passions she had long denied.

His mouth slanted against hers, his arms pinning her tightly onto him. She shoved against his chest, the heels of her hands forced against his muscled strength, but she might as well have been trying to push back the passing of time. His embrace, far from painful, felt right and good and, most powerful of all, inevitable. She had been right to worry—a kiss would only be the start . . .

Chapter One

New Orleans
August, 1830

The moment Adam Gase stepped into the casino, he felt a tingling at the base of his neck, as though something important were about to happen.

Or maybe it was just that he wanted it to. He'd been out of prison one month and had yet to get near the revenge he was after. Maybe tonight was the night.

From the doorway, he took a careful look at the long, crowded foyer of the casino, at its mahogany-paneled walls and sparkling chandeliers. La Chatte de la Nuit, it was called.

"As fine a place to try your luck as any in Louisiana," someone in town had said.

But Adam was not seeking easy money. He was after the owner, Catherine Douchand.

"Bonsoir, m'sieur."

Adam glanced at the speaker, a tall, broad-shouldered man in frock coat and stiff-necked shirt. One of the employees, he decided from the assessing look in the man's eye, a watchman doubling as greeter at the gambling hall.

Unable to speak the language of the Creoles, Adam nodded a response, considered for a moment asking to

5

see the casino owner, then decided to look for himself. She was there, all right. The word on the streets of the city was that the beautiful Mademoiselle Douchand, rarely a visitor to town, was *always* there, drawing the men into the casino as much as did the cards and roulette.

She must be quite a woman to attract such a crowd on a steamy summer's night.

Especially when an evening of sharing her company with the other gamblers was all that they dared. If fortune smiled upon them, they might even share an intimate laugh, but nothing more.

"You know these Creoles," an American had told him over a glass of brandy. "They like beautiful women. And they like to possess one of their own."

She was, his hushed voice had added, widely known as the mistress of Emile Laverton, New Orleans's most mysterious and sinister resident. Others had agreed, but none had been willing to say anything else about the man. Adam saw they were afraid.

Her association with Laverton, not her beauty, had brought him out tonight. She would lead him to his enemy. For Adam, that would be enough.

To confront her—and better yet, her lover—he had donned suit and tie for the first time since his farce of a trial more than two years before. He had never been comfortable in the restrictions of such clothes; hard-muscled after the years of convict labor, he found himself even more uncomfortable now. But wearing a tight collar and restricting coat was the least he would do to get his hands around Emile Laverton's throat.

Making his way through the throng, he came to a sudden halt in the doorway to the main salon. The woman he had heard so glowingly described was standing a dozen feet away on the far side of the roulette table which centered the room, dark-suited men surrounding her as befitted a great beauty. Apart from a few servants, she was the only one of her sex he

6

had observed in the casino, but she would have drawn a crowd anywhere.

From the doorway Adam could see every turn of her lovely head, every twist of her silk-clad body, every shift of her thick-lashed eyes. The descriptions, he thought, had not done her justice.

Hair as black as the night rested against the stark white covering her shoulders. Her gown was high-necked, long-sleeved, and fitted to her frame, unlike the bosom-bared, full-skirted styles of the day.

Or at least the styles as Adam remembered them, his recent past having been spent in an uncivilized cypress swamp, his companions sharp-toothed alligators and jailers with twenty-foot whips. He'd had no dealings with women of any kind, beautiful or not, and had not sought them out during his few days in town. He had a great deal of catching up to do.

Beginning with Catherine Douchand.

At the end of the table, the croupier set the wheel in motion and called, *"Messieurs, faites vos jeux!"*

The gentlemen tossed their bets onto the red-and-black squares, and as gold coins began to pile high they turned their attention from their hostess to the spinning cylinder. More coins joined the stacks already in place.

Adam kept his eyes on the mademoiselle. Despite his avowed purpose for tonight's visit, the sight of her reminded his body of pleasures long denied. He could not draw his eyes away.

The nearest of her admirers bent a fair, slick-combed head to hers and whispered something only she could hear. She threw her head back, her swan neck arched and her breasts thrust against the confining silk of her gown, her silvery laugh issuing above the din. It was a distinctly feminine sound, softening the harsher noises of male voices, the rattle of the roulette wheel, the roll of dice.

Even the whirling cylinder could not hold completely the attention of the men beside her. It was no matter that they staked their fortunes on wherever the fickle ball might drop; a beautiful woman was not to be ignored.

The cylinder began to slow.

"Rien ne va plus," the croupier warned, and the betting ceased.

The wheel came to a stop, and a hush settled over the crowd.

"Dix-huit, rouge, pair, manque." As the croupier called out the winning combinations, he used a small rake to pull the coins into the pouch beside him. Few players were able to claim success.

No wonder Catherine Douchand laughed. By Adam's calculation, the casino had taken in several thousand dollars on that one spin of the wheel—and the wheel would spin half the night.

"La Chatte de la Nuit, she's called," said a man close by. Like Adam, he was staring at her. "Cat of the Night," he translated with a sneer for his ignorant American listener. "Like the name of the establishment. It is a name well chosen, *n'est-ce pas?"*

Adam ignored him.

The speaker persisted. "A true French beauty, worthy of a Paris salon. But one, alas, who is unattainable. We can do no more than admire her from afar. And honor her beauty and grace."

There was a trace of regret in his voice, and a slurring of speech as though he'd been sampling more than once the wine offered on silver trays by the casino's waiters. It was the alcohol, Adam suspected, that made him speak so volubly to a stranger, and an American stranger at that.

He spared a glance at the man, who, like himself and the other gamblers, was dressed in a black frock coat, a stiff white collar and black silk tie at his neck. He was young, no more than twenty-five, ten years Adam's junior, but there were lines about his mouth and eyes and a flush to his skin that gave evidence he had lived hard in those few years. Like most Creoles Adam had seen.

The man was short, his head coming just above Adam's shoulders, but as he leaned forward on the balls of his feet, he had a truculence about him that went with his height.

"There are many stories of La Chatte," he continued "It is said she came from nowhere, an orphan . . . a product of the convent, one story goes, but others say such is an *impossibilité*. No one claims to know her intimately." The regret was more evident than before, as though he would volunteer to investigate the mystery, if only the opportunity presented itself.

"Not even Emile Laverton?"

The man's expression changed from warm speculation to surprise and more, to a trace of fear. It was the same fear Adam had discovered in town.

He shot Adam a warning look. "It is a name that is not spoken lightly, m'sieur."

No, Adam thought, *I do not believe that it is. And for just cause.*

"There are those," the Creole continued, "who believe Laverton is no more than a ghost, an imagined figure about whom dreadful stories are told." He shrugged, once more the Gallic man-about-town. "As for myself, I prefer not to join in the talk of such a one. Life is much too short, do you not agree? I give no thought to whether or not he is real."

Life was short, all right, but Adam was willing to take a large portion of his remaining time to find the elusive Laverton. To find him and, after learning why justice had been scorned two years before in a New Orleans courtroom, maybe carry out a little justice of his own.

He turned his attention back to Laverton's mistress. She had not moved from her position, but he sensed she knew everything that passed in the large, smoke-

9

filled room, including his interest. He doubted she could know the cause. Let her believe he was like the other fools, interested in sampling her charms for the challenge she presented. His cause was his own; she would learn it soon enough.

Giving in for a time to his instincts, Adam savored the sight she presented. Her skin was dusky above the white throat of her gown, her eyes almond-shaped and an unusual shade of violet, like the night shadows in the Louisiana swamps. She was a woman who could give a man great pleasure, although he wondered how much pleasure she would take for herself. Despite her provocative appearance and the closeness of the men, she seemed to hold herself aloof, as though she were laughing both with and at them all at once.

Even while he reminded himself of his objective, he felt his body tighten, and he knew the old urges had not been beaten from him. She was, no matter her own purpose or desires, a woman made for providing satisfaction.

She settled her eyes on him. They were unreadable, but they lingered too long for idle curiosity. She was the first to look away. It seemed a victory to him, albeit a minor one.

He turned his attention to the crowds of men. Gamblers and pleasure seekers were all he saw, but he was not disappointed. He had not expected the mysterious Emile Laverton to be present tonight, but it could do little harm to mingle and perhaps learn where he might be found. If anyone was brave enough to tell what they knew.

Adam had no fear. He was beyond such weakness, just as he was beyond the call of the gambling tables around him. The room in which he stood was the casino's largest and most elegant. Crimson velvet and damask hung in graceful folds at the open windows, giltwork decorated the walls, and overhead hung a pair of glittering chandeliers that matched the ones

10

in the foyer.

A gentle night breeze sifted through the windows and eased the damp heat of the August night.

To his left were a half dozen small tables, at each of which two men devoted their lives and fortunes to the demands of *écarte,* a card game preferred by the Creole aristocracy. The less elegant Americans—or at least the less pretentious—could be found at the poker and faro tables on the opposite side of the salon. In the center were the roulette wheel and a second table devoted to the roll of dice; at the latter both Creoles and Americans mixed to try their gambling luck.

It was said the duc d'Orléans introduced the game of craps to Louisiana when he visited shortly before the turn of the century. Like many other vices, the game had taken hold in what was then a Spanish territory. Adam wondered if it were the climate which caused decadence to thrive.

"M'sieur," said the young speaker who had drifted away for a moment and then returned, a glass of wine in his hand. "This is your first time at La Chatte, is it not? Allow me to introduce myself. Gaston Ferrier, at your service."

Adam's natural politeness forced him into a nod, but nothing more. He had no idea whether or not he would be recognized, but there was no reason to announce himself to a listener who might take the news of his presence to Laverton. Surely, for all the hell Laverton had brought, he would remember Adam's name.

"Excuse me," he said. "The tables beckon."

Turning his back on Ferrier, he set about touring the casino and listening for snatches of conversation that might help in his search. The main salon extended across the back of the main building. Doors near each end opened onto side rooms, where cards, billiards, backgammon, even dominoes beckoned. In the room to the east a long table was laden with the savory food of the area—boiled shrimp and crayfish, fish fillets in

11

rich sauces, pots of gumbo, thick slabs of roasted beef, crusty breads, cakes and beignets and charlotte russe, and at one end a variety of wines for those who did not choose to wait for the waiters to come around.

In the wide foyer between the two smaller rooms, a circular staircase extended to the private quarters on the second floor. Having been told that La Chatte lived at the casino, Adam assumed her room could be found somewhere up those stairs.

Something about the layout seemed familiar to him, as though he had been there before. But such was impossible. The casino had been built the year he bought his land and he'd been too busy at his labors to investigate its reputed grandeur.

Mademoiselle Douchand's establishment was not in the city itself, but had been built in the specially incorporated nearby town of Carrollton, begun as a neutral ground where the usually quarreling French and Americans could meet for recreation. At La Chatte anyone's money was good, even that of a man just out of jail. Thinking how different his present surroundings were a brief month after he'd received his freedom, Adam could barely keep the disgust from his face.

Not so long ago he had been a simple planter with no more cares than the weather and the condition of his sugarcane. He had not turned from the call of a poker table when the occasion arose, but neither had he sought out a game of chance. Live and let live had been his creed.

He had changed, and he wondered if the marks on his body were evident in his eyes. Probably. Certainly the gray streaks that had appeared at the temples of his otherwise black hair provided evidence that he was a troubled man.

Walking through the rooms, he heard nothing that could help his search for Laverton. Occasionally he stopped to ask a question or two, but as had been the case in town, no one claimed to know the man. It was as though Laverton moved with the shadows, as though he did not exist. As though he had not set up Adam on false charges of slave smuggling two years ago. As though Adam's imprisonment had been no more than a nightmare.

Adam had scars to prove such was not the case, and he had evidence that, while not admissible in court, was more than enough to convince him of Laverton's guilt. Why had he been cast into hell, and by a man he had never met? The unanswered questions ate into Adam's gut. Laverton existed, all right. For a while. The need for revenge ate into Adam's soul.

Thus he had sought out his enemy's whore. She moved about the rooms as he did, but their paths did not cross. Her white gown drifting among the black suits, she was like a luminescence in the dark.

Only their eyes met on occasion, and he saw she was aware of him. As the evening wore on, he found himself looking for only her and was disappointed when she did not appear. Close to midnight he watched her stand once again by the roulette table and decided it was time to make his move.

"Messieurs, faites vos jeux!" came the call.

Adam edged his way around the table, tossed a coin carelessly toward the cloth, and by determined maneuvering managed to take the coveted place at La Chatte's left.

"Américain," someone hissed, as though his origin was enough to explain his rudeness.

Adam shrugged off the intended insult. At this late hour there were few of his kind still present at the casino, but he had grown used to being among unfriendly folk. And he had another, more compelling cause to pursue.

Catherine Douchand was as tall as the Creole Ferrier, her clearly defined body sleek and slender. Up close he could see the smoothness of her skin and the

13

reflection of the chandelier light as it caught in the dark curls of her hair.

The Cat of the Night.

She was truly well named. Unmindful of the whirling wheel, Adam gave his attention to her.

"Rien ne va plus," said the croupier from across the table.

The gamblers quietened, and Adam was aware only of the rise and fall of La Chatte's breasts as she took slow, even breaths.

"Dix, noir, pair, manque!"

Adam paid scant attention to the coins shoved in his direction.

"You have won, m'sieur," she said.

He was startled by the sound of her voice. It was soft and thick, like sweet-flowing honey, and came from deep in her lovely throat. Yet there was a contempt beneath all the softness that did not escape him. For an instant he was tempted to place his hands around that throat and squeeze against the disdain.

He could do it. None of the burly guards he'd seen at the edges of the room could stop him before he pressed the life from her body. But her death was not the one he was after. For her he would prefer . . .

Adam stopped himself. What kind of a temptress was she to turn him so quickly from his need for revenge?

Again came the call for bets to be placed. Carelessly he took a half dozen coins and placed them on the table. Again the spin, and again her voice.

"You are most fortunate tonight. Are you not interested in the winnings?"

Adam shrugged. "Not especially." He leaned close where no one else could hear. "I am far more interested in the woman beside me."

Her eyebrows arched. "A foolish mistake, m'sieur."

Adam answered her with a smile and was pleased to see a flash of unrest in her eyes. She was not so

14

unmoved by him as she would have him believe.

For the next hour he continued to place careless bets against the turn of the wheel, always far below the thousand-dollar limit set by the house. He lost occasionally, but far more often he won, and the stack of gold coins on the table in front of him continued to grow. A hush settled over the crowd, and more men joined those already around the table to see if one of them could at last break the casino.

It was unfortunate that he was an American, their sentiment seemed to indicate, and side bets were placed among them as to whether or not he would continue to win.

More than once the croupier cast a questioning look at La Chatte, as if to ask whether the bets of the incredibly lucky gambler should be accepted. Each time she nodded without expression, despite the casino's growing losses. Half the night's profits, he estimated, and was forced to a grudging admiration for her coolness.

He grew weary of winning. Gambling gold held no attraction for him; he preferred to earn his way by different means.

"I have one more bet to place," he said at last when the coins in front of him grew to an impossible amount. Never had he seen more money in one place.

"I wish to wager it all."

Low murmurings sounded around the perimeter of the table.

Catherine Douchand turned her head to him. "Impossible. You have several times our limit before you, as you well know, m'sieur."

"I'm not after your money. I've something else in mind."

Her violet eyes clouded. "What could you possibly want that I would be willing to grant?"

"An audience with Emile Laverton."

Surprise played across her face and a heavy silence

15

settled on the room.

"Impossible!" she said.

"Please don't insult me by claiming you do not know him."

"Whether I do or do not is none of your concern." She turned as if to order that the game continue.

"Surely it is not an association that brings you shame."

A delicate pink colored her tawny cheeks and made her all the more beautiful. When she looked up at him, he was startled by the rage she could not hide. "Shame! How dare you use that word to me?"

Somehow Adam had stirred emotions of great volatility, emotions that the enigmatic La Chatte would have preferred to keep hidden.

Around him he heard the whisperings of the men, and he knew from their tone they were against him in his request. La Chatte had her protectors other than Emile Laverton.

"I dare a great number of things. I repeat," he said firmly, "where is Laverton? Your answer against my gold."

"If I knew where he could be found, I would never tell anyone who demanded to know as you have done. Not for all the money at La Chatte."

Her head was tilted defiantly up at him, and he read in her expression an intense loyalty to her lover. Unlike so many mistresses Adam had heard of, she cared for the man who kept her. She cared deeply.

Adam was seized with a desire to grab her lovely shoulders and shake until the answer spilled from her lips.

With her flowery scent teasing his every breath, he admitted to an even wilder desire. He wanted to cover her mouth with his and kiss her until she moaned for release. He wanted to drag her from the salon and to her upstairs room where, in private, he could make her talk. This beautiful, defiant creature belonged to

16

Laverton, did she? What a sweet and satisfying revenge it would be if for one night Adam made her his own.

He had been so long without a woman, and this one, her eyes blazing in daring defiance, her slender body held in rigid anger only inches from his, was the most desirable creature he had ever seen.

She would talk to him, all right. Eventually.

Something of his thoughts must have communicated itself to her, for he heard her sharp intake of breath and read alarm in the depths of her eyes.

La Chatte was as unnerved as he was by their confrontation, and he forced his emotions under control. She could give him answers, most certainly, and, equally enticing, a chance for a revenge he had not considered. But not here. Not tonight. He had waited two years for this campaign. He could afford to be patient for a day or two.

His lips twisted in a smile. "I have changed my mind, mademoiselle," he said huskily. "Forget Emile Laverton. I ask for what every man in this room desires. One kiss from La Chatte."

"Mon Dieu!" a nearby gambler cried out.

The previous look of surprise on her face was as nothing compared to the shock she presented now. "Don't be a fool."

"I am willing to pay much," he said, gesturing toward his stacks of gold coins.

"I am not for sale."

"I am not buying you. Only one kiss."

A shadowed expression replaced her shock. "I have given my kisses to only one man," she said with quiet severity. "I do not seek another."

One man. Adam almost laughed at the ludicrous lie. She might now save herself for her lover, but surely through the years he could not have been the only one.

"Listen to my offer." The advice took in the others in the room. "One turn of the wheel. All of my winnings for one kiss. I take both or nothing."

17

Around the table, quiet men watched and waited for La Chatte to make up her mind, their full attention on her. It was as though Adam spoke for them all. For a moment a wildness flashed in her eyes, the wildness of a doe stalked by hunters in the swampy woods. If Adam had not known better, he would have thought she was afraid. But such was impossible. The woman of Emile Laverton would never show such emotion.

He witnessed in grudging admiration her quick, successful struggle to compose herself. She did not want to appear weak to the crowd, nor to the man who had become her adversary. Most of all, he was certain, she did not want to appear weak to herself.

At last she laughed sharply, and there was in the sound none of the silvery softness he had heard before. "You really are a fool."

"You pick the number," he said.

She hesitated.

"Do you fear kissing another man so much?" he asked, goading. "Or are you afraid you'll enjoy it?"

Her breathing became irregular, and her breasts rose and fell enticingly. "I do not fear you," she said. "Give me a coin."

He chose a hundred-dollar piece and placed it in her palm, his fingers lingering against the warm dampness of her skin. Jerking away, she tossed the coin on the table; it landed on the seven.

"Only one wager this time," she instructed the croupier. "Spin the wheel."

News of the stakes spread to the side rooms, and the gamblers crowded into the main salon. Side bets were placed, but gradually all talk ceased, leaving only the rasping sound of the cylinder and the rattle of the ball to fill the air.

Adam kept his attention on her and on the tiny beads of moisture forming above her upper lip. He'd lick them away before he claimed his kiss.

18

The roulette wheel slowed, slowed, slowed, and at last the ball dropped. Adam did not take his eyes from her mouth. La Chatte stared straight ahead, her body erect, her head held high.

"Sept!"

All remained quiet around them as she slowly turned to look at him. "Again, m'sieur, you have won. My congratulations." She lifted her face. "Claim your final winnings and then leave." She did not close her eyes, choosing to stare up at him in defiance.

He slipped one hand around her narrow waist and pulled her against him, bending his head to hers, her softness curving into his taut frame, the heat quickening in his loins. He studied her eyes, which were not simple shadows of violet after all but pools of light and dark, gold points shining in their plum-colored depths. He looked for signs of emotion, but at this moment she was remarkably good at keeping her feelings from those eyes.

His gaze dropped to her lips. They were full and pressed tightly together. A man would have to soften them with his own lips and tongue to draw the complete pleasure that they offered. Adam vowed to do just that. But not with an audience. For such a softening, they must be alone.

He lifted his head and eased his hold on her waist, with great reluctance letting his body separate from hers. "Ah, but I did not stipulate where or when," he said. "There is nothing in the rules of La Chatte that says my winnings must be claimed on the spot. Correct me if I am wrong."

Her eyes widened as around them whisperings began again.

"But . . ." she began.

"My preference is for a more secluded place."

She stepped away and stared at him in open contempt. "Impossible."

"Do you go back on your word?"

The whisperings grew louder.

"Never," she said. "Only a man does such a thing."

"You sound bitter, mademoiselle. If you have truly kissed only one man, I wonder what in your limited experience has made you so. Unless that one man has proven less than kind."

"You go too far. We will clear one of the side rooms if you insist." Her look said more than her words that she considered him as reprehensible as the lowest reptile in the swamp.

She turned from him. His hand on her arm stilled her.

"My preference is also for a different time."

She whirled to face him. "You are worse than a fool. You are insane. No one tells La Chatte what to do."

"I have dozens of men who can swear you agreed to the bet. It is not my fault that you failed to make the particulars clear."

She broke away from his stare and glanced around the salon, for the first time openly acknowledging there were witnesses to their confrontation. And for the first time since he'd set eyes on her, he knew for certain she was unsure of herself.

"We cause a scene, m'sieur. This is a matter between the two of us."

"I could not agree more. But the hour grows late. I will call on you within the week to settle the wager."

He drew away from her before she could protest, and the crowd parted, allowing him to make his way out of the room and down the foyer toward the front door.

"M'sieur!"

The sound of her voice stopped him at the casino entrance.

She stood behind him a dozen feet away, as proud as ever. "You have forgotten the gold. My man will gather it for you. Never should it be said that La Chatte held back on a bet."

20

With that pronouncement, she whirled and made her way up the curving stairs. Toward her room and her bed. Adam wondered if Laverton awaited her there. The image of her disrobing for her lover burned in Adam's mind.

Tomorrow, he vowed. He would have her kiss tomorrow. And much more. He would not be denied.

He turned toward the door.

"Bastard! Halt!"

He glanced over his shoulder toward the shouted order, which came from the main salon. Gaston Ferrier, flushed and weaving, stood in the doorway, his hands clinched at his sides.

"You're drunk," said Adam.

Ferrier staggered toward him. "I have been in a side room, m'sieur, and have only now heard of your reprehensible behavior."

Each of the Creole's words was pronounced with great deliberation.

"If you must make a fool of yourself, do it at the tables," Adam said.

"That I cannot do," he said with a shrug. "I have lost everything." With obvious effort he pulled himself upright. "Everything but my sense of decency. You have insulted the lady, a woman honored by all who listen and watch. In so doing you have insulted me."

Adam could see where Gaston Ferrier was headed. Having abandoned his pride at the card table, he hoped to redeem it here. Damned fool Creoles with their damned fool sense of honor, he muttered. *Code Duello,* they called it. He called it absurdity.

"Go home and get some sleep, Ferrier," he advised.

Ferrier held his erect posture, his red-rimmed eyes blazing with indignation. "I am doubly insulted, m'sieur. Only one course opens itself to me. We must meet on the field of honor."

Adam sighed in disgust. Behind Ferrier a crowd of

men waited for his response. Even La Chatte had paused halfway up the stairs.

"Am I to understand," he asked, "that you have challenged me to a duel?"

"Mais oui," Ferrier intoned with great pomp and deliberation. "Honor demands that I not be denied."

Chapter Two

From her vantage point halfway up the stairs, Cat Douchand regarded the scene.

Honor! she thought in disgust. What did men know of honor? The real kind that went beyond politeness and society's rules, the kind that went to the heart?

She answered her own silent question. They knew nothing.

Below, the foolish young Creole Gaston Ferrier pressed his point. "Your answer, m'sieur? I demand satisfaction."

It was not the first such challenge to be issued at La Chatte de la Nuit, and she knew it would not be the last. But this one was of special interest to her, since it involved the American.

One of the casino's men pushed through the throng spilling from the gambling rooms into the foyer. Coming up behind Ferrier, he glanced at Cat. For a moment she considered letting him interfere, then something made her motion him away. Like the rest of the onlookers, she wanted to see how the arrogant stranger would respond.

Gripping the banister of the stairway, she waited. She knew what he should say to the demand; it was a long-honored tradition in Louisiana that no man deny another the chance to avenge his honor, no matter how inappropriate the challenge had been. But the American did not act like other men.

Through the years she had operated La Chatte, its patrons had been content to engage in mild flirtations with her or to regard her from afar. Fear of the man they took to be her lover and protector stilled anything more. The American had shown no such fear. If she had not been so upset by his boldness, she might have admired him. Except that she did not waste admiration on men.

One private kiss. She shuddered at the thought of being alone with the strong-willed man—alone and in his arms. She had read in his eyes a determination to claim more than just the kiss; the realization of his desire had shot through her like a bolt of lightning. And he had known.

He might as well have demanded the deed to La Chatte, for all she was willing to pay, but he had placed her in an awkward situation. Too many had witnessed his challenge, and her pride was at stake. Like Gaston Ferrier, she had her honor to uphold.

But that did not mean she would purr for him when he claimed his prize. For the past decade the few people close to her had shortened her name to Cat. Cats purred, all right, but they also scratched, as the American would find out if he went too far.

Below, just as she had expected, the unorthodox stranger waved his hand in disgust at the foolish Creole. "Go home," he advised his adversary, "and sleep it off. You'll be glad in the morning you did."

"Bastard!" Ferrier hissed, undeterred, and proceeded to demand the American meet him at dawn at the Oaks, the wooded area of New Orleans that had become infamous for its duels. Because of Ferrier's drunkenness—she learned earlier he had indeed lost everything at the tables and had taken the loss badly—the slurring of his words muted their force.

Despite his inebriation, she knew that the Creole

onlookers, descendants of the city's French settler sided with him. Louisiana had been a state for eightee.. years, yet the enmity between French and Americans had not abated. They gambled with one another and occasionally shared a drink, but they rarely called each other friend.

Her eyes rested on the American. His hair was as black as hers, except that streaks of gray marked his temples. He seemed too young for such coloring, no more than thirty-five. She wondered if suffering had brought the streaks. There had been moments earlier when she passed him in the casino before he spied her; at those moments there had been a strange kind of bleakness lingering in his cold blue eyes.

She felt a flicker of sympathy for him, then brushed it aside. She must not allow his problems to soften her heart. All creatures suffered. It was a part of life. Sometimes she did what she could to relieve that suffering, but not when the victim was a man who seemed more than capable of caring for himself.

As the American turned to leave, the enraged Ferrier stumbled toward him.

"Go home," the Creole was advised for the second time. "I will not duel with you."

Ferrier did not slow his pace until he reached the man he had selected as his enemy. His hand grasped the American's shoulder and whirled him around. Drawing a white glove from an inside pocket, he slapped his face.

The murmurings among the onlookers grew louder.

The American shrugged, drew back his fist, and with one blow to Ferrier's jaw sent the foolish young man to a crumpled heap at his feet.

Cries of outrage at such barbarity filled the foyer, but the American seemed unimpressed. He stepped back as several men came to Ferrier's assistance, his eyes drifting up to hers.

Damned foolishness, he seemed to say.

Agreeing, Cat did not allow herself to respond.

For what seemed to her the thousandth time this evening, his gaze slid over her face, down the length of her, and back again. What unsettling eyes he had, she thought for the thousandth time, ignoring as he did the furor over the fallen Creole. But Cat was skilled in keeping her thoughts to herself, and she merely looked coolly at him.

He gave her a mock salute, mouthed "Tomorrow," and headed for the door. The croupier from the roulette table called from the back of the throng for him to wait and made his way toward him, a heavy leather pouch in his hand.

"Your money, m'sieur."

The American hesitated, as though the gold had little meaning for him. What a strange man he was. How different from anyone she had met.

With a shrug of his shoulders, he took the pouch and, nodding briefly to Cat, he was gone.

Tomorrow, she thought as she stared at the door closing behind him. For the second time a shiver of unrest unsettled her as she thought of what awaited her. *Tomorrow.* If she didn't know herself better, she would think he had made her afraid . . . or worse, had aroused in her an anticipation of their next meeting.

She brushed the idea aside as madness. The man was no more than a boor to claim his winnings when and where he chose. She would pay off because she had no choice, but he would get only what he had won. She planned not to touch him with her hands. Arrogant as he was, he might expect her to swoon and beg for more than just the one kiss. Cat swooned for no man. Not anymore.

She should have handled the scene differently. "Claim your winnings, now or never," she should have said.

But it was too late for regrets. Cat had learned long ago the wisdom of not looking back.

She hurried up the stairs, leaving the fallen Ferrier his friends. A light shone from beneath the closed doo. at the back of the second floor. Good. She needed something to occupy her mind.

Knocking lightly, she entered and stared at the figure of a man seated behind the broad desk. He was using her study as he often did, to take care of his own business. Cat was happy to provide him with the privacy that he demanded.

And he always seemed glad to see her, even if he didn't show it with an expanse of enthusiasm.

His head was bent, and she saw that his brown hair was thinning on top. He was nearing fifty, she reminded herself. It was time he showed the signs of his age. Even in the seclusion of the study, his spare body was as always immaculately clad in a black suit and sharply tied cravat. Not in almost nine years had she seen him wrinkled or casually attired.

"Emile," she said from just inside the doorway, "it is good to see you tonight."

Emile Laverton looked up, but the expression on his sharp face did not soften.

"Come in, *ma petite chatte.*"

Emile had always called her his kitten, even in those early, dreadful days before she told him her name. She had never asked why. He was the one who had shortened her name to Cat.

"I wish to go over the books, if you have no objections," she announced, pulling up a chair in front of the desk and brushing a recalcitrant curl from her forehead.

"You know I do not mind, but is it not late?" He reached for the cheroot resting in the ashtray beside him and took several shallow puffs as he waited for her to answer. Smoke curled about his hard-lined face. Anyone else seeing him right now would think he was a demon. Cat knew he was not.

"The hour is of no consequence," she said. "I would

be unable to sleep."

Emile's gray eyes rested speculatively on her. "There was trouble tonight."

"Michael told you?" she asked, referring to the Irishman who served both Cat and Emile.

"He mentioned an unusual wager."

Cat experienced a moment of irritation that she should be spied upon by Michael O'Reilly and the report taken immediately to Emile. She brushed the feeling aside as unworthy. At the lowest point in her life, Emile Laverton had provided the strength she needed to exist. Through the years he had served her with unfailing loyalty. She must have no secrets from him.

"You know how the Americans are," she said lightly.

"Perhaps I do. But tell me, Cat, how do they seem to you?"

"Gauche." She remembered the lean face of the American drawing close and his whispered demand for a kiss. "Arrogant."

"Could it be," asked Emile softly, "that my invincible kitten blushes?"

Emile knew her too well by far, she thought, and was surprised by an unusual irritation with him.

"I'm weary of dealing with men who are driven by lust. And forever grateful that you are not prey to such impulses."

"I detect a certain sharpness in you tonight."

She drummed her fingers on the desk. "Only because you will not let me forget the foolishness of the evening."

"I wish to know if you plan to settle the wager."

"Of course. Don't I always?"

"I have never known you to do otherwise. But tonight's wager was different, and the postponement . . ."

His voice trailed off into insinuations about what she might experience with the American.

"If I am not pleased with the terms that are presented, I shall pick the time and place."

"That will not be necessary. Tell me the name of this man, and I will see that he bothers you no more."

The hardness of his voice startled her.

"Michael was not very thorough tonight or else he would have reported that the man did not give his name. Please allow me to handle this, Emile. I will not have it said that I ignore my debts."

"No one speaks ill of *ma petite chatte.*" Again his words were edged with hardness.

Cat stirred restlessly. Enough time by far had been spent on the American.

"We waste the hour, my friend. Shall we get to the books?" She turned up the oil lamp on the desk. "I think you will be pleased at the profits of the past week."

She felt a glow of pride. Even considering tonight's loss at the roulette table, she was adding greatly to her account.

With no more argument, Emile reached for the record of accounts she kept in the top drawer of the desk. She watched him open it to the figures under discussion, enjoying the slight widening of his eyes, the quirk of his thin lips. Emile never showed quite so much emotion as he did when receiving news of financial success.

Not that La Chatte de la Nuit belonged to him now. He had made her a loan of the casino four years ago, had even let her decide on its design, and she had long since repaid him for his investment. The title was in her name; all profits were now hers. Still, she liked to keep him up to date as to her finances. He seemed to appreciate her efforts.

Cat kept unerringly accurate and complete figures. It was a skill she had learned long ago and one that she had never forgotten. Tonight, with an image of midnight-blue eyes stubbornly remaining in her mind, she gladly concentrated on the unemotional exactness of the columns of numbers. It took the two of them close to an hour to go over the casino's receipts and expenditures, the latter including costs of the food and drink served in one of the side rooms.

"You do not have to provide such a lavish repast for the gamblers," said Emile.

It was an old argument between them.

"I want no one to go away hungry. Broke, yes, if gambling is how they choose to lose their funds. But their stomachs, if not their pockets, should be full." She smiled, not wanting to sound charitable. "I am certain the tables I set out bring them back again and again."

Emile shrugged. "Do as you wish. You have succeeded far beyond my expectations. I must not argue with your accomplishment."

Oh but she had so much more she wanted to do. The money was only a means to an end. Emile knew of her ambition. He did not like it, but he understood.

Excusing herself, she bade him good night. "Will I see you tomorrow?" she asked as she opened the door.

Emile shrugged. "I have business to see to. Perhaps not."

Experience told Cat she might not see him for days. She knew not how he spent the time away from her. She knew of no one who did, with the possible exception of Michael O'Reilly. Some doubted the elusive Emile even existed; others spread rumors of illegal activities, ugly enterprises which would not bear the scrutiny of the law. Cat paid no attention to the stories; she knew in her heart they were lies.

"Cat," he called as she was about to leave. Something in his voice caused her to turn. "This American may not be so easy to handle. I do not have to tell you to beware of him, as indeed you must beware of all men."

"You do not have to tell me. I will be all right," she said, and slipped throught the door, closing it

30

behind her.

Alone once again, she caught her breath. How certain she had sounded, how strongly she believed what he'd said. She wanted to mean her confident words. But Emile's warning had sharpened the worries she had fought against ever since that accursed bet had been made.

Despite her determination to give the American a chaste payoff for his outrageous wager, she could not stop her heart from quickening each time she thought of him. She could still feel the press of his fingers at her waist as he pulled her against him, his thighs brushing against hers, his . . .

Stop! she warned herself. She was never given to such musings about a man. Never! Such considerations were dangerous, and she must not let them take over her mind.

One nagging thought bothered her. Why had she not told Emile that the stranger asked about him? It was an unimportant detail, certainly, and one that Michael had most likely already reported. So why not mention it herself? But she had been accused of feeling shame over the relationship, and she had lost control. For some reason she did not understand, she had been unwilling to tell her old friend how much the American had unnerved her.

It was possible she sensed there would be trouble if ever the two met. Bad trouble. She did not want to consider what it would concern, or what might be the results.

She hurried down the long hallway toward her room. Two people huddled beside her door. So intent had she been on her memories she had not noticed them.

Ben Washington, the free man of color who had been her friend as long as Emile, was bending his hulking frame toward his woman Delilah. The two were arguing in tones so low she could not make out the

31

words, but Cat could tell by the way Delilah's fists rested upon her ample hips that she was not pleased with what her man had to say.

"We always argue," Delilah had once told her. "Except in bed. When a man offers the kind of loving Ben does, a woman would be a fool to put up a fight."

It was a confidence that Cat had neither invited nor welcomed.

She walked closer to the pair.

"You're nothing but a dumb darkie," Delilah was saying.

"And you think a little white blood makes you a genius," Ben threw back. "It doesn't make you anything but confused."

Light from a double-candled wall scone illuminated the woman's coffee-colored, high-cheeked face. She was beautiful, as were many of the mulattos of the city, beautiful enough to serve as mistress to a rich white man, but she had chosen the ebony-skinned Ben for her mate. If a preacher had ever spoken words over them to legalize their living together, Catherine didn't know it. Their marital situation was their business, not hers.

The two lived in a separate building behind La Chatte. Ben was a handyman, driver, guard, messenger—whatever Cat needed. Delilah supervised the kitchen and the serving of food in the casino, and on occasion served as Cat's personal maid.

"Forget that gris-gris nonsense," Ben was saying as Cat drew near.

"It is not nonsense," Delilah said. "The mam'selle is in need."

This argument over Delilah's belief in voodoo was a common one between her and the churchgoing Ben.

"How am I in need?" asked Cat.

The two jumped apart as though she had caught them doing something wrong.

Delilah's rich brown eyes met hers. "We're all in

need, Mam'selle Cat. Even Ben."

"I take care of my own troubles," he said. "There is no need for any superstitious charms."

His voice was a rich baritone. He spoke well, rarely resorting to the *gombo* used by most of the coloreds in the city. But then he had spent his youth on a trading vessel and had been exposed to the languages of the world.

"Bah!" was his woman's reply.

"Please tell me," said Cat, "what danger prompts you to make the gris-gris."

"I did not say there was a danger," said Delilah, who now avoided Cat's steady gaze.

"Need, then. What is my need?"

"There was a problem tonight," the young woman responded. "I was there. I saw."

"The American," said Cat. "He is not a problem." Her words held more conviction than she felt.

"I hope in my heart that you are right," answered Delilah. "But what if Mam'selle Cat is wrong?"

Cat studied her face for signs that she was playing some sort of joke, but Delilah looked serious. Deadly serious.

As serious as Emile had sounded when he questioned her about the wager. What had gotten into everyone tonight? She included herself. The stranger had been at the casino no more than a few hours, yet he had managed to upset an inordinate number of people.

She fought against impatience. "Do not concern yourself so. Like Ben, I can take care of myself."

"She is a stubborn woman," said Ben, nodding toward Delilah.

"And you are a man who is blind," argued Delilah.

"I thank you both for your concern," said Cat, suddenly overcome with weariness, "but the greatest danger right now is that I will fall asleep on the spot."

Delilah stepped near. "Forgive me, Mam'selle Cat. I will help you prepare for bed. All is locked up below.

33

Everyone has gone."

Cat waved her away. She wanted nothing more than to be alone, to crawl into the great feather bed awaiting her and forget all that had transpired during the evening. Most of all she wanted to end the speculation about what might happen tomorrow.

Reluctantly Delilah departed, Ben close behind. As they descended the stairs, Cat heard once again the argument over the special gris-gris Delilah wanted for her mistress.

Slipping inside the darkness of her room, she listened for sounds of movement. All was quiet.

"Balzac," she whispered, expecting to be attacked at any moment.

There remained no response. She eased her way to the nightstand and fumbled for the lucifer that would light the oil lamp beside her bed. After completing the task, she turned to survey the room. It was far different from the opulence of downstairs. A simple oak headboard and nightstand, a frame over the bed for the essential netting to hold out the hungry mosquitoes, one four-drawer chest, over which hung a mottled mirror, one cane-bottom rocking chair by the window, and a wardrobe for her few dresses, black for day and white for night, and the clothes she wore when she rode. Nothing more. No pictures on the wall, no overstuffed furniture where she might recline in her idle hours.

Cat had no idle hours. Neither did she pamper herself, except for the feather bed, and that only because she needed her rest in order to keep up with the demands she put on herself. Creature comforts were for others. Not for her. Even the counterpane was a simple quilt she had found in the marketplace.

Kneeling, she peered beneath the bed and saw the object of her search—a tiny golden kitten curled into a sleeping ball, a stray she'd found crying behind the casino two weeks ago and had taken to her heart.

Balzac's rest boded ill for her. He would wake soon, refreshed. He would want to play the remainder of the night.

She needed Delilah's gris-gris, all right, but as protection from a ferocious kitten.

She kicked off her slippers and tiptoed to the wardrobe, where she worked at the buttons concealed in a placket down the front of her dress. After discarding her silk undergarments—chemise, slender petticoat, and stockings—she slipped into a plain cotton nightgown, washed her face in the cold water from the pitcher on the chest, and proceeded to run a brush through her hair with relentless thoroughness. She braided the black tresses into two plaits and glanced at herself in the mirror.

Some enchantress she was. She looked more like a schoolgirl. She laughed, a giggle unlike the throaty laughter she saved for the gamblers, but the giggle died almost the instant it was born. How foolish she was being. She had left girlish innocence behind when she was seventeen, almost ten years ago to the day. What a strange anniversary to remember, and she wondered what Emile would say if he could know her thoughts.

"Beware of men," most likely. It was an admonition that he gave her often, but it was one she did not need.

Without warning, tiny claws pierced the toes of her right foot, and she jumped, inadvertently kicking her attacker. He leaped away, back arched, and looked up at her with astonished eyes, as if to say *Mama, what did I do wrong?*

She leaned to pick up the golden bundle of fur. "Forgive me, Balzac," she said, holding him aloft and peering into his wide green eyes. He stared back, unblinking. "I meant you no harm. Of course you can claw at my foot. Anytime you choose."

She cuddled him against her chest and was rewarded with a tiny mew of protest. Not so easily was he won over.

"You're hungry, I'll bet." She glanced toward the windowsill and saw the small bowl of finely minced food which Delilah had been instructed to leave each night. When she moved closer, she saw that beside it was a small cotton bag stuffed with what she could not imagine. Powdered bat wings? Eyes of frogs? Anything might appear in one of Delilah's charms.

Cat smiled. Over Ben's objections, the woman had managed to leave her gris-gris after all.

She pulled the chair close to the bowl, and sat with Balzac in her lap. She picked up a small bite of food between forefinger and thumb and let the kitten lick it away, then repeated the process. Eventually he grew impatient with such slow feeding, and she placed him on the sill beside the bowl. Tiny teeth worked at the nighttime feast.

Cat looked out at the starry moonlight. For a change the sky was not overcast, and she allowed herself to enjoy the silvery luminescence of the August night. A breeze tugged at the window's curtains and cooled her cheeks. Below her, the sign for the casino banged against its frame.

She leaned forward until she could see the sign. It was white and gold-bordered; instead of letters, it bore the image of a large black cat with narrow green eyes that stared down upon the passersby. It needed no words. Everyone looking for a game of chance knew about La Chatte de la Nuit. She had seen to that since it first opened.

Unlike Carrollton's other gambling halls, which were simple brick structures unadorned except for scarred tables and the accoutrements that went with separating men from their fortunes, La Chatte was grand. Like the buildings of New Orleans, plaster covered the brick walls in the style of the Spanish. On either side of the main building were expanses of lawn, dotted by oak trees that provided shade. As a result, La Chatte was cooler inside than the rest. And it was far more successful.

Which was exactly what Cat wanted.

Her thoughts turned to the home of her childhood, pillared and stately, and to the graceful, moss-draped oaks which cast shadows across the symmetrical lawns on either side. When she had been planning the construction of La Chatte, that home had been in her thoughts, although the casino sat close to the road, not set back in the trees. There was no river at the front, no levee, no Bayou Rouge at the back.

She took comfort from the memories of that land, so near and yet so far, and knew she always would.

She stroked behind Balzac's ears.

"We make a great deal of money, *n'est-ce pas?*"

Balzac purred.

"But then we have a need for it."

Balzac did not reply. She placed him in her lap and began to rock slowly, but her tumbled thoughts would not let her rest.

Beware of men. She definitely would. Emile Laverton was the only man she knew who was not a hypocrite. Plantation owners kept their quadroon mistresses in city apartments and their white wives toiling away in the country while they waited for their lord and master to return. Most of the men losing their fortunes in the casino had wives and children who made the real sacrifices.

Even the American probably had a wife waiting for him to grant her a brief time with his body, to enjoy—or endure—the passion he had left over after the hours spent with another woman in town.

And he expected her kiss! Hate for him welled in her heart, surprising her with its intensity. She had no idea what there was about him that aroused such feelings.

Except that for a little while tonight he was making her examine her feelings and, at least in private, reaffirm the cause that drove her on. Without knowing it, he was making her look into her soul.

No one tells La Chatte what to do, she had told him, as though she were the guardian of her destiny. What a farce. She was trapped by her circumstances, by her past, and by the very private wishes for what lay ahead.

She lifted Balzac and nestled him at her throat.

"Little boy," she whispered, "we have our plans, do we not?"

Balzac's rough tongue licked at her skin, and she shivered. "What a rogue you are." She carried him to the bed, and after folding back the quilt, she slipped beneath the thin top sheet. Balzac curled on the pillow beside her.

"You're the only male I need in my bed," she whispered after turning down the light and tugging the mosquito netting into place. "You might scratch and even draw blood," she said into the dark. "But you don't leave scars. Not like a man."

Chapter Three

Emile Laverton leaned back in the desk chair of Cat's casino study and stared at the tip of his cigar glowing in the dark, his mind wandering over the earlier happenings downstairs. Such ponderings in the solitude of night were far from unusual for Laverton, and as a rule much to his liking, smoking cigars and watching over Cat ranking high among the few pleasures he took from life.

Tonight he took little comfort in his thoughts.

He had been sitting in the same place since she left hours before. The night was comfortable, far cooler than the usual stifling oppressiveness that was common to August in southern Louisiana, but the air contained hints that heat and humidity would soon return.

Twisting to look out the window at his back, he saw pink fingers of light stretching into the sky above the distant dark outline of trees. Dawn would be arriving shortly.

Laverton settled back in the chair and took a deep draw on the cigar. He did his best thinking just before dawn.

He didn't need much sleep and never had—a half-hour doze taken here and there sufficed. It was one of the ways he was different from other men.

Another was that he had a particular obsession for

seeing to details. Especially details concerning Cat.

Right now one detail was eating at him. Who in hell was the American? Laverton did not believe for one instant that the stranger had really been willing to gamble a few thousand dollars against a kiss from Cat. And he meant that as no insult to her. Maybe one of the foolish Creoles, in a moment of gallantry, might have felt that way. Not an American.

And especially not one from the East. Reporting to him earlier in the evening, Michael O'Reilly had placed the stranger's accent as native to one of the New England states—New York, maybe, or Pennsylvania. New Englanders were the worst kind for practicality and hard work.

He puffed at the cigar, and the glow deepened.

So what was going on? If the man meant any harm to the *petite chatte,* he'd be dead before he could draw many more breaths.

A knock at the door brought an end to his reverie. "Come in, Michael."

The door opened, and for an instant light spilling from the hall outlined the squat, broad-shouldered figure of the Irishman who served as Cat's assistant at the casino. In truth, he was on Laverton's payroll, too, a fact she probably knew but had never discussed. Unlike most women, she didn't ask questions or put up arguments over subjects she considered none of her concern.

Cat trusted him, and he in turn protected her. In ways she could not imagine.

"Thought you'd be awake, your lordship," Michael O'Reilly said wth his usual flourish as he closed the door behind him. "Thought you might be wanting to talk."

"Have a seat," said Laverton.

O'Reilly made his way in the dark to the chair Cat had occupied when she was going over the books. Neither man suggested lighting the lamp.

"Tell me again about last night," said Laverton, flicking an ash into a bowl on the desk. "Everything."

O'Reilly needed no more prompting as he described the scene at the roulette table, including the lean, hard look of the American and the brash way he had treated the woman Michael called Mistress Cat.

Laverton listened in silence. Michael had a knack for re-creating overheard conversations, even a day or two later. It was a skill that had served Laverton well on more than one occasion. Nothing he heard tonight, however, pleased him, except that Cat had not been flattered by the man's approach, merely flustered and insulted. She wasn't a woman who cared for the attention of men.

So why had she neglected to mention the American's interest in the whereabouts of the elusive Emile Laverton? The question was one he had considered most of the night.

"He asked others in the casino about you, too," Michael said, as though he could read his employer's mind.

"And what did he learn?"

"No one knowing exactly what you look like, your lordship, much less where you bide your time, they could hardly give him an answer."

Of course they couldn't. Laverton carefully nurtured his anonymity, using a back stairway at the casino so that no one could see his comings and goings. Not even Cat knew the whereabouts of his office in the city.

"And," O'Reilly added, chuckling, "none seemed too interested in talking about the subject, either. A man would think they were afraid of no more'n the name."

Again, Laverton was not surprised. But if none of the Creoles wanted to discuss him, why the American's persistent questions? More than ever, his interest in the stranger was piqued.

In his various business endeavors he dealt with men from the East, most of them his enemies by the end of

41

their acquaintance. Some of them still lived, but none, he thought, who would be foolish enough to seek him out.

He felt a sudden rage that someone bent on causing trouble could invade ground he considered both his province and Cat's refuge. The hand holding the cheroot trembled, and he crushed the cigar into the bowl, the fiery tip extinguished into ash. Just so would he like to crush the American.

He got hold of himself. He must think. Somewhere in his memory lay the clue that would give sense to last night. Casting his thoughts over the past weeks and months, he could recall no one who fit the stranger's description. The answer lay in the man's motivation. Money or a woman—one of them had to be at the root of his search.

Laverton was tempted to rule out money, the stranger being far too unconcerned with the gold he had won. A woman, then. Perhaps the loss of honor. A family member seeking revenge for some harm that could be laid at Laverton's feet. The possibility existed.

Maybe it was the stranger's honor that needed avenging. A glimmer of an idea occurred to him. He remembered a planter a couple of years ago, an American who stood in the way of Cat's foolish dream. He couldn't remember the man's name, had never laid eyes on him. He had paid others to do the work of ruining him.

It had been an impulsive action, the first of this particular kind, but if things had worked out, he would have brought Cat the happiness she was after. When they didn't, he'd decided to let the matter rest. He would help her in other ways. Besides, through the success of the casino, Cat was helping herself. She might never achieve her goal—Laverton hoped she did not—but working toward it was bringing her more contentment than he had ever seen in her.

His tapered, manicured fingers stroked against the

sparse gray stubble on his cheek and he thought in passing he would need to shave. "Do you remember a trial of a year or two ago?" he asked Michael. "As I recall, you made some of the arrangements."

"Doing my duty, your lordship. And an interesting duty it was, seein' as how you'd never asked me to do anything quite like it before."

"Who was the defendant?"

O'Reilly thought a moment. "Adam something or other. Ah, yes, Adam Gase. Never saw him, you understand. There never was a need, not with the others doing their work so well. You always say not to take unnecessary chances. I try to go by what your lordship says."

"That's one reason why I pay you so well, Michael. Where is this Adam Gase now?"

"Haven't heard. Far as I know, he's still behind bars."

"But there's a chance, I assume, he could have been released."

"Always a chance," O'Reilly said, his broad, flat face split by a grin, "the justice system being as unreliable as it is. With these Americans in charge, it's hard to put a man away for good."

"Recall any of the principals involved?"

"There was that old fool of a judge. Name slips me mind at the moment."

"You surprise me."

"I've got me flaws," said Michael, sounding miffed. "The judge is retired. Quit the bench right after the trial, as I recall, but I'll get a name for you. There was a witness, too. Him I know. Sean Casey."

O'Reilly spoke the name with pride. They stuck together, these Irishmen, thought Laverton. As well they had to. The Creoles didn't think much of them as a group, especially one with Michael's patronymic. More than sixty years ago Alejandro O'Reilly, nick-named "Bloody," had led a band of Spanish soldiers to occupy the territory after the land was given by the French king to Spain. The name had been well earned, and memories were long in the state.

"Sean Casey," Laverton repeated. "We've used him a time or two in other pursuits, have we not?"

"That we have, your lordship. A sailor who hates the sea, he is, and glad for the work. Paid him right well, you did, too. The lad took to drinking and carousing, that glad he was to stay on shore. Haven't seen him in a while."

"Find him. And check on Adam Gase. If he has been released, we wouldn't want any loose ends lying around that could lead to us."

"Will do." O'Reilly stood, then hesitated. The first rays of the day filtered into the smoky room, casting shadows on his ruddy face. The dark suit revealed in the light was ill-fitted to his stocky frame, Laverton thought with disgust as he cast a studied glance over the man. Still, the Irishman was not hired for his sartorial splendor.

"One other thing," said Michael. "'Twas a bit of a ruckus as the American was leaving. Got into a fight with one o' the Creoles."

"Details, please."

"Gaston Ferrier by name. Lost everything at cards and had a cup of wine too many. Took offense at the way Mistress Cat was treated and challenged him to a duel. Being the uncouth creature that he is, the American landed him a facer."

"This Ferrier. He has a family?"

"Heard talk of a wife and baby."

"There would be, of course," said Laverton.

The existence of the woman and infant was a fact Cat would know before long, and one she would act on. A foolish habit of hers, but a harmless one.

He reached for the humidor and extracted another cigar. O'Reilly took it as an act of dismissal and left.

Laverton studied the cigar and dropped it back into

the container. All the thinking of the night had left him with a craving more imperative than another cheroot. It was one he didn't have very often, but when it came upon him, usually when his peace of mind was disturbed, it was best acted upon.

He wanted a woman.

Except for Cat, he didn't particularly like women, but he had need for them. She thought he was without lust, but she was wrong. At fifty he had lost neither capacity nor desire. Sometimes a whore would do, one who knew how to use her lips and tongue where he most wanted them. At other times he preferred taking his pleasure with a virgin.

Tonight he wanted neither. He had a woman waiting, a lady, she called herself, and in the eyes of New Orleans society, so she was. But not with him. She liked it when he penetrated her flesh. She admitted craving sex with a dangerous man.

When he first learned of her existence, he had gone after her. Being more than a little foolish and a great deal vain, she had been easy to seduce.

"You're like a snake," she had told him. "Sleek and slithery when you come to me. When we make love, you hardly make a sound."

He had not known whether she meant the comparison as a compliment, but he did not much care. They met in secret, using the apartment he kept in the heart of New Orleans known as the Vieux Carrep. Twice he had gone to her, but they had both decided such a rendezvous was too risky. Slaves talked. Her husband might find out.

Laverton was no more eager to reveal his affair with her than was she. Not just yet.

He rose, brushed at his coat, straightened the black tie at his throat, then quiet as a shadow, strode out of the room and down to the casino stables, where a horse was waiting for him.

He studied the sky, which had changed from black to

45

deep blue since he glanced out the window a half hour ago. He had best be on his way. By the time full daylight came to New Orleans, he wanted to be riding the lady instead of the blood bay.

In the servants' quarters next to the stables, Delilah lay in her man's arms and listened to the sound of a horse being ridden away. That would be M'sieur Laverton, she thought with a shudder. She always felt better when he was gone.

Not that he had ever harmed or threatened her in any way—if she discounted the time he tried to take her in the barn and she pulled a knife. That had been almost two years ago and he hadn't tried again. Still, he frightened her, and she didn't know why.

Maybe it was the lean, foxlike look of him . . . or the way he watched everyone around him as if all were his prey Whatever the reason, she was on edge when he was close by and relieved when he was gone.

Ben's broad gentle hand cupped her breast and his low, even snore broke the stillness of the small bedroom. Delilah snuggled against his naked body, knowing she was well loved. She and Ben might have their differences over the nature of things, but not about each other.

Her mama would have disapproved of her only child's taking up with a man black as the night. Delilah was seven-eighths white—an octoroon, daughter of a quadroon mistress and a French planter. Her voluptuous beauty was a fact she accepted without vanity, as she accepted the blue of the sky. Her skin was the color of coffee and cream, and her ebony hair thick and straight. Her looks and her blood heritage made her almost respectable, certainly good enough to serve, the way her mother had done, as a white man's town woman.

Delilah wanted no part of such an arrangement. She

had seen her mama suffer and waste away when the planter had decided to be faithful to his wife. Yellow fever had taken both man and wife. Delilah had not mourned.

She had met Ben five years ago at a Sunday dance in New Orleans's Congo Place. Along with a crowd of her people, slaves and free alike, she was dancing the bamboula under the shade of a sycamore, the tom-toms thrumming to a wild African beat. Ben had stepped close, his big body blocking out her view of the other men. She had been with him ever since.

A kind and loving man, he would never leave her, and she would never leave him, not even when he most exasperated her, as he had done tonight.

She shifted beneath the light covers.

Ben snorted awake. "What are you up to, woman?"

She decided on the truth. "I'm worried about Mam'selle Cat."

"Miss Cat can take care of herself. And if she can't, there's old Ben here and Mister Emile to see to things."

Delilah smiled to herself, "old Ben" having reached the ripe age of thirty-eight. "That could be what's worrying me," she said.

"Don't you think I do well by Miss Cat?"

"You know what I mean."

Ben was silent for a moment, not rising to the argument she presented to him. They disagreed about Emile Laverton. Ben did not claim to like the man, but he did swear that as long as Laverton drew breath, Catherine Douchand would be safe.

"You know why M'sieur Emile does not care for you, Ben? It's because you're incorruptible. An honest man. He doesn't know how to deal with such."

"Delilah, you talk nonsense in the early morning."

"It's when I speak the truth."

"So speak the truth. Why are you worrying about Miss Cat?"

Delilah paused before answering. Stretching naked

beside Ben, she felt the muscled expanse of his chest against her shoulder, his powerful leg resting possessively over her own legs, his hand on her breast. Ben was her strength and her pleasure and her joy.

"She's leading a wasted life."

A low laugh rumbled in Ben's throat. "Miss Cat's got more money than the two of us will ever see."

She ran her fingernails through the coarse hair on his chest and flicked at one of his nipples. "Since when did you judge happiness by money?"

He caught her hand in his. "You've got a point, woman. But Miss Cat is working toward something. And she's getting close."

"She's running *from* something, more to the truth."

Ben sighed. "I shouldn't 'a told you about all that. It keeps giving you ideas."

"I'd have some of them by just watching. She's lonely, Ben. She needs a man like you."

"What is she going to do with a black man?"

Delilah hit him in the chest. "You know what I mean."

Ben chuckled. "What do you want me to do, woman? Go out and pick her out one? It's hard for me to tell whether a white man is good-looking or not. They all look pale and kind of sickly."

"Even the American?" Delilah asked softly.

"Maybe not so much as most. You getting ideas for yourself?"

"I like my man black as a raven's wing. You know that. I'm just thinking of Mam'selle Cat."

"Don't be matchmaking, Delilah." Real warning was in his voice.

"It wouldn't do me much good if I *was,* now would it? She's lying upstairs alone in a big old feather bed and swearing that's the way she wants things. She's not about to take advice from me."

"Just remember what I said. That woman's had troubles enough in her life without getting more

48

from us."

She did not respond, hoping her silence would be taken for acquiescence. But Ben was wrong, and so was Mam'selle Cat. Matchmaking was exactly what Delilah *was* doing. She had seen the man for her mademoiselle.

The American was not good-looking the way the Creoles could be. He was too lean and hard and a little frightening in his intensity. Not Laverton frightening, exactly, although she couldn't put into words the difference between them. The American had something about him that she liked—integrity, maybe, although she did not know why such an idea came to her mind.

And he was the only man she had ever seen who could outmaneuver Mam'selle Cat. Standing beside him at the roulette table a few hours ago, her mistress had been decidedly unnerved. It had been enough to give Delilah faith that beneath the assured exterior of La Chatte beat the heart of a real woman. An unhappy one, too.

That was why she had prepared the gris-gris. Ben thought she was making a charm to keep the mam'selle from harm, as did the mam'selle. Again, both were wrong. She had made up the most potent love potion she knew about, wrapped it in cloth, and placed it on the windowsill where it could summon the power of Oshun, goddess of love. One way or another, Mam'-selle Cat would get herself a man.

Preparing to rise, Delilah smiled into the gathering daylight. What would Ben say if he knew she had used such a potion to capture him?

Chapter Four

Still conditioned to the hard bunk of the penal camp after a month of freedom, Adam spent the hours between midnight and dawn tossing and turning in the bed at the comfortable New Orleans hotel room he had rented for the week. Only when the first light of day began to lighten the darkness was he able to drift into troubled slumber. He dreamed he was back in the camp.

The dream was a familiar one. Clad in blue-striped convict garb, he was caught in quicksand, his feet and manacled ankles sucked beneath the soft ground at the edge of a wide and murky bayou. Tall brown grasses as high as his chest grew in the shallows around him and brushed like boar bristles against his body. In vain he tried to free himself, but he was caught as if in a vise. Steadily the water level of the bayou rose until it covered the iron bands grinding against his skin, and higher until it lapped halfway up his calves.

A fine, chill mist blurred the marsh that lay to his right and the expanse of rising water to his left, casting a ghostly vagueness across his world. Still the bayou did not cease its rise. The more he tried to pull free from the bayou bed, the deeper he sank, the thick, hungry sand inching as high on his legs as the water had been a moment ago. Unable to free himself, he watched the bayou, fed by some unseen source, deepen . . . deepen . . . deepen until it reached his waist.

As he stared in helplessness at the iron bands around his wrists and the thick chain that linked them, he quickened his struggle.

Suddenly through the grass drifted a knotted cypress log. As it neared, Adam saw the log transform into a swamp alligator, twenty feet in length, its wide-spaced eyes inspecting him with terrifying intensity. The primordial beast drew within a yard, jaws open, teeth jagged and bared.

"Slay the demon!" a gravelly voice yelled out from close beside him. "He's your supper, brother, or you are his." The hated voice broke into wild laughter.

Adam jerked his concentration away from the alligator and stared through the mist at the guard who had become his mortal enemy. He loomed on horseback so close Adam could reach out and grab his leg . . . if only his hands were not shackled. Brother Red, his bald head glistening in the falling rain, sat astride a black stallion, a leather whip as long as the alligator dangling at his side, a gloved hand gripping the hide handle.

The threatening jaws of the alligator closed just as the whip rose in the air, and Adam knew it was the guard who presented danger to him, not the reptile. With a snap the leather strip curled high into the gray, wet air and arced toward his back. Adam threw his hands upward and wrapped his fingers around the knotted tip in exultation. Like the log, the whip became a living thing, and he found himself gripping the cool, moist slipperiness of a cottonmouth.

His scream of terror was muffled by the laughter of Brother Red.

He flung the snake away from him and fell backward, landing in the rising bayou. At last the sandy bottom gave up its hold on his legs as the water folded over him like a blanket. Exhausted, he lay back and accepted the comfort it offered. But only a moment. Death would not find him such a willing victim.

"No!"

His mind exploded with the cry of protest, and he realized he was sitting upright in a bed, his naked body bathed in his sweat.

His eyes darted wildly about the small room, and his heart thundered in his chest. He half expected to see the rough panels of the pen that had been his home for two years and the bunks of the half dozen convicts who had shared his quarters.

And of course there would be Brother Red, the sadistic, Bible-quoting guard who prayed to the heavens while he tortured his fellow man. Brother Red was always the worst part of the dream, as he had been the worst part of the camp.

Adam pulled back the mosquito netting and stared into cruel brightness, his mind assimilating with maddening slowness what his vision took in. He was alone in a morning that appeared to be half gone. The sunlight streaming through a lone window revealed a scarred four-drawer chest; beside it, a ladder-back chair holding Adam's clothes, and on top a porcelain pitcher and bowl resting on a crocheted doily. A mirror hung on the wall over the chest. On either side of the gilt frame hung matching faded portraits of women wearing high-necked dresses and faint smiles. Either of the subjects could have been a traveling man's homebound wife who waited patiently for his return.

The only other furniture in the room was the bed, its tangled covers pulled loose beneath him to reveal the ticking of a down mattress.

Adam willed his breath to slow. He was in a New Orleans hotel room, safe except for the imagined horrors of his dreams. He wondered how long it would be before he slept again in peace.

The answer to his unspoken question came quickly.

The restlessness would last until he learned why Emile Laverton had wished him harm and, just as important, until he brought the man to justice.

Justice. Adam put a more accurate name to it. Until he brought Emile Laverton to his death.

He rose from the twisted bedclothes and moved stiffly to the chest. He bathed in water from the pitcher, not minding the trickles that ran down his chest and legs and darkened the straw mat covering the floor. He dried with a small hotel towel adequate for no more than an eight-year-old child. For Adam, it was a luxury.

His shaving implements were stored in the small valise he had placed in the bottom drawer. After lathering face and throat, he was forced to look into the mirror as he ran the sharp edge of the razor over his skin.

Haunted eyes stared back.

Two years ago he had been a man who enjoyed life, a gentle, peaceful man who worked hard to make his plantation profitable. He had planned one day to find himself a wife.

The Adam of that long-past time was a stranger to him now. He had seen the depravity of man . . . had found it in his own heart. He suspected that joy was lost to him forever. But not satisfaction. He would take great satisfaction in bringing his enemies to a just end.

And there was La Chatte de la Nuit, the beautiful Catherine Douchand. In his mind he was back at the roulette table, the raven-haired temptress at his side. He could see her violet eyes flashing up at him in anger and defiance, her slender body still with an indignation that made it all the more provocative beneath the covering of white silk. La Chatte offered a special pleasure that sweetened the bitter taste of revenge. He would not be denied.

Raking a comb through his tousled hair, he pulled a clean shirt from the valise. Long, tanned arms went into the sleeves. At least, he thought as he worked at the buttons, his body had not wasted away during the long months. Inhuman work—work that had killed the weaker prisoners—had toughened his muscles and given him an extra endurance beyond any he possessed before the nightmare began.

He remembered well the day a constable from the city, accompanied by a half dozen burly guards, came to the plantation and on the steps of the main house ordered that he be put under arrest. So many for one innocent planter, he remembered thinking, as though the number of his persecutors made the injustices against him all the worse.

Confused by charges that could not possibly be true, Adam had given in to rage, had fought the iron bands they tried to put around his wrists. One of his men—a good worker and a friend—had run to his rescue, and the bullet Adam suspected was meant for him had instead struck the innocent man.

Adam had more than the injustices against himself to avenge.

Hurriedly he finished dressing. In brown shirt and trousers and brown boots, he was more at ease than he'd been in last night's restrictive wear. He needed one last item before he left the hotel—the pouch of coins he had won at roulette. The handsome sum must be deposited into his New Orleans bank account at once.

Last night he had scoffed at his winnings, but he had not been thinking clearly. Gambling gold could be put to good use on his needy land.

His banker, Reginald Odom, an Easterner who had come south before Adam, agreed.

"You've worked miracles," Odom said a half hour after Adam had arrived in his Chartres Street office and after their business was done. A spare, neatly dressed man with brown hair combed back from his high forehead and a Vandyke beard adorning his chin, he stared in admiration at Adam, who was seated in front of his desk. "Keeping Belle Terre going when even I thought it would have to go on the market—that was quite a feat."

Adam shrugged away the compliment. "Tom Jordan's the best manager and overseer in the state."

"Don't deny the part you played. Your men, black and white, were loyal, Adam. Damned if I've seen anything like it. They couldn't have known you would try to free them the minute you got back to Belle Terre."

"I'd been owned by a sadistic guard for two years, Reginald. No man should have to endure such a thing."

Adam's efforts on behalf of the Belle Terre workers, begun through correspondence with Odom as soon as he was released, thus far had proven less than satisfactory, Louisiana law working against him as it had during his quick trial. To receive their freedom, slaves must have reached the age of thirty and be able to prove they'd been above reproach for the previous four years. Under the direction of a lawyer recommended by Odom, a young man named Joseph Devine, the papers had gone through the courts on only one of Adam's men.

"A miracle of speed," Devine had commented when Adam met him on the trip into town.

Adam wasn't satisfied, and he'd asked Devine to continue his work.

"Where's the freed slave now?" asked Odom.

"He stayed on to work for wages. It was his decision."

"Admit the truth, Adam. They all stayed on while you were gone, didn't they?"

"One or two went looking for greener pastures. Maybe they just wanted a boss who wasn't in jail."

Odom's answering laugh was more like a bark. "You know what would have happened on most of these sugarcane plantations without an owner on the premises for two years? Desertion, that's what. Slaves

56

running, free hands looking for more secure employment. And I'd hate to think of the looting."

"As I said, I left a good man in charge."

And he had. Tom Jordan, a fellow American, had been with him from the beginning, had learned the tricks of planting and crop rotation and harvesting alongside his boss.

Adam thought of the run-down house and weedy grounds of the plantation. Despite the work it needed—or maybe because of it—he knew that if he ever were to find peace again, it would be there.

Belle Terre wasn't the largest plantation on the Mississippi, nor was it likely to be the most profitable. When he bought it, years of neglect had brought the place close to ruin. But coming upon it on his travels across the country, he had seen the potential. And the natural charm of the moss-draped oaks and the dark-leafed magnolias had stirred something in his soul. With family dead and nothing to draw him back to Pennsylvania, he had invested his inheritance in it. The owner, a stern-faced Creole, had seemed glad to let it go.

Adam had been bringing it closer to its former grace and beauty when the constable arrived. Jordan had kept the fields producing during the years of his incarceration, making enough profit to keep creditors from the door, but there had been no time for anything else. When Adam learned that his sentence was shortened from ten years to two, his first act of freedom had been to hurry to Belle Terre, where he saw with sadness that the house and grounds had fallen once again into disrepair.

He'd spent three weeks there working, assessing priorities on what had to be done, figuring the cost against the anticipated income from the fall harvest, and trying to rest. He was breathing free air; he should have been able to relax. But the air wasn't truly free as long as Emile Laverton went unpunished, and Adam had ridden into town.

"Did you know I had a good offer for the place?" asked Odom.

Startled from his musings, Adam was immediately alert. "When?"

"Not long after the trial. I got word to Jordan, but he said you wouldn't be interested."

"Who offered?"

"Don't know. It was made anonymously through the president of the bank, but with Tom saying the place wasn't for sale, the matter was dropped. I always wondered how he knew what you wanted done out there."

"We managed," Adam said, declining to give further details on the unorthodox way he and Tom had remained in communication. "Think you could find out who wanted to buy Belle Terre?"

"Sorry, Adam. You know I'll do everything I can to help you, but I was told the buyer did not wish his name known. The bank must respect that confidentiality." Odom hesitated, studying Adam thoughtfully. "You don't think it could have any bearing on your arrest, do you?"

"I don't know what to think. I'm investigating anything and everything I can."

Odom shook his head slowly. "I can't believe anyone would wish such hell on another human being simply for property, and pardon me for saying it, Adam, but run-down property at that." His next words came with great caution. "It *was* hell, wasn't it?"

Adam knew the man was asking out of friendship and concern, but he wasn't ready to talk about those years.

"There's something you can answer for me," he said. "What do you know about Emile Laverton?"

The banker's eyes widened in surprise. "Emile Laverton! That's a name I don't often hear spoken above a whisper. What have you got to do with him?"

58

"That's what I want to find out."

A frown creased the pale skin between the banker's thin brows, and he stroked at his neatly trimmed beard. "He's not a man to cross, if rumor is correct. His name has come up on occasion in connection with a shady deal or two, but there has never been anything openly said—or charged—against him. Never even seen the man myself. You don't think he had anything to do with your arrest, do you?"

Hate welled in Adam so strongly that it threatened to smother him, and he could not answer at once, his knuckles white against the arms of the chair as he fought for control. Odom had asked a simple question, nothing more. Adam was stunned by the violence that the contemplation of Laverton could arouse.

"He had everything to do with my arrest," he said at last.

Odom could not have missed his torment, but all he said was "How? Was he at the trial? Damned shame I was out of town when it all happened. I might have been able to do something to help you."

"It was a setup, Reginald. Pure and simple." He stared at his old friend and saw concern in his eyes. "You were best far away."

"Accepting that he could have done such a thing, why would he bother? What did he stand to gain?"

"As I said, that's what I intend to find out."

"He's a slippery bastard. You'll need lots of proof. Have you got anything that will stand up in court?"

Adam shook his head. "But I know, all right." For a moment he wanted someone to share the burden of his knowledge, and he found himself talking about the convict he knew only as Cotton. Not much older than Adam, he was already in the camp when Adam arrived. He kept to himself, as much as a man could who slept with six other men in a ten-foot pen and who was chained with them on work crews during the day. Adam had been there a year when Cotton began to talk.

"I know about your trial," he said one steamy night as they lay in adjoining bunks and listened to the laughter of the drunken guards. "I was supposed to be there."

Adam's skin crawled, and he forced himself to remain still while the convict talked.

"Smuggling slaves, wasn't it?" Cotton asked.

Adam had told no one in camp of the charges against him.

"It was me supposed to testify against you, but I changed my mind. I see he got someone else." Cotton fell silent.

"Who?" Adam asked. "Who got someone else?"

But Cotton was through talking. Adam promised him his ration of food each night, said he would pay him handsomely on the outside once their respective sentences were done, and, when bribery failed, had thrown himself toward the man's bunk and wrapped his hands around his throat, willing to squeeze a name from him if he could. It had taken three prisoners to pull him off. Cotton still refused to talk.

Two months later Cotten fell ill with malaria and told Adam he needed to confide in someone "before the good Lord condemns my soul to everlasting hell."

Cotton wasn't the first convict Adam had heard turn to religion in his final moments, but it wasn't the preachings of Brother Red that had brought him to seek redemption. It was fear of death.

He sat beside Cotton's bunk during that last night he was on earth and held his fevered hand. And he listened. The convict had been approached by one of Laverton's men—"Knew 'im well since I'd done a job or two for the bastard"—to testify against someone he had never met. He spelled out the testimony he was to give against Adam, the same testimony that had eventually been given after Cotton was already in the camp.

"Got cold feet. Only time I'd been in court was when I was the one on trial. Couldn't see goin' there of my own free will." But he'd ended up there anyway, on charges of stealing a woman's purse. "You were set up, man, but so was I. I stole more'n a few things in this life I never got caught for. But not that purse."

The words were forced now, but Cotton seemed unable to stop until his tale was done. "Wily old Emile wanted me out of the way. Didn't want me shooting my mouth off when you finally did come before the judge. He got me about as far out of the way as a man can get. Funny, ain't it, the way we ended up together? Couldn't hardly believe it when I heard your name."

"Why are you telling me all this now?" Adam asked.

A sigh came from deep within Cotton's sunken chest. "You've got strength about you. More'n most. You'll get the bastard. Get 'im for me, too."

"I will."

Adam saw the man had little time left, but he could not hold in one last attempt to learn all the convict could tell. "Why was I set up, Cotton? What is this all about?"

"You'll have to ask Emile."

Cotton had talked no more. He died within the hour.

A hundred miles from the camp and a year later, Adam stared at the respectable Reginald Odom and said, "I plan to do as he suggested. I plan to ask Emile."

"Be careful, Adam. You play a dangerous game."

But Adam was beyond taking care. He stood to leave, thanked Odom for his patience and concern, then paused at the door. "One last question. If you can't help me with Laverton, what about his woman?"

For the first time in their meeting, Odom looked uncomfortable. "His woman?"

"Catherine Douchand. Surely you have heard of her."

"Her connection with Emile Laverton is only rumor, I believe."

"It's more than rumor. I met her last night."

"So it was at La Chatte de la Nuit that you won your gold. Rather unusual. More money is left there than is ever carried out."

"Mademoiselle Douchand gave every appearance of being prosperous. I don't imagine I dented her finances very much." He studied the banker. "You're being evasive, Reginald. Do you know anything about her or don't you?"

"I've seen her, of course," he answered, refusing to look Adam in the eye.

"Am I asking you to betray another confidence? The woman's a whore, Reginald. She's sold herself to Emile Laverton."

"Catherine Douchand . . ." Odom stopped. "I am not at liberty to discuss her, Adam," he said apologetically. "But she is not to be judged as harshly as you are doing."

"There we disagree." He stood and shook the banker's hand. "Thank you for your help. If you decide there's something about the offer for Belle Terre that you can tell me, let me know."

"Be careful, my friend," warned Odom. "You've had a rough time. Don't get so carried away with paying old debts that you let it ruin the rest of your life."

"I haven't got much of a life until I can put a few things to rest."

Adam let himself into the main room of the bank just in time to see the door to the president's office open. Standing in the doorway with her back to Adam was a woman in an ill-fitting black dress, her dark hair pulled into a bun at her neck, a black bonnet on her head. She gave the appearance of being in mourning. A widow, he thought idly, and not a very attractive one.

She turned just as she lowered her veil over her face, but not in time to keep Adam from recognizing the lovely and delicate profile.

La Chatte de la Nuit. Depositing her gains from the

previous night at the casino, Adam was certain.

He stood stunned and watched her shake hands with the banker. The dress truly was an ugly thing, hanging limp against her body and disguising her slender frame. And the magnificent hair that she had worn loose was twisted into a knot so tight it pulled her skin taut.

What kind of a game was she playing? Women wore veils in New Orleans as protection against the omnipresent mosquitoes. La Chatte was protecting herself from prying eyes.

Was a visit to the bank the only business she was about? He doubted she was looking for him so that she could settle her debt, although, Adam thought with a smile, she would probably choose that dowdy dress when the occasion arose.

Adam decided what he must do. He would follow her. Only when he discovered her destination in New Orleans would he let her know she had been recognized.

Chapter Five

Cat hurried through the small bank lobby and onto Chartres Street, whispering to herself in vexation at the unexpected turn of events. The arrangements she had come to make—certainly not the first of their kind for her—were usually seen to with little of her personal intervention, but not today.

She should have expected problems to arise. Since the confrontation last night at the roulette table, and the resulting wager, nothing had gone right. Even going over the books with Emile, usually a time of satisfaction, had not erased memories of the American. Sleep had eluded her until almost dawn, and just as she was drifting into the balm of unconsciousness, memories of the foolish wager at last blurred by exhaustion, Balzac had laid siege to her right braid.

Before leaving the casino, she had gone so far as to stuff Delilah's gris-gris in the pocket of her day dress, hoping against reason to ward off any more problems. Thus far she had experienced none of its supposed benefits.

Tired and out of sorts, Cat found her setback at the bank difficult to accept.

She ought to forget the whole thing, hurry back to La Chatte, and, after depositing her lilliputian tiger outside her door, crawl back in bed and pull the covers over her head, but that would be admitting defeat. Cat could not do such a thing ever again.

Considering the unexpected turn of events, she was vaguely aware of a figure exiting onto the street behind her, but she did not look back. No one could possibly recognize her in the gown and bonnet she chose for the world outside the casino; it was her guarantee of privacy.

Walking briskly down the crowded brick sidewalk— the banquette, as it was called in the city—she went over the latest scene that had her upset.

Her request to the bank president Raymond Wardwell had been simple. He was to set up an account in the name of Gaston Ferrier's wife to tide her over the difficult days ahead. Cat had arranged several such accounts for the families of foolish young men who lost all at La Chatte. Each time she made only two stipulations: the husband was not to have access to the account, and the source of the money was never to be revealed.

"Madame Ferrier will not accept your charity," Wardwell had warned after listening to her presentation in the privacy of his office.

"It is not charity," rejoined Cat. "I want only to return a portion of her husband's foolish losses."

"I know this family personally. Madame Ferrier, whose own family is without funds to help, believes her young husband can do no wrong. The import business he inherited from his father has long thrived, despite several poor decisions on his part. She will look on your offer as unwanted and unneeded charity. In her mind, her husband will provide."

"Not after last night," said Cat in disgust. "He put up his business on the last turn of the card. He had already lost his home to one of his friends, one, I might add, who accepted his written promise with great speed."

"I say only what his wife will claim. She will not use the generous allowance you have set up in her name."

66

"Not even for their baby?"

"You know yourself, Mademoiselle Douchand," Wardwell said, his lips twitching in a smile, "how stubbornly proud the Creoles can be. Two courses are open to you. One, keep the money for your own account. Two, visit the woman yourself and present your arguments."

"Impossible."

"It is your decision to make. I believe that in person you can persuade her the money you offer is rightly hers." The banker's kindly stare rested on Cat. "And rightly her infant son's."

How well Wardwell knew her, she thought, but then he was among the few who knew her past. At times it seemed he could read her mind. "You do not play fair," she said.

"I tell you only what you will think of later. You are a good woman, Mademoiselle Douchand," he said. "I know you will regret not doing all that you can."

Cat looked away from those soft gray eyes, her gloved hands twisting in her lap. "How old is the child?"

"Six months, I believe."

Pain clutched at Cat's heart. What a particularly vulnerable age was six months, especially if his mother were thrown onto the streets, a not unlikely occurence under the circumstances. Cat held little hope Gaston Ferrier would care for his family—not a man who drank and gambled the night away and who pledged his honor and his life in defense of a woman who was little more than a stranger to him.

And his infant son was only six months old.

An image of what he must look like had flashed in her mind—rounded pink cheeks, dark wisps of hair with just a touch of curl, fingers that instinctively clutched at anything in reach, and most vivid of all, laughing brown eyes that stared in wonder at the world.

How quickly laughter could fade from a baby's eyes. Picturing those eyes closing, she gave way to impulse. "I will go," she had said. "Tell me where they reside."

Hurrying along Chartres Street, ignoring the shop windows with their displays of bonnets and fine French shawls, she berated herself for reacting with emotion rather than rationality, yet she was honest enough to realize she had no choice. Wardwell was right. She must do all that she could.

In the ill-fitting dress and with the veil secured firmly beneath her chin, she moved in and out of the pedestrian traffic on the *banquette*. No one gave any special attention to her, the men showing more interest in the numerous yellow- and scarlet-gowned females strolling down the way than in a dowd in black, and the women dividing their interest between the shop windows and the men.

Perspiration pooled between her breasts, and she could feel the day's heat against the back of her neck. She quickened her step as if in so doing she would cool the air.

"Mam'selle," a familiar voice called out, "have we entered a race?"

With a start of guilt, Cat remembered that Delilah had been waiting for her outside the bank. She had been so caught up in reliving the scene with Wardwell that she had forgotten all about her.

Coming to a halt, she waited for the speaker to reach her side. "Forgive me, Delilah. My thoughts were wandering."

"Thinking again." Delilah, clad in a plain black dress similar to Cat's, straightened her *tignon,* the head kerchief that black women were required to wear when they moved about the streets. "Such a serious activity will give you wrinkles."

"And what if it does? I am not a vain woman."

Delilah's nose wrinkled as she studied her mistress's gown. "This I already know. But is it always necessary to hurry through the streets without taking enjoyment?" She cast a quick glance behind them, then looked slyly up at Cat. "Could you not stroll through the market? Perhaps have beignets and cafeᴘ au lait, or a bowl of jambalaya? The time is after noon."

"You know I never do such things." Cat stared down at the shorter woman, whose chocolate eyes stared right back. "You're up to something, Delilah. What is it?"

Delilah shrugged her rounded shoulders in innocence. "I am hungry. Nothing more, mam'selle. If you dine, then I can also."

Cat inhaled. New Orleans air was always redolent of a hundred tantalizing odors—spices and fresh-harvested seafood and baking bread, rich chicory coffee and gumbos, and the familiar staple, rice and red beans with sausage and ham. Certain as she was that Delilah was not completely truthful, she wouldn't mind postponing her business for a short while. Perhaps they could wander through the market . . . buy a few food items for La Chatte . . . treat themselves to the warm, sugar-coated beignets.

She brushed the thought aside. Ben, driving the carriage, was taking care of the marketing. They were to meet him in less than an hour at the north end of Place d'Armes, the central city square that separated St. Louis Cathedral from the Mississippi River. According to the banker, the Ferrier home was located two blocks away on a fashionable section of St. Anne Street. She had just enough time to tend to her business before the appointed meeting time with Ben.

Cat took a coin from the same pocket that held the voodoo charm and pressed it into Delilah's hand. "Treat yourself to what you want. I'll meet you at the carriage."

Delilah was better off shopping alone, Cat thought as she hurried away, since she would be free to purchase the strange ingredients for her gris-gris—

away from her mistress's skeptical gaze and the scornful eye of Ben. Besides, Cat did not want or need company when she met with Madame Ferrier.

Turning onto St. Anne Street, she found the house quickly. Two stories high, it was similar to the buildings on either side, pink stuccoed brick with wide windows both upstairs and down. The openings were blocked by pots of aromatic plants; from the street she could smell the rosemary. Across the second story was a gallery, twenty feet in length, its wrought-iron grillwork mindful of the Spaniards who had once ruled the city.

A young black girl opened the wide gate that served as a front door, and after excusing herself for a brief conference with her mistress, returned to escort Cat inside.

Cat passed through the wide porte cochere, and entered into the open courtyard, the patio that was the heart of the home. Tropical shrubs and magnolia trees bordered the stucco walls and a fountain, its waters unmoving and covered with a fine, dull scum, filled the center, and the carriage that should have been at the far edge was not there.

Looking for her first good sign of the day, Cat hoped the absence of the equipage meant Gaston Ferrier was not at home. In all likelihood, he had not returned since the disaster of last night.

The servant escorted her up the wide stairway and through a hallway onto the long, narrow gallery, where Madame Ferrier awaited. A small and pretty, fair-skinned woman with dark hair tucked neatly into a bun, she was seated on a wrought-iron chair beside a matching table at the far end, watching with worried brown eyes as Cat approached. Cat estimated her age at not above twenty.

"Mademoiselle Douchand," she said in a small, curious voice. Her gaze drifted briefly over her visitor's drab gown. "The name is familiar. Have we met?"

70

"I think not," responded Cat, lifting the veil of her bonnet. "I've come about your husband."

"Oh," Madame Ferrier whispered as she studied Cat's face. "Is he all right?"

"He is, as far as I know, in good health." Except, she added silently, for a possible sore jaw where the American had struck him and, if he had any conscience at all, a very heavy heart.

"Then why . . ." The young woman's voice broke, and Cat could read her mind. Despite her appearance, was this the other woman, Gaston's *chère amie* whose existence she had long suspected?

"I am the owner of La Chatte de la Nuit."

"You are . . . La Chatte?" Again, she took in Cat's gown, only this time with genuine surprise.

"I am."

Madame Ferrier's pallid skin furrowed in worry. "Is Gaston in some kind of trouble? I know that he likes the cards too much, but he has assured me that wagering is only a harmless pastime."

Cat could see no way to soften the bad news. "He has gambled everything away."

The young face tilted upward, an expression of concern dissolving to disbelief. "Not everything. Gaston would not do such a thing."

"Everything."

Madame Ferrier clutched at the arm of her chair. "But that would mean the business . . . the house . . ." Her eyes flew to the dark, open doorway at her left.

Once again she looked at Cat, a spark of rebellion in her wide brown eyes. "How do I know you speak the truth?"

"You don't. But why should I lie? You will find out from your husband soon enough.

"Has the notorious La Chatte come to cast me and my child onto the streets so soon?"

Cat sat in an adjoining chair and placed one hand on the woman's arm. "Of course not. It is not I who hold the deed to your home, but the man with whom your husband gambled. Even if I did, I would not behave as you charge."

"Are you saying you did not profit from last night?"

"I can make no such claim. The casino took a major share of your husband's losses."

Madame Ferrier jerked away and stood, looking down at Cat with contempt. "Then you have come to gloat. If," she said with great emphasis, "what you claim is true."

Cat heaved a sigh. As she had expected, the interview with Madame Ferrier was not going at all well; she should have stayed with her first inclination to go back to La Chatte.

"I came to offer my help," she said, standing. "For you and your son." Before the distraught young woman could protest further, she went on to tell of the account that had been arranged in the name of Madame Ferrier.

"Gaston will provide," responded his wife, shaking her head stubbornly.

What foolish creatures women could be, Cat thought, especially those who are young and still believe in the power and goodness of love.

"He cares deeply for me and his son. I will show you." Before Cat could protest, Madame Ferrier whirled through the doorway and returned within the minute, a blanket-wrapped bundle in her arms. Behind her stood the servant who had opened the gate.

"Our son Jean Claude," said Madame Ferrier.

Cat edged backward. "This is not necessary, Madame Ferrier."

The young mother shifted the infant to her shoulder, and the blanket fell away to reveal a round head covered in silky black curls.

"Oh," whispered Cat.

The infant turned to the sound, his eyes as wide and wondering and smiling as Cat had imagined they

72

would be.

"You can see how beautiful he is," said Madame Ferrier. "Never would my husband do anything to harm him. Or," she added with bravado, "to harm me."

Cat knew she should have turned and hurried down the stairs and onto the street and as far from the beautiful Jean Claude as she could. She was transfixed. How many years it had been since she stood this close to a baby.

Before she could protest, the infant was in her arms and his mother was stepping away.

"Hold him," Madame Ferrier ordered. "He is a loving child. He knows no strangers."

Cat scarcely heard what the woman said, her own mind clouded by the unexpected and unwelcome turn of events.

"I can't—" Her voice broke.

She was caught by the sweet-sour smell of the child and by the soft, small size of him. She tried to thrust him from her, but her muscles refused to respond to her silent pleas. Despite her distress, she could no more separate herself from Jean Claude than she could fly from the gallery.

Rounded brown eyes stared up at her, and Cat could do nothing but stare back. Pale-pink lips curved into a tentative smile, revealing a single white tooth emerging from the lower gum. Instinct demanded that she hold him close, and she felt a burgeoning warmth in the vicinity of her heart.

She bent her head, her lips close to the infant's cheek, and she was swept by a feeling of déjà vu. Just so had she held another child . . . just so had curious fingers tugged at the collar of her gown . . . just so . . .

She pulled herself to the present. What madness had come upon her, she thought in a haze of confusion that bordered on terror. Unmindful of Jean Claude's cry of surprise, she shoved him roughly back into his mother's arms.

"I can't . . ." she began, then swallowed, willing herself to gain control.

Whirling away, she started toward the doorway leading to the stairs. A dark shadow in the opening stopped her progress halfway. The shadow moved onto the gallery and became a man. Hatless, he stood ten feet from her, his legs slightly apart, arms loose at his sides. Gaston Ferrier, she thought at first, then realized the newcomer was far too tall and lean to be Ferrier. He took a step forward, allowing sunlight to fall across his features, and her eyes focused on the hard planes of the man's face. The American stared back.

"You!" she said. Instinctively she backed up until she bumped against the wrought-iron table.

"Mademoiselle Douchand," he said with a slight nod. For a long moment his eyes lingered on her, studying her as though he had never seen her before.

Cat was trapped by the stare, caught between it and the infant held in his mother's arms behind her. It seemed an eternity before the American shifted his attention from her.

"Madame Ferrier, please excuse me for intruding, but when no one answered downstairs, I took it upon myself to make sure nothing was wrong."

The servant made an attempt to explain, but her mistress waved away her words.

"You have come at an awkward time, m'sieur," Madame Ferrier said.

"Again, I apologize."

He walked the length of the gallery toward the women, his boots striking softly against the cypress floor. Lowering her eyes, Cat took in the brown shirt and trousers that fit with great efficiency, defining rather than concealing the contours of the body underneath. He appeared more at home in the casual clothes than he had in last night's frock coat, but no less handsome—if one liked the hard, rugged look that

74

he presented.

Something about him gave the impression he'd been traveling a long, difficult journey—one that was not yet complete.

His legs were longer than Cat had remembered, and more muscled than she had imagined, but the width of his shoulders was the same as her mental image of him.

So were the gray-tinged black of his tousled hair and the deep blue of his eyes. He moved with graceful determination as he closed the distance between them, and she knew without doubt there was not a spare ounce of fat on his frame. When he came to a halt beside her, his trouser leg brushed against her skirt, she wondered if he planned to collect his debt there and then.

He stared down at her and she could read the message deep in his gaze. *Later.* She was caught in his spell.

At last he looked away. "Madame Ferrier, allow me to introduce myself. Adam Gase."

He glanced back at Cat, as though he expected some kind of reaction from her at the announcement of his name. As far as she knew, she had never heard of him.

"M'sieur Gase," Madame Ferrier said, her baby held close. "You startled us."

"Forgive me," he said, "but I have business with Mademoiselle Douchand. She is such a busy woman that I feared I would lose her in the street crowds."

As Cat listened to him speak, she shook off the trance that had overtaken her when she saw him. Or the shock, she thought, giving it a more accurate name.

"You were listening in on a private conversation," she accused.

Again came the studied look. "I did not want to intrude upon you and the child."

So he had seen her hold the baby. He must have observed her confusion, just as he could read her distress now. No doubt he had heard her offer of money, too. Did the man have no sense of decency?

Anger came to her rescue. Enough was enough.

"We will take care of our business, M'sieur Gase, some other day." She turned to Madame Ferrier. "And as to the account I spoke of, it is there for you to use. I ask only that you think of your son."

Fastening the veil once again over her face, she said to the servant, "Please stay with your mistress. I will let myself out."

As though a strong wind were at her back, she hurried along the gallery, down the stairs and through the porte cochere. She needed to put distance between her and the child . . . and between her and the American Adam Gase. The tall gate at the street brought her to a halt and she fumbled at the handle.

"Allow me," a deep voice said over her shoulder.

"No," she said, but the latch proved unfortunately stubborn. She could hear the steady breathing behind her; to cover the disconcerting sound she rattled harder at the wrought iron. Strong brown hands covered hers; even through her gloves, their warmth startled her into a cessation of her struggles.

"Allow me," he repeated.

Cat jerked away from his touch, knowing she was behaving foolishly but unable to do otherwise. La Chatte was always cool and unflappable, she told herself, always mistress of every situation—until Adam Gase came on the scene.

Conceding temporary defeat, she stepped aside, and with a wave of her hand indicated he should proceed. As he moved close, her gaze fell on the strength of his chin and she could make out the faint shadowy stubble on his lean cheeks. In spite of the way she mingled with the gamblers at the casino, ten years had passed since she last allowed herself to study a man so closely, and she could not look away.

His black hair brushed against the collar of his shirt, which was open at the throat. Such thick hair it was, made distinguished by the gray at his temples. Fine lines radiated from his eyes. Worry lines, she thought, not lines of laughter. Adam Gase was not a man who often laughed. She could not look at his lips.

His neck was strong and burnished to a coppery brown by the sun. Curls of hair were visible just below the hollow of his throat. Somehow she knew his chest would be dusted with similar curls. They would be wiry, she thought, but not so stiff as the faint beard that darkened his face.

She sensed the moment he turned to gaze down at her. Slowly she lifted her heavy lashes and through the thin veil met his stare. She was startled by the hunger in his eyes, and startled more by her immediate response, the beginnings of warmth deep inside.

A breeze filtered from the courtyard, carrying with it the sweet scent of magnolias.

"Catherine," he said, his voice a husky whisper.

At the sound of her full name on his lips, she swayed toward him, her body inches from his, her hands longing to lift the veil. She came close to whispering his name. From overhead came the cry of the infant Jean Claude, and Cat returned to her senses, the inner warmth turning to a more acceptable and familiar chill. She gave silent thanks for the gossamer shield that hid the pinkness staining her cheeks.

"M'sieur," she said, stiffening, "you forget yourself. Or could it be you wish to collect your debt"—she hurled the word at him—"here at the gate?"

Slowly his lips curved into a challenging grin. "You won't get out of our wager so easily, Catherine."

"You have no right to call me by that name."

The grin died more quickly than it had been born. "You speak to me of rights?"

The bitterness in his voice matched anything she could say to him, and the hunger in his eyes was quickly replaced by a hard, uncompromising glare.

Adam Gase was a changeable, enigmatic man, and,

77

Cat suspected, a dangerous one, but she refused to look away. "I speak to you of common courtesy. It is a quality you seem to lack."

"It is a quality I do not find particularly important. Not right now. I could call you mademoiselle, but it seems far too formal, considering what we will share. Do you prefer Cat? Or La Chatte? You seem more like a Catherine to me."

"What nonsense you utter." A thought struck her. "How did you know I was here?"

"I, too, had business at the bank this morning."

"You recognized me?"

"It would take more than that ridiculous dress and veil to hide you from me, Catherine."

Cat stirred nervously and shifted her attention to the wrought-iron gate. "You should have not followed me here."

"I would have followed you much farther than the Ferrier home to get what I want."

Cat could not keep from looking at him once again. There was no mistaking the meaning in his eyes. Speechless, she threw herself past him; this time the gate opened with ease. She brought herself to a halt just in time to keep from bumping into a matronly figure on the crowded banquette in front of the Ferrier home. Behind her she could hear a deep-throated chuckle.

She turned in the direction of the Place d'Armes, realizing that it must be time to meet Ben and Delilah.

"Bastard!"

The epithet rang above the noise of the passing pedestrians and she was startled to see directly ahead of her the rumpled figure of Gaston Ferrier, his jaw swollen and discolored, his angry stare directed to the man standing in the shadows at the gate. She doubted he had recognized her, so intent was he on finding the man who had brought him shame.

"*Américain . . .*" he continued, "you dare to come to my home? It is what I should have expected from such as you."

Cat backed toward the stuccoed wall, leaving the two men to face each other across a distance of ten feet. Others on the walkway likewise moved from between them, but no one strayed very far. Around them, a muted chorus of murmurings began.

"Ferrier, I did not know until a few minutes ago that this was your home." Adam Gase sounded disgusted both with himself and with the young Creole.

"You lie, like all of your kind. You hoped to wait, perhaps, and catch me by surprise."

An ugly smile spread across Ferrier's bruised face, and a triumphant gleam lightened his eyes. "It is just as well," he continued. "Name your weapon and I will see that it is provided. We will settle our debt of honor here and now."

Chapter Six

"We settled this last night," Adam Gase said sharply. "Go inside to your wife and child."

Around the men, the murmuring ceased as the crowd waited for Gaston Ferrier to respond.

Cat looked from one man to the other, Gase physically strong and coolly in control of himself, and the bruised and disheveled Ferrier close to exploding from anger.

"I will see that pistols are brought," the Creole said, his voice tight, his dark eyes blazing. "If you trust that I will not deceive you in some way. You may ask anyone you wish to inspect the weapons."

He nodded to a distinguished-looking Frenchman in the crowd behind Gase and then nodded toward the house. Cat watched in growing alarm as the man, accompanied by a bonneted woman, let himself in through the gate.

The American held his arms from his body. "As you can see, I am not armed. And I won't take one of your guns."

Though his open coat and breeches were wrinkled, and his tie was missing from the partially unbuttoned shirt, Ferrier managed to pull himself up with great dignity. "Once again you insult me, m'sieur, to refuse my challenge. Indeed, you insult all with the blood of

81

France in their veins."

"Mon Dieu," came a cry from one of the men who watched. "What you say, Ferrier, is true."

"The only insult," Gase said in disgust, "is directed from you to your family."

"This is a business for men, not women and children," said Ferrier. "Last night you took me by surprise. I will not let you do so again."

The gate to the Ferrier home opened with a creak, and the Frenchman stepped onto the banquette, a wooden box in his hands. He stopped between the two men. "Gaston, do not worry about Madame Ferrier. My own wife tends to her now."

He lifted the lid to the box. Cat was close enough to see the pair of dueling pistols nestled against the red velvet interior. Half stocked in figured walnut, each was decorated with a silver scroll plate down the side. They looked expensive and deadly, just the sort of weaponry that Gaston Ferrier would fancy.

"I took the liberty to see that they were loaded. You must, m'sieur," he said to Gase, "have someone act as your second and inspect them."

"I'll do it, by damn," yelled another man from the crowd, this one dressed in a fringed leather shirt, his face half covered by an unkempt brown beard. "You Frenchies gotta be watched."

"*Un Américain,*" sneered Ferrier.

"A Texican," bragged the newcomer as he picked up one of the guns.

Cat caught Adam Gase's eye. "You can't . . ." she began.

He shook his head briskly.

The Texan took his time inspecting the gun, then lifted it to his eye as if taking aim at the crowd. Ignoring the gasps of surprise, he handed it to Gase. "This un'll do just fine."

For their part, the crowd pulled back to give the duelists more room and found themselves mingling

82

with the carriages that had come to a halt close to the fray.

Gase stared down at the pistol, then lifted his eyes to his challenger. Cat saw no sign of fear on his face, only disgust and pride.

Ferrier took a half dozen steps away. "I believe this is the proper distance." Turning his back, he said loudly, "If a volunteer would kindly count to three, we will turn and fire."

The onlookers who had been behind the men scurried into the street. Holding her place next to the wall, Cat cast a hurried look among the crowd, seeking someone, anyone, who could halt the absurdity. Stupid, stupid men.

"Un!" someone shouted.

Gase looked at Cat. "Please move, mademoiselle. You are too close to the line of fire."

"I will not take one step until you both cease this nonsense," she said.

He shrugged in response.

"Deux!"

Cat thought of Jean Claude and of the American who only a few minutes ago had seemed so powerful. He looked terribly vulnerable now. "Do something," she pleaded.

"If you must remain there," he said, "at least drop to the ground."

With a cry of exasperation, Cat stepped between the two men. "Stop, I say," she demanded, but her words were overpowered by the loud, deep *"Trois!"* that came from the edge of the crowd.

Ferrier whirled, pistol raised and cocked. The air was rent by the roar of gunfire, from which direction Cat could not tell. Belatedly, she did as she was ordered and dropped to the ground. Eardrums close to bursting and her nostrils burning from the acrid smoke, she took a minute to realize she had not been hit.

Eyes closed, she berated herself for so stupidly

thinking she could intercede between two men bent on destruction. She became aware of a figure bent beside her.

"Are you all right?" the American asked.

She nodded, at the same time admitting to relief that he was not sprawled out dead on the banquette. She found she could not speak.

"Fine shootin', partner," said the Texan, who stood behind him. "Unless you were aimin' for something a mite more vital."

"Fool," Gase muttered, and Cat did not know whether he meant her or Ferrier, or the second. He could even have meant himself.

Forcing her eyes to the left, she saw the Creole crouched on the ground, his left hand holding the bloodied sleeve of his right arm. She watched as a pair of men came to his rescue.

"I hadn't meant to shoot," Gase said, low, as if he talked to himself, but his eyes were locked with hers. "I was afraid where his bullet might land."

"You were worried about me?" she asked shakily.

His answer was lost as the gate to the Ferrier home creaked open, and Madame Ferrier hurtled onto the walkway. Close behind was the Frenchman's wife, her bonnet aslant as though she had been in a struggle of her own.

"Gaston," Madame Ferrier cried, and hurried to her husband's side. "They kept me from you, my love. What have they done?"

"He is not injured badly, madame," one of the men said. "It is only a flesh wound."

Ears still ringing, Cat tried to stand but found her legs could not bear her weight. Gase pulled her upright and cradled her against his side, giving her the strength that she could not give herself. She was powerless to pull away, and together they watched as Madame Ferrier pressed kisses to the bruised face of her wounded husband.

Around them the excited whisperings grew, and Cat heard more than one comment that the *Américain* had not paid Ferrier the respect of turning his back during the count.

But he had not planned to shoot, Cat wanted to argue. *He fired because I was stupidly in the way.*

She held her silence, knowing the agitated onlookers would not listen.

"Please," Madame Ferrier said above the whispers, "carry him inside where I can care for him."

Ferrier moaned as he was lifted between the two men who had been inspecting his wound. As they bore him past Cat, his face a scant two feet from hers, he opened his eyes. With the sunlight directly on her, she knew he could see through the filmy veil.

"La Chatte," he whispered in startled recognition. "You are with . . . with him?"

"I . . ." she began.

Madame Ferrier stepped between them, her chin held bravely high, but she could not hide the tears that blurred her eyes.

"You could have killed him," she said, her scathing glance taking in both Cat and Adam Gase. "I do not know what has caused this terrible thing. I know only it is my poor Gaston who has behaved with honor. My dear husband . . ." Her voice broke and she could not continue.

"Sir," said one of Ferrier's bearers, "please take the mademoiselle and depart. Your presence causes only further distress for his wife. It is doubtful that the authorities will be much interested in what has taken place."

Cat heard mutterings of agreement, along with the whispered words "La Chatte de la Nuit" drifting across the crowd. Gaston's cry of recognition had been heard.

"The man gives good advice. Let's get out of here," Gase said and, without allowing her a chance to argue, pushed his way through the onlookers. Feeling very much like a puppet, she barely managed to keep her feet on the ground as he continued to hold her tight against his side.

"You need quiet and privacy," he said when they were a block away from the scene of the shooting. The walkway was empty of other pedestrians, the excitement having drawn them quickly to the front of the Ferrier home.

"I can take you to my hotel room," he added.

"No!"

He came to a halt and stared down at her. "I won't rape you, if that's what you're worried about."

Cat felt the blood return to her brain, and once again her thoughts formed a semblance of order. "Such a thing was far from my mind," she said with less than complete honesty, then added, "although I have no proof you speak the truth."

"Now that's the Catherine I know."

"You do not know me at all, M'sieur Gase."

The look he gave her said more than words that such a situation was only temporary.

"I can return you to your room at the casino," he said.

And, she thought, *tuck me cozily in bed.*

Cat shook her head, unable to contemplate the half-hour ride to the outlying town of Carrollton. The afternoon shadows were lengthening, but in the late summer, night was still several hours away.

She glanced up the street which crossed St. Anne. Rue de Bourbon, the sign read. Emile kept a small home not far away. He had told her of its location, in case she was ever in need of a place to stay in the Vieux Carré.

He was rarely there himself, he had assured her, but he maintained a pair of servants who kept the place open and stocked with food and drink. Cat wasn't a drinking woman, but a snifter of brandy sounded wonderfully appealing to her right now. She could send

86

word to Ben and Delilah where she would be.

She hesitated a moment. Adam Gase had asked about Emile last night—before he changed his mind about the wager. She had sensed then that there was trouble between the two men. Nothing she had learned since about the American indicated he would back down from a confrontation with her old friend. She had always considered Emile invincible, but against Gase she was not sure.

Still, Emile said he was rarely at the Bourbon Street residence, and she would like a moment to rest.

Making her mind up quickly, she gave Adam the directions to the house, omitting any reference as to its owner, and within a few minutes they had arrived.

The house was much like Gaston Ferrier's, only slightly smaller and somehow grander, the plants around the courtyard greener and fuller, the fountain burbling with flowing water, the walls more recently painted. Escorted upstairs by a black woman who had said nothing after hearing her name, Cat found even the furniture at the end of the shaded upstairs gallery more comfortably upholstered than the wrought-iron chairs she had shared with Madame Ferrier. Further, the pieces looked as though they had seldom been used.

Walking slowly close to the iron railing, she removed her hat, veil, and gloves and tossed them onto a low cypress table, the legs of which had been carved to resemble the clawed feet of an alligator. When she took her place on the small settee, Adam Gase passed up the chair she had assumed he would take and sat beside her, ignoring the sharp look of disapproval she threw his way.

She tried to relax, but in the heat of the afternoon her heavy gown clung damply to her skin. Worse, with Adam Gase sitting so uncomfortably close, she found herself suddenly and inexplicably nervous.

The brandy was soon served, and the servant, requested to send a message to the waiting Ben, departed without a word.

Taking one of the glasses from the table, she closed her eyes for a second and was unsettled by the image of a bloodied sleeve flashing across her mind's eye.

"Ferrier really was not badly injured," the American said.

Curse the man. Could he read her every thought?

Swallowing more of the amber liquid than she had planned, she closed her watering eyes until the burning sensation abated and she could once more breathe without fear of coughing. She dared a glance to her left and found the American settled back and watching her with great deliberation.

"It is rude to stare, M'sieur Gase. But rudeness is not something that seems to concern you."

"No, it's not. How else can I figure you out?"

"I am not a puzzle to be solved."

"Or a prize to be opened, I suppose."

Cat gripped her glass. "What an absurd thing to say."

"No more absurd than your stepping between two dueling men."

Cat felt her face flush. "I had not planned to do so," she said defensively. "But neither of you seemed inclined to halt the proceedings."

"And you were so certain your orders would be obeyed."

Cat's short laugh was without humor. "Believe what you wish. I acted without thinking."

"Yet you do not strike me as a woman who acts impulsively. Until today I would have thought your every action calculated."

Cat contemplated the polished surface of the table. "And so it is. I made a mistake. It all seemed so foolish."

"And so it was." He helped himself to another glass of brandy and settled back once again to his perusal of her. "And so it was."

Cat stirred nervously, wishing he would look at something else. "I owe you an apology for something I just said." Her fingers stroked at the skirt of her gown. "I am aware, m'sieur, that you tried to stop the quarrel. It was not your fault that Ferrier would not listen."

"I'll accept your apology if you drop that ridiculous *m'sieur*. My name is Adam."

"I do not care for such familiarity."

He shifted toward her. "But I saved your life. Or at least it is possible that in wounding the determined Gaston, who quite likely is a bad shot, I kept him from hitting you. For that I claim a reward. My name on your lips."

Brushing at a tendril of hair that tickled her cheek, Cat turned to him. "You are an impossible man. What could you possibly expect to get by following me?"

He grinned. "We both know the answer to that."

Cat's exasperation grew. "M'sieur—"

"Adam."

She refilled her snifter and took a sip. The brandy, joining with surprising smoothness the liquor that had gone before, began immediately to do funny things with her brain. "Adam, then," she conceded. "Are you satisfied?"

"The name will do for a start."

An uncomfortable silence settled between them. "Enough questions about me," Cat said. "It is apparent that your roots go back to some other part of the country. Are you traveling through the city?"

And when will you depart? Surely, she thought, he could hear the unasked question in her voice.

"Louisiana is my home."

"Oh." She made no attempt to hide her disappointment. "But not New Orleans."

"What makes you so certain?"

"Because you mentioned a hotel room. And I have not seen you in La Chatte before. Most men who can afford to do so eventually visit the casino at least once."

"My residence is a few miles upriver, although I've been away for a couple of years."

A picture of roiling brown water flashed in Cat's mind, and she shuddered.

"Did I say something to upset you?" Adam asked.

"I do not care for the river."

"That's rather unfortunate, since the city is several feet below sea level. One break in the levee and you would find the Mississippi covering your backyard and, I would guess, much of the casino's first floor."

Cat swirled the brandy in her glass. "I may not care for the river, but I will not let it chase me away."

"There's not only the Mississippi. Southern Louisiana is laced with swamps and bayous. Does the casino mean so much to you that you stay with all that hated water around?"

Taking another sip of the warming liquor, she turned to face him. "I have my reasons for staying. Again I must say you ask too many questions."

"You answer damned few of them. Why did you offer Madame Ferrier money?"

"So you *did* listen in," she said indignantly.

"It's another example of how rude I can be."

His lips twitched into an almost smile, and she found herself, despite her indignation, almost smiling back.

What extraordinary eyes he had, she thought . . . so watchful, their color dark blue like an early-evening sky, yet with tiny pinpricks of light relieving the darkness. What was even more extraordinary was that she would notice such a thing.

"I can't quite figure you out," he continued. "Would you tell me about the money for Madame Ferrier?"

She welcomed his bluntness; it was something she knew how to handle. "It is none of your business."

"Of course it isn't. But I still want to know. Do you make a habit of offering settlements to the wives of foolish and destitute men?"

Against her better judgment, Cat heard herself

90

say, "Sometimes."

"A curious habit for the owner of a gambling hall. I don't believe I have ever met anyone quite like you." His words held a taunting quality.

"I don't imagine you have."

"How do you determine who will benefit from your largesse?"

"That, m'— Adam, is truly none of your concern."

His voice took on a solemn tone. "Is it perhaps when there is a child involved?"

The question struck her with its closeness to the truth and she turned from him, fighting the impulse to throw the remaining brandy in his face. "Enough. Please leave."

He shifted closer until his thigh was pressed against hers and his breath was warm on her neck. "I didn't know whether you were going to take that infant and run away with him or toss him back at his mother. I got the feeling you didn't, either."

"You don't know what you're talking about. I don't like children."

"Liar." A glint lightened the dark blue of Adam's eyes. "I saw the way you looked down at him. For a moment you were like a picture of Madonna and child."

Cat laughed sharply. "What an imagination you have." Her head reeled from the brandy and all that had happened before and, she admitted, from Adam's nearness. "Please leave."

"I doubt you really want me to go. Otherwise you wouldn't have asked me to a place we could be alone."

"I . . ." Cat could think of no response, unable as she was at the moment to remember just exactly what had been in her mind when she suggested the Bourbon Street house as their destination.

Resting his empty glass on the table, he leaned toward her, his right arm draped across the back of the settee, the fingers of his left hand lightly touching the side of her neck. She jumped as though he had burned her.

"I would like to claim my winnings now." Again he stroked the skin between her ear and the collar of her gown.

She closed her eyes, and the dizziness grew. "Please leave," she repeated. "It would be unkind to take advantage of me this afternoon after all that has happened."

"But we have already established that I am not a kind man. Or am I merely rude? Either way, kiss me, Catherine."

Kiss me, Catherine. The words seemed to come from the past. If only they had, she could push them from her mind as she had long ago learned to do and continue with her life.

But there was a man at her side, a very determined and attractive man. She had known from the moment she saw him through the smoke-filled air of the casino that he wanted far more from her than she could possibly give. A kiss would be only the start.

Like the tides on the shore, Cat felt herself drawn to him. It took all of her strength to pull away and to stand. A moment passed before she could speak.

"If you won't leave, then *I* must do so."

Before he could respond, she hurried toward the stairway, her step unsteady but determined. It wasn't until she reached the cool shadows cast at the side of the courtyard by a late-blooming oleander bush that he caught up with her.

His hands gripped her arms and pulled her back against him. "Now, Catherine. The time to pay your debt is now."

He turned her to face him. His eyes burned down into hers, and her breath caught.

She swayed toward him. Perhaps he was right. She should let him kiss her. Then he would have no excuse to be around her ever again.

She tilted her head upward. "I don't suppose you will settle for a kiss on the cheek."

His eyes moved to her lips. "Hardly. I have paid much for this moment."

"But last night," she said, confused. "you took your gold. I made certain that you did."

"There are other ways for a man to pay. Far more costly than anything won or lost at the turn of a roulette wheel."

His fingers roamed upward to her shoulders, caressing her throat and stroking her ears, then moving toward the tight bun at the nape of her neck, and she forgot to question his curious words. Before she realized what he was about, half the pins were removed from the carefully crafted coil and she felt a loosening of her hair.

"What—"

"Shh," he whispered as he removed the remaining pins, and the long curls tumbled to her shoulders and against her back.

He buried his hands in the thickness, freeing his thumbs to stroke her cheeks. "Better," he said. "You look more like a woman who wants to be kissed."

"Who said—"

"Shh. *I* say, Catherine. I can read it in your eyes."

Cat's breath grew ragged and she found she could not deny his charge.

"I've been a long time without a woman, Catherine Douchand." His eyes glittered with unmistakable desire. "You are temptation indeed."

His head bent closer. Cat's heart pounded and the warmth inside began to build once again. She had agreed to this, she told herself, had known he would try to arouse her with his words and with this touch, but heaven help her, she had not realized just how much she would be willing to comply.

He cradled her face. "Say my name."

"Adam." Her voice was no more than a whisper.

He looked at her tenderly—she could find no other word to describe the soft warmth in his eyes. His mouth covered hers, so sweetly and gently that at first it seemed he was putting scant pressure on the touch, as though he planned to break the kiss . . . little more than a brushing of lips . . . concede the debt was paid, and depart.

Cat held her breath, not knowing what she wanted him to do.

As the wondering words drifted through her mind, the kiss became more urgent, his touch firm, his hands wandering lower to stroke her back and pull her into a hard embrace. Fright seized her, and her own hands spread in protest against his muscled chest. How thin the cloth seemed and how close his skin. She could feel its warmth, could feel the pounding of his heart that matched her own quickening pulse.

Trembling, Cat understood why she had been so dreading this moment . . . not because she expected his touch to repulse her . . . not because he might claim far more than just a kiss. She had feared her own weaknesses, and feared a return of passions she had long denied.

She had been right to worry. Her body tingled, and the silent admonitions faded. No longer shoving against him in protest, her traitorous hands sought the contours of his chest and the muscles that constricted in response to her strokes. Trailing her fingers to his throat and to the hair at the nape of his neck, she felt his unyielding body press against her breasts as the embrace deepened.

His tongue traced her closed mouth and, unable to deny him, she parted her lips and he slipped inside. She met the invasion with her own tongue and, just as she should have admitted would happen, all the repressed desires of the past years exploded within her. He was so strong and masculine and demanding, and she forgot why she must refuse him.

She inhaled the manly scent of him and he seemed a part of her. She gripped his shoulders and held herself as hard as she could against him, her breasts swelling with the need for him to caress her. Every part of her body seemed on fire.

He broke the kiss and his lips trailed across her cheek and ear, settling against the side of her neck.

Mindless with need, she was still aware of the movement of his hands against her back. Stroking fingers and palms drifted inexorably lower until he cupped her buttocks and held her tightly against him. She was tall enough to feel the pressure of his enlarged manhood against her lower abdomen. He bent his knees and the pressure moved between her thighs.

She had only to lift her skirt . . .

The thought was like a blast of cold air striking against her fevered body, and the passions fled. Catching him by surprise, she wrenched herself from his embracing arms and whirled to hide the shame that must surely be evident on her face.

Dazed, she struggled for air, her fingers gripping at a thin branch of oleander for support. Dying desire became humiliation. She did not spare herself in placing blame. She had heard the leaves of the shrub she held on to were deadly poison, but they could do her no more harm than she could do herself. If she had ever once doubted such was the case, she had only the past torrid seconds in Adam Gase's arms to prove that such was the truth.

Gradually her breathing settled into its rhythmic regularity, and her heart ceased the pounding that was almost a pain.

"Catherine," said Adam behind her. He stroked her arm. The gesture was gentle, as though he wanted to make certain she was all right . . . as though he cared.

She wondered how long it would take her to turn and face him. The speculation ended with the sound of someone descending the stairs behind them.

"Mister Laverton say it all right if you sometime want to stay the night, Miss Douchand," the servant said. "Will you be here? If so, I'll need to tidy things up a bit."

Cat found her voice. "No one will be staying. Our business is done."

The woman's footsteps retreated to the upper floor.

"This is Emile Laverton's home?" Adam's voice was as hard and unyielding as she had found his body to be only minutes before, but it was not nearly so welcome.

She shifted to face him. "It is."

"Funny," he said. "When we first arrived, I decided it was not regularly lived in. Of course I did not see the bedroom. I would imagine that is the room the two of you use."

"How dare you."

"Surely by now you know I dare a great deal."

He knelt at her feet and she stepped away nervously, wondering what he could be up to. Surely he would not go so far as to—

He stood and extended his hand. When she drew back, he took one of her hands and placed a dozen hairpins against her palm.

"So you can tidy yourself. There's not much I can do about your swollen lips. Anyone looking at you will know right away the cause."

Cat drew herself up proudly. "It was, as you should remember, the payment of a debt."

"It was far more than that, and you know it." His dark eyes fell to her gown. "Tell me, does Emile order you to dress in such a god-awful manner?"

"No one tells me what to do." To her own ears, her brave words sounded hollow.

"Surely a lover would feel free to make suggestions." He looked back into her eyes and she saw he fought against a great rage, as though there had been no tenderness between them, as though there had been no warmth.

Adam believed she was Emile's mistress. Could that be the reason for his fury? Could he possibly be jealous? But that would mean he had developed an interest in her that went beyond claiming her sexual favors. Such an idea was unthinkable . . . or was it? Cat asked herself why she cared what drove him to act as he did.

"Miss Cat, are you all right?"

She looked past Adam and saw Ben Washington and Delilah standing in the doorway that opened onto the street. Taking a deep breath to steady herself, she said, "I'm fine, Ben. M'sieur Gase was just leaving."

Ben's broad, dark face bore a decidedly skeptical expression.

"When we got the message you were here, I tried to tell him you could take care of yourself," said Delilah.

"Of course I can. Go on out to the carriage and I'll join you in a minute. I need to"—she spared one brief glance at Adam—"tidy myself before we begin the ride home."

Adam turned to leave, then paused. "Give my regards to Laverton. Tell him we'll meet before long."

With a nod to Ben and Delilah, he was gone.

Cat stared at the emptiness of the section of outer walkway visible to her from the courtyard. Her thoughts tumbled, and she wondered once again if Adam could possibly care for her.

A darker question ate at her. How did she really feel about him? In the space of a few short hours he had set loose emotions that she had spent years burying. She had no idea how such a thing could have come to pass. Surely that fault lay in herself rather than in him. Adam Gase was insensitive and demanding and inquisitive and rude. The list could go on and on, except that she might begin to include traits that were better left unassessed.

The one sure thing she could hope for was that she never saw him again.

She hurried up the stairs to retrieve her bonnet and

gloves, and twisted her hair into an untidy knot, the pins embedded with unnecessary force into the tangled mess. She was downstairs in less than a minute, the bonnet jammed firmly atop her head. As she pulled the veil into place, she glanced at the watchful Delilah who stood close to the outer doorway. Outside Ben was readying the carriage.

Cat pulled on her gloves and patted at the pocket of her skirt. "I'm afraid your gris-gris isn't keeping me out of trouble," she announced. "I've come close to being shot and then . . . Well, never mind."

"You brought it with you?" asked Delilah.

Cat confessed that she had.

Delilah grinned, her dark eyes twinkling. "It's possible you're wrong, Mam'selle Cat. If you were to ask for my opinion, I'd say that little charm was working just fine."

Chapter Seven

As he strode down Bourbon Street, determined for the time being to put as much distance as possible between himself and Emile Laverton's house, Adam wondered what had come over him that he could so quickly let himself be distracted from the cause that had taken over his life.

He should have been questioning Catherine about her lover's whereabouts. Hell, when he learned who owned the house—something he should have figured to begin with—he should have searched the place to find out anything he could about the man.

So what had he done? Asked her about everything *except* Laverton, and then cut out without so much as an inspection of the courtyard. Since meeting Catherine Douchand, he'd learned pitifully little—except that like the other fools of New Orleans, he was vulnerable to her charms.

Any woman who spent her nights flirting with a casino full of men . . . any woman who let herself be called the ridiculous name La Chatte de la Nuit . . . any woman who served as mistress to a bastard like Laverton was not a woman he should be concerned with—except, as he had decided last night by the roulette table, to take to bed.

He could still feel her responding to his kiss. One

moment she had been holding herself stiff and the next she was all softness and warmth and flowery scents. He'd forgotten guards and justice and revenge. He kissed her because it had been so long since a woman had been in his arms . . . because she was a soft and desirable creature . . . because he was a man and she was a woman and they were doing only what was right for them to do. For one feverish moment he had known she was kissing him for the same reason.

When she wrapped her arms about him and touched him with her tongue, he had almost lost control and taken her without waiting for the niceties of a bed.

It wouldn't have been rape. She had wanted him as much as he wanted her—a fact that made her all the more a puzzle.

The one thing for sure he had learned was that, whatever his other shortcomings, Laverton had chosen his mistress well. There was an air of both innocence and experience about her that would entrance any man.

So what kind of a game was she playing with him? And why had she tried to give money to Madame Ferrier? Perhaps the greatest puzzle of all concerned the Ferrier infant. Accustomed nightly to facing a casino full of drinking and gambling men, why was she so frightened of holding one small child?

The questions ate at him as he made his way to the livery barn where he had stabled his gray gelding Keystone. By the time he arrived, he had decided on one more visit to the casino. Laverton could be there . . . or he might find someone who could be forced into telling his whereabouts. If he rode fast enough, he would get there well before the Douchand carriage arrived, well before Catherine could rouse anyone to keep him from searching the place.

The late-afternoon traffic was light on the road leading from the Vieux Carré to the community of Carrollton. As he rode up to La Chatte, which was situated like a pearl in a long row of plainer gambling houses, he was struck again by its familiarity. Something about the symmetry of the narrow front gallery and of the side yards reminded him of another place, another setting, but anxious as he was to get inside, he gave little thought to the puzzle.

Above him the black cat on the casino sign swung gently in the late-afternoon breeze. Tethering Keystone to a standard close to the street, he found the front door locked, the hours of operation posted as dusk each night or seven P.M., whichever came first, until an hour after midnight.

Making his way down one side of the building, he noted the outbuildings to the rear, including a stable and a small house he assumed served as quarters for the servants. Away from the others and closer to the casino was the kitchen, smoke curling in a diffused gray ribbon from its chimney, and he could imagine the bustle inside in preparation for the spread of food Catherine laid out for her guests.

A brick path led from the kitchen to the casino and to a back door. Without knocking, he tried the knob. It turned easily in his hand and he slipped inside a small pantry and all-purpose storage room, its walls lined with high and low cabinets. He glanced through the doorway at his left; the scent of wine was strong in the brick-lined room. Here barrels of port and burgundy and chardonnay were decanted into handier vessels for serving to the casino's guests. It reminded him of a similar room at his plantation Belle Terre.

Directly ahead was a narrow hallway which ran behind the main room to the casino. Light spilled into the area, and from somewhere in the casino's interior issued the sound of male voices; they would be setting up the tables for the night. He gave La Chatte's owner credit; she was not miserly when it came to hiring an adequate staff.

To his right Adam spied a back stairway leading to

the private quarters on the upper floor. If Laverton were anywhere nearby, he would be up there.

He took a step toward the stairs.

"Now where might you be heading?"

Adam halted, at both the sound of the voice and, more imperative, the prodding of what he took to be a gun at his back.

"The front door was locked," he answered with a shrug.

"Which should have told a thinking man that the place was not open for business."

Whoever the speaker was, he sounded angry, he sounded Irish, and he sounded very sure of himself.

His body tense, his senses alert, Adam said, "My business here does not concern gambling."

"I'm doubting you'd be delivering supplies." The gun poked hard against his side. "I'm doubting it would be anything Miss Cat wants. Now why don't you just turn around, kind of docile-like, and—"

Docile-like came hard for the prison-toughened Adam, and he shifted on one foot away from the gunpoint, at the same time jabbing his elbow into the speaker's rib cage. Taking advantage of his sudden counterattack, Adam whirled and slammed his fist against the man's jaw. The blow would have felled most men, but the stocky gunman, his head knocked back, shook it off and brought his pistol level with Adam's heart.

Rubbing at his chin, he gestured for Adam to back up several steps. Adam took a hard look at his opponent. He was short and broad, built like a boulder, a scrapper who'd be difficult to take down. The sleeves of his shirt were rolled back over hairy, muscled forearms; his close-set eyes were eager with enjoyment in the confrontation; his nose was flat, as though it had been broken a time or two. Adam looked at the gun and complied.

"Need any help, O'Reilly?" a burly black man said

from the door to the hallway.

The red-headed Irishman shook his head. His words were directed at Adam. "Are you making a habit of fistfighting hereabouts? I'm not so easy to take down as the lad last night."

Adam glanced at his stinging hand, reddened about the knuckles from the blow. "So I found out."

"Now I'll ask you again, polite-like so you'll know how it's done. Where were you heading?"

There was nothing polite in O'Reilly's tone of voice, and nothing cordial in the hard stare he leveled at Adam.

"I'm looking for Emile Laverton."

O'Reilly's broad, flat face broke into a smile, but his eyes remained cold. "Now that's better. But not entirely satisfactory. There's no one living on the premises going by the name o' Laverton."

"But he has business here. And I need to find him. Right away. He wasn't at his place on Bourbon Street . . ."

The Irishman's eyes registered surprise.

". . . and I rode out here."

"What makes you think he'd be at a closed casino? Supposin', of course, anyone around here had ever heard of such a man."

"We both know the answer to that."

O'Reilly paused, his studied glance moving to the stairway. The hair on the back of Adam's neck prickled, just as it had done when he entered the casino last night, and he shifted to match his line of vision to O'Reilly's at the same moment a shadow disappeared toward the top steps.

"You may be in luck, Mr. Gase."

Adam stared at the vacant stair where someone had stood only moments before, then slowly turned to face O'Reilly. "So you know my name."

"Made a point of it after the fracas with the Creole. Foolish men, the French, but then so are Yanks. Got to protect Miss Cat from 'em both, you understand."

Adam was certain the protection offered by the tough-looking Irishman extended to Laverton.

"You said I was in luck. Any of it good?" he asked.

"Depends upon what you're really wanting, now don't it, Mr. Gase?" O'Reilly gestured with the gun toward the stairs. "Let's go up and find out."

Adam went first. Reaching the second floor, they emerged onto a dimly lighted hallway, closed doors halfway down either side. At the far end he saw the wide stairway leading to the main entryway of La Chatte. Another closed door was to the right of the back stairs. It was the latter door that O'Reilly indicated as their destination.

Adam moved slowly in front of the Irishman, his palms sweaty, an anxious knot in the pit of his stomach. He'd waited two long years for this moment. A million ideas had occured to him as to how it should be played. None of then ended with Emile Laverton's good health.

He turned the knob, and the door slid quietly open. Adam stepped inside, the armed Irishman close behind.

"Bonjour, M'sieur Gase," said a figure from behind the facing desk. With the light from the window falling across his back, his features were in shadow. Leaning forward, he turned up the lamp on the desk and smiled at his guest.

Adam tightened his fists at his side. With narrowed eyes he studied Emile Laverton. Thinning brown hair, a spare, neatly clad body, a lean, almost emaciated face—nothing to indicate what a monster he must be. Nothing except the eyes. They had little color and no depth, making him seem sightless, but Adam knew beyond doubt that the moment he stepped into the room Laverton had taken a quick, thorough perusal of him from graying temples to dusty boots.

And he'd seen the hate in Adam's eyes. There had

been no attempt made to hide it.

"Will you be wanting me to stay?" asked O'Reilly. Laverton shook his head.

"I'll be right outside," the Irishman responded, and Adam heard the door close quietly behind him.

"Take a seat," Laverton said, gesturing to the chair opposite the desk. "Perhaps you'd like a cigar." He reached for the humidor.

"This isn't a social call," said Adam. He thought of the friend slain during his arrest, remembered the sadistic guard Brother Red, heard the sound of a whip cracking in the air, and was surprised he could be so calm.

As calm as Laverton, who must have seen from the fit of his visitor's clothes that he was unarmed. But Adam could easily crush his enemy's throat with his bare hands. If he were quick enough, he could accomplish the feat before O'Reilly realized anything was amiss and ran with gun blazing into the room.

But then Adam wouldn't learn the reason he had been thrown into hell for two interminable years.

Laverton lit a cigar and studied the burning tip. "If you've come about casino business, I'm afraid I cannot help you."

Adam walked deeper into the room. "Why did you do it?"

A puzzled expression settled on Laverton's face. "Why did I do *what*, m'sieur? You will have to make yourself plainer."

"The arrest . . . the trial . . . the sentence—all of it."

"Perhaps," said Laverton, his thin lips curving into a smile, "you mistake me for someone else."

"I've made no mistake." Another step brought him within three feet of the desk. "Why did you have me thrown into prison?"

"I am not an officer of the law, or of the court. You most certainly have made a mistake." Still calm. Still slightly puzzled, as thought Adam were some kind of mental deficient who must be dealt with patiently.

"Ever hear of a man called Cotton?"

"Cotton? An unusual name, and one that is unfamiliar."

This time he probably spoke the truth. Laverton would not bother himself with someone so lowly as the poor soul who had died in the prison camp. He'd leave negotiations with such as Cotton to subordinates like the armed Irishman.

"It's the only name I know," said Adam. "We didn't have a formal introduction. It was hardly necessary, considering we were chained together in a work gang during much of the day and crammed into a shed together at night. As you can imagine, we got to know each other rather well. Cotton told very interesting stories. About false charges of smuggling slaves, about setup trials conducted in haste. About you, Laverton," Adam added, closing the distance between them, his hands spread on the desk, his body leaned forward. "And about me."

He stared down at the seated man. Laverton stared back with the same empty eyes that had watched Adam since he walked into the room. Laverton's neck rose thin and beckoning above the stiff collar of his shirt.

"Really, m'sieur"—Laverton flicked an ash into a brass bowl on the desk—"I do not know what you are talking about. This Cotton must have made some kind of mistake."

"Mistake? You keep using that word. I'd say you are the one who has made a mistake."

While he spoke, Adam admitted to a rage building inside him, a fury that he could not contain with the civilized speech that was passing between him and Laverton.

With a sweep of his arm he knocked the humidor and ashtray and a scattering of papers from the desk; they fell with a clatter to the floor.

"I could kill you," he said. "I could strangle you with

my bare hands. I would take great pleasure in the act."

The door to the hallway opened. "Trouble, your lordship?"

Laverton studied Adam for a moment, then looked past him. "No, Michael. An accident, that is all."

"Looks to me—"

"An accident, Michael," Laverton repeated. After a pause, the door again closed.

Laverton glanced at the humidor and at the cigars which had spilled across the carpet. "My, my. You have a dramatic way of showing your displeasure, M'sieur Gase."

Adam stood upright, the moment of rage passed, dissipated in the foolish gesture of clearing the desk.

"I'm glad to see you admit to something, even if it's knowing my name."

"I have Michael to thank for the information. He is a fine man. Crude, of course, and abominably dressed, but he performs each of his tasks well. You say you could kill me. I assure you, m'sieur, you would be dead within the minute if you tried such a thing."

"You do that very well, Laverton."

"Do what?"

"Play the fop. Expensive suit, expensive cigars, clean hands. No dirt, no calluses. A Creole gentleman. Is this the side you present to Catherine?"

Laverton started, the first anxious reaction Adam had received since walking into the room. "We will not discuss Mademoiselle Douchand." Laverton's order cut like a knife through the air. "Do so, and you risk your life."

Staring into Laverton's pale eyes, Adam was reminded of a cold fog coming off the sea.

"If you think to frighten me, think again," he said. "I'm beyond frightening. There's a funny thing about facing death daily for two years. It loses its power over you. There are times it seems a friend; you'd welcome it if you got the chance, because the reality of life has become so horrible. Ever experience anything like that?"

"My experiences are no more of your concern than yours are of mine."

In that instant Adam saw what he must do.

"I really had planned to kill you. Eventually, after you'd confessed everything I have to know. But that would be too easy for you. A quick shot . . . strangulation . . . a knife. There are a number of ways to take revenge, but all of them ultimately unsatisfactory. And all of them could lead me back to the prison camp. It's in that swamp that the real punishment lies. It's there that you need to go, not to your grave."

"You seem to have given this imaginary crime of mine a great deal of thought, M'sieur Gase, as well as the retribution. But I am not worried by your threats. Neither of us, it would seem, has the power to frighten the other."

"If you are truly untroubled—and I'm not completely sure that's the case—it is only because you don't know what awaits."

"None of us can know what the future holds." Laverton glanced toward the door, then back at Adam. "That is why I employ someone like Michael. And he is not the only one, I assure you. He is, however, the most . . . civilized."

"The United States Army wouldn't do you any good, Laverton. Not now. You had me thrown in prison without just cause and without a fair trial. No man should have such power over another. A good friend was killed when those thugs came to arrest me. You will pay."

For a moment Laverton's foxlike face was set in a look of pure malevolence. "I am fully capable of protecting myself—and those I care for. With or without help. Be warned. Go too far and it is I who will seek revenge."

"You've got me shaking in my boots, Laverton. So

much so that I'm having a hard time not laughing out loud. I'm after justice, if there is any such thing. Somehow I'll prove my innocence and the part you played in sending me away. There's a guard, a preacher he calls himself—Brother Red—awaiting you out there. His sermon is a whip, and he has a painful message to deliver. It's not one you ever forget."

Adam strode around the desk and gripped Laverton by the collar, pulling him out of the chair. The older man was no match for his strength and made no attempt to struggle in his grasp.

"I took it for two long years, Laverton. I wonder how long you will last."

Their eyes met. Laverton did not blink, did not show the least sign of fear. Neither did he speak, letting the icy hate in his stare say far more eloquently than words that the battle lines between the two men had been drawn.

The cold metal tip of a gun pressed against the side of Adam's neck.

"You'd best be letting his lordship go, Mr. Gase," Michael O'Reilly whispered in Adam's ear. "Wouldn't want to take off your head here and now. 'Twould make a mess on Miss Cat's desk."

Adam slowly did as he was instructed. Laverton straightened, smoothing his tie and the lapels of his coat. Neither Michael nor the gun moved.

"Mr. Gase was just leaving, Michael," said Laverton.

Michael stepped away, the gun lowered to his side. "I'm a little disappointed to hear that."

Adam glanced at the Irishman—at his broad, flat face with its broken nose, at his barrel chest and arms the size of posts.

"We'll meet again," Adam assured him. He glanced back at Laverton, who was once again seated behind the desk. "I'm sure we all will."

Without waiting for either man to speak, Adam strode quickly out of the room and slammed the door behind him. If they wanted to gun him down, he couldn't do much to stop them. Somehow he didn't think that was their way, not right here in the lighted hallway where his blood would stain the expensive rug—despite O'Reilly's talk of ruining the desk. Dark alleys would be more their style.

He made a silent vow. No longer would he go about the streets unarmed. He wasn't by nature a fighter, but he was learning. He needed to guard his back better. And he was decidedly against sneaking through back doors.

He headed for the front stairway just as Catherine appeared at the top step, bonnet and gloves in hand.

"Adam," she said in surprise, her violet eyes wide, her lips, he was glad to note, still slightly swollen from their kiss. And her hair was definitely untidy where she had hastily pinned it back in place.

"Good for you, Catherine," he said as he drew near. "You remember my name."

Her glance cut to the closed study door, then back to him. "What are you doing at La Chatte, M'sieur Gase?" she asked with exaggerated politeness.

"Talking to the man that's never there."

"Emile—"

The name was soft on her lips. The rage he usually directed at Laverton he found directed at her and at himself because, against all reason, he wanted to pull her into his arms once again.

"The evil one, or so he's known on the streets. The elusive one, the ghost. The bastard. And, of course," he added cruelly, "the lover of Catherine Douchand."

"You don't know what you're talking about," she said, her expression one of rage that matched his own.

"Where is my error? In the character of Laverton? Surely not in the relationship between you two. You're an experienced woman." He glanced at the Persian carpet which ran the length of the hallway and at the gilded sconces on the walls. "You live a life of

110

decadence. Surely you're not trying to deny it."

"Get out of here. I'll call for help."

His hands gripped her upper arms, and he pulled her hard against him. "Cry out, Catherine." His head bent closer. "Now."

She struggled in his grasp. "Let me go," she said, her voice more a plea than a command.

"Is that really what you want? Or would you prefer I drag you behind one of these closed doors and give you what you wanted the last time we met?"

Giving her no time to respond, he covered her lips with his own in a hard, searing kiss that told her more than words how ready he was to carry through on his threat. Hot desire knifed through him. This time her fists pounded against him, and she twisted to free herself from his embrace.

He thrust her away. "Perhaps the time is not yet ripe, Catherine, but it will come. We will make love. You know it, and so do I."

With a nod he hurried down the stairs.

Cat rubbed at her bruised lips, her thoughts in a turmoil as she stared at the departing figure. She struggled for breath. She wanted to hurtle after him and rain imprecations down on his head. She wanted to slap the proud look from his face. She wanted never to see him again.

She wanted . . . She did not know what she wanted, and her indecision tore at the tattered remains of her peace. Trying to attribute her confusion to the effects of the brandy, she knew the slow ride back to Carrollton had served to sober her. Whatever bewilderment she suffered was because of the departing man.

The door to the study opened, and Laverton emerged. "I heard voices," he said from the end of the hall.

111

"The American from last night," said Cat, hating the shakiness in her voice. "He was just leaving."

"Any problems?"

Cat shook her head. "He's gone. My business with him is done."

"Without, I assume, complications."

"There were no complications." Never had she lied to Emile, she thought, but how could she describe the confusion that beset her, and the yearnings she felt each time Adam was nearby? She'd thought all such feelings were long dead. In the space of a few hours she'd found she was wrong.

"Has he never mentioned my name?"

Cat started guiltily. "He has asked your whereabouts."

She felt Emile's hard gaze as she spoke.

"And nothing more?"

"Nothing." *Except,* she thought, *to accuse me regularly of being your mistress. It seems to matter a great deal to him.*

She wanted to ask Emile what his conversation with Adam had been about, and why Adam was filled with such rage. But in all the years they had known each other, she had never questioned him about his business. She could not bring herself to do so now.

Emile spoke in the smooth, sure voice she had come to know well. "Nevertheless, my dear, I must warn you to guard yourself well against the man. Do not let yourself be alone with him."

"I shall be careful," she said, then added, "I need to change for tonight. Please excuse me." Avoiding Emile's steady eye, she let herself into her room. The orderliness of her private quarters would help her thoughts to settle once again. She had duties to perform, guests to entertain, and most of all, her old resolves to call forth to give her strength.

Time had always been her friend. It would be so again.

She threw bonnet and gloves onto the bed and pulled the pins from her half-fallen hair. If only her hands did not shake . . . If only her heart did not continue to pound . . .

We will make love.

The man was absurd.

She glanced into the mirror and was startled by the wounded darkness of her eyes.

You know it, and so do I.

She knew no such thing. Julien had taught her years ago that men were not to be trusted. She'd been so young, so in love. And he had abandoned her in her time of greatest need.

She had not thought of Julien's name in years and cursed Adam for making her do so today.

She pulled at the buttons of her gown. A scratching from the hallway stilled her undressing. She opened the door and stepped aside to allow Balzac to enter, his perambulations on the upper floor having obviously come to an end when he heard her arrive.

She barely glanced at the small golden figure prancing inside. Closing the door, she looked downward as the kitten deposited a misshapen object at her feet. Recognition dawned, and with it came dismay. He had slain a mouse, and he had brought it to her.

He looked up proudly. *Mama,* he seemed to say, *haven't I been a good boy?*

Staring at the broken body of the rodent, her eyes on the trace of blood at his neck, Cat burst into uncharacteristic tears.

Chapter Eight

Arriving back in New Orleans too late to begin any interrogation at the courthouse, Adam settled for a bottle of brandy in his hotel room—a full decanter which he was prepared to empty if it took all night. He hadn't been drunk since the age of sixteen when he and a couple of his Pennsylvania farm friends found a jug of corn liquor in the abandoned belongings of a hired hand who had run off with the mayor's daughter.

Man and wife had never been heard from again, as far as Adam knew, and their names were long forgotten, but he remembered the liquor and the following day's gut-emptying illness in great detail.

On this night nineteen years later he chose a fine French cognac, an appropriate choice since he was about to nail the hide of the Creole Laverton to the nearest jailhouse wall. The more he considered today's confrontation at the casino, the more he admitted that Laverton was exactly what he should have expected—a sharp-faced man of almost effeminate habits, a carefully turned-out gentleman who sat alone in a semidarkened room and waited for others to do his dirty work—a man of few words, most of them soft-spoken threats.

Two glasses later, his contemplations turned to another Creole, one equally unsettling but in a far different way. At the moment parading herself before the gamblers at La Chatte, Catherine was best thought of through a haze.

Think of her, he did—of the full lips that responded to his kiss, of the curve of her body as she pressed herself against him, of the desire she had not been able to keep from the depths of those remarkable violet eyes. She'd come alive in his arms, like an enchanted princess in a child's fairy tale who needed only the kiss of her true love to awaken her to the joy of life.

Drawing deeply on the brandy, Adam wondered what in hell had come over him. A princess and her true love, for God's sake. Ever since he watched her hold that baby, a glow of unutterable love in her eyes and then a shadow of unutterable despair, he had been unable to disregard a fanciful thought or two about her.

But he must have been wrong. The light on the gallery had been poor. La Chatte, a temptress to half the men in New Orleans, was hardly a sleeping innocent awakened by his kiss. She'd given herself to a criminal in return for the casino and for the comfortable life it provided; Adam was as sure of the fact as he was that the cognac went down a hell of a lot smoother than corn liquor ever could.

Pacing the length of the room, he paused and held the glass up to the lamplight, the amber liquid reminding him of a woman's dusky skin in the darkness of the courtyard.

Laverton's courtyard, he reminded himself as he tossed back the drink and reached for another. Catherine needed to know that in aligning herself with that fox-faced bastard, she had made a poor bargain. As the contents of the cognac bottle decreased, Adam convinced himself more and more that he was the one to teach her. Bedding her would be more than a pleasure, he concluded long after midnight; it would be a duty.

What had been purely a desire for revenge was taking on new aspects. Whatever the truth about her behavior at the Ferrier home, Catherine was a far more complex woman than he had at first suspected, and certainly more so than her reputation indicated. Rather than grieving when Laverton inevitably met justice, she should be glad. By the time Adam pulled off his boots and fell on top of the bed covers, he had decided he was doing her a damned fine favor by showing her what sex with a real man could be like.

He awoke the next morning to several realizations: first, that he had done some foolish speculating about the nobility of his lust; second, that for the first time since his release from the work gang he had slept the night through without dreaming; and third, that French cognac provoked as uncomfortable a head and stomach as the hired hand's jug.

He took a long time to change clothes and a longer time to shave. Pulling on his last clean shirt, he decided he would need to find a laundry soon or else toss out what he'd brought from Belle Terre and find the nearest clothing store.

What he needed more than clothes, however, was a gun. A tobacco-chewing dealer in weaponry was located not far from the hotel; after careful study of the available stock, Adam settled on a double-barreled percussion holster pistol he was assured had proven popular "with them Texicans. They ride over to N'awleens every now and then for a little civilization. Don't seem to take to it much, though."

The dealer aimed with unerring accuracy for the brass spittoon on the floor by the display case. "They leave about as loud-mouthed and bragging as when they come in."

Adam also purchased a holster, which he wore strapped against his hip. He wanted Laverton's men to

117

know he meant business, just in case he hadn't made his point clear enough yesterday in the study of La Chatte.

A cup of chicory coffee helped him forget the worst of the cognac's effects, and the morning air, still holding a trace of the nighttime cool, helped clear the pain from his head, helped him decide what to do.

When he'd first come to town earlier in the week, he'd concentrated on learning all he could about Laverton. His questions had led him to La Chatte. Today his investigation would take a different direction.

He made his way to the headquarters of the city next to the St. Louis Cathedral, planning to read over the written report of his trial and learn if there were any details he might have forgotten that could help him now. But he didn't need the names of the participants; they were burned in his memory.

"Those records are two years old. They'd take hours to locate," a pasty-faced clerk said with a sniff. "We will take your request, of course. Come back at the end of the week."

Adam leaned across the scarred counter separating them. "What about Judge Osborne?" he asked.

"Judge Lawrence Osborne retired more than a year ago." The clerk's watery blue eyes blinked at Adam through a pair of wire-framed glasses.

"Where can I find him?"

The clerk's lips pursed. "I am not able to give out that kind of information—even if I knew it, which I most assuredly do not. The less said about . . . well, never mind."

"Have you got something against the judge?"

The clerk shook his head, one finger pushing at the glasses on the bridge of his nose. "It is not my place to judge a judge." He considered a moment, then with a grimace said, "It is most unfortunate that Osborne has taken to drink, especially considering that he is a former member of the court."

Adam scowled. "Maybe he has a lot to forget. Maybe he's worried about some of the justice he dispensed coming back to him."

"You sound, sir, as if you, too, do not approve of the man."

Adam remembered the swift gavel that had ended each protest of his own hastily chosen attorney and the narrow, tight lips that had pronounced sentence with no delay after the sole witness had taken the stand. The entire proceeding had taken place in less than an hour; reliving it, he gave in to a moment of rage.

"I'll see him burn in hell."

The clerk's eyes widened. "Sir," he said, fidgeting with the neat stack of papers on the counter in front of him, "please watch your language. You are in a government building."

Adam almost laughed. Calmer, he asked about the prosecuting attorney.

"Drowned in a boating accident only a few months ago."

Only one officer of the court remained: the bailiff Johnnie Taylor, who, he was assured, should be on duty at the courthouse.

Adam remembered Taylor as a short, balding man with a nervous twitch in his left eye and a gimpy walk.

He found him walking slowly down the corridor outside the courtroom where the farcical trial had been held. Except for Taylor, the hallway was deserted.

Adam approached him from the rear and recognized his uneven gait right away. Squat and broad, he wore gray shirt and trousers, both pulled tight across his backside. A half circle of sweat stained the shirt just above his belt, and a gun was holstered to his meaty right thigh.

He'd gained weight since the trial, Adam thought, most of it gone to flab. Adam knew just the remedy for removing excess fat: two years under Brother Red's crucifying whip.

"Hello, Johnnie," Adam said when he was close.

The bailiff turned. "Wha—" His left eye twitched mightily in recognition.

"I hoped you would remember me," Adam said.

Behind Adam a door opened and closed, and a pair of dark-suited men with the self-important look of attorneys strode past, too deep in conversation to note anyone else.

Taylor stared at their departing backs, as though he might call for help, then turned his attention once again to Adam, his gaze resting for a moment on the newly purchased gun. "Heard you'd got early release."

"You don't look very pleased."

"Just surprised. You're looking fit for a man just out of the swamps."

"I'm feeling fit, too, Johnnie. At least reasonably so. And angry. You ever get so disgusted with anyone that you could shoot him down and not feel a twinge of conscience?"

Beads of sweat broke out on Taylor's high, lined forehead. "Now, Gase, you know I was only following orders of the court."

"Of course you were. But I always got the feeling you knew what was going to happen ahead of time. Like someone who had read the play before showing up at the opera house. Each time Osborne barked an order, you were already moving to do what he said. You got me in and out of that courtroom so fast, I barely had time to dust off my chair."

Taylor took a step backward on his good leg. "What you getting at?"

"That the whole thing was staged, with me as the appointed victim."

"Ain't never seen a defendant yet that didn't swear he was innocent. Don't appear you're any exception."

120

"I'm an exception, all right. I've come back for the justice that was missing before. And I need help. You willing to help a mistreated prisoner who wants to see the righteous rewarded and the guilty punished? Are you willing to do as you've sworn to do and really uphold the law?"

The bailiff glanced nervously up and down the hall, a trickle of sweat running down the side of his face. "You got to be crazy."

"A little," said Adam, figuring there was no harm in encouraging Taylor's fear. "I'd say it's best you humor me, answer what I ask, and then I'll be on my way."

"You were tried in open court—"

"So where were the spectators? Where was the jury? As I recall, there was just you, a couple of attorneys, and the judge."

"Osborne ain't working no more," Taylor said hurriedly.

"Neither is the prosecutor, I hear. A boating accident, wasn't it?"

"That's what they say." Taylor's left eye fluttered like a flag in a stiff wind.

"No need to ask about the lawyer brought in for me. He was too stupid to follow orders and get them right." Adam shrugged. "I guess that leaves only one participant unaccounted for—the witness. An Irishman named Sean Casey, as best I recall." On purpose he sounded unsure, as though he couldn't remember if he got the name right, as though the name hadn't been part of a litany of names that filled his nighttime thoughts in the prison camp.

"That's right, isn't it?" he asked. "Casey was his name."

Taylor gave a tentative nod. "Best as I can recall."

"I imagine you recall, all right. It didn't take Casey long to tell his story. Have you ever seen a case tried in an hour before?"

"I wasn't watching the clock."

"I know. You were just following orders. Now you've got one more to consider. Tell me all that you can about Casey . . . or anyone else who might know him. You'll sleep better nights, Johnnie, helping me now. Satisfy me that you've told all that you can, and just maybe I won't be visiting you again."

An hour later, Adam was making his way on foot down the busy levee walkway that ran alongside the Mississippi. Food and clothing stalls had drawn a large crowd of shoppers on this sunny August afternoon, and he had to hold on to his patience as he found his progress slowed.

The walkway was a symphony of sound: the rattle and squeak of horse-drawn carriages on the nearby street, an occasional blare of a trumpet announcing an auction or the arrival of fresh seafood, the insistent tolling of church bells, and most of all the cry of the vendors hawking their wares.

Every time he came into the city he was struck by its festive air.

As he moved downriver, the crowd gradually thinned and the area through which he passed took on an ominous air—swaggering sailors with bottles in hand, women hawking wares that had nothing to do with clothing or food, pimps watching them at their recruitment. He was in the area known as the Swamp, the one part of New Orleans where society feared to visit. And with good reason, Adam thought as he made his way determinedly forward. The place was a haven of whores, drunks, gamblers, deserters, cutthroats and thieves.

Just the sort of place where he would find a man like Sean Casey.

Taylor had directed him to a saloon on the edge of

the Swamp. "Casey's a seaman. At least he used to be. Lots of 'em hang out there. Could be you'll find him. That's the best I can do."

Adam had no choice for the time being but to follow through on his recommendation. He found the place on a side street. Like the surrounding buildings, the one-storied ramshackle affair was constructed of rough planks flimsily thrown together. A poorly lettered sign hung above the open door:

DRINK EMPORIUM
LADIES WELCOME

Inside, only the sunlight from the doorway and from two small windows located on the side walls provided light. As his eyes adjusted to the smoky gloom, Adam saw a dozen tables scattered about the half-filled room. A bar extended across the back; behind it a mustachioed bartender, rag and glass in hand, eyed him carefully. Around him conversation was desultory, except for the high-pitched laughter of a woman somewhere to his right.

Adam strode to the bar and ordered a whiskey.

The bartender put the order and an open hand in front of Adam, who caught the hint and paid promptly for the drink.

With residues of last night's overindulgence still lingering, he ignored the whiskey.

"Business seems slow," he said.

"Picks up later."

Adam cast a careful gaze around the room before turning back to the bartender. "I was hoping to find a man."

"So are most of the women who come in here. Didn't figure you for that sort, somehow."

Adam ignored the implication. "A particular man. I haven't seen him in a couple of years. An Irishman.

123

You get many Irishmen in here?"

"We get all kinds."

"Sean Casey one of them?"

"Could have been. It's a common enough name."

"This Sean Casey does odd jobs from time to time. Not particular about the nature of the work or the man who hires him." Pulling a twenty-dollar gold piece from his pocket, he flipped it in the air, then spun it on the counter beside the whiskey glass.

"I'm most anxious to talk to him," he said.

The bartender waited for the coin to end its spinning before he spoke. "Could be he comes in here some. If it's the same Sean Casey, of course."

"Tall, heavyset man with a red beard—or at least he had one the last time we met. Hair shaggy and red as the beard. Talks with a brogue. The back of his left hand bears a scar."

The bartender pocketed the coin. "Beard's gone. Or at least it was the last time he was in here."

"When was that?"

"Yesterday afternoon."

Adam admitted to a growing excitement. "Any way I could get in touch with him?"

"Any way I could get another coin?"

"You value your information."

The bartender shrugged. "I get the feeling you do, too, mister."

Adam tossed another coin his way. "I'll want to see him today."

Without comment, the bartender snapped his fingers and a small black boy came running from the shadows of the saloon. Bending, the man whispered an order to the boy, whose bare feet beat a quick retreat for the door.

"May take a spell," he said, then gestured for Adam to take a seat at one of the tables for the wait. "If Casey don't want to be found, he can lose himself real easy like in the Swamp."

Adam selected a table at the side of the room and sat with his back to the wall. From this position he had a clear view of the door. He knew from the prickles on his neck that Casey was about to approach, even before the tall shadow darkened the doorframe.

Sean Casey was exactly as Adam remembered him, tall and broad and bushy-haired, except that he was minus the beard. He lumbered toward the bar, his gait that of a sailor away from the sea. "You sent for me, Ralph? What's going on?"

The bartender nodded toward Adam. "You got company."

Casey turned toward the side table, a frown on his grizzled face. Even in the subdued light Adam could see the instant he was recognized.

He stood and nodded toward one of the chairs. "Sean, I've been looking forward to seeing you. It's been a long time."

Casey's stare took in the holster at Adam's hip.

Adam rested his hand on the gun. "Don't cause any trouble. Just have a drink with me and a little talk. It shouldn't take long for us to conclude our business."

The drone of conversation in the saloon faded as the two men took each other's measure.

"Have a seat," said Ralph from behind the bar, "and I'll get you a whiskey."

"Do as the man suggests," Adam said. "As I said, the only thing I'm after is information."

Muttering his disgust, Casey threw his heavy frame into the chair to Adam's right. "I ain't saying a damned thing."

When Ralph brought him the whiskey, his scarred hand gripped the glass and he downed the drink in one gulp. "I'll be needing another," he said. "Throat's too dry to talk."

Adam nodded toward Ralph. "Just leave the bottle."

Casey poured himself another drink, this one full to the rim, and swallowed half before setting the glass on the table.

From the background came the sound of renewed talk.

"That wasn't a very nice thing you did, Sean, lying about me under oath. Didn't your mother tell you back in Ireland that lying was a sin?"

"Leave me mother out of this. The old woman's dead now and in her pauper's grave." He gulped at the whiskey and reached for the bottle once again. "So's me old man, matter of fact."

"Please accept my sympathies."

Casey eyed him from beneath shaggy brows. "You ain't interested in my troubles."

"True, but I am interested in your lies."

"I told what I saw."

"Think again, Sean," Adam said softly, but there was no mistaking the hint of steel in his voice. "We both know you gave false evidence against me. But you can make up for that terrible deed. You can tell the truth now."

Casey blinked and concentrated on the newly filled glass.

"Were you well paid?" asked Adam, leaning back in the chair.

"I ain't talking."

"It's been two years, Sean. Two long years." He studied the frayed open collar of the Irishman's shirt and the deep lines carved into his ruddy skin. "Times have been hard, haven't they? The money must be long gone. Unless you've done other jobs for Emile Laverton. Is that what you've done? Worked for him?"

"The son of a bitch . . ." Casey caught himself.

"Did he cause you trouble?" asked Adam sympathetically. "And after all you did for him."

"Money was supposed to last. Other jobs, he said,

would be coming my way. Keep me from having to ship out again." The man's voice was slurred by the whiskey.

"I thought you were a sailor."

"Was. Hate the damned ocean."

Adam considered a moment. "Laverton was supposed to get you land work, was he? You should have known he was not a man you could trust."

"I'm a damned good hand," he said, as though he were talking to himself. "Do what I'm told. Dependable, that's Sean Casey."

Adam ventured a guess. "Except when you're drinking."

Casey jerked his eyes toward Adam. "That's a friggin' lie."

"Lies can cause a man a lot of trouble, can't they, Sean? We both know that." This time he was the one who reached out to refill the Irishman's empty glass. "What you need is a little money. To help yourself get on your feet. Then you can get a job to your liking. Inland. Texas, maybe. I hear there's opportunity there for a man like you."

Casey's eyes took on a wily look. "Money, you say. How much?"

"A hundred dollars. In gold."

Greed lightened the Irishman's stare. "Where might you be keeping it?"

"I'm not carrying that much money with me into the Drink Emporium. But it's not far away."

"What're you wantin' me to do for that much gold, kill a man? I'm not the one for killing. Never done it before."

"I told you from the beginning, just talk, that's all. To me and to whoever I say. Talk about Laverton and what he had you do."

"Can't."

"Why not?"

"Never met a man bearing that name."

Adam felt a crush of disappointment. "A moment ago you called him a son of a bitch."

"Didn't mean him exactly."

"Somebody hired you to lie about me. For him."

"I'm not denying I was hired."

Again Adam ventured a guess. "It was another Irishman, I'll bet. Michael O'Reilly. Have you two known each other long?"

Casey nodded once. "Came over on the ship together."

Adam realized he had been holding his breath and let out a long sigh of relief. "Michael's looking prosperous these days, isn't he?"

"He's not been around in some time," Casey said harshly.

"Believe me, Sean, he's taken good care of himself. It's too bad he forgot about his old friend."

He lapsed into silence and let Casey think about his fellow countryman for a minute or two.

Again came the wily look in the Irishman's eyes. "Make it two hundred and we're in business."

"Agreed." Adam had been prepared to go much higher, but he didn't see the point in letting Casey in on the information. "There's one catch. I'll need a witness to our conversation. You above all people should know how valuable a witness can be."

Casey hesitated. "I got bad feelings about this. Like someone walked over my mother's grave."

"Two hundred, Sean. In gold."

Adam could almost hear the grinding of the Irishman's brain as he thought through the proposition. "No weapons," he said at last.

"Agreed. But we'll have to meet at a place of my choice."

Casey's grin revealed a row of yellowed teeth. "You don't want to bring all that money into the Emporium

128

without that pistol at your side?"

"I don't." Adam went on to make the arrangements. Casey was to meet him on the river side of the Place d'Armes in two hours. Reluctantly, Casey agreed to leave the Swamp.

Adam took the bottle away from the Irishman and pushed away from the table. At the bar he handed the whiskey to Ralph, along with more than enough money to pay for the drinks. "See that he doesn't have anything but coffee. And food, if you can get some. I need him sober."

Another coin brought a nod from Ralph, and Adam departed. He would get the gold and a witness—the lawyer Joseph Devine, if he were available—then head for the square. By the time he arrived at the bank, the front door was already locked and he had to bang for ten minutes before anyone inside heard him.

Opening the door a crack, a clerk answered with a curt, "We're closed, m'sieur."

Adam shoved his way into the lobby. "Tell Mr. Odom that Adam Gase is here."

"Sir"—the clerk's voice rose—"we are closed."

"Let Mr. Gase enter," Odom said from his open doorway.

In the privacy of the banker's office, Adam explained what he needed. Odom was skeptical of the plan— "Bribery, that's what it is, and it's a dangerous course," he said in protest—but Adam insisted and was soon carrying a small bag of gold close to his side as he hurried down Chartres Street toward the office of Joseph Devine. He hoped the attorney lived up to his name.

Adam found Devine seated behind a cluttered desk. His grip was firm, a good sign, Adam thought, trying not to consider how young the short, slender attorney looked. His sandy hair was worn long against the collar of a starched shirt, and the tanned face looked as though it seldom needed the touch of a razor.

For a minute they discussed the work Devine was doing on behalf of the Belle Terre slaves, then Adam turned the topic to the Drink Emporium and Sean Casey. "I'll need a witness to whatever he says. You may have to testify in court."

"I certainly hope so. I've never met this Laverton, but if only half the rumors about him are true, he ought to be locked away for life."

"I plan to do my part to make that happen."

The afternoon sun was bearing heavily down on the old city as the two men hurried along the banquette. Adam could hardly believe it was only yesterday that he had followed Catherine along this same route after seeing her in the bank. In the distance, rising like a welcoming arm into the sky, was the steeple of St. Louis Cathedral.

Lurking close to the cathedral, around the corner behind the city headquarters, was a building he hoped never to enter again—the Calaboso, New Orleans's city jail. It was a hellhole of cold, damp cells and of desperate men, many of them chained to one another, and all around them the fetid smell of degradation and despair.

He stopped once, to take the gun from its holster and nestle it inside his shirt. The metal was cold against his stomach.

"I'm not supposed to be armed," he said in answer to Devine's questioning glance.

"And now you're not?"

"Look at it this way. Casey wasn't supposed to be lying under oath."

"You have a point. Ever thought of studying law?"

Adam grinned. "I'm a simple planter."

"You're about as simple, Mr. Gase, as the Louisiana code of laws. And I can assure you that it is as complex a set of statutes as you're likely to find."

They reached the Place d'Armes just as the church bells were tolling. The square was a wide stretch of grass and maple trees surrounded by a wrought-iron fence. They let themselves in through one of the intricately designed gates, the echoes of the bells giving a solemn, stately background to their arrival, and walked quickly along one of the pathways to the far side, the part of the square closest to the Mississippi. Few people were about, and they found a cypress log bench near the southwest gate.

The time went by slowly, and Adam began to question Devine about the participants in the trial.

"Nothing suspicious about the prosecutor's boating accident," the lawyer said. "He went out when a storm was threatening. Always did think he knew more than anybody else."

"What about Lawrence Osborne? Why did he retire?"

"There are rumors, of course. It's known he found a particular liking for Jamaican rum. There are those who said he was worried about something or someone. As far as I know, no one complained when he stepped down. At the end, he couldn't seem to make a decision from the bench."

"Too bad he didn't have that kind of trouble when I knew him."

"He lives not far from here," Devine said. "In a place right behind the Opera House. Not seen about town much, though. One of the lawyers at the courthouse said he was doing a great deal of traveling. Visiting family, mostly. When he's in town, he pretty much keeps to himself."

The talk gradually died; by the time they had waited an hour and a half, Adam decided Sean Casey had made other plans.

"Damn," he muttered as he paced the path in front of the bench. "I never should have let him get out of

131

my sight."

"Perhaps something happened to him," Devine said.

"Something happened, all right. Something called Emile Laverton." Adam made up his mind what to do. "Here," he said, thrusting the gold into the lawyer's hands. "Keep this for me. I've got to find the drunken fool again."

Devine watched as he took the gun from beneath his shirt and slipped it back in the holster. "I'll go with you."

"You've done enough."

Adam walked with Devine as far as his office, then hurried on toward the Swamp and the Drink Emporium. Just as the bartender had predicted, the saloon was rowdier in the growing dusk than it had been earlier in the afternoon.

"You're out of luck," said Ralph as Adam approached the bar. "He shipped out."

"What in the hell do you mean? Casey sat right at that table and said he never wanted to go to sea again."

Ralph avoided Adam's cold stare. "He was convinced to change his mind."

"How? With a knife to his throat?"

Ralph did not respond.

Adam tried again. "Did he happen to mention the name of the vessel?"

"Not that I recall." He shot a hard look at Adam. "You can flip all the coins you want in my direction, but I can't tell you more than I know. One of the regulars came by and said he saw Casey boarding a schooner not more than a half hour ago. Supposed to go out on the evening tide."

"Is the man who saw him still here?"

"Nope. And I don't know where to find him, neither."

There was fear in his voice and in the depths of his eyes. Somehow Laverton, or his deputy O'Reilly, had gotten to him, too.

The journey on foot back to the hotel was taken slowly, Adam making sure to stay with crowds and away from dark alleys even as he let his bitter thoughts take hold. For the rest of his troubles he could curse Emile Laverton; tonight he had only himself to blame. He'd held the evidence in the grip of his hand, and stupidly he had let it get away.

Walking into the lobby, he was still trying to decide what to do next. Another trip to La Chatte? What would be the purpose? He would only watch Catherine move about the casino charming a hundred other men. He might unnerve her, all right, but just as certainly he would unnerve himself.

Maybe he would find Laverton upstairs, but what good would that do? None, until he decided what to say to him. He was enraged enough and strong enough to attempt to beat a confession out of him, but he doubted Laverton would ever talk. Besides, after the threats he had issued so firmly last evening, Michael O'Reilly or someone like him would not likely let him get close to that study.

What he needed to do was get away from this damned city for a day or two. Belle Terre beckoned. He could think there in the comfort of his home, and he needed to check in with Tom Jordan, maybe work the fields himself. It wouldn't hurt him to sweat a little of New Orleans and Carrollton out of his system.

Maybe, as he put the gelding Keystone through his paces on the night ride, the fresh air would clear his mind.

First, though, he would find out for sure whether Judge Lawrence Osborne, retired, was out of town as Devine had suggested, or if in reality he was holed up in his townhouse nursing a bottle of rum.

After settling his bill at the desk, he took the steps two at a time as he hurried upstairs to pack.

133

Chapter Nine

The next two days went by slowly for Cat, who kept expecting Adam to burst through the doors of La Chatte and upset her with more of his outrageous behavior. She was both relieved and disappointed when he did not.

Her disappointment came, she told herself more than once, because until she saw him again she could not tell him her opinion of his crude promise outside her bedroom door.

We will make love.

What was she supposed to do, sit around pining for him to return and carry through on his words? He did not know her at all if that was what he planned.

Cat had not pined, but she found her nightly chores in the casino more tedious than they had ever seemed to her, and she caught herself looking over her shoulder with exasperating regularity to see if a particular pair of dark blue eyes were watching as she worked.

She even grew sharp with Delilah. "I'm not sure the shrimp was fresh last night," she said on the morning of the third day since she'd seen the upsetting American. They were standing in the storage room just inside the casino's back door and taking an inventory of their supplies.

Both were dressed in their work clothes, plain black

135

dresses and white aprons, Cat slender and sylphlike beside the shorter, full-figured servant.

"All the seafood was fresh off the boats, mam'selle," Delilah replied. "Same as usual. The delivery man swore to it, and they tasted all right to me."

"Maybe we ought to try another supplier."

Delilah's velvet-brown stare rested on her. "I believe it is not the shrimp that bothers you, Mam'selle Cat."

Cat opened a high cabinet door and stared at the folds of white linen tablecloths and napkins. "I can't imagine what you're talking about."

"It's the American. A man like that gets under a woman's skin."

Cat slammed the door closed. "Adam is *not* under my skin."

Delilah shrugged. "Whatever the mam'selle says."

Cat contemplated the innocent look cast up to her and wondered at the obsequious tone in Delilah's voice. In the four years they had worked together at the casino, Delilah had been loyal, helpful, and quick-thinking, but she was *never* obsequious.

"What do you know about Adam Gase?" asked Cat.

It was Delilah's turn to open the cabinet and count the store of linen.

"I've seen the m'sieur twice in my life," she said as she ran her fingers over the tablecloths. "The night he came here and the other afternoon in New Orleans.

Cat stared at the fine-featured profile of the servant. "I get the feeling you're not telling me the complete truth."

Delilah closed the cabinet and turned to look at Cat. "It is the truth that I did not know him before he came to the casino and won the wager with you. And I know of no one who could tell me more about him than you already have discovered."

Her face softened. "But I also know that M'sieur Gase is the only man in four years who has walked into La Chatte and made you think about something other

136

than making money. I know that he's put color in your cheeks that I have not seen in all the years we've worked together. What I don't know is why he came around here in the first place, except that you're a fine-looking woman, mam'selle. There are some things you don't have to put much thought to in order to understand."

The two women stood in the stillness of the room and looked at each other. Outside, Cat could hear the metallic click of shears as one of La Chatte's workers trimmed the shrubbery growing close to the back wall. In her mind she was standing outside her bedroom door; she remembered the image of a sharply honed, bronzed face leaning close and of a pair of midnight eyes that saw past her shield of indifference and into her restless soul.

She spoke in a voice little above a whisper. "Why do men not leave us alone, Delilah? Why can't we live our lives apart from them in peace?"

"A few of us, Mam'selle Cat, are able to do just that in the convents. For most, such a place does not offer a complete existence."

Cat looked away. Delilah knew she had spent several years with the Ursuline nuns in New Orleans, at first regaining her strength from the incident that had almost taken her life and later helping in any way that she could—keeping their books, ordering supplies, supervising the day-to-day running of the convent in ways the sometimes impractical nuns would not consider. But it had not been a complete existence, and with Emile's help she had left to open La Chatte.

A somber mood fell over her, displacing the impatience and uneasiness that she had suffered for days. She knew the cure. Today was Sunday, the one day of the week that the casino remained closed. The hour was early; she could saddle her mare, ride into the country, and still return before dark.

Sometimes she rode with Emile, but he was not here today and she could not wait to find out if he would appear. She had not taken such a ride since last spring. Much too long to stay away from the place of her dreams—the run-down sugar plantation where she had spent so many happy years and one tragic day. The place she planned to own one day soon.

She would ride to Belle Terre.

Cat rode well, and she rode fast. Julien, like so many Creoles a born horseman, had taught her. She had learned to ride astride, a fact that had shocked Julien's father, Gerard Constant. It was only one of a long list of things about her that he had never prized.

The mare, a black Arabian named Raven, had been a gift from Emile when she made her final payment on La Chatte.

"Ride her to your plantation," he had said. "She will carry you swiftly and surely and return you safe."

Emile did not approve of her dream; he thought the run-down Belle Terre a sorry reason to hoard her money and had more than once told her it would not bring her the pleasure that she sought.

But never, with all the power that he could wield over her, had he done anything to impede her quest, and for that alone she would forever be grateful.

The day was warm, but for a change the sultriness that usually lay like a heavy hand over the countryside was not present. She wore denim trousers and a pale-blue shirt, her hair in braids tucked under a brown straw hat pulled low on her forehead. Anyone seeing her would think she was one of the Cajun girls who sometimes rode through the swampland of southern Louisiana or, if the glimpse was a quick one, maybe a boy. An onlooker would never take her for the sophisticated owner of La Chatte.

The route that Cat regularly chose followed a winding dirt road through the wooded landscape; sometimes she cut cross country through rolling fields of high, wild grass, Raven flying with a speed and smoothness to match her avian namesake, tail high, her black sleek coat shining with sweat in the southern sunlight.

Always Cat stayed away from the river. Someday, when Belle Terre was hers, she would make her peace with the river. She would take the public road in front of the house, the road close to the levee. She would turn toward the row of live oaks leading to the main house, dismount and step onto the gallery, and with no one to stop her walk in the front door.

But that day was still in the future. Until then she would take the old, familiar route.

Cat loved the feel of bunched and extended muscles under her, exhilarated in the wind against her face. And at the end was the one place in the world that would always be home.

An hour's ride away from La Chatte, she turned for good away from the seldom-traveled roadway and wound through the open countryside. The first sign that she was drawing near her destination was a thickening of oaks directly ahead and to her left a line of willow and cypress that marked the bayou which ran behind the plantation. She reined Raven to a walk and allowed herself to enjoy the sight of the scattered wild shrubs and the carpet of clover and graceful fern that lay between her and the nearest stand of trees.

The air was heavy with the scent of late-blooming magnolia and with the fertile odor of the wilderness. If scent could be a color, she mused, then Louisiana air carried the color green.

From somewhere up ahead came the distinctive *pip-pip-pip* of a woodthrush, followed by the rest of his loud, liquid song. In answer to the concluding trill was the insistent cry of a mockingbird.

Glancing up into a boundless blue sky, Cat stilled an urge to call out to the birds. Instead, with a click of her tongue and a prod of her booted heels, she urged Raven to race across the open grassland and into the protection of the oaks.

In the cooling shadows she felt the beginnings of the excitement that always came over her when she approached the plantation. She guided Raven through the trees and stopped at the edge of the field that extended from behind the main building of Belle Terre to the Bayou Rouge, so named because of the red cast of its slow-moving water.

She felt no sense of inconsistency that she should fear the Mississippi and welcome the closeness of the bayou. Along the latter's banks she had known happiness, while the river . . . She brushed the memories from her mind.

From her haven of moss-draped oaks, Cat stared across a hundred yards of weeds and mottled patches of grass to the back of the two-story brick-and-stucco structure that had once been her home. Long gone was the small, separate room where she had slept. It had been constructed because by Creole standards it was unseemly for an unwed female to sleep under the same roof as an unwed male.

Such a foolish consideration. A separate bedroom had not kept the worst from happening.

She looked at the main house with a critical eye. The American who had purchased the plantation four years ago ought to be shot for letting the grounds go, for letting the paint flake on the stately walls of the house, and most of all, for not giving in to her offer to buy the entire estate.

Four years ago—the instant she heard that the widower Gerard Constant had put the sadly neglected plantation on the market—she had made her first offer. She was unwilling to borrow more than a modest sum from Emile, and she'd been outbid. She had not known the new owner's name, never wanted to know anything about him or the family he must have brought to the land.

Two years later, with the casino a great success, she'd made another offer through the banker Raymond Wardwell.

"Don't deal directly, Cat," Emile had advised. "Since you are determined to carry through on your plans, let the bank handle your affairs. You will be taken more seriously and stand a greater chance of success."

She had known her dear friend was trying to protect her from personal rejection, and she had agreed to his request. Again she had failed. All Wardwell had told her was that the owner was away for an extended period of time but his representative swore the place was not for sale. This year in the bank president's office she had heard the same story.

But Cat had faith. Belle Terre looked worse than she remembered it, and she was prepared to name a far greater sum than ever before. And just maybe she would skip her intermediary Wardwell and talk to the owner in person—if he had returned. Time and patience, as well as the continued success of La Chatte, would see the fulfillment of her dream.

On her visit last spring, in a moment of frustration and longing, she had approached a woman servant she saw drawing water at the cistern. She had asked about the owner, but the woman had appeared nervous, refusing to answer any of her questions directly, except to say that the man was without family. Cat had received the definite impression that wherever he was, the American was in trouble.

She had pinned her hopes on the news. Whatever was going wrong for him, her money would certainly help him out. Unless he were as obsessed with the land as she—a possibility she could not even consider—then he would have to agree eventually to her generous terms.

She sighed, and reined Raven along the boundary marked by the oak grove and toward a path at the back side of the clearing. The path wound through a tangle of saplings and shrubs, stopping at the mossy bank beside the bayou.

As a child she and Julien used to steal down to the water—against strict orders—and pretend that every log was an alligator, every floating twig a snake. Sometimes they were right, and they would go running back to the house, half laughing, half terrified the way only children could be. Even then, Julien had sworn to protect her.

She dropped to the ground and tied the mare close to the water. Raven drank greedily for a moment, then accepted with pleasure the handfuls of grain Cat had brought in a saddlebag.

Her own lunch was a cold biscuit, a thick slice of ham, and a canteen of sweet lemonade that Delilah had prepared. She left Raven in the shade beside the Bayou Rouge and carried the repast toward a ramshackle gazebo that lay between the water and the main house. Gerard Constant had erected the gazebo beside what was then a man-made lake stocked with fish. Peacocks had wandered the surrounding grass, and for a while two black swans had graced the shallow water.

It was the year Cat moved to Belle Terre. She had been three years old, and her mother had been alive.

What a magical place it had seemed to her, and despite the hard times that had followed it still carried the patina of that old shine.

Cat climbed the rickety steps of the octagonal structure, the cypress floor creaking under her boots. Munching on the biscuit and ham, she stood beneath the frame of what had once been a shingle roof and stared toward the main house. Twenty-four years ago she and her widowed mother Marie Douchand had come to the plantation, owned by her distant cousin Gerard, to help care for his invalid wife Louise and for their children, five-year-old Julien and his older sister Arianne.

"Your father Henri was a great man in France,"

142

Marie had often told her, "but the money that was once his was embezzled by a dishonest business partner. We may be poor relations in Louisiana, but we can always hold our heads high. Never forget that your papa was a nobleman. The blood of the aristocracy flows in your veins."

Marie had refused to reveal more about Henri, only that his death and the ensuing poverty had forced her to bring her infant to the New World. She had tried to find work in New Orleans to supplement the waning funds she brought with her, but at last had agreed to the offer to help at Belle Terre.

"We must be grateful to Cousin Gerard," she had warned, and Cat had tried. But Cousin Gerard—even as he admitted them to his home, letting them dine at the long table with the rest of the family and share in their talk—had made great demands on Marie. In every way she had to cater to the whims of his ill-tempered wife and spoiled daughter.

Julien had been the pleasant one, always a smile on his lips and a suggestion of youthful adventure. As the years passed, Marie had turned grim from the demands of her lowly position at Belle Terre and eventually from ill health, and Cat had looked to the handsome, fun-loving Julien for companionship. It was only natural that she had fallen in love.

Julien was gone now, still in Paris as far as she knew, and Arianne, married to a man twice her age, lived on a neighboring plantation to the north. All the rest were in their graves.

Remembering, Cat gripped the splintered railing that she leaned against; for her efforts a sliver of wood embedded itself in the pad of her right forefinger. The pain brought her thoughts momentarily to the present, and she worked for a full two minutes before extracting the splinter. Sucking at the sore spot, she thought that she had never known much good fortune in the gazebo. Here she had told Julien she loved him; here she had told him good-bye.

Ten years had passed since that day, but it seemed like yesterday, and once again she was a free-spirited girl of seventeen. An orphan for five years, she had learned to run Belle Terre the way Marie had shown her, the way Madame Louise Constant should have done. She kept the household accounts, she ordered the supplies, she saw to the cooking and serving of the meals. She came to regard Belle Terre as her own.

"And it will be one day," Julien had sworn the night he met her in the shadows of the deserted barn. They were lying side by side in the hayloft, her head against his arm.

Cat knew what went on between a man and a woman. She'd been told by Marie shortly before her death. Knowing the end was near, her mother had spoken sweetly, lovingly, of her husband and had assured Cat she had nothing to fear from the marriage bed.

The hayloft was not what her mother had been thinking of—even in the throes of love and awakening desire, Cat had known that much—but she went without a worry in her heart. Julien was her ray of light. He would not bring her harm.

When she was with him, she felt a curious, curling warmth inside that was both upsetting and pleasing, like the deep hunger one felt before sitting down to a sumptuous meal.

But when Julien leaned close and brushed his lips against hers, she knew this hunger was different from any she had known. In what had been a bold move for her, she returned his kiss, then settled against him and waited for what would happen next.

His hand touched the lace of her dress that tickled her throat, then moved downward to her breast.

She was startled by the power of that gentle touch and drew away with a whispered "No."

Julien was insistent. "Yes," he said, pulling her once

144

again in his embrace.

"Trust me, Catherine." His fingers stroked where they had been before, and she did not push them away.

"Kiss me, Catherine." His breath was warm on her cheek and her young heart pounded.

"All will be well," he assured her.

Of course it would. With love warming her as much as his touch, she had given herself to him as he asked. He had been gentle and affectionate, a young girl's dream. The pain had been brief and unimportant, and if the pleasure was not exactly what she had expected, she blamed herself for wanting too much. She did not love him any the less.

Most of all, she trusted him, trusted the sweet assurances he whispered in her ear. She had opened her heart to him, and told of her secret longing to live on Belle Terre with him forever. Julien and Belle Terre. In her mind they were one and the same. She belonged to them and they belonged to her.

During the following week, they met two more times in the hayloft. Caught up in her awakening passion and her need to belong to him, she could not stay away, and oh how dearly insistent he was that she had become everything to him.

But Cat had not been raised to be deceitful, and she grew apprehensive.

"I can't meet you like this again," she told him one midnight as she lay on the uncomfortable hay, her hands smoothing her wrinkled skirt, her eyes carefully avoiding the sight of Julien fastening his trousers.

"Why not?" he asked bluntly, and she realized that he was not as sensitive to her feelings as she would have liked.

Wanting to tell him she felt ashamed of their secret meetings in the hayloft, she put her feelings into words she hoped he would understand.

"I do not like to betray your father in such a way."

"My father," Julien answered in disgust, "likes to

145

order everyone about. But he cannot tell me whom to love. What we do is our concern, and it is not wrong."

In her heart she disagreed and silently swore not to meet him again, putting him off with embarrassed hints that the wrong time of the month was near. A week later he pressed her for another late-night assignation. Unable to shake off the feeling that trouble lay ahead, she agreed only to meet him the next morning in the gazebo. There she tried to tell him of her fears.

"I love you, Catherine Douchand, and I always will," Julien had sworn as he clutched her hand against his pounding heart.

"And I love you. Forever and forever."

Their undying love had not lasted the day.

Julien approached his father and, filled with worry, Cat had listened in growing horror outside the parlor window to the words that passed between father and son. They had not known she was there; later she wondered whether their words would have changed had she made her presence known.

"I want to marry Catherine," Julien had declared.

"What foolishness is this?" Gerard replied, astonishment heavy in his voice.

"It is not foolishness, Papa. She belongs at Belle Terre."

"As a servant," he replied, and the eavesdropping Cat realized the older man's astonishment had become contempt.

"As the mistress," Julien angrily insisted. "She loves the place as much as you or I. And I have pledged her my love."

"Foolish puppy. What do you know of love?"

Without eyeing him, she could see Julien pull his slender body up to its full height, one that measured only slightly greater than hers.

"I am a man now, Papa. Catherine and I have known one another," he announced proudly while Cat listened in shameful surprise.

"You have had your way with the girl?"

"Three times."

As though the number mattered, she had thought. Even at the time, trying desperately to cling to her faith in him, she had known he was bragging.

Gerard laughed. "It is clear you have my blood flowing in your veins, Julien. You make me proud."

"Then you give your consent?"

"Of course not. She is not worthy to be your wife. Your *chère amie,* if you insist, but not your equal. You must marry one who is pure. A woman of wealth. Belle Terre needs outside money. It is a fact I have always made clear to you."

"Marriage to someone else? It is not possible."

"Nothing else *is* possible, Julien. You say you are a man. It is time you made the decisions of a man and not of a lovestruck boy."

"But what about Catherine?"

"Perhaps some arrangement can be made. Use discretion if you cannot control your lust. Later, when you are safely wed, you can set her up in town."

Julien had continued to protest, but Cat knew that he was engaged in an argument he could not win. Worse, the longer he talked to his father, the weaker became the determination in his voice, and at last she realized that her undoing was not her beloved's outright betrayal but a gradual acquiescence to a stronger will. Crushed, she had stumbled away . . . back to the gazebo where Julien had so recently embraced her . . . back to the last place she had known happiness.

An hour later Julien found her there.

"He is a devil," he declared as he strode up the steps. "Never did I expect such a response."

Dying inside, Cat turned a cool eye to him. "Perhaps your father knows best."

Julien stirred nervously, refusing to look her in the eye. "What do you mean?"

147

"He believes I am not a suitable wife, *n'est-ce pas?*"

"He speaks foolishly, like an old man who has forgotten what it is to love."

"He speaks like a man who wants to protect his son and his land. Belle Terre is a small plantation. It could serve a family well, but it does not support your father in the manner he would like to enjoy. Does he not keep a quadroon in town? Does he not gamble with the other planters?"

"My father's habits are not mine, Catherine."

But Cat had known they would be, sooner than he would admit, and she had told him good-bye.

"I shall move to New Orleans. There must be work for me somewhere. I am a fair seamstress and I know well how to keep books. My training here will serve me well."

The words had broken her heart. To leave Julien . . . to leave Belle Terre. For all the difficulty they presented her, the Constants were her only family; except for them, she was alone in the world. She had thought never again to experience such despair.

But she had been wrong.

Cat moved out that evening, in a carriage provided by a determined and openly grateful Gerard.

"You will see that this is the right thing to do," he had told her when she came down the stairs with the valise that contained all her belongings. Twenty-four years ago, at the age of three, she had not arrived with much less.

He forwarded her money for a small apartment until she could become self-sufficient and said it was best that they not hear from her again.

"Julien will suffer if you persist in seeing him. You understand."

Cat, head held high, assured him that she did.

Two weeks later she heard that Julien had sailed for France to meet with a family long associated with the Constants. A wealthy family, she was sure, and one with an eligible daughter. More than a year later, she heard he was married, but by then she was in the depths of such agony that she no longer cared.

If it had not been for Emile . . .

Cat stood in the gazebo, her eyes blurred with unshed tears, and forced the memories to fade. Some things were simply too painful to recall.

Seldom did she ever think of Julien, and of those few bittersweet moments in the hayloft, never. So what was wrong with her now?

She hurried down the gazebo steps, strode past the cypress cistern towering on the far side of the depression that had one time been a lake for fish and swans, and headed for the trees shading the bayou.

When she was in the protective shadows, she knelt on the soft, grass-covered bank and, tossing her hat aside, splashed cool water over her face. She knew what was wrong. Adam Gase. He had touched her face and she had trembled. He had kissed her and she had been consumed by desire.

Worse, by filling her thoughts with long-forgotten memories and needs, he had reminded her of the loneliness that she usually was able to hold at bay.

Delilah had been right this morning. He made her think of things other than making money. He brought color to her cheeks.

She stood and pressed her fingers to her lips, remembering Adam's kiss. The years had dimmed many of her memories of Julien, and the harsh events of long ago had taken the tenderness from his lovemaking, but she knew in her heart that he had never done anything that had affected her half so much.

A rustling in the bushes startled her from her reverie, and she turned to see the tall, lean figure of a man.

"Adam!"

"Good afternoon, Catherine."

What was he doing here? Stunned, she could think

of nothing that made any sense. It seemed, almost, as if by thinking of him with such intense concentration she had summoned his actual presence.

He stepped close and stared down at her. She stood rooted to the bank, powerless to move. The look in his eyes was one she had seen before—taunting, curious, and still more. Definitely more.

Chapter Ten

A shaft of sunlight piercing through the branches of a cypress made him easy to see. Her throat was tight, and she could do no more than stare at him as he stared back at her.

He was dressed in the brown shirt and trousers he'd worn the day of the duel, the day he'd taken her to Laverton's house. A thick lock of hair, as black as Raven's mane, fell across his forehead, and the gray at his temples gave him a powerful and devilish look. His eyes, glittering beneath thick brows, roamed over her blue shirt and britches, rested on the braids which lay across the rise of her breasts, then settled on her face.

"Couldn't stay away from me?" A crooked grin broke the harshness of his expression. "I'm flattered."

Despite his taunting words, he didn't look flattered, and he didn't look surprised; he looked very, very pleased, like a hunter who'd found a plump and helpless rabbit in his trap.

But Cat was no rabbit, as he should already have learned. Through the pounding of her heart, she found her voice. "Are you suggesting I've been following you?"

He shrugged, his shirt tight across broad shoulders. "I was out riding." He gestured downstream and she saw, no more than twenty yards away, another horse tethered close to the water beside her mare. So intent had she been on her own troubled thoughts, she hadn't heard him arrive. But then he probably hadn't wanted her to hear.

"I'd doubled back," he continued, "when I saw you walking by the cistern." He took a step toward her, and then another, until he stood so close she could see nothing but him. "Knowing your Creole penchant for fine manners, I figured it was only polite to say hello."

He reached out and she watched, spellbound, as he lifted one of the braids, his fingers brushing against her shirt. Her skin tingled, and the tingling spread to the pit of her stomach.

"Nice," he said softly, his eyes again roaming, and she knew he meant more than her hair.

She slapped his hand away and stepped backward. The heels of her boots sank into the mud close to the water's edge, and she swayed. He put out a restraining hand and gripped her arm; again she slapped it away, this time being careful to edge sideways, being extra careful to step out of his reach.

"You are a liar," she said. "We both know that you were following me. The only thing that surprises me is that you did it with such skill."

"I do a lot of things with skill."

Cat's face warmed and, worse, so did other parts of her. Her legs trembled as she turned away from him.

"Go home to your wife," she said harshly, "or your mistress, whichever you choose, only leave me alone."

"No wife, no mistress," he said. "Only you." He paused. "Tell the truth, Catherine. Are you watching me for Laverton or for yourself? I can't see him sending you when he has his Irishman to run his errands. Which leaves the conclusion that you have taken me at my word."

She whirled on him. "What do you mean?"

"You want to make love."

Cat itched to slap him. "You conceited bastard. I

don't need you for my pleasure."

A look of rage robbed his face of all gentle goading. "For a minute there, I had forgotten you already have a lover." He moved toward her, his hands coming at her so quickly, steel fingers wrapping about her upper arms, that she had no chance to defend herself. He pulled her roughly against him. "You tell me how much pleasure I bring."

His mouth slanted against hers, his arms pinning her tight in his demanding embrace. She shoved against his chest, the heels of her hands forced against his muscled strength, but she might as well have been trying to push back the passing of time.

His lips, moist and firm, moved against hers, demanding a response. She tried to hold herself back, tried to restrain the thundering of her heart and the coiled desire that threatened to ensnare her.

She did not welcome these sensations, did not want them, did not need them, her mind screamed even as her body betrayed her with its own command that she wrap her arms around his neck and melt against him in surrender.

Still she tried to fight him and herself, tried to hold herself stiff, tried to quell the frissons of passion that raced through her body. Everything she had ever believed about herself—that she controlled her destiny, that she could live without knowing a man—was proved wrong for all time if she once gave in. *Everything!* But, God help her, his lips were so wonderfully warm against hers, and demanding in a way that was frightening only because the demands could be so easily met.

He was doing this to hurt her, he had as much as said so . . . to prove that he was a better man than Emile. What a fool Adam was. He was the only man to incite the tempests of desire that were raging through her—and with no more than a kiss.

She'd been so lonely for so long—she admitted it at

last—and his embrace, far from painful, felt right and good and, most powerful of all, inevitable. The heat he was generating inside her laid waste the chill of denial that was her source of strength.

With her senses shredded, she found her hands pressed to the nape of his neck, the warmth of his skin teasing her palms, the coarse strands of his hair taunting her fingers. Her breasts were taut and full against him; unable to hold herself rigid any longer, she shifted slightly, felt her nipples harden as they rubbed against his sinewy strength. She was aware of everything about him at once—the manly scent of sweat, as though on his ride beneath the cloudless sky he had absorbed the sunlight, the bunching of his muscles as she curled against him, the low moan in his throat that had nothing to do with pain and everything with desire.

She felt his hands against her back, pressing her tight, kneading small circles on either side of her spine, then spiraling down, down, down to the curve of her waist and on to the flare of her buttocks, increasing the pressure of his hold. She felt his thighs against hers, felt the swell of his body, knew his reactions were as volatile as her own.

His tongue worked at her lips and she gave him entrance, dancing her own tongue against the sweet invasion. This time she was the one who moaned. She drew in ragged, hot breaths and her body trembled with all the repressed emotions that had been dangerously loosened when once before he had claimed her in just this way.

She splayed her hands against the tight muscles of his upper back and, taking his lead, drew hard circles with her palms. He broke the kiss.

"Catherine," he whispered hoarsely into her open mouth, his breath mingling with hers, then repeated her name, only this time with more insistence. He ran his tongue down her neck to the open throat of her shirt, licking at the pulsating hollow before trailing to a beaded nipple that protruded against the cotton shirt.

He sucked at the thin cloth and she felt as though she were already naked beneath his assault. Which she soon would be, here on the grassy bank behind Belle Terre. Through the haze of passion one rational thought occurred: a grassy bank was no better than a hayloft.

"No," she cried out, hoping to sound out her rejection of him with all the power that was in her, but the word came out a plea.

Slowly he lifted his head and his eyes burned into hers. Again she held herself stiff, an act which took monumental strength considering the melting warmth with which he surrounded her. "No," she managed again.

He eased his embrace but he did not let her go. "You can't walk away now. We've gone too far. For whatever reasons, I have watched you, wanted you, I know only that we will make love. And it will be good."

She was startled by the raw need in his eyes, by the frank certainty in his voice.

"You promised . . ." Her voice broke.

"Don't you know that I'm not the only one who can't stop?" He bent his head and brushed his lips against hers. "Don't you know that if you ride away you'll be filled with an emptiness that won't go away?" He outlined her mouth with his tongue and his hands stroked her upper arms. "Don't you know that we're doing no wrong in seeking pleasure in this rotten world?"

His bitterness struck her as much as his need. Somehow he had known troubles to equal hers, and she felt a oneness with him that was close to her undoing.

"Adam," she whispered. She studied the lips, the lean cheeks, the tousled black hair, and at last the burning midnight eyes that were close to her. "You don't know what you're asking."

"And you, my beautiful, puzzling, tempting Catherine, don't realize the pleasure we're about to share."

But she couldn't bring herself to do as he wanted. Men offered the promise of pleasure in such dark, seductive words, but they delivered lasting pain.

She shook her head. "I can't."

A look of harsh rebellion savaged Adam's face. "Don't play the coy innocent with me, Catherine. I know it for the lie it is."

Frightened, she pulled away. "You said—"

"I won't take you by force. You've let me know already what you want."

He seized Cat's hand and dragged her away from the water and into the trees; she was powerless to stop him. They came to a halt in the shadowy dimness that seemed close to night, shifting dapples of sun the only evidence that it was still day. They stood on a bed of wild grass and clover; above them stretched a canopy of leaves. Again she heard the cry of a mockingbird; more, she heard the pounding of her heart and knew true fear—not of Adam and what he was about to do, but of a small voice inside that told her he was right.

She wanted him; if he gave her no choice, then she could tell herself what happened could not have been avoided, no more than she could avoid the storms that came off the ocean. The storm inside her was as violent as any that the winds of nature had ever propelled upriver. If she gave in to its raging, then perhaps she could forget thought, forget yesterday and tomorrow, forget everything but Adam.

Suddenly she was back in his arms, his head bent close, his lips moving against hers as he spoke. "We will make love here and now. You will give yourself to me, Catherine. Willingly and with great passion."

Hot fingers worked at the buttons of her shirt, pulling it from the waistband of her trousers, thrusting aside the pale-blue cloth to reveal her breasts, full and waiting, their tips darkly pink and erect. The look in his eyes as he stared at her nakedness was as erotic as anything he had yet done, and Cat's head rolled back in submission. Pleasing him with the fullness of her body, she took great pleasure for herself.

He bent his head further until his tongue laved the tip of one nipple; his teeth bit gently, and then with open mouth, he sucked and brought her to a searing ecstasy. Her blood flowed thick and hot in her veins, and with her knees trembling, she clung to his powerful shoulders.

When he moved to the other breast, her hungry hands found the open throat of his shirt. His skin was as hot as the sunlight, smoothly taut over bunched muscles, and she was swept with a need to feel more of him. Pulling at the buttons, impatient, she heard a ripping sound and was rewarded as the folds of brown cotton cloth parted and she could stroke the contours of his chest. His own nipples were tight and hard; she rubbed her thumbs against them, felt the rippling of his body as he trailed kisses to the valley between her breasts and whispered against her moist skin, "You are more beautiful than I imagined, Catherine. You've made me forget."

His words, half heard in her love-drugged mind, burned against her skin, as did his lips and his tongue. She tugged at the tail of his shirt; he helped her pull it from his body, tossing it aside before removing her own shirt. Foreheads touched as they stood leaning against each other, and they fought for breath. He pulled back and again stared at her nakedness. In turn, she stared at him. Coils of black hair curled at his throat, then thickened across the width of his chest before thinning at the band of his trousers. The dim light could not hide the bronze color of his skin, as though he worked in the sun half dressed. She leaned close and wet first one nipple, and then the other with her tongue. He tasted salty. She thirsted for more.

His hands cradled her face and she shifted to look up at him. Again raw desire darkened his eyes to the shade of a moonless night sky. She leaned close and rubbed her breasts against him.

He reached for her braids, and she saw that he was trembling. "You look like a young girl," he said in a voice as unsteady as his hands. He worked at the plaits, one at a time, until they were loosened; his fingers combed through the black tresses, which lay against her ivory skin like a stain of ebony ink on parchment. "But you're a woman." His hands cupped her breasts. "A very desirable woman," then, almost to himself, "and it's been so long."

She arched her back into the firm nest of his palms. *Ten years?* she wanted to say. *Has it been ten years?*

But that was thinking back, and she could not do such a thing. The moment was everything. Adam was everything. *No wife, no mistress.* He was as alone as she. Knowing little more about him, she knew that he would do as he promised and bring her great pleasure. How little of that had been in her life.

When his hands worked at her trousers and briefly, too briefly, brushed against the pulsating juncture of her thighs, she felt a momentary panic. But she was no longer a child and the decision was made. He was right, as he seemed to be far too often. Neither of them could walk away now. Steadying herself by holding on to his shoulders, she stood still as he knelt to pull off her boots, then slowly inched downward the britches and white silk undergarment that she herself had fashioned to wear when she rode . . . eased the clothing away from her waist, past the triangle of soft black curls that hid the growing moistness of her most private self, lingered for a moment, his hands working against her thighs before continuing.

At last she stood completely naked before his kneeling figure. With Adam she wanted to be bold— she had lived her adult life in such a manner—but when

158

he bent his head to kiss her thighs, she found herself overcome with a sudden shyness that bordered on panic. She dropped to her knees in front of him and pressed her lips to his, and as he embraced her, the panic fled.

"Later, Catherine," he said huskily. "When you want it."

He laid her gently on the bed of grass and clover, then pulled the rest of his own clothing from his tall, lean frame. At first the mat beneath her tickled, but she soon forgot it as she watched in fascination, knowing that she was looking at a splendid form. His hips tapered neatly from his waist, his thighs and calves strongly muscled. Black hair dusted his lower legs.

Her gaze moved slowly back up to the part of his anatomy that she had carefully avoided on her first perusal. Like her, he had a patch of thick hair at his lower abdomen, but then all similarity ended.

His manhood was a marvelous thing, and a tingle of fear shot through her. Knowing that her body would soon enfold his, she wondered if somehow she would disappoint him.

As if he could read her doubts, he dropped quickly to the ground beside her and pulled her against him. She forgot her fear. She wrapped her arms around him and stroked his back, her fingers trailing along unexpected ridges. He grew still.

"Adam . . ."

For just a moment she sensed a return of the bitterness that she had seen more than once in his eyes and heard often in his voice. "Pay no mind to my flaws, Catherine. I'm not incapable of performing as a man."

She was puzzled, and could only whisper, "Flaws?"

He shook his head as if in anger. "Later. Not now. God, not now."

His lips covered hers and she forgot what had puzzled her, knew only the power his stroking, seeking hands, the potency of his mouth as it roamed over her face and neck and breasts.

When his fingers at last trailed to her inner thighs, she parted her legs to show him that she welcomed his touch. His massage was gentle, yet he set loose such a torrent of aroused passion in her that she thought she was losing her mind. Never, never, never had she felt anything like this. For him she truly was innocent, although it was a truth he would never accept.

She cried out in dismay when his fingers abandoned her pulsating flesh.

"Together," he whispered into her tangled hair. "Together is better."

Levering himself on top of her, he slipped inside so quickly that she forgot to be afraid.

Her body jerked involuntarily at the hard fullness of his intrusion. He held her tight for a moment, whispering her name and soft assurances, more sounds than articulated words, that all was right and good.

Slowly he began to thrust himself deeper into her. She experienced a moment's discomfort but nothing comparable to what she had imagined when she saw his size. The discomfort passed. Somehow Adam managed to touch the throbbing point where his fingers had been, and she knew only a return of mounting ecstasy as she matched his rhythm with thrusts of her own. She had not known lovemaking could be like this.

And then she could not think at all. Clinging to his sweat-slick body, she let rapture overtake her. All vestiges of control forsaken, she was a wild thing under him, crying out and only dimly realizing she was crying out his name. The passion came in quickening, velvet-dark waves, and when it reached its height, her mouth pressed to his burning neck, her arms gripped tight around him, his own ragged breath hot against her ear, his own rapture matching hers, she knew that Adam had been right. It was better together.

She could not speak and was grateful that neither

could he. Enfolded in his arms, she waited for her heart to cease its pounding and at the same time willed the moment to last. One thing she told herself: when sanity returned, she would not experience regret. Too much of her life's energy had been expended in such a fruitless waste.

Gradually her breathing slowed and she felt him pull away and stare down at her. He opened his mouth to speak, seemed to reconsider, and bent to brush a kiss across her lips. It was a tender gesture, almost a loving touch, but of course that was absurd. She and Adam did not love each other; they did not even know each other very well.

And yet they shared secrets that neither could deny. As taunting as he usually was, as disregarding of her wishes, he could not claim she had no effect on him. He was as shaken by what had happened between them as was she.

So what did he expect her to do now? She had no idea; she knew only that she did not want him to pull away, and her hands moved once again to his chest and up to the back of his neck. His skin was hotter than it had been when she had first caressed him; she remembered thinking he seemed to carry the sun.

"Tell me what you're thinking," he said, his eyes locked with hers.

The question unnerved her, and she said the first thing that entered her mind. "That you're different."

"Different?" His voice was silky in a cool kind of way, not at all comforting, and the warmth in his eyes died, leaving only a shuttered expression that she could not read. "How am I different? And from whom?"

From my first love. The words would not come. She moved her hands from his neck and settled her gaze on his gray-streaked hair. "I meant that you don't wear a hat. Most men in this heat do."

"And I thought you were about to compliment me. My mistake." He lifted himself away from her and, sitting, stared down into her eyes. "As for the hat, Catherine, I haven't worn one in two years. The sovereign state of Louisiana did not see fit to include it as part of the uniform."

A cool breeze wafted against her damp body and she felt a sudden chill. "I don't know what you're talking about."

"Maybe it's time you had all of your curiosity satisfied."

The words were like a slap. He shifted until his back was to her; in the shadowed light she could make out the white welts that crisscrossed his otherwise brown flesh.

Her first reaction was a gasp, not of revulsion but of shock and dismay. He had been beaten. And, from the looks of the scars, some of them far more faded than the others, often over a long period of time.

She ran her fingers along one long, pale ridge. He jerked away. "I am not a freak," he said, and turned to face her once again.

Frightened by the look in his eyes, she edged farther from him.

"I didn't think you were," she said in her defense, but the words came out weak, as though she were not certain what she meant.

He harbored such mean thoughts of her, always, even now after the tenderness they had shared. He'd been a gentle and thoughtful lover, but only until he was satisfied. She felt an urge to cry—for his suffering and his harshness and for the humiliation that washed over her. She sat and crossed her arms over her breasts, the urge for tears giving way to an urge to laugh— hysterically, uncontrollably, and for a long, long time. How cruel men could be. The wonder was that she had ever forgotten.

Somehow she found the strength to be calm. "What happened to you?"

"Hasn't Laverton told you?"

She brushed the damp, matted hair from her face. "Always Emile. Why, Adam? Why?"

"I can't believe you don't know."

"Know what?" she cried out in frustration. "What am I supposed to know?"

He opened his mouth to speak, then, just as he had done when their lovemaking ended, he changed his mind. He stood, gathered her clothes, and laid them beside her.

He turned to dress himself, but Cat could not let the matter go so easily. "What is going on between you two?" she demanded.

As he pulled on his shirt, he glanced down at her. "I could ask you the same thing. Only I already know, don't I?"

"You don't know a damned thing." The bitterness in her voice matched any that had been in his. "It's a rotten world, you said. You were right. It's rotten because of men like you."

She stood, refusing to show any shame in her nakedness, and quickly dressed, then hurried toward the water's edge to retrieve her hat.

She heard his footsteps against the soft ground as he followed. As he always seemed to be doing. She felt a rush of longing to throw herself into the water and wash the smell and feel of him from her, but she knew that nothing would wash him from her mind.

As she twisted her hair into a knot atop her head, she jammed the hat firmly in place. She looked at him one last time, saw that his shirt was opened, saw small rips in the fabric where she had pulled at the now-absent buttons. How eager she had been to get at his body, she thought, and her cheeks flushed with shame.

"Surely this ends things between us," she said. "You've satisfied your curiosity about me. I am no better than you thought. I've nothing left to give you, Adam. Nothing."

She turned and hurried along the narrow path that

ran beside the Bayou Rouge. Pulling the reins free of the thick log where she had tethered Raven, she mounted. To her surprise, Adam grabbed at the bridle and stared up at her.

"This doesn't end anything."

She thought about reaching for the crop and slashing him across the face. But then she remembered the ridges.

I am not a freak.

Such a thought had never occurred to her, but it *had* occurred to him. Adam had known a shame that must have come close to hers. What was wrong with her that she could hate him and at the same moment feel such a flood of sympathy that she wanted to offer him comfort and understanding?

"Please leave me alone, Adam," she said, not bothering to hide the desperation in her voice.

"I can't do that." He moved his hand from the bridle to her thigh. "And I don't think it's what you really want."

She stared down at the leather-brown skin. *You want me,* she thought. *Until you have other plans, other desires.*

Unable to give him an answer, she jerked at the reins. Raven responded with a sharp bob of her head. Well-trained Arabian that she was, she started in motion as her mistress directed, moving around the gelding and toward the band of trees.

Cat did not look back to where Adam remained standing. She only hoped he did not choose the same route back to town. She had sworn not to regret what had passed between them, but she found it a vow she could not keep.

Most of all she regretted the weakness in her voice when she asked him to leave her alone.

Chapter Eleven

Adam watched as Catherine disappeared into the tangle of trees and brush, her slender back proudly straight, her long legs gripping with provocative sureness the black Arabian mare she was guiding away from the water's edge, and away from him.

Regret washed over him, not because he had made love to her, and not because they had parted with harsh words. What he rued more than anything was that the time had ended so soon.

"You're a fool, Adam Gase," he whispered under his breath.

He pulled off his shirt, tying it around the pommel of Keystone's saddle, and mounted, reining away from the stand of trees and toward the path leading to Belle Terre, but his thoughts went another way.

Catherine Douchand was the most exasperating, annoying, unpredictable, puzzling woman he had ever known. She was also the most enticing, beautiful, tender, and passionate. More, she was vulnerable. How in hell he could consider the wealthy, worldly woman known as La Chatte de la Nuit vulnerable he had no idea, yet that was how she seemed to him. When she held the Ferrier baby and then rejected him, when she looked at the infant's wounded father, when she gazed up at Adam and accepted the inevitability of their making love, he'd seen signs of fragility—the softening of her lips, the warming of her eyes.

At times before today, even the unconscious way she shifted her head and shoulders had seemed to say the burdens of the world were heavy to bear. The moments had passed quickly, but they added to the aura of mystery surrounding her.

He had told her that the two of them would be good together, but he'd had no idea of the overwhelming effect she would have on him.

It made no difference that more than two years had passed since he had a woman. He'd never made love to a woman like her. She was innocent and knowing at the same time, her body tight, as though she had not held a man before. But she was no virgin. Maybe Laverton was not one to seek her favors often. Maybe he preferred her to do other things for his gratification.

Adam thrust the ugly thoughts from his mind. While Catherine lay in his arms, she was loving and lustful, sensitive to his touch and eagerly seeking touches of her own. She responded the way a woman ought to respond to a man. And he'd been caught by more than just her passion. She'd made love to him as though they were the only two people in the world . . . as though they knew each other as well as they knew themselves . . . as though giving pleasure assumed importance beyond any other consideration.

When he'd shown her the scars, she was shocked, but in a sympathetic way, and he realized for certain that she knew nothing of where he had been. No pity had been in those remarkable violet eyes, only concern. A man could get close to a woman like that.

Too close.

The thought occurred to him that she might be nothing more than a very skillful actress. But which character was the real Catherine—the warm and tender woman who had lain in his arms or the brittle, flashing-eyed beauty who taunted the gamblers at La Chatte?

166

She'd accused him of following her, but that was absurd, no more than a ploy to cover the fact she was watching Belle Terre . . . watching for him. Had she been sent by Emile? Or was she on a mission of her own?

The mysteries surrounding Catherine continued to grow. The exasperating thing was that the more he knew of her, the less he understood.

Circling the wide lawn behind the main house, he dug his heels into Keystone's flanks and headed for the fields of cane that lay directly east. The sun, halfway down the horizon behind him, burned hot against his bare neck and back and he remembered her asking him why he never wore a hat.

Someday he'd tell her the truth. Too long in the shadows of a swamp, he liked the feel of the sunlight against his skin.

Adam glanced up at the blue sky. Not a cloud to be seen, if he did not consider a low white line in the direction of the river. He loved the sight of that clear sky. As far as he could remember, it had rained for the two years he'd spent in the swamp. Such was impossible, of course—his chest and arms were brown as bark from the hours he'd spent outdoors—but that was the way he remembered things. Just mist and rain and fog—and gray clouds of mosquitoes that came at a man like a judgment from the beyond.

He was beginning to understand the heathens who had worshipped the sun as the source of warmth and light, and of life itself.

Understand them, yes, but not join them. Today he had discovered something that was for him warmer, something far more soothing—Catherine's hands and lips. She brought comfort when she most excited him.

Catherine Douchand, mistress to the man he'd sworn to destroy. For a thousand reasons he should stay away from her, but one overriding thought ate into his gut. He wanted her again. She made him forget—

the one woman who should stand as a bitter reminder of the past.

"Adam Gase," he repeated, "you're a fool."

With a sudden burst of speed, he guided Keystone to the tall, swaying cane. The rows flanking the cane were wide—six feet, twice the space hollowed out by the other planters along this stretch of the Mississippi.

But Adam wanted room for a two-mule team to work the rows, one of the innovations he knew would eventually increase the productivity of Belle Terre.

Before his arrest, he'd been filled with plans—windrowing to protect the stalks from an early frost, crop rotation to ensure the soil remained rich and fertile, steam mills with double rows of iron rollers to extract the maximum juice from the ripe cane, vacuum pans to replace the open-kettle system for boiling the syrup.

Idea piled on top of idea, each exciting him as much as the last, all of them convincing him he could make a success of a run-down plantation. Most of his plans came from the vast study he'd undertaken concerning this new kind of farming, a man from Pennsylvania knowing more about wheat and corn and apple trees than cane.

After four years, most of the ideas needed as much work as they ever had. Even with Tom Jordan handling things, in the second half of his ownership he lost much of the improvements he had gained in the first.

But the cane was coming back. He slowed Keystone's pace as he rode down the black-dirt row and studied the high stalks and narrow, arched leaves of the healthy plants. A warm breeze stirred the field, setting up a murmuring of leaves that sounded like bees. With the right amount of rain in the remaining days of August and a cool, dry fall, the cane would be ready for harvest by mid-October.

He mustn't let his hatred of Laverton make him forget the full tally of his priorities, which, taken in no particular order, included proving in court that he'd been falsely charged and falsely convicted; contriving for the real culprit Emile Laverton to suffer his just punishment; harvesting, processing, and selling at a profit the year's crops; restoring the main house to at least a livable condition; seeing that the men and women who worked for him were adequately taken care of. And deciding what to do about Catherine.

It seemed a formidable list for a man just out of jail, especially when he wanted to work his way through it before Christmas. Adam had to smile.

He paused and took a deep breath of the sweet Louisiana air, looked up to catch a glimpse of a heron flying low across the cane, its white wings stark against the late-afternoon sky. Such scents and scenes were why he'd stayed in the South, why he'd purchased Belle Terre. His view of the world might have changed, along with his view of himself, but he felt the same about the country. He was going to stay.

Over the rustling leaves and the hum of the ubiquitous mosquitoes, he heard a deep baritone voice singing out a vigorous rhythmic chorus of words— part Creole French, part African dialect, part English, and, as far as Adam was concerned, in general untranslatable. But he got the message. One of the men was working hard and speeding his labors on with a joyful song.

Adam urged Keystone into a trot. They rounded the far end of the row and he saw the worker, shovel in hand, standing ten yards away in a shallow ditch that ran perpendicular to the rows, his concentration on the task of digging at the packed soil beneath his feet. He was dressed in the usual clothes of a field hand—a swath of cloth to cover his private parts and a pair of soft black boots stuffed with hay. Massive shoulders and upper arms and thighs gave testimony to his physical strength. His coarse hair was trimmed short, and his black skin was glistening with a fine sheen of sweat.

Adam recognized him as the one Belle Terre slave that Joseph Devine had been able to provide with papers of freedom. Bodeen he was called, Bodeen Constant after the man who had owned his mother.

Adam rode up on him from the rear. The singing stopped, and Bodeen glanced over his shoulder. A grin split his dark face and his white teeth shone.

"Massa Gase," he said, "what you be doing out here?"

"Listening to the music, Bodeen. Just listening to the music."

"No charge for that, Massa Gase." Bodeen's grin traveled to his black eyes. "No charge a'tall."

He commenced to sing and dig again, scooping dirt from the edges of the ditch, keeping the level shallow to avoid hitting the water table which lay close to the surface of the southern Louisiana land.

Adam watched him for a moment, then dismounted. He secured the reins over pommel and shirt, then slapped the gelding on the rump and sent him in the direction of the stables on the far side of the house.

"Mind if I take a turn?"

"Don't mind, no sirree," answered Bodeen without a flicker of surprise. In the few weeks Adam spent at Belle Terre after his release, he had found physical labor a pleasure—or at least a way to work off two years of built-up anger and a way to consider what he ought to do.

Unlike most of the planters, he'd worked shirtless alongside the men. He'd caught a few stray glances at his crisscrossed back; somehow the marks had become a badge of honor to the slaves and free men alike, more than a few of them bearing their own scars from the previous owner, Gerard Constant, and his overseer.

Adam would never inflict such wounds on other human beings, any more than he intended to own them any longer than necessary. Louisiana laws might work

170

against him, but no matter the cost, he intended to carry through on his promise to free the slaves as soon as they reached the magic age of thirty.

Bodeen was only the first. Immediately after receiving his freedom from the court, he'd accepted the employment Tom offered him at Belle Terre. Tom swore that the man's output of labor had increased.

Adam dug in silence for a full five minutes, Bodeen taking a rest in the shade of a hackberry which grew on the far side of the ditch. The stretch and pull of muscles cleared out the tensions in his system and the worries from his mind.

He did not slow until he had tossed a foot-high pile of dirt onto the rim of the ditch. Wiping at his brow with a forearm, he glanced at the placid Bodeen.

"Did Tom send you out here?"

Bodeen shook his head. "Drainage, Massa Gase, drainage, that's what sent me. We need all we can get. Rains gonna come in the next few days, and we gotta take that devil water away from the cane and down to the bayou. Otherwise those stalks'll rot. Can't get no sugar from rotted stalks. No sugar means no money coming in."

"Which means no wages. Right?"

"Right. Man's gotta take care of hisself and his family."

Adam anchored the tip of the shovel into the ground and leaned on the handle. "I didn't know you had a family."

"Don't. Not yet. But I got my eye on a woman sweet enough to make these fields dry up from pure jealousy. There's curves on her body that old river ain't never seen. And that ain't all. She can cook a meal so fine, it confuses a man whether he should take her to the kitchen or take her to the bed."

"That could be a real problem."

Bodeen laughed. "I worked everything out. We takes us a little pleasure first. We eats afterward. She's even got me helping with the cooking and the cleaning. The way she puts it, she helps me in the bed, and turnabout is fair play. She's a real stickler for fair play."

"She sounds like quite a woman. Is she at Belle Terre?"

A shadow of seriousness settled on the black man's countenance. "Tacey's one of yours. Works in the house."

Adam remembered her from the few evenings he'd spent inside. A small woman with indeed more curves than the Mississippi. Quiet when she served the food and polite, always offering a shy, friendly smile when he spoke to her. He couldn't imagine Tacey ordering the brawny Bodeen to help in the kitchen. Funny what a man was willing to do for the woman he loved.

"I don't suppose she's thirty, is she?" he asked.

"Eight years to go before that day gets here. I know what you're thinking, Massa Gase, but ain't no way the law'll let her be free."

The two men looked at each other for a moment.

"We'll work something out," said Adam.

"Maybe . . ." Bodeen paused. "Massa Gase, how come you were charged with bringing in more slaves against the law? That's the last thing on this earth you'd be likely to do."

"A good question. I'd like the answer myself."

"You got any idea who mighta brought all these troubles on your head?"

"I've got more ideas than proof. In the white man's world, proof is everything. Even if it's a lie."

Bodeen uncoiled his long, broad body from the shade and stood. "Tell you what . . . You figure out a way that my woman can be free like me, and I'll help you with whatever you got to do. Dig a ditch"—he nodded slowly as he spoke, his brown eyes narrowing—"or maybe dispense a little justice. I don't need no white man's proof, neither, Massa Gase, to know where the justice oughta go."

172

His broad, blunt-fingered hands flexed against his bare thighs, then curled into fists as he added, "Whatever you say is good enough for me."

He bent, picked up a hoe that had been lying beside the hackberry, and joined Adam in the ditch. The two worked in unison for the next hour without speaking, Bodeen's dark face hiding all signs of his thoughts, Adam's concentration turned toward the mindless task of shoveling dirt. Only the sound of their heavy breathing and the caw of an occasional bird disturbed the constant hum of the breeze in the cane.

When the sunlight began to dim, Adam tossed his shovel onto the high ground and climbed from the ditch.

"Time for us to call it quits," he said.

"I'll be along directly." Bodeen stared up at Adam. "Remember what I said about helping out. Justice is something a man like me thinks about. Givin' and gettin'."

"As Tacey would say, fair play."

"Right," agreed Bodeen.

"I'll remember your offer. Thanks, Bodeen, but right now it looks like I've got to work on the problems myself."

He turned on his heel and set a course that took him past the canebrake, past the dilapidated gazebo, and across the expanse of the grass that lay between the tree-lined Bayou Rouge and the main house. The breeze was cooler now that the sun was lower on the horizon, and it carried with it both the hint of rain and the scent of summer clover.

Forgetting the conversation with Bodeen and the session of hard work, Adam thought of Catherine, her silken, golden skin pressed against the green, sun-dappled mat that had formed their bed, her black hair spread wantonly about her head, her eyes burning up at him. Would he ever again smell clover without thinking of her?

Someone waved to him from the back door of the house, and he recognized the stocky figure of Tom Jordan. Tom, who had traveled with him from Pennsylvania and accepted the job as manager of a plantation whose needs were as foreign to him as those of a farm on the moon. He'd studied alongside Adam and had proven a true friend.

Adam returned the wave. Tomorrow, he thought, he would have to turn over full management once again to Tom, the way he did each time he rode into town. But for only a few days, not two years. Never again would he leave his land for so long—except to be lowered in his grave.

Tomorrow he would ride back to New Orleans and try once again to find Judge Lawrence Osborne, try to find out why the trial had been so rushed, try to find out how much Osborne had been paid. And by whom.

He'd see Catherine again. He didn't doubt it for a minute, nor did he doubt what he would say. After he told her what had happened to him, what her lover had done, he'd ask her what she thought he ought to do about it. He'd find out her opinion on fair play.

Chapter Twelve

That night, after a hard ride back to the casino, Cat fell into her feather bed and slept the dreamless sleep of the dead. It was as though at rest she could not deal with the enormity of her weakness at Belle Terre any more than her wakeful mind had managed to deal with it during the day. She awoke later than usual, no more rested than she had been when she pulled the covers over her head ten hours before and warned Balzac to leave her alone.

Whether the golden ball of fur had complied or not, she did not know, lost as she had been in deep unconsciousness, but the expression in the unblinking green eyes staring at her from the neighboring pillow as she awoke held a hint of hurt feelings. She cuddled the kitten guiltily, placed him gently on the floor, and arose to pull on one of the black cotton dresses she wore for her daytime work. She hurried downstairs, hair knotted at her neck, and out to the kitchen behind the casino. Balzac scrambled on short legs in her wake.

She found Delilah supervising the pair of women whose job it was to prepare the casino food. They were kneading dough for bread, and the large room was filled with the rich odor of loaves already in the brick oven beside the low-burning fire.

"No breakfast this morning," she announced to the

watchful Delilah. "Just coffee. I've decided to do something about the floor in the main salon."

Delilah's eyes widened. "What does the mam'selle have in mind?"

"It needs a good scrubbing."

"But we did that—"

"And polishing. The whole place is looking a little run-down, don't you think?"

Delilah stared at her for a moment and did not disagree.

Cat grabbed up a thick cloth as a hot pad, took the coffeepot from the edge of the hearth, and poured the steaming dark liquid into the ceramic cup that she regularly used. The brew was bitter and soothing.

So much for sustenance, she thought as she lifted a tin pail from its hook on the side wall opposite the fire; it was time to keep herself occupied. Scrub brushes and rags were stored in a shed outside, along with the mild soap she used on the casino's cypress floors. In ten minutes, aproned and with a white kerchief tied around her hair, she was on her knees in one corner of the salon, a cautious kitten standing just far enough away to avoid the periodic splashes of the scrubwater as the brushes moved from bucket to floor.

Cat threw herself into the work, making no comment when Delilah joined her. Ben and two other workers moved the tables as the two women made their way slowly across and down the room, the rasp of the brushes against the wood and the occasional slosh of water the only sounds. Cat paused every half hour or so to wipe the sweat from her brow, then renewed the scrubbing with all the fervor she'd given it at the beginning. She did not allow herself to think beyond the result she was achieving on the floor.

I've done this sort of work often enough, she reminded herself more than once, and there was absolutely no reason for Delilah to regard her with such bemusement—although, as the morning progressed, she admitted silently that she might be going beyond the usual pace she set for herself.

The cleaning was complete before lunch—a light repast of warm bread and cheese and hot tea—and the polishing begun. She threw herself into the work as zealously as she had throughout the morning, but this time she could not control her thoughts quite so well. If she happened to see a pair of dark, mocking eyes staring back at her in the luster of the wood, she rubbed all the harder until the vision was gone. If she heard a man's voice, deep and low, whispering her name in her ear, she hummed a wordless tune in rhythm with the polishing rag.

When they were finished and the gaming tables once more in place, she stood back and admired her work. Never had the cypress boards looked so fine.

"Whatever's bothering the mam'selle," Delilah said from beside her, "I hope it's settled by tomorrow."

"Why?" Cat said without thinking, then wished she had denied that anything was on her mind.

"You'll have us whitewashing the walls and replanting the flower beds."

Cat waved aside the words. "The floor was in bad condition, that's all. It's not right to let a place get run-down. Not right at all."

She did not wait for a reply, but instead hurried out to the kitchen for an early supper of fish soup and another cup of tea.

It was Ben who saw to it that a bathing tub was waiting for her in her room when she went upstairs. It sat on a thick mat at the foot of her bed, steam rising from the surface of the water. "Take your time, Miss Cat," he said at the door. "Let the men lose a little money before you come down. Maybe not come down at all. Take the night off."

"Nonsense," said Cat, pulling the kerchief from her head. "I'm not in the least tired."

Ben gave her a skeptical look but did not dispute

what he obviously took to be a falsehood. When he turned to depart, muttering under his breath, she did not ask him what he said.

She undressed as quickly as she had dressed ten hours earlier and lowered herself into the hot water. Her hair was the first to receive her attention, then she soaped the rest of her body twice. Anyone watching would think she was trying to wash off some kind of stain, she thought—something hard to remove, like the scent of a man or the lingering touch of his hand.

It was the closest she had come all day to re-membering—except for the reflection of a man's eyes and the sound of a man's voice—and a heaviness settled in her heart. What had she done?

Weariness overcame her, and she could do no more than lie back in the water, her damp hair spread over the edge of the wooden tub, and try to understand the memories of yesterday.

She had been out of control. Nothing else made sense. Adam had stirred something deep inside her, a need she hadn't known still existed, and she had been powerless to resist. She must draw comfort from the acceptance of her helplessness. Her temporary help-lessness. Surely he would not see her again.

But he had said that he would. And thus far in their brief acquaintance, he had done everything that he planned.

What if she were no stronger the next time she was with him? She had no reason to think that once he pulled her into his arms, she could find the will to tell him no.

Just as she'd been unable to deny Julien—until it had been too late.

Enough, Cat told herself. Such maundering could do no good. She stepped out of the tub, dried herself, and, dressed in her silk undergarments, brushed her hair. Never did she let one clear thought into her mind.

She wielded the hairbrush with all the vigor she had

given to the salon floor. When her hair was dry and hung in lustrous curls against her shoulders, she put on her uniform for the night—white silk, high-necked and long-sleeved—and hurried down to greet her arriving guests, moving from room to room, from cluster to cluster of gamblers, never staying in one place too long, never noticing exactly to whom she spoke.

If her laugh seemed a little brittle from time to time and her eyes flashed with a shallow, desperate light, no one seemed to notice.

There was some talk of Gaston Ferrier and the duel, although only two days after the shooting the men were already turning to other scandals, other gossip. The Creole was healing well, someone reported in her hearing.

"A brave man and an honorable one," another observed in French.

"The man's an imbecile," another countered.

Opinion appeard divided between the two views. No one mentioned the fact that La Chatte had been present at the scene, nor that she had left with the American who had been challenged. But Cat was certain that they knew.

Throughout the evening she drifted past the tables, watching the play, laughing at witticisms that were not funny, fending off suggestions for games beyond the salon. For a Monday, the casino was extra crowded, but under her guidance there was ample food and drink for all. Occasionally she looked toward the front door, half expecting a tall, dark-haired figure to appear. When he did not, she told herself she was glad.

Only when the gamblers were gone and the rooms neat and clean once again, did she allow herself to slow down. Watching the last of the workers depart, each bidding her good night, she stood at the base of the stairs, unable to take the first step. As tired as she was, she knew she could not expect another night of dreamless, deadening sleep. Fresh air, that's what she

179

needed, a stroll in the night.

She turned, walked through the deserted rooms, and, unlocking the back door, stepped into the moonlight. Her route took her to the side yard of the casino, a stretch of grass and moss-draped live oaks smaller but much like the side yard of Belle Terre. The night air was cool and sweet, a welcome change from the smoky interior of the casino. She took a deep breath and caught the scent of coming rain. It was a common enough occurrence, New Orleans never remaining long without a shower or two. In the stillness she heard only the whir of crickets and the rustle of wind in the leaves.

As she stood beneath the spreading branches of the largest oak she wrapped her arms about herself, and imagined she was once again in Adam's arms. She might call herself a thousand kinds of fool, but she couldn't forget the press of his lips on hers or the heat of his body as he held her close.

If that was all there was to remember, then she might have been able to accept her attraction to him. But of course Adam had not stopped with a kiss. And neither had she.

A door opened, and she turned toward the small house at the back of the lot. Delilah, still in the black silk dress she wore to serve in the casino, stepped into view. She closed the door behind her and walked across the lawn toward Cat.

She did not speak until she stood close. "The mam'selle looks like a ghost in the dark."

"Do your voodoo beliefs include ghosts, Delilah?"

"I do not accept all of the teachings, mam'selle. I do not worship the serpent, nor do I engage in animal sacrifice. But there are many mysteries in our world which cannot be explained by the white man."

"Such as?"

"The power of the gris-gris."

"Yours did not seem to save me from harm."

Delilah's black eyes were warm and thoughtful. "Has the mam'selle suffered a great trouble?"

"I don't know," Cat answered honestly.

"I am certain of this much," said Delilah, a smile twitching at her lips. "If the mam'selle keeps up the way she has today, we will all be in an early grave."

Cat answered her smile, then looked away, her gaze straying absently to the swaying moss that hung like spun silver from the low branches of the tree. The smile died. "Tell me, Delilah, is there a charm to keep a woman from . . . wanting a man?"

"Some things even the voodoo cannot change. Wanting a man is one of them. If it were the opposite you were asking—something to help bring you desire . . . oh, that would be different. I would have the potion that you need."

"I'm afraid," Cat said, half to herself, "that would be like throwing matches onto a fire. But I can't . . ." Her voice broke.

"What is it that Mam'selle Cat needs? I will do what I can."

Caught as she was in her own thoughts, Cat only half heard the offer. "I've always held myself apart from the gamblers," she said as though her actions needed defending. "A laugh, a little conversation, that is all. And no one ever pushed for more . . . no one until—"

"—the American," Delilah finished for her.

"He's different from the others."

"So I have observed."

"They come here to try their luck at the tables, but I do not believe Adam ever cared whether he won or lost at the roulette wheel. Certainly he didn't care for the money. I've seen sorrow in his eyes, Delilah, such sorrow as would break your heart. He'd deny it . . . but I know."

As she looked at Delilah, she thought of the one other certainty she held concerning Adam. "He never thought I would tell him no."

"He is, as you say, different from the others." Delilah took her mistress's hand, holding it for a moment as she spoke. "He is also good for Mam'selle Cat."

"I wish I could know that for sure . . ." Cat hesitated, and from the recesses of her mind came the one worry she had not been able to accept or forget. "What happened yesterday . . . You know, don't you? It could happen again. And I cannot, must not conceive a child. Not Adam's. Not any man's."

"There is among the gris-gris of my people a potion that can make the babies stay away." Delilah's voice held a businesslike calm, as though her mistress made such a statement every night.

Once she'd freed her fear, Cat could not let herself be soothed. "Are you sure? What if I'm already—"

"You must give me your trust. It was my own mother who gave me the secrets. She said only once did she fail to take the powder, and you see before you the result. I will have it for you when you wake." She smiled. "Have no fear, mam'selle. The condition of barrenness is not permanent. When you have decided to bear a child, you need only throw the powder away."

Sadness swept over Cat. "No, that's one thing I will never do."

"This is a decision that only Mam'selle Cat can make. Be assured that what we have discussed tonight will not be repeated. Not even to Ben. He would not approve of another gris-gris, regardless of its purpose."

"Thank you, Delilah. If stories are already circulating about me and the American, they can be only rumors. It is no one's business what I do. And," she said with a rueful smile, "I would not want anyone else to doubt that I am unobtainable."

Not even Emile, she thought with a shock. He had warned her away from men. What would he think if he knew what had happened yesterday? She did not want to disappoint him; he had been a dear friend for so long.

182

She stopped herself. Emile was far more than a friend. He was her salvation.

She bade Delilah good night and returned once again to the casino, locking the door behind her and hurrying up the back stairs.

Maybe everything would be all right, she told herself as she tried to still her worries. Maybe Adam would not come again, and if he did . . . if the same thing happened, she would accept it for what he had said it was: pleasure in a rotten world. It was a sentiment that Cat could surely understand. No emotions other than the needs of the flesh would involve them. She was a mature woman, no longer a young girl with dreams of true love; it was not to be expected that she would forever deny herself such moments again. She had been fooling herself if she thought that she could.

Cat felt her worries lift. Through the years she had learned to handle every situation, had adjusted to life's troubles, had learned to enjoy what she could and to endure what she must. How easy it was to endure Adam when she was with him . . . no, not endure but *enjoy*. And he was damnably hard to forget when he was gone.

She stepped into the upstairs hall and saw that the light spilled from the open doorway of the study.

Emile smiled out at her. "Cat, do you not want to talk tonight?"

As usual, he was immaculately dressed in black coat and tie, brown hair combed back from his sharp, clean-shaven face. Cat felt a sense of relief at his beckoning. Emile never disappointed or hurt her or pushed her to do things she could not accept. And he would not push her to tell her secret thoughts.

If she asked him what he knew about Adam—questions Adam himself had suggested she ask—Emile would tell her the truth. He would not ask why she wanted to know.

She joined him and settled into the chair in front of the desk.

Emile was the first to speak. "Michael tells me you were busy today. So much effort expended upon a floor when you have servants to do the menial work."

"I didn't see Michael."

"You know how he comes and goes. Tell me, *ma petite chatte,* why all the frenzy? Are you troubled?" He leaned forward, his arms on the desk, and watched her narrowly. "Usually it is a man who upsets a woman so, but in your case, surely not."

His probing surprised her. "I went to Belle Terre yesterday," she said, a note of defensiveness creeping into her voice. "You were not here to ride with me, but I needed to go. It had been a long while since my last visit."

"You are free to ride where you choose. Have I ever said otherwise?"

"No," said Cat, "but I know you do not approve of my desire to buy the land."

"Only because I do not believe it will bring you the happiness that you seek."

This discussion over her plans was an old one between them—and the only one in which they disagreed.

"So you went to the land," continued Emile. "Such visits usually do not bring you to your knees with a bucket of scrubwater at your side."

Cat stirred nervously, a vague sense of uneasiness overtaking her. Wanting . . . needing to ask Emile about Adam, she found that discussing him over the desk in her study—where she usually went over the accounts—betrayed what they had shared.

It was a foolish, romantic notion, and she brushed it aside. "I met the American, Adam Gase, on the plantation grounds. He had followed me."

Emile sat in silence for a moment. "Is this what he said? That he followed you?"

"He did not deny it when I accused him of riding after me."

Emile waited for her to continue and at last she did, choosing each word with care. "We argued. He's had troubles that he thinks you know something about."

"M'sieur Gase is a confused man, my dear. He has believed lies about me." Emile picked up the lighted cigar from the desk ashtray and inhaled deeply, blowing a haze of gray smoke into the air and staring at the glowing tip. He looked back at Cat. "They are lies he claims to have heard in prison."

"Prison?"

"Perhaps he neglected to mention he is a convicted felon and only recently released. I suppose it could have slipped his mind. He wants to harm me, Cat. I fear that because of these twisted plans of his, he might want to hurt you, too."

"But how?" she managed. "Why?"

"Who knows how such a disturbed mind might work?" Emile hesitated. "I can see he has also neglected to tell you he owns Belle Terre."

The news hit her like a slap.

Emile did not stop. "He has accused me of causing his arrest, although he cannot come up with a reason for my doing such a ridiculous thing. He seeks revenge. When he visited here and talked to me, he said he would do anything to get it."

"Revenge," she whispered, and let the meaning of Emile's words eat into her mind. Adam owned Belle Terre; he believed she was owned by Emile. And he wanted revenge.

Her head reeled from the news. Adam had been so gentle when he held her . . . so loving. Could it all have been solely to get back at Emile?

It was Adam who called the world rotten. The sentiment was one Cat could share, now more than ever. She was struck with such an unexpected pain that she thought she would faint.

Emile poured a glass of brandy from a decanter on the desk and walked around to Cat. He lifted her limp hand from her lap and wrapped her fingers around the drink. "Here. You have had a nasty shock."

Cat did as she was instructed, barely aware of the burning sensation as the brandy slid down her throat.

Adam . . . Belle Terre . . . prison . . . revenge. The words pummeled like fists into her thoughts. She kept coming back to revenge.

"I have done nothing to harm the American," said Emile.

"I know," she said, her voice barely above a whisper. But Adam believed the stories that Emile had labeled lies. They had brought him to La Chatte . . . and to a game of roulette.

A knock at the door startled her. Michael entered. "Sorry, your lordship. I'll come back later."

Cat stirred. "There's no need. The hour is late. I should leave." She spoke as if she were caught in a nightmare in which nothing seemed quite real. She tried to rise and found that she hadn't the strength.

Adam . . . revenge.

And she had harbored plans for making love to him again.

"It's just that I have learned something," continued Michael. "Something that will be told to the public tomorrow. Something your lordship might be wanting to hear tonight. It's about the American, Gase."

Emile took the glass of brandy and set it on the desk, then placed his hand over Cat's. His palm felt cool and damp. "If you think it's important, Michael, then by all means tell us what has happened."

Michael closed the door behind him and stepped deeper into the room. Cat looked over her shoulder and watched him as he spoke. "The police caught him today skulking around Judge Osborne's house. Or I should be saying, the *late* Judge Osborne's house."

"I had heard rumors of the m'sieur's death. A shooting, was it not?" Emile asked, his eyes steady on the Irishman.

"That's right, your lordship. And Gase was wearing a gun."

"What do the police believe he was doing there?"

"The constabulary being the fine organization that it is, they already know. Mr. Gase right now is deep in the confines of the Calaboso. They've charged him with killing the judge."

Chapter Thirteen

Lost and alone, Adam floated through a darkness as deep as despair, searching for a ray of light, for solid ground under him, for a sense of order in a formless world. He tried to call out but found himself without a voice and, worse, without a hope in his pounding heart. What was the purpose, he asked his dreamself, of screaming into the void if there was no one to hear? And what was the purpose in hoping if his nightmare had no end?

The clatter of metal on metal jerked him awake.

He swallowed hard as the noise disappeared into the dark, and drew deep, settling breaths, pushing from his mind the dreamworld of endless night and accepting the dimness of awaiting day. He was back in the Calaboso where he knew was housed all the order he could ever expect—three stone windowless walls, a fourth of iron bars, and beneath him a hard mat atop a harder floor.

The jail had lost none of its relentless efficiency since his first arrest: a dismal room at the front for questioning by the police and a cold, damp cell at the back to let him think over his answers. And all around him, other cells. A few, like his, housed prisoners awaiting trial. Most were packed with red-jacketed men—debtors, felons, runaway slaves—chained and separated only by color, not by the severity of their crime.

His stay before had been brief—a frantic night before the trial and a night of rage afterward. Then followed a fast wagon ride to the swamps and a slow two years until freedon.

It wouldn't go the same way again. This time they would have to kill him, a condition that offered strong possibilities of coming to pass. This time he wasn't charged with smuggling slaves; this time the charge was murder. The penalty for murder was death.

Again the clatter from one of the adjoining cells; he recognized it as the scraping of metal against the iron bars—a tin cup probably. He had one somewhere on the floor. Some poor, unseen soul was making the noise, a wordless protest against the dark, a demand for food and water, a cry for someone to care.

Don't bother, Adam could have told him; *they'll come when they'll come.*

He sat cross-legged on the mat, his back against the stone wall, and considered his plight. Yesterday had begun early with a fast ride through the fields and an even faster one from Belle Terre to Judge Osborne's New Orleans home. He'd taken care to wear his holster and pistol, both clearly visible to Laverton or one of his thugs.

He'd slipped through the gate and made his way through the late-morning shadows of the judge's courtyard.

"Halt, m'sieur."

He'd turned to see a gun pointed at his chest. At the other end of the gun was a stern-faced policeman with a cold cast to his eyes.

He should have rushed the man, taken him by surprise, at least attempted an escape.

But he had tried to explain. "I'm looking for Judge Osborne."

"You did not knock at the gate."

Adam had been turned away from there too many

times, but he had not thought the policeman would understand.

"Your name, m'sieur."

"Adam Gase."

Another uniformed man appeared and said, "It is the one that the housekeeper spoke of."

"Where is Osborne?" asked Adam.

"You know as well as we do, m'sieur, that he is dead. Such a look of innocence you should save for the court," the first officer said. Extending his hand, he added, "Your gun, *s'il vous plaît.*"

Still another policeman appeared, and another, as though they had all been waiting for him to arrive. Surrounded, he had complied.

In an airless room at the Calaboso he'd been interrogated. Again and again the same questions were thrown at him, first by the police and later by an attorney for the state. "What were you doing there? Why did you want to see the judge?"

And Adam's response: "To find out why I was convicted so quickly of a crime I did not commit. Osborne knew I was innocent. Why was no one allowed to testify in my behalf? I wanted answers. He could not answer them dead."

"Your animosity toward the late justice is evident, Mr. Gase. Revenge is an ancient motivation," commented the lawyer, a portly, middle-aged man named Samuel Carlile. "And so is greed. Tell me, please, where you were during the afternoon hours Sunday."

"Is that when Osborne was killed?"

"Just tell us where you were."

Sunday. Yesterday. Adam remembered a clearing in the woods and a pair of violet eyes staring up at him. Attorney Carlile did not understand his sharp and bitter laugh.

"I want my lawyer," Adam said. "One of my choosing this time. Joseph Devine."

Carlile was unable to get more out of him and finally

agreed. "We are not out to persecute you, Mr. Gase," he said before the manacled Adam was led from the room. "You will have access to a complete defense as allowed by the law."

Adam had met the declaration with a skepticism that was with him still.

His thoughts were interrupted by the groan of a door being opened; a shaft of light cut through the dimness outside his cell and he heard the creak of a cart, the shuffle of footsteps, the sharp cry of "Breakfast! Everybody up!" Adam's first full day of incarceration had begun.

Shortly after a breakfast of coffee and corn pudding, shoved unceremoniously through the briefly open cell door, he watched as the chained work crews shuffled out, parading past the iron bars, each man wearing a red jacket, red trousers, and nothing to distinguish him other than a name badge pinned to his chest.

An hour later he was surprised when a jail guard reopened the cell and announced that his lawyer awaited.

"Get along with you," the guard said, hand on his holstered gun as he led Adam past the dim cells lining the corridor. As he walked, Adam could feel the watchful eyes of the few men remaining in their section of the jail, but no one spoke. Close behind him came the heavy footstep of the guard, a swarthy man almost as wide as he was tall.

Adam was led to the same interrogation room that Carlile had used the day before—a small, square room whose bare floor was barely adequate for a six-foot-long table and two cane-bottomed chairs. Its only decoration was a folded umbrella resting in the corner.

Joseph Devine rose from one of the chairs. His slight figure was clad in a black suit, starched shirt, and black cravat, his fair hair combed neatly back from the tanned, even-featured face. Adam was struck again by his youth.

Joseph greeted him with a warm handshake and a quick, disgusted look at the manacles around his wrists.

"Can't you take those off?" the lawyer asked, glancing at the beefy guard.

"Against the rules." The guard's narrow eyes stared hard at Adam. "The kind of bastards we get in here are trickier than a cottonmouth. Can't give 'em no slack."

His body filled the doorway and he gave all appearances of remaining in place until it was time to return Adam to the cell.

"Close the door as you leave," answered Joseph coolly as he set a small leather satchel atop the scarred table. "I'll let you know when I'm done."

"I ain't—"

"It's against the rules for you to remain." Joseph shot a sideways glance at the guard, who stood a foot taller than he did and outweighed him by a hundred pounds. "Mr. Gase has the right to a private consultation with his legal representation."

The guard blinked twice, his thick lips curled downward, then without a word, he slammed the door closed behind him. A key clicked loudly in the lock.

"He's probably afraid you'll take that umbrella and jump him," Adam said.

A flash of appreciation came and went in the lawyer's blue eyes, which were two shades lighter than Adam's. "An old lawyer's trick, scaring the police. But we usually resort to it only after we've lost a case."

"Get prepared then. You're going to lose this one."

"It would seem you're not filled with false hopes."

"I don't feel hope of any kind. Don't forget, I've been down this road before."

"And don't you write me off as a failure just yet." He indicated for Adam to take one of the chairs, removed a small quill case and notebook from the satchel, and pulled the second chair up close. "Tell me what has happened, including what you told Carlile."

193

Adam settled into the chair, his legs stretched in front of him, his manacled hands resting on his thighs. "I'd spent the weekend working at Belle Terre . . ." he began, leaving out the details of Sunday afternoon, "and decided to make one more attempt to confront Osborne."

He began with his ride into town the next morning and described everything he could remember, including the size of the policeman's gun that was pulled on him in the judge's courtyard. Joseph's quill scratched against the open notebook as Adam spoke, his only comment a grunting sound from time to time.

"I'm not sure it was wise for you to talk so much to Carlile," he said when Adam fell silent.

"I've done nothing wrong." Even to Adam the words sounded stupid. He'd done nothing wrong before.

"Unfortunately, the police and the prosecutor do not believe you."

"It's another setup, Joseph."

The lawyer set the pen down and frowned at Adam. "I only wish it were."

"I know it is. Laverton has done it to me again."

"Don't get me wrong, Adam. I'm still on your side, but you were the one prowling the town with questions for anyone you thought could help you. You were the one who made a nuisance of yourself with the housekeeper. Laverton had nothing to do with that."

"If I did bother the woman, it was at worst ungentlemanly behavior on my part, but that's hardly a crime."

"The judge was shot in the head and his room ransacked. Your gun could have been the one used. And you could have been looking for the old Spanish doubloons that the judge collected. As payment for the years he put you away."

"Is that what the police believe?"

"It's one of the possibilities they are considering."

"Why did I return?"

"You did not find the gold."

"Returning would be incredibly stupid.'

Joseph hesitated. "There are those who believe revenge is stupid, too."

"Do you believe I'm guilty?"

"No. But I will not serve on the jury."

"Then I'm to have an open trial this time."

"Right away. The state looks with disapproval on the removal of a judge, retired though he may have been and never having garnered much respect."

Again Joseph picked up the quill, drawing meaningless circles on the paper where his notes had stopped. "If only you had an alibi other than simply being at Belle Terre. Neither the word of your slaves nor of Tom Jordan will do you much good, although we'll certainly call Tom to the stand."

Adam looked sideways at the lawyer and said quietly, "I've got another alibi."

Joseph stared at him in astonishment. "Not someone in your employ?"

"No." Adam let out a long, slow breath of air. "Definitely not someone in my employ."

"Good God, man, why haven't you said anything before?"

"She won't testify."

"She? You were with a woman?"

"That's one way of putting it."

"The two of you were—"

"I don't intend to describe the afternoon."

A small smile crept onto the lawyer's face. "At least it's an alibi a jury of men will accept. Surely you plan to identify her."

"La Chatte de la Nuit." Adam watched the surprise in the lawyer's eyes.

"Emile Laverton's—"

"Exactly."

Joseph considered the news. "Were you together the entire afternoon?"

195

"Long enough to prove I didn't shoot the judge."

"I'll speak to her," said Joseph, confidence edging back into his voice.

The lawyer's enthusiasm made Adam regret he'd ever mentioned Catherine. "Don't bother, Joseph. You won't get close. And it might be dangerous."

Joseph brushed the advice aside. "Don't forget, I sent the guard running. I'm tougher than I look."

"You don't know who or what you're dealing with. To you and most of New Orleans, Laverton is a shadowy figure, a mystery man with a bad reputation. I've met him. He's a bastard. I wouldn't put anything past him."

"I will, of course, be careful."

Joseph repacked his satchel and reached for the umbrella. "Mustn't forget my weapon. It was beginning to rain just as I got here."

"You're a stubborn man, Joseph Devine."

"All part of the profession. You'll learn to appreciate me before the end of the trial."

He knocked at the door, which was opened immediately, and nodded good-bye. "I'll get back as soon as I can."

It was with foreboding that Adam watched him leave. Joseph thought he was tough, but he was a mewling infant compared to the kind of men Laverton hired. Laverton himself, if pushed to it, could shoot him down and regret only the mess that his bloodied body made.

Not that it would come to shooting. Laverton was too slick for anything so obvious. More likely, threats would be used against the lawyer himself or against someone he loved.

Back in his cell, as morning dragged into afternoon, he let in the thoughts he'd been holding at bay, ponderings about the beautiful and enigmatic Catherine Douchand. If Joseph's visit wasn't forestalled by one of Laverton's thugs, how would she receive him?

How would she react when asked to tell the police or, if necessary, a jury, that she had lain with Adam at the moment Judge Osborne was killed?

Adam feared he already knew the answer.

He must forget her concern for Madame Ferrier, forget her tenderness with the Ferrier child, and, most of all, forget the seemingly innocent way she'd fallen into his arms. He must remember only that she had kept him occupied while someone killed Lawrence Osborne.

He found it hard to believe she hadn't known what was taking place. Catherine was far more devious than he had given her credit for being. She and her lover had played him for a fool. The realization ate like a poison into his system. How in hell he could have let himself be distracted by her, he couldn't—

Adam brought himself up short. He knew exactly how. She'd looked up at him with those wide and wounded violet eyes, her lips parted, her body provocatively clad in britches and a clinging shirt, and all he'd been able to think about was getting her into the woods.

And afterward, he'd wondered just how much she knew concerning Laverton, wondered what she thought about fair play, about his seeking justice in an unjust world. If he had ever put the questions to her, he could imagine the manner of her response: her lovely head thrown back, her graceful neck arched, a silver laugh of ridicule escaping from her slender throat.

His hands itched to get around that throat.

He stopped himself. What if he was wrong about her? The idea wasn't completely insane. Perhaps she had been ignorant of the shooting. Perhaps even now she was telling Joseph that she would be glad to testify in Adam's behalf. He'd like to believe that such was the case, and for reasons that went beyond gaining his freedom. He'd like to believe that she was more innocent than she seemed.

During the next two days, as he waited in apprehension for Joseph to return, Adam relived Sunday afternoon a hundred times. The longer he waited, the more certain he was that things had not gone well at the casino. Too late, he swore that Catherine would never fool him again.

On the third morning of his incarceration, the behemoth guard again came to call, escorting him in silence to the interrogation room. He entered to see Joseph sitting at the table, his back to the door. The door slammed shut behind him and the key turned in the lock.

Slowly Joseph turned to face him. His right eye was badly bruised and there was a bandaged cut on his left cheek. Adam's first thought was that he did not look so youthful anymore; the second, a wish that he had Laverton and his hirelings in the room with him. He had rage enough to take them all on at once.

And then he'd like a private visit with Catherine.

"You were right, Adam," Joseph said with a shrug and then a grimace. "I must remember not to do that for a while."

Adam imagined the unseen bruises on the young lawyer's body. "I'm responsible for this. I never should have told you about her."

"You tell your lawyer everything, Adam. It's another one of the rules."

"We're dealing with people that don't admit to any." He pulled up a chair and set close by Joseph, his manacled hands on the table. "Tell me what happened."

"I went to the casino right after I left here, but no one answered the door. When I went back that night, I couldn't get close. A hard-looking Irishman kept at my side to make sure. And Mademoiselle Douchand retired early, not long after the place opened."

Adam nodded toward his bruised eye. "When did that happen?"

"Later, when I left. The Irishman tried to convince me I shouldn't return."

"His name is Michael O'Reilly, in case you want to press charges."

"One case at a time, Adam. He would only swear I was making a nuisance of myself. And he wouldn't be far wrong. I was not quiet in my insistence that she talk to me."

"You've been recuperating since then, haven't you? O'Reilly did a thorough job."

"Not so thorough. I still plan to call the mademoiselle to testify."

"Don't bother. She'll only lie. There were no witnesses to our meeting."

"Which was held where?"

"In a stand of trees behind Belle Terre."

Joseph nodded in understanding.

"With a little clover thrown in." Adam felt like a fool for remembering such a detail. Under other circumstances, he'd be a cad for telling it to someone else, for even hinting at what had gone on between him and Catherine. But in setting him up, she had wiped out all considerations that might be made in her behalf. Gone was his hope for her innocence. "Believe me," he added bitterly, "she won't admit to what happened."

"Then *you* will have to."

"She'll say I'm out to ruin her reputation. She'll say it's part of my revenge. Make no mistake about what's happening here, Joseph. They've got a grip on my balls and they're squeezing."

"We'll just have to squeeze back."

The lawyer spoke bravely, but the marks on his face gave more eloquent evidence that any success on their part would be difficult to come by.

Adam made no attempt to argue. Let Joseph take what encouragement he could from the impossibility of the case he must present.

Adam knew the way things would go—mounting

evidence against him and little rebuttal allowed. He didn't want Catherine to testify. She would only lie. She was good at lying. She had made him wonder about her, made him forget about the rottenness of the world. He wouldn't forget again.

Adam appeared in court on the following Monday, clean-shaven and dressed in a somber suit Joseph had obtained from Belle Terre. Outside, the rain poured down on the already sodden city. As they made their way through the hallway behind the courtroom, Joseph told him the weather had been bad since his arrest.

"Bodeen predicted rain," said Adam. "It's a good thing we widened the ditch. About the only good thing that happened Sunday afternoon."

He saw Catherine as soon as the bailiff Johnnie Taylor escorted him in past the judge's bench. She was seated in the back row of the half-filled courtroom, alone, veiled and wearing the loose black dress she'd worn before.

The sight of her shook him. He hadn't expected her to be within a mile of him ever again. Coming here was a brazen act, even for her, and for all her shortcomings, he hadn't taken her for one to gloat. He didn't bother to tell Joseph who she was. There seemed little point.

He nodded to Tom Jordan and Reginald Odom, seated together in a middle row, then took the chair beside the lawyer, whose bruises had faded to a mottled puce. The cut on his cheek was barely visible from more than three feet away.

Joseph leaned close. "Judge Williams is hearing the case. He's a fair man and widely known to be honest."

Adam listened without comment, glancing for a moment to his left at the double rows of jurors, all black-suited men with solemn mien and the light of self-righteousness in their eyes. He looked back at the black-robed judge, whose desk sat on a raised platform twenty feet away. With his full head of gray hair and kindly brown eyes, Williams had a benign look about him, but that would do Adam little good. President Jackson himself could have conducted the proceedings, and still the outcome would have been foreordained.

It was an outcome that Catherine had come to watch. He could imagine the triumphant expression she wore beneath the veil.

The witnesses moved through quickly. The pasty-faced clerk from the city records office was first. He'd brought documents concerning the first conviction and went on to describe Adam's visit less than two weeks ago.

"Mr. Gase was real angry," he said with more enthusiasm than Adam thought necessary. "Wanted a transcript of his trial. Actually cursed, he did."

"Do you recall his exact words?" asked the prosecutor, Carlile.

"I'll see him burn in hell," yelled the clerk, then settled back in the witness chair with an embarrassed grin. "That's what he said. In just that tone. I warned him right away to cease using such language. He behaved right away when he saw I wouldn't put up with any of his nonsense."

"Who was the *him* that Mr. Gase referred to?"

"Oh, Judge Lawrence Osborne. He made that clear enough."

"Your witness," Carlile said to Joseph as he sat down.

Joseph stood. "What was Judge Osborne's reputation in town? I believe you spoke of it to the defendant."

"I object," Carlile said.

"Sustained," said the judge.

Joseph tried again. "Did Mr. Gase ask about anyone other than the judge?"

"I believe he brought up the prosecuting attorney. I told him that man was already dead." The clerk looked at the jury. "That was one he couldn't get to."

"Thank you," Joseph said with a shake of his head. "That will be all."

Johnnie Taylor was next. "He caught me out there in the hall," he said in response to a question from Carlile. "Wanted to know everything I could remember about the trial. Said he was after justice, but I was thinking at the time what he was after was plain old revenge."

Joseph shot to his feet. "Objection."

"Sustained," said Judge Williams. "Mr. Taylor, please answer the questions without further comment."

"Did he say anything else?" asked Carlile.

"Mentioned a gun." The bailiff's left eye twitched. "Asked if I was ever upset enough to shoot down a man."

Again Joseph rose to his feet, but Adam put a hand on his arm and pulled him back to the chair. "Forget it. He's right." Adam could feel the noose tightening around his neck.

The bartender from the Drink Emporium replaced Taylor. "He came in asking for Sean Casey."

Carlile gestured toward the trial documents which were lying on the table in front of him. "The same Sean Casey who testified against him two years earlier."

"Objection. The witness couldn't possibly know if this Casey was the same man."

"Overruled."

"It was the same," said the bartender. "Heard Casey say so himself. Mr. Gase bought him a bottle of whiskey, asked him a lot of questions."

"Objection. There's nothing in this testimony, Your Honor, to indicate the meeting had anything to do with Lawrence Osborne."

"Sustained."

The bartender persisted without instructions. "Got old Sean so shook, he took the first ship out. And he was a man who'd sworn to give up the sea."

Adam held Joseph in place. "Give it up. He's close enough to the truth."

The next witness was a surprise. Madame Gaston Ferrier, looking slight and innocent in a lace-trimmed amber gown, her wide dark eyes staring out from a small, delicate face, sat on the edge of the chair.

Joseph stared openly. "What a lovely woman. Don't tell me she intends to say you threatened her."

"She'll say I gunned her husband down."

Which proved close to the truth. Over Joseph's repeated objections, Carlile managed to get in much of her testimony about the unorthodox duel. She also added that he had entered her home without permission shortly before accosting her husband on the street.

"Objection," protested Joseph.

"Sustained."

But the evidence of Adam's brashness was firmly planted in the jury's minds.

"Your witness," said Carlile.

"Madame Ferrier, was it not your husband who challenged the defendant?" Joseph asked, and rather gently, Adam thought.

"That is true, M'sieur Devine," she said, her eyes lowered. "My husband would testify himself, but he is still too weak."

Adam muttered under his breath, and Joseph shot him a warning look.

"But I stood on the gallery and watched him shoot Gaston. He did not turn his back, as a gentleman would have." Her voice grew weaker. "I held my baby and saw everything."

"Was it not also true that Mr. Gase was trying to stop the duel?"

Carlile rose to object, but Madame Ferrier, her slender shoulders lifted, was already speaking. "It is possible, but who can say for certain what was in the mind of the *Américain?*"

"Give it up," Adam advised for the second time.

"Thank you, madame," said Joseph. "That will be all."

After a solemn lunch in an area behind the courtroom, neither Adam nor Joseph eating more than a bite, Osborne's housekeeper, a gray-haired widow named Elizabeth Land, gave even more damning evidence—of repeated visits by Adam and demands that he be allowed inside the judge's house.

"He was after the judge. I saw that right away. Poor man."

Adam knew she did not mean him.

"Or," she added tremulously, "he was after the Spanish doubloons. Everyone knew the judge collected them."

Joseph shot to his feet, got his objection sustained, but as with Madame Ferrier's testimony, the damage had been done. If Adam had not already harbored a sufficient motive for killing Osborne, there was also the cache of priceless coins.

Several members of the jury shifted in their chairs. Not for the first time, Adam wondered how Catherine was enjoying the spectacle, but he refused to turn around to see if she remained in the courtroom. Even if she were present, he would not be able to see behind the veil—to look for the smile of satisfaction, the light of triumph in her eyes.

A growing fury ate at him, and he forced her from his mind before he found himself leaping over the railing behind him and going for that lovely throat.

"This next question will be difficult, Mrs. Land. Please answer the best you can. It was you who found the body, was it not?"

Mrs. Land dabbed at her eyes with a knotted handkerchief. "His Honor was in the study. I brought him a cup of tea, as I always did. And some of those beignets he was always so fond of. I had just got back from the market with them, as a matter of fact. So fresh they were still warm. I figured that's why I didn't hear the gunshot. With all the neighbors being away—some of them just gone for the afternoon and the rest spending the summer at their places on the lake—well, with most everybody being gone, there wasn't anybody to hear when the poor man . . ."

The widow's voice broke.

Carlile paused before continuing. "That was on Sunday, right? A week ago yesterday."

"It was. He'd only got back into town an hour before. Been visiting his sister in Tennessee as he did sometimes. Looked kind of peaked to me when he got back. Said the journey was more uncomfortable than ever. He got aches from time to time. Said a drop or two from the bottle did him good. And I said it wasn't my place to judge him." She caught herself. "I didn't mean that as a bit of humor, Mr. Carlile."

"I did not think you did, Mrs. Land."

Someone stirred behind Adam, but he did not look around. From the corner of his eye he could see the bailiff, seated between him and the jury, turn his attention to the spectators.

"Now what time was this, as best as you can remember?"

"Three o'clock. The chimes from the church were sounding just before I went in. You can hear 'em real nice from our . . . from the late judge's place, ringing in the hour every Sunday afternoon."

"Tell us what you found."

"That poor man was stretched out behind the desk. The room was a wreck. Someone"—she glanced once at Adam—"got in real fast through the window that His Honor always kept open. I just know he was after those doubloons the judge thinks—pardon, the judge *thought* so much of. Didn't get 'em, though. My coming must have caused him to run sooner than he planned." This last was said with a shudder.

The rustling on the spectator side of the railing grew louder. Johnnie Taylor rose from his chair, and Adam shifted to see the source of the commotion.

The view that met him pushed all other considerations from his mind. Catherine Douchand, veiled and drably gowned, was marching with a determined stride toward the front of the court.

Chapter Fourteen

Cat spared only a quick glance at Adam as she made her way toward the railing that separated the spectators from the court.

Sunday afternoon. The words burned in her mind. Until a few minutes ago, she'd thought the judge had died last Monday. Simpleton that she was, she'd been unable to believe Adam's guilt, unwilling to accept without any doubt that he had used her only for revenge, a revenge that he had turned on the judge. She'd come to watch the trial and hear for herself the evidence against him. An unrecognized spectator, that's all she was, one of the many curious men and women who crowded into the courtroom.

But the murder had taken place Sunday afternoon. Everything had changed.

She passed row after row of gawking onlookers, some no doubt recognizing her, most wondering who the rude intruder could be. She kept her eyes straight ahead.

"What is the meaning of this disturbance?" The barked query came from the bench.

What, indeed, Judge Williams? Cat thought.

A public spectacle was what she was—she who treasured anonymity when she was away from La Chatte—but she couldn't sit back and watch Adam

207

suffer for something he did not do. Rising from that bench had been difficult to do, but remaining quiet would have been impossible.

She stopped at the railing directly behind the defendant's table, carefully avoiding a second glance at the watchful Adam, her attention instead directed at Joseph Devine.

"Mr. Devine," she said, loud enough for the judge to hear, "you must stop this ridiculous trial at once." Her voice hesitated only slightly. "M'sieur Gase was with me Sunday afternoon."

Her bare hands gripped the top rail. Wondering idly where her gloves could be—she must have dropped them in the aisle—she listened to the furor she'd set loose.

"I object," shouted the prosecutor, Carlile.

"Mademoiselle Douchand," demanded the judge, who'd made more than one visit to the casino and obviously saw through her disguise, "I ask again, what is the meaning of this interruption?"

Defying earlier instructions from Judge Williams, the jurors chattered among themselves, and the bailiff was yelling for her to step away from the rail.

All spoke at once.

"Your Honor," said Joseph Devine, trying to speak above the din, "I request that a new witness be called right away."

A disappointed "oh" came from the witness chair, where Osborne's widowed housekeeper still sat.

Adam was the only principal in the drama who did not say a word.

Cat kept her eyes straight ahead. To anyone watching her as carefully as he, she gave the appearance of being unruffled by the chaos she had caused. In truth, the courtroom turmoil was nothing compared to what she was feeling inside.

More orders, more shouts, none of which she paid attention to, all her concentration directed to remaining upright and calm.

"Overruled" came the judgment from the bench concerning Devine's motion she be allowed to take the stand at once.

Devine did not look particularly upset, and Cat could sense that the tenor of the trial had shifted in Adam's favor. Still carefully avoiding a glance at Adam, she took a seat on the bench directly behind the railing.

With decorum settling once more on the courtroom, Carlile concluded his questioning of Mrs. Land and called the arresting policeman, who put Adam's gun into evidence. The weapon, he said, was taken from the defendant as he arrested him in the late judge's courtyard. "A mean-looking character the suspect was, if I ever saw one," he commented before Devine could object.

"You arrested him on Monday," Devine said when it was his turn to examine the witness.

"That is correct."

"And Judge Osborne was killed on Sunday."

"Correct."

"I have no further questions," said Devine.

Carlile, with a weary shake of his head, said that neither did he. He rested his case, and it was Devine's turn to call witnesses to the stand.

At last Cat found herself swearing to tell the truth.

"Take your time in answering the questions, Mademoiselle Douchand," said Devine.

She nodded once at the attorney, whom she remembered from earlier in the week at La Chatte. A fair, handsome young man with determination in his eyes, he'd caused some kind of disturbance, but Michael had assured her it was because he lost all his money at cards.

It would seem that Michael had lied.

For the other witnesses, Devine had issued his questions from where he was seated. For Cat, he came forward to stand at her side, a sympathetic look in his eye.

"Please state your name for the court."

"Catherine Marie Douchand."

"Owner of the casino known as La Chatte de la Nuit."

"That is correct."

"Are you aquainted with the defendant?"

"He came several times to the casino."

"Tell us where and when you last saw Mr. Gase."

Cat found she was most in control if she kept her eyes on the questioning attorney and not, definitely not, on the solemn defendant whose stare bored into her.

"It was Sunday, a week ago. Out in the country. Behind his plantation."

"And what were you doing there, mademoiselle?"

"I often ride out to Belle Terre. I find the place lovely. And the ride gets me out of the city for a while."

"I see. Where exactly did you see him?"

"I was giving my horse a drink at the bayou that runs behind the plantation. He saw me and asked what I was doing there." She squeezed her hands together, keeping them firmly anchored in her lap lest she show her nervousness. "I did not know at the time he owned the land where we stood."

From the corner of her eye she caught a shift of Adam's body as he leaned forward against the table.

"Can you give a time of the meeting?"

"Only an estimate. I'd taken a lunch along and had already eaten. The sun had dropped slightly. I'd say it was about two o'clock."

Carlile stood, but Devine continued without pause. "It could have been an hour before or an hour afterward, could it not?"

"Possibly."

"Which would have put your meeting anywhere from one to three in the afternoon. Sunday a week ago."

"That is correct."

"The time period during which Mrs. Land testified her employer was slain."

"I can only say, Mr. Devine, that he could not possibly have been in town. He was with me."

"Could you have been seen by anyone else at this meeting?"

"I doubt it. There was a row of trees separating the bayou from the back of the plantation. The area was quite deserted." Cat had to force her voice to remain strong.

"Lift your veil, please, Mademoiselle Douchand."

Cat hated the shaking of her hands as she complied. Tucking the veil against her bonnet, she dropped them immediately back to the folds of her black gown.

"Now look at Mr. Gase."

Cat did as she was told. She could not stop an intake of breath as he met her stare. His eyes were so dark and deep. He seemed to be peering inside her soul.

"Can you positively identify him as the man you met behind Belle Terre?"

"I can," she said barely above a whisper.

"Your witness," he said to Carlile, and returned to his seat.

"Mademoiselle," the prosecutor said, rising and striding to exactly where Joseph Devine had stood, "you testified that you had already met Mr. Gase several days earlier at your casino."

"I did not say when, but yes, it was several days before my ride to Belle Terre."

"That night at the casino, he won some kind of bet, did he not?"

"I see the stories have spread," she said, turning her attention to him.

"You are a well-known woman in New Orleans. And men, being what they are, will gossip."

Devine rose to his feet to object. "Overruled" came from the bench.

"You were also present at the duel which Madame Ferrier has already discussed."

"Yes."

"It would seem you have more than a passing acquaintance with the defendant."

Cat did not respond.

"Pardon my intrusion into delicate matters, Mademoiselle Douchand, but could it be that your feelings are involved here?"

"Objection," shouted Devine. "Mademoiselle Douchand's feelings have nothing to do with her testimony."

"Sustained."

Cat found herself looking once again at Adam. The gray at his temples was more prominent than she remembered, and there were shadows under his eyes. *He hasn't slept well,* she thought and wondered, if she'd been forced to answer the prosecutor's question about her feelings, just what would she have said?

"Why did you come forth this afternoon?" asked Carlile. "Why not earlier?"

"Because," she said, once again shifting her attention to him, "I did not know when Judge Osborne was killed. As soon as I heard Mrs. Land's testimony, I knew I had to speak."

And it had mattered not one whit whether Adam had made love to her in the woods to get back at Emile. Nothing had mattered—not the public exposure nor the questioning she was sure to endure—nothing except seeing him free.

"Did you and Mr. Gase spend a long time together beside the bayou?"

"An hour perhaps. I don't believe it was any longer."

"And the two of you were alone?"

"We were alone."

"Would you tell the court how you passed this hour?"

A snicker was heard from one of the spectators.

"Objection," said Devine. "They could have been counting alligators, for all we know, or discussing the price of sugarcane. What happened does not change the fact that they were together."

"You have made your point well, Mr. Devine. The objection is sustained."

There, it was over, Cat thought, waiting for the humiliation that must come from her public admission of being alone with Adam in the woods. Surely there wasn't a listener in the room who had trouble figuring out what she and Adam had done.

But she found that she was not ashamed of what had taken place, at least not ashamed that anyone else should know. Her regrets came from within.

At last she was allowed to return to the back row. Head high, veil still tucked away from her face, she made the long walk slowly, ignoring the curious looks of the crowd.

Devine tried for an instructed verdict of not guilty, but Judge Williams ruled in favor of the prosecutor's objection. The attorneys gave brief arguments, Carlile's slightly overreaching Devine's in length, but there was a desperation in his words that said he knew what the jury would decide.

They were out no more than ten minutes. None of the spectators left.

"Not guilty," the foreman said.

"Good show!" one of the spectators shouted.

Everyone seemed to stand at once and Cat hurried from the courtroom, trying to get away from the crowd.

Adam caught her halfway down the corridor, his hand gripping her arm so hard that she could not pull away.

"We need to talk," he said.

Cat could not look at him. "I've done all the talking I need to this afternoon, Adam. Let me go."

"No." He pulled her to an alcove at the side of the

213

hall, away from the gawking crowd.

She was forced to turn her head. Again their eyes locked. He seemed to have lost the tiredness she'd noticed in the courtroom; his face held all the rigid, intractable power she had seen every time they met. But there was something more, something in the depths of his eyes, a puzzled tenderness as though, not understanding the woman that he held, he still could not let her go.

The noise of the passersby retreated. For a moment she was alone with him back at the bayou, her breath caught by the look he gave her, an insistent warmth spreading from the pit of her stomach throughout her body.

She shook away the image. "People are staring," she said.

"You don't give a damn about them any more than I do."

"I thought that I did."

"We're both learning some things about ourselves, aren't we, Catherine?" The grip of his hand on her arm lightened until it became a caress.

She did not try to argue against what they both knew to be true; nor did she try to pull away.

"Let's get out of here," said Adam. "Name the place, only make it private. And not the house you took me to last time. I'd take you to a hotel"—his mouth twisted into a wry grin and her heart quickened its beat— "except that the state was providing me with lodgings and I don't have a room."

"I do."

Cat startled herself with the admission, and she hurried on. "I did not know if the trial would continue for another day, and it seemed foolish to keep Ben waiting around to take me back."

"What about your maidservant?"

"I sent Delilah back with Ben. I was not afraid to stay alone."

"I wouldn't think that you would be. What does surprise me is the interest you had in the trial."

"It shouldn't. I know about your imprisonment and about why you came to the casino, Adam. I thought you might have . . . done what you had done at Belle Terre to get back at Emile. And to hurt me. I thought that maybe . . ." She could not go on.

Adam was silent for a moment. "We definitely need to talk."

She looked past him to a cluster of men in the middle of the hall. She recognized Joseph Devine and the banker Reginald Odom, but the third, a stocky, plain-faced man in shirt and trousers, she had never before seen. "Your friends are waiting."

"Let me introduce you to my manager at Belle Terre."

It was Cat's turn to say no.

"Wait here, then. I'll be quick."

True to his word, Adam joined the men for no more than a minute, shook their hands, and as they headed for the door, he returned to her.

"Is your hotel within walking distance? It's still raining outside."

"I'm not afraid of the rain." Her only concession to the weather was to lower the veil.

Adam grinned and locked his arm with hers. Outside, the rain had turned to a fine mist, and she was surprised to find there were still a few hours remaining to the day, gloomy as it was. She would have guessed it was midnight.

Neither spoke as they hurried along the banquette. The crowd was thin and no one paid them any mind. Cat had selected an unfashionable hotel a half dozen blocks away on Royal Street. Except for a lone clerk behind the desk, the lobby was empty. Cat asked for her key, unmindful of the questioning look on his face as he looked behind her to the waiting Adam.

They were going upstairs to talk, she told herself. He

wanted privacy; that was the only reason she was bringing him here.

Liar, she thought.

She embarrassed herself by fumbling at the lock. Adam covered her bare hands with his own and took over; the warmth from his skin matched the growing warmth inside her.

Preceding him into the small room, which was dimly lit by the waning sunlight filtering through one window, she reached for the bedside lantern.

"Leave it," Adam said. "We can see well enough."

"To talk."

"To talk," he agreed.

She gestured toward a chair by the window and sat on the opposite end of the bed, her back against a post, her hands in her lap.

Adam pushed up the sash, and a whisper of fresh, damp air rushed into the room. He glanced back at her.

"Aren't you going to take off that hat?" he asked.

Undoing the pins holding it in place, she stroked her hair back into its neat bun, but a stubborn tendril fell against her cheek.

Adam settled into the chair, his long legs stretched out half the length of the bed. With the light coming from behind him, she could not see his face clearly.

"That's still the most godawful dress I've ever seen," he said.

Brushing at the beads of moisture that had caught on her skirt, she wondered if he planned to request its removal, too.

"But you were the most beautiful sight I've ever seen, standing there behind me in the courtroom."

"I couldn't keep quiet."

"Even though you thought I wanted to hurt you Sunday."

Cat caught her breath. So here they were, she thought, brought by his blunt words to the core of what lay between them. She tilted her chin upward and looked directly at him, wishing she could see his eyes. "Didn't you?" She spoke the words bravely, defiantly, to cover the dread in her heart. "Isn't that what your approaching me has been all about from the beginning? To get back at Emile?"

"It was when I made the bet. I was ready to hurt anything and anyone connected with him." He sat straight in the chair. "By Sunday I wasn't thinking of revenge."

"I'm supposed to believe that?"

"It's the truth. I'd lost my concentration concerning a lot of things long before Sunday. And all because of you."

Cat's pulse quickened. "Why, Adam? Why?"

"Damned if I know."

"At least you aren't trying to sweet talk me into believing I've bewitched you with my charm."

"I'm just trying to understand what's going on between us. Why were you out at Belle Terre that day?"

"I said why in court. The ride gets me away from town."

"You also said the plantation was . . . what was the word, *lovely*, I believe. You surely got a better look than that. The place needs more work than I've had time or money to give it. There are a thousand other places you can ride to out of New Orleans that offer more to see. I repeat, why Belle Terre?"

Cat stirred nervously. "You're wrong if you still think I was following you. Until earlier in the week, I didn't know you had anything to do with the place, much less owned it. The truth is, I used to know the family that lived there before you. I've always had a fondness for Belle Terre."

Her voice almost broke at the half truth, and she stood. "I'm not sure I like this talk you wanted. Maybe you ought to go."

"The only thing I'm sure of is that I can't get you out of my mind. I've never felt like that about any woman before, Catherine. Never. You've bewitched me, all right."

"Is that supposed to be a compliment?"

"It's the truth." He stood and began to walk slowly around the bed. "I've had damned ugly thoughts about you, and you've had the same about me."

"You're wrong about Emile."

"To hell with Emile. Today there's only me and you. We can't stay away from each other, can we?"

He came to a stop behind her and leaned close, his breath warm on her neck. "Can we?"

"I . . ."

His lips burned against her skin and moved to the spot just behind her ear. Cat shivered and felt herself leaning into the kiss.

"No," she confessed, "we can't."

His hands kneaded her shoulders, but his touch was gentle, as though he held a fragile flower that he treasured. He nibbled at her ear. "Are we good for each other, Catherine? Or are we bad?"

"Adam . . ."

His hands shifted to her hair. The pins dropped to the floor, and the freed curls fell against her shoulders as she felt his fingers working at the back buttons of her gown.

Chapter Fifteen

Suddenly shy, Cat shifted away from his active hands.

"I'm not sure . . ." she began.

"Oh, yes you are."

His voice was deep and insistent and much too close to her ear for her to think of an answer.

Another step, and she turned to face him. Looking into the depths of his eyes, flashing with hunger, she felt the floor shift under her and knew that facing him had been a mistake. She could not look at him and declare they would not make love again.

"What have you done to me, Adam?"

"I'd like to think . . ." He paused, then reached out to take a strand of hair between his fingers. Stroking back and forth, he whispered, "It's like silk. Everything about you is like silk."

"You didn't answer my question."

His eyes met hers once again. "Only because I could ask the same thing."

Cat's first instinct was to turn her head and kiss his palm, but that would be a gentle gesture, a provocative, silent plea between lovers. And they were not, could not be, lovers. The word had a ring of permanency to it, a commitment. Adam was not a permanent part of her life; they'd made no pledges to each other, had said no words of love.

They had made love—it wasn't the same as loving, as Cat well knew. They would probably do so again. But that was all. Their lives were crossing for a while, nothing more.

There was a part of himself that Adam held back. But then there were things she, too, held secret . . . things she could never tell another human being. A few already knew, but they would never betray her trust.

Cat viewed him solemnly, willing him to see she faced him now with as much open honesty as she could manage. "I did not set out to change anything about you. I did not even want to see you again after that first night at La Chatte."

Adam stepped close and spread his fingers in her hair, lifting the long black curls, studying them as though they held some kind of magic.

"But you came to the court today. Knowing the truth, you spoke out. You can't imagine how I felt when I saw you walking up the aisle and then listened to your words. Such sweet embarrassment was in your voice—"

"I thought I had that disguised," Cat said, the embarrassment returning. "Anyway, it didn't last long. I knew what I was doing."

"You know what you're doing now, too. I'm beginning to know what's in your thoughts very well." His eyes burned into hers. "You can't imagine how much I want you."

His hands rested against her shoulders, fingers massaging the base of her neck. He was standing so close she could feel the heat of his desire as it permeated her own tingling body. She felt weak and strong at the same time, wanting him to overpower her and at the same time fighting a craving to throw herself into his arms and make love to him the way he had made love to her beside the Bayou Rouge.

Throughout the interminable days and nights since

then—long hours of recrimination and regret—she had suffered, fearing that beneath those shadowy oaks he had sought a cruel kind of revenge, that the sweetness he'd shown her at Belle Terre had been only another way to lie.

Men always lied to women they planned to use. For all his troubles—real or imagined—Adam could be no different.

Cat searched his face for a sign that, more than wanting her, he needed to hurt her in some way. Even now, even after what she had done for him today. If she could see the ugly edge of vengeance behind his passion, then perhaps she could push him away, could order him to leave and hope that he would obey. His treachery would be her salvation, would keep her from falling completely under his spell.

She saw nothing but desire, the raw need of a man for a woman, the same raw need that she felt gnawing inside.

"Ah, Catherine," he said, his thumbs stroking her cheeks and the edges of her parted lips. "Beautiful Catherine, dear Catherine. What thoughts roam through that head of yours?"

She had no answer; as his hands caressed her and worked their magic, she slipped beyond rational thought.

"Give yourself to me again," he whispered huskily.

And then she was in his arms, his mouth open against hers, his tongue thrusting deep into the dark, moist interior, touching her own tongue, the roof of her mouth, her teeth, then returning to dance against her tongue. His hands shifted to cradle her face, his breath teasing her cheek.

Trembling, Cat felt a surge of longing, a mixture of loneliness and desire that was at once painful and sweetly promising. He had called her *dear,* and for the while she could believe that she was, so gentle was he and so tender.

How did he do this? she asked herself. How did he arouse such naked needs—the need to be held, the need to be loved, the need to be as one with him? Why was she so easily persuaded that she was right to share his quest?

When his hands moved to her shoulders and then lower to caress her breasts, she stopped asking herself how and why. Her body arched against his palms and she felt her breasts swell, her nipples harden. She broke the kiss and whispered, "Yes, Adam. Yes."

She rested her hands against the lapels of his coat and found the rough texture of the cloth unsatisfying. She wanted to feel the contours of his chest, the wiry curls of hair that darkened his already tanned skin, the sleek, hot skin pulled tight over sinewed muscle. Slipping her fingers inside the coat, she played with the buttons of his shirt. Last time she had torn his clothes open; this time, more skilled, she unfastened the shirt with quick dexterity and pressed her hands against his body. She heard the intake of his breath, felt his heart pounding beneath her palm.

"I want to look at you," he said. "Naked. Lying on the bed. I want to look at you."

Cat had never been with a man on a bed, a thought that struck her with unexpected absurdity. She pushed the idea from her mind and pressed her lips against his chest. His skin was hot as fire.

"You just want to get me out of this godawful dress," she whispered.

He chuckled. "You're getting to know me very well."

Even with her face resting against his body, she could picture the softened expression that he must be wearing, the glint in his eyes, the slight, provocative smile on his lips. He was right. She was getting to know him very well. And she, too, wanted to see him lying naked on the bed.

She pushed away. "I've got rather a large number of clothes on," she said, her own eyes smiling up at him.

"Hadn't you better get started?"

"The last days have been hell, Catherine. I'd like to take my time."

"Whatever you want."

"I'll remember you said that."

He kissed her briefly, then surprised her with a grin of appreciation. "There is something to be said, however, in favor of your advice." As he spoke, he removed his coat and tossed it aside.

"I'll remember you said that," she answered, repeating his words.

She turned to present her back to him, and for the second time he began unfastening the buttons of her gown. She felt each brush of his fingers, even through the chemise, and her head rested to one side as she waited for him to finish. He pushed the gown from her shoulders and down her arms. With a moment of assistance from her, the folds of black gabardine fell in a pool at her feet. The chemise came over her head, and the petticoat joined the gown on the floor. That left only her stockings, a pair of white silk drawers, and her black slippers.

"You didn't exaggerate, did you?" he asked. "There *are* a lot of clothes."

She bent to remove her shoes, then slowly turned to face him. His eyes trailed from her lips to her throat to her bared breasts. He stroked the taut nubs with his thumbs, and again Cat's head fell to the side. She closed her eyes and gave in to the sensations he was arousing, the tingling that began in her breasts and grew to a warmth in the pit of her stomach. If Adam was in a rush to undress her, she decided, there was no way she planned to complain.

Her only difficulty was remaining upright when her knees threatened to buckle under her.

As usual, he sensed her difficulty. "I think you like me to touch you."

Her only answer was to bite at her lower lip.

"Here," he said, pulling her into his arms, "let me do that." And he did, his teeth nibbling against her mouth, his tongue licking, his own lips brushing against hers.

His expert hands worked at the tape holding her final undergarment in place. He kneeled to ease the drawers down her legs. His face was close to her thighs, his gaze like heat on her body as he studied her.

Cat rested her hands on his shoulders while he removed her stockings. At last she was naked, as he had wanted. Through the shirt she could feel the tautness of his muscles. She thought of the scars that marked his body. Now she knew where he had got them—from lashings in prison, although she still did not know why he had been there.

It didn't matter. He was making love to her with such incredible tenderness, as though he . . .

Adam stood, and the tenderness came to an end. "You're driving me insane. I was wrong. I can't take my time."

Lifting her into his arms, he laid her on top of the bedcovers; in an instant he had removed his own clothes and was lying beside her. He pulled her hard against him, his hand raking down her side, rubbing against her breast, their legs tangling, his mouth on hers, then burning against her cheeks and down her throat.

He seemed to touch her everywhere at once with a savagery the past days and years had created in him. He whispered words she could not understand, isolated sounds of elation and hunger, blended to an animal intensity. He made her share that same desperate need. She forgot tenderness or how much it had meant to her. She raked her hands over his chest, across his abdomen, against his thighs—such powerful, muscular thighs. His body was hard and contoured in sinewed planes that made her feel soft and feminine and burning with fiery hunger for him.

"Adam," she whispered more than once, her voice unrecognizable as her own. His name became a plea for more.

He gave her what she craved, with his lips and tongue and with his hands, kissing and caressing, teasing the hardened tips of her breasts, with light kisses and then with the laving of his tongue until she heard herself cry out. Her body pulsed for him, moistening itself in eagerness for his entry.

His hand explored downward, massaging her stomach, tickling the pubic hair, and at last teasing her throbbing nub while one finger thrust its way inside her. She writhed beneath his touch; she was a feral creature who demanded fulfillment, but she was no more wild than he.

Taking his shaft in her hands, she stroked and caressed him. He moaned her name. Their ragged breaths blended and her heart beat so strongly that she thought it might burst. When he shifted on top of her, it seemed the most natural thing in the world to part her legs and lock her ankles around his buttocks. He kissed her as he entered, then pressed his burning lips to the side of her neck.

The thrusts were quick and deep, then quicker and deeper as she arched to meet him. There were no secrets between them, nothing held back; there could not be when a man and woman shared without compromise such a melding of needs. Passion mounted into a frantic craving for completion, reached at last. With their sweat-slick bodies clinging, the fine raw edge of rapture slowly dissolved into the satin contentment of satisfied desire.

Adam held her tightly, his face pressed to her tangled hair, and she listened as their breathing slowed. Unwinding her legs from his body, she lay still beneath him, marveling that such a strong, powerful man could rest so lightly on top of her. At last he edged away and lay on his back beside her, his gaze directed at the ceiling. She felt a chill as the early-evening air hit her still-fevered body.

She must have shivered unknowingly, because suddenly he had wrapped her again in his arms. Enfolded thus so gently, she thought to kiss the sweat from the hollow of his throat and then irrationally decided that such an action was far too intimate for her to contemplate. She wanted his tenderness, but if she gave it back in turn she would be telling him that what she was experiencing with him went beyond the pleasures of the flesh.

Cat squeezed her eyes closed, fighting an impulse to cry and laugh at the same time, knowing in her heart that she was drawn to him in ways she had not known existed, ways he must never realize.

How absurd her life had become. She had opened herself to Adam without compromise, and here she was fearing to reveal to him the emotions he had unleashed in her. Fiery passion was what he wanted to see, not tenderness.

She must fight the feelings in her heart—feelings she could not, would not, give a name to. Naming them would be the start of accepting them. He would never understand what a heavy toll such an acceptance would take on her after he was gone.

She shifted away from him; he resisted her movement at first, and then lessened his hold. She lay beside him, but even in the waning light which drifted through the window behind him, she hesitated to look his way. Only their breathing broke the stillness.

Cat was too inexperienced at pillow talk to know if such a time of repose and reflection was to be expected. After a full minute of feeling his eyes on her, she could stand the silence no longer. "You're quiet, Adam. That isn't like you. Don't you have anything to say?" The words came out more harshly than she had intended.

"Tell me what you want to hear." He stroked her hair. "I could tell you more than you can imagine. How you made me feel strong and whole once again, made me feel clean after the degradation of imprisonment, made me feel alive."

Her eyes darted to his face, but in the dimness she could not read his expression; could it possibly match the fervor of his words?

Of course it could; Adam was still caught by the throes of passion. Cat had come into his life at its lowest ebb; whatever she gave him would be like sustenance to a starving man. Such sustenance could have been given by any woman, not just her.

He'd called himself bewitched; she recognized his condition as loneliness.

She shivered, and he moved closer. "I'd like to get beneath the covers," she said, drawing away.

"Whatever you want." He shifted his weight, loosening the counterpane where it was tucked in at the headboard, and Cat eased her body beneath its comforting warmth—and its comforting concealment.

Adam's long, lean body remained disconcertingly on top of the covers. Cat trained her eyes on the bedpost.

"I never did get a good look at you lying on the bed," he said.

"You were too eager." Again her voice was harsher than she meant it to be.

"I wasn't the only one." He matched her tone.

"No," she said, smoothing back the damp curls from her face. "You weren't the only one."

She could feel his eyes on her profile; she sensed the tension in him, feared what he would say next.

"Why do you stay with him?"

He took her by surprise, and yet she should have known. Always Emile. Her lover, or so Adam believed. No amount of denial on her part would make him change his mind. Frustration . . . anger . . . disappointment all stirred within her.

"What I do is my business."

"It's becoming more and more mine."

"Only because our lives are intertwined right now. Why is it that men think they can tell women how to live their lives, and do not grant the same authority to them?"

"Quit changing the subject, Catherine."

"I thought I was staying very much on it. My relationship with Emile Laverton is none of your concern."

"He'll hurt you."

And you think you won't? She swallowed the words. He might think she was feeling sorry for herself, and that she most definitely was not.

"No man hurts me, Adam. Especially not Emile. He is the dearest person in all the world."

"Damn it, Catherine, it doesn't sound as though we're talking about the same man."

"I don't know what stories you've heard about him, but they're lies. I know they are. No one knows him as I do. You're so blinded by a need for revenge against him that you can't see clearly. Revenge is stupid. At my lowest moment, even I—"

She broke off.

Adam's laugh was hard and ugly. He seemed hardly to have heard the despair in her voice.

"What if I prove that I'm right about him and you are wrong?"

Cat could take no more, and she sat upright, turning her back to him, holding the cover close against her body. "You can never, never, never convince me that he is not my friend." Her voice quivered with emotion. "He came along at a moment when . . ." She could not go on.

She felt his hand on her arm, and she stiffened. "Do not ever speak of him to me again."

"He killed Osborne, or had him killed. It's my guess Michael O'Reilly pulled the trigger, but he was acting under Laverton's orders."

"Impossible." Cat covered her ears to shut out his words.

"He's using you, Catherine."

228

"Stop."

"He sent me to prison on the basis of false testimony that he paid for. He's not worth your loyalty. Or anything else from you. Leave him."

She rocked back and forth at the side of the bed, still able to hear what he said, anguish tearing at her heart. Adam asked too much of her; he did not understand.

"Stop," she said again. "Stop, stop, stop." And then, lowering her hands, she whispered, "Go away."

She sat for a moment, holding herself very still and waiting for him to respond, but all she could hear was his measured breathing. At last he got up from the bed, and she listened while he pulled on his clothes. She felt cheap and used. She'd given herself to Adam freely and willingly and with complete abandon, and in return he demanded concessions from her that she could never make.

He could see his words tormented her.

He did not care.

Adam was that most dangerous kind of man—a man with a cause. Cat knew too well what havoc such a one could raise. Julien Constant had placed his plantation and his family above her. Adam was obsessed with revenge.

The irony of it was that Adam, too, owned Belle Terre.

Adam owned Belle Terre. The thought would not go away. Emile had probably known for a long time. There were times she thought he knew everything. Was it possible Adam was right, that Emile had . . .

She could not go on. Any conclusion to the thought was too horrible to contemplate. All she could wonder now was whether she would ever ride to Belle Terre again.

Adam paused at the door. "I don't want to leave this way, arguing over someone like him."

"You don't owe me anything," she said. "We each had a good time. A celebration that things went the way they should have in court." At that moment she meant what she said.

"Is that what your life is all about? Celebration?"

"Of course," she snapped, her head held high. "And good times. Ask anyone in New Orleans, and they'll tell you all about the infamous La Chatte . . . if they haven't already."

"I don't believe you're the kind of woman you're describing now. Not for a minute."

"Believe it, Adam. You asked if we were good or bad for each other. We're both. Good for a while, and then . . . Well, figure it out for yourself."

"That's what I'm trying to do, Catherine. That's what I'm trying to do."

Adam hesitated outside the room, feeling like a bastard for leaving so abruptly and at the same time wanting to put distance between him and Catherine. What was there about her that made him want to caress her and strangle her at the same time? She was warm and loving and good—it was there in her eyes when she wasn't playing a part; it was in the way she shared in their lovemaking. He'd seen it time and time again when she was away from the casino.

But she was a fool about Emile Laverton. When he'd tried to tell her the truth, she had refused to listen. When he had continued, there had been real despair in her voice.

Emile is the dearest man in all the world.

Adam pictured the cold-eyed scoundrel who had threatened him in the casino study. He tried to imagine anyone—man or woman—not seeing Laverton for what he was. No wonder he kept himself from the public eye.

Could she possibly love him? The idea filled Adam with such a rage that he could hardly keep from storming back into the room and shaking her until she came to her senses.

Feeding his rage was a sense of exasperation. The way he saw it, a man knew how things were with another man. Good, bad, or in between, they let themselves and their purposes be known.

But with a woman, especially one as puzzling as Catherine, things were different. A man had to guess much of the time why a woman behaved as she did, and nine times out of ten he'd be wrong.

Adam had to get Catherine out of his system. He had to forget about the way she curled against him, the way she looked up at him with such sweet abandon, forget the delicate contours of her face and the seductive power of her body and the way her lips felt under his.

What he needed to remember was the way she'd pulled away in the bed and ordered him to leave—which, by damn, was exactly what he would do.

He stormed down the stairs, through the lobby, and onto Royal Street. Forgetting Catherine would be as difficult as proving the guilt of Laverton. For all his efforts since getting out of jail—the first incarceration, he thought bitterly, not the second—he'd let all his possible witnesses get away from him, had alerted Laverton to his plans, and had fallen under the spell of the bastard's mistress.

Rather a bad show for a man who had vowed vengeance with all the strength of his soul.

The rain had ceased, and the evening air held a sweet, damp coolness that was typical of the city after an early-September shower. The crowds that had been missing on his walk with Catherine from the court to the hotel were now on the banquette, and the Royal Street vendors were once again hawking their wares. Walking quickly past the wrought-iron gates of the townhomes along Royal, Adam wondered if Joseph Devine could still be in his office. He needed some money—the cash he'd been carrying at the time of his arrest had been taken from him along with his gun.

Surely the police had turned over his possessions to Joseph.

He'd see the lawyer, pay the stable for a week's care for Keystone, and ride straight to Belle Terre. During the next few days he would leave the renewed investigation of Lawrence Osborne's murder to the New Orleans authorities.

He turned down a less traveled side street, a shortcut to the law office. The route took him past an alley opening onto the street. As he strode past, he saw a movement, a shadow. Cursing the fact that he was unarmed, he whirled away but not in time to avoid the blow delivered to his head.

He fell to the ground in unconsciousness.

Chapter Sixteen

"He's coming around, your lordship."

Adam heard the words through a fog of pain. As he struggled to consciousness, he tried to figure out where in hell he was . . . how he came to be slumped in a chair, his arms bound behind him . . . why every muscle in his body ached as though he'd been chopping cypress back in the prison camp . . . why someone was pounding a hammer against the back of his head.

He shook his head—a mistake—and waited for the hammer to slow. The last thing he remembered with any clarity was leaving Catherine's hotel. They'd made love and then they'd fought—a natural progression for them. He remembered the street, remembered a plan to visit his lawyer's office, and then nothing. Until now.

"You should not have hit him so hard, Michael. I grow impatient."

Another voice, deeper, sharper, and one he recognized.

Adam attempted to lift his head, to open his eyes, to demand to know why he'd been knocked out and brought here. The hammers multiplied, and he held still.

"M'sieur Gase is having difficulties," the sharp voice said. "Help him."

Footsteps shuffled behind him, and the rim of a glass

233

pressed hard against his lips and teeth. He swallowed, gagging at the sharp whiskey as it cut its way down his throat, then swallowed again. The second time he did not gag, but he felt the beginnings of nausea as his stomach fought against the alcohol.

He forced himself to look up, forced a grim smile to his mouth. Staring at the man sitting behind a desk directly in front of him, he said, "We meet again, Laverton." His voice came out weak, even to his own ears.

"M'sieur Gase, welcome. You must feel yourself honored. Seldom do I invite anyone to my private offices."

The whiskey began its work, slowly clearing Adam's mind if not easing his discomfort. The hammers stopped, replaced by a metal vise that had his head in its grip, and the throbbing pangs became a steady agony. Ignoring it, Adam gave a brief glance at the room. He had to move his head slowly or else the threatening blackness of unconsciousness would return. Rough cypress walls, a wide oak desk with chairs on either side, closed cabinets to Adam's right, at Laverton's back a window covered with a shade thick enough to preclude anyone's looking in or looking out. To the left was a closed door.

The only ornamentations rested on the desk: a dim light on the corner nearest Laverton's right hand, a humidor, and a small brass bowl holding a crushed cigar. The heat in the room was oppressive, the odor unpleasant with stale smoke.

He let each image, each sensation, slowly press itself against the back of his mind as he fought against the misery of nausea and pain.

It was a dismal place—the lair of a predator, a sanctuary more suited to a denizen of the Swamp than to the sharp-faced, fine-suited man sitting opposite him. Adam suspected that the Swamp was most likely where he was right now, not too far from the Drink

Emporium where he had met with the witness Sean Casey.

Somewhere close by, the murky Mississippi wound on its journey to the sea, flatboats and barges and frigates clogging the outgoing tide. On the surrounding streets were the derelicts that went with that river trade. Right now Adam's world consisted of just himself and the man he had come to hate.

He heard a stirring and twisted to glance behind him, paying in pain. The squat, spread-legged figure of Michael O'Reilly blocked the door to the outside. Adam corrected himself. He should have known to include the Irishman. Looking back at Laverton, he forced himself to sit tall. "I'm to feel honored?" His head reeled, but he kept his voice strong. "You have a strange way of extending hospitality. It doesn't give a man much chance to decline."

"As you can guess, m'sieur, I do not like to be told no."

Adam strained to free his wrists, but rope held them tight. "As part of all this honor, could you instruct your lackey to untie me?"

Laverton nodded once. Michael came from behind, and Adam could feel a cold blade against his skin as the rope was sliced. Suddenly freed, his arms fell lax. Slowly he brought them forward, pain rushing through his strained muscles. He rubbed at his wrists.

"Perhaps you are wondering why I asked you here," said Laverton.

Adam stared into Laverton's pale, emotionless eyes. "The question crossed my mind."

"I wish to know your intentions concerning Mademoiselle Douchand."

The question took him by surprise. "As I recall, the last time we met you did not wish to discuss her."

"But that was last time. Tonight I do."

"Too bad. Tonight I don't."

Laverton's eyes narrowed. "You would be foolish to

235

challenge me. You are not among friends."

"I'll try to remember that." Adam began to rise, but strong hands shoved him back into the chair. The cold, flat side of the knife pressed against his neck. O'Reilly hovered by the arm of his chair.

"Do not make me angry, m'sieur," said Laverton.

"I'd hate to upset you," said Adam. "I can see where that might be unwise." *For now,* he added silently, while the knife was so close to his throat.

"It is always unwise. Surely you have learned that. If it had not been for my impetuous *petite chatte,* you would at this moment be preparing for a return to the prison camp. Or perhaps the hangman's noose."

Adam started forward, felt the knife turn slightly, the sharp edge aimed at his throat, and forced himself back in his chair, forced his rage to subside. The threatening pressure of the knife eased, but Michael remained close by, his arms loose at his sides, the weapon held prominently in his right hand, the blade glinting in the glow from the desk lamp.

"She's impetuous enough to want the truth to be known. Unlike you. And brave enough to step forward in public."

"She did not ask my advice."

"I didn't think that she had." Adam adopted Laverton's unemotional stare. "Is she really your kitten?" he asked. "How well do you really know your mistress? She doesn't seem to know a hell of a lot about you."

"I did not ask you here—"

"You didn't ask me here at all."

"—to speak of my relationship with the mademoiselle. Rather, it is you who bother me. You play with her emotions. I will not have it."

Adam could detect no jealousy in Laverton's words, only determination. "Catherine is free to do as she chooses. I have forced her into nothing."

"She is a vulnerable woman. I will not have her hurt."

"I'd say you're a little late for that. True, I don't know much about her, but she doesn't strike me as being the happiest woman in New Orleans. I've seen shadows in her eyes . . . heard laughter that didn't ring true. More than once I've thought she is playing a part. I still think so."

"You are wrong, M'sieur Gase. She was contented with her life before you appeared. I want her to be so again."

"Contented, eh? Is that why she disguises herself whenever she goes into town? Is that why, except for the gamblers at La Chatte, she keeps herself away from the world?"

"She has dreams for which she sacrifices. Foolish dreams, I am sure you would agree, but they are hers, nevertheless. Once she has put them aside, she will enjoy the life she has made for herself."

"What dreams do you mean? I might not find them foolish at all."

"They are none of your business. Nothing about her is your business. You must stay away. You will never see her again." His eyes narrowed, their pale color darkened by an intensity of feeling that startled Adam with its suddenness and with its depth. "I will kill you if you do," added Laverton. "The only reason I hesitate to do so right now is that your death, coming so soon after your wild accusations concerning me, might cause her some discomfort, might plant doubt in her mind. Nothing permanent, I am sure, but I see no necessity for her to lose so much as a night's sleep over someone who is insignificant to her happiness."

Adam kept a tight rein on his anger. "Is *insignificant* your word or hers?"

"We have not discussed you."

"What do you discuss?"

237

An edge of impatience flashed across Laverton's face. "For someone so close to the blade of a knife, m'sieur, you choose foolish questions indeed."

"If she were my woman, I'd be filled with rage that she'd been with another man."

"She is not your woman."

"And she's not yours, either, is she?"

The remark was a shot in the dark, an impulsive remark born of anger and frustration, but Adam knew right away he'd hit upon the truth, as unlikely as it would have seemed to him only a few hours ago. He shook his head at the realization. "Whatever your relationship is, you can't claim her as your mistress."

"I make no claims one way or the other. You are the one who persists in seeking labels. Give up, m'sieur. You cannot begin to guess what the mademoiselle and I mean to each other. Or what her life is all about."

But Adam couldn't give up. "What you did to me is connected to her, isn't it? And to Belle Terre. She said tonight she had known the former owners."

Laverton smiled, a slight curl of his thin lips that did nothing to soften his face. "Enough. I grow weary of your speculations. As, I am sure, the mademoiselle most certainly does, especially if you attempt to accuse me of terrible deeds."

"Like killing Judge Osborne? You set that up, didn't you?"

Laverton did not respond.

"You don't have to answer. I know the truth, although once again I find myself short on proof. Tell me, Laverton, what hold do you have on her?" asked Adam. "I don't get it."

"There is much that you 'do not get,' as you so inelegantly put it, M'sieur Gase. Surely even you can understand what I say. Do not see her again. Do not attempt to draw her away from me. You will not win. And you may not continue to live."

Adam sat forward in the chair, expecting O'Reilly to

come forward again with the knife, but the Irishman made no move toward him. "You're not frightening me now any more than you did at the casino. I told you then that I wasn't afraid to die. There are far worse things. Like letting you get away from me."

"You persist in a hopeless cause."

"Not so hopeless. Look at it from my viewpoint. Most of the people involved in the trial have already been punished: the prosecutor drowned, the witness abducted to sea, the judge shot. None of it happened directly by my hand, of course, but my coming back to town certainly precipitated Sean Casey's sudden departure and Osborne's death. By my reckoning, that just leaves you and Michael."

Laverton waved his hand. "I grow tired of this discussion."

"You issued the invitation, remember? If you have nothing more to say, tell your hoodlum here to get out of the way so I can leave."

Laverton's eyes flicked to O'Reilly. "First you were a lackey, Michael, and now a hoodlum. You seem to be falling in M'sieur Gase's estimation."

O'Reilly slipped the knife into a sheath attached to his belt. "Your lordship, if you please . . ." In one smooth motion he jerked Adam to his feet and planted a solid fist into the midsection just below his ribs.

Adam doubled over, clutching at his stomach as he struggled for breath.

"A man's got to demand a little respect, your lordship," O'Reilly said.

Adam forced in shallow gulps of air, once, twice, until the endeavor seemed less like forcing a rod down his throat, and drew himself upright. He glanced at Michael and then at Laverton, contempt hard in his eyes.

"If you two gentlemen are through with your demands, I'll be leaving."

"Do not think to impress me with your toughness,"

said Laverton.

"Here I was hoping you were wetting your elegant trousers. I shouldn't underestimate how tough *you* are." He glanced at O'Reilly, then back at Laverton. "Or rather, how tough your thugs are."

He was pleased to see a flicker of irritation in the pale eyes staring up at him.

"Do not forget our discussion tonight," said Laverton.

"And there's something *you* shouldn't forget," Adam said. "The way Catherine came forward at the trial to defend me. She must have known you wouldn't approve—whether you discussed her testimony or not. I don't know if she meant to do so or not, but she managed to ruin your plans."

Figuring that was as good an exit line as he was liable to come up with, Adam let himself out through the door that the Irishman had been guarding when he first came to. Just as he had expected, he found himself on one of the streets of the Swamp. At night and unarmed, his head still aching, his muscles sore, his stomach in a knot from O'Reilly's solid punch.

He rubbed at the base of his neck and felt a crusted lump. He winced, wondering if he wasn't getting soft after a couple of months away from the regime decreed by Brother Red.

Adam took to the center of the walkway, refusing to skulk in the shadows to avoid the cutthroats and thieves who scurried like vermin in the night. Ignoring the dark figures he could see moving past him in the street, the occasional gruff talk, the high-pitched laughter and cries of whores, he walked fast, self-confident, as though he were in the best of condition and, even better, as though he carried under his coat all the weaponry of General Jackson at the Battle of New Orleans.

Besides, if Laverton ran true to form, he'd probably have O'Reilly trailing him, watching where he went.

Making sure he stayed away from his *petite chatte*. The Irishman could see he got back to the center of town in safety.

Catherine wasn't Laverton's mistress. The thought brought a lightness to his step.

Do not see her again.

Would Laverton never learn? He'd see her again whenever he wanted to—or whenever she let him, Catherine being the stubborn woman that she was.

Maybe he could return to the hotel and . . .

Several possibilities came to mind, each a pleasure unto itself. He needed to get back to Belle Terre for at least a week or two of uninterrupted work, but surely a delay of an hour or two wouldn't bring ruin to his crops.

Regardless of how the night ended, he needed cash; for that he would seek out Joseph Devine. And for all his brashness at the moment, he wouldn't mind the comfort of his gun. Then perhaps a trip to the market and a stop by the hotel desk. And then . . .

Do not see her again.

Which was exactly contrary to what Adam intended to do, despite his avowal only a few hours earlier to avoid her company for a while . . . to get her out of his system . . . to remember only that she had ordered him to leave.

But he hadn't liked the way they had said good-bye. And he was getting damned tired of being ordered around.

It was true she had defended Laverton with a fervor that had enraged him, had called him the dearest man in the world, but she had testified in open court for the man he was trying to ruin.

Whether she admitted to Laverton's bastard ways or not, she certainly realized there was no love lost between Adam and him. Despite her wish for privacy, she had publicly sworn to spending time with him in seclusion—and the avidly listening public had drawn the correct conclusion.

One thought stayed in his mind above all others. She wasn't Laverton's mistress. So who or what was she? And how could she possibly have had any connection with his imprisonment, an imprisonment he'd already decided she knew nothing about until she saw the scars?

Adam's lips twitched into a smile. He'd never solve the riddle of the real Catherine Douchand by staying away from her. And it mattered little what Laverton commanded.

What was she doing right now? Thinking of him? Trying in vain to sleep? Tossing about on the bed where they had made love? The truth was she was probably sound asleep. He wondered if she slept naked . . .

Whoa, old boy, he told himself. *You're not going back for another roll on the bed.*

He was returning to the hotel because he wanted to see her again—and Laverton, order or no order, had nothing to do with his return. In a burst of impatience, he lengthened his stride down the middle of the walk, daring anyone to stop him and hoping that Michael, with his short, muscle-bound legs, could keep up with his pace.

Chapter Seventeen

Cat lay on the rumpled cover of the hotel bed and gave up on sleep. Maybe the problem was that the hour was too early—not even ten, and she was used to staying up long past one. Maybe she was hungry, having skipped the past two meals. Maybe she missed Balzac, who nightly curled into a golden ball on the pillow beside hers.

Or maybe she couldn't forget that the bed was where she and Adam had made love only a few hours ago. The cover still carried his scent.

Ridiculous thought. She had brushed him completely from her mind as soon as he had walked out the door. Well, almost as soon. And almost completely.

At first she had concentrated on not bursting into hysterical sobbing, and then on ignoring the ache in her heart. He said such terrible things to her—always about Emile . . . always lies. They had to be; she could not believe otherwise.

Still, the moment he was gone she had wanted him to throw open the door and stride back into the room, had wanted to forget about their arguments, had yearned to let him hold her through the night.

In view of all the new and unsettling things that were happening to her, that would be one she would find a comfort.

With a sigh, Cat accepted her longing for him as fact and not haunting supposition; the thought that missing him kept her awake was not ridiculous at all. She had a weakness for Adam, nothing more, but it had her almost out of her mind. Knowing what might happen between them after the trial—should the impossible happen and he would be free—she had gone so far as to bring Delilah's gris-gris into town, packed beside her white gown in the small valise.

But he had left. And she was unable to sleep.

Not that she needed to see him again tonight. It was best that he was gone. She needed time to sort out her thoughts, and she didn't want him thinking she was available whenever he chose to want her.

She sat up, propping herself against the headboard with both pillows at her back, and decided that what she should have packed in addition to the pregnancy-preventing potion and her nightwear was a good book.

She glanced around the small room, at the chest of drawers, at the chair by the door, at the bedside table with its dimly lit lamp. Even in the pale light filtering through the window, everything looked austere, even ugly. Funny, she hadn't thought so when Adam had been in the room.

She glanced down at the high-necked nightgown and at the black braids that rested across her breasts. What would he think if he could see the sophisticated La Chatte now? He made fun enough of her drab widow's garb. Cat knew the answer. He would say she was dressed like an innocent schoolgirl. He would say her sleeping wear was as inappropriate as the black dress.

He was good at saying things that hurt.

And yet . . . Cat sighed. He had a dear way of calling her Catherine, of drawing the name out with great care, his voice rich and deep. No one had called her by her full name since she had left Belle Terre. She had thought no one would again. She was Cat. La Chatte. Mademoiselle Douchand. Except to Adam.

The room was warm and close, and she shifted to the side of the bed nearest the window, stood, and pulled the curtains aside to stare into the night. A full moon shone overhead and cast a silver glow onto the city below. A lover's moon, she'd heard it said. It was a stupid thought, and she shoved it aside. Men didn't think such romantic nonsense, and women would be far better off if neither did they.

The window opened onto Royal Street, and she watched an occasional carriage clatter by, as well as single riders on horseback. In the space of a few minutes she counted twenty such riders and a dozen carriages, but at this hour there was little foot traffic on the banquette.

She twirled one of the braids and wondered if Adam had ridden back to Belle Terre. If he had started out soon after leaving her, he could be there by now. If he took the river road and if highwaymen did not set upon him.

Highwaymen, for heaven's sake! Adam was smart enough to watch out for himself.

Then she thought about Belle Terre. For a while she'd been thinking she could never return there, not with Adam as the owner, but that had been the conclusion of a woman who admitted defeat. Cat had been such a woman once, but she had changed.

As far as she could tell, he didn't know she had offered for the plantation. And so he shouldn't, if the bank had honored her request for anonymity. What would Adam say when he found out? As he most certainly would, because she planned to keep upping the amount, over and over, as long as she could or until he gave in—whichever occurred first.

Her dreams must not be allowed to die. And she liked the idea of Adam giving in to her.

A dark figure moving rapidly along the walkway directly below caught her eye. Something about the long-legged stride seemed familiar. She caught her

245

breath, and her fingers pressed against her lips. Could it be . . . Heart fluttering, she felt briefly like the schoolgirl she resembled.

It couldn't be Adam, and yet it was. What was he doing so close by? He couldn't possibly be on his way to her room . . . not now after he'd been gone so long. Could he believe she had spent those hours pining for him? The fact that she had been doing close to that only served to increase her agitation.

She fell back from the window, afraid he might see her in a spill of moonlight. He would be up the hotel stairs in a minute or two. What could she do to get away from him? Her eyes flew around the room. Where could she hide?

She thought of the gown. He would have chance enough now to taunt her about the misplaced look of innocence.

She wouldn't let him. She would tell him to keep his mouth shut, to get away from her, to—

A pounding against the door stopped her thoughts.

"Catherine," he called. "Are you awake?"

If only she'd brought a wrapper. Maybe she had time to throw on her dress.

Again came the pounding. "I know you're in there. The desk clerk said you hadn't left."

If he kept up the noise, she wouldn't be the only one on the floor who couldn't sleep. The man had no sense of decency.

She moved to the door and said, "Go away, Adam."

"No." He pounded again.

Her panic grew. "You'll wake up everyone in the hotel."

"Then let me in. I find it a little unsatisfactory talking to you through the door."

Oh he did, did he? Cat's panic subsided into stubbornness. "I have no intention of satisfying you again tonight, Adam. Wasn't that perfectly clear when you left? Pound all you want. I'm not opening

246

the door."

Her declaration was met with silence. Could he possibly have given up so soon? Good, she told herself. She really wanted him to leave.

She stepped away from the door and dared to approach the window. Pulling aside the curtain, she watched for his appearance once again on the banquette. One minute became two and then three, and still no Adam. What was he up to? she wondered. Getting his own room when he found he could not share hers?

A key turning in the lock startled her, and she whirled. He was inside and closing the door behind him before she could cry out.

"How did you—"

"The desk clerk. I paid the bill, said there was a little misunderstanding between us earlier and I feared you were not well."

Cat forgot both panic and stubbornness and concentrated on her anger. "A swooning female? Is that what you told him?"

In the filtered moonlight she saw him grin. "Something like that."

"What have you got to be so cheerful about? I told you I would not—"

"I know, Catherine." His voice softened. "You will not satisfy me. That's not why I returned."

Walking past her, he turned up the lamp, and she saw for the first time that he was carrying a basket.

"I've brought you a late supper. I was afraid you neglected to eat. You really need to take care of yourself."

She shook her head in disbelief. "I have been taking care of myself for several years now."

"And doing a damned poor job of it."

"I'm a better judge of that than you, Mr. Gase."

He glanced at the rumpled bed. She could have sworn his mouth twitched as he smoothed the top cover and set the basket directly in the center.

"Croissant and cheese, some cold, boiled river shrimp, cleaned, of course, and a bottle of white wine. I hope it's what you like."

Gripping the post at the foot of the bed, Cat tapped her bare foot against the carpeted floor. If anyone could outdo her in stubbornness, it was Adam. "I cannot approve of your being here like this," she said. "Not after all that we said to each other."

Which was a lie, but she could not tell him the truth, that she had been thinking of his return ever since he left. Right now, she could barely admit it to herself.

He stepped close and cradled her face, his thumbs stroking her cheeks. "I couldn't let today end with the quarrel. You sacrificed a great deal for me at the trial. You made sweet love to me afterward."

Cat felt her knees grow weak and her heart began to pound. She held on to the post for dear life.

"And what you got in return was a lecture," he continued. "I've been judging the way you live your life the way I was judged, taking the word of others without real proof. And it's not my business anyway, is it?"

It could be, she wanted to say, and surprised herself with the thought.

"The troubles I've got with Laverton are my own," he said.

His touch was gentle against her chin.

"Tonight I should have kept them that way," he added, then brushed his lips against hers.

The kiss lingered long after he had lifted his head. Cat stared at him in wonderment. He hardly seemed like the man who had left her only a few hours ago.

He smiled warmly. Ripples of pleasure coursed through her.

"What is it you Creoles say?" he asked. *"Bon appétit."* His hands dropped to his side as he stepped away.

She fought to keep from swaying toward him.

"What are you saying?"

"Just that I hope you enjoy the food I brought you. I'm riding out now for Belle Terre."

Admitting to a rush of disappointment, Cat felt like an idiot child. "I see," she said. She drew herself upright, and cast a sharp look at the basket. "You shouldn't have bothered."

"It was no bother." Adam's gaze locked with hers. "You do want me to leave, don't you?" The question in his eyes was as suggestive as the question in his voice.

Cat could not bring herself to ask him to stay. That would be like begging. And she did not beg.

"I said so, didn't I?"

"So you did." He walked around her.

Staring after him, she saw that the hair above the collar of his coat was matted with what she took to be dried blood. For the first time she realized that his suit was wrinkled and stained, as though he'd been in a fight or had been rolling around on the ground.

"You're hurt."

He looked at her and shrugged. "There's a lot of danger on the streets, Catherine."

"It's a rotten world," she said, echoing the thought he himself had expressed.

"For a while this evening I forgot. When I left here, I got a quick reminder. I was jumped from behind."

Cat longed to stroke the lock of black hair from his forehead. "Did you see who did it?"

"That's nothing for you to worry about. I'm taking care of things."

"Shouldn't you at least let me wash off the blood?"

"There's no need," he said, and she could see he did not want her ministrations. From her he wanted something entirely different. And even that, not now. "I'll take care of it when I get home."

Which was, of course, Belle Terre.

Cat was reminded sharply of the reality of her situation. Here she was offering him sympathy and, if he made the least move, a great deal more. And afterward he would ride back to the place she treasured above all others in the world, leaving her to a lonely hotel room.

What she needed to do was keep things in perspective.

"Then," she said coolly, "you'd better get started. You've got a long ride."

"Right." Adam stood by the door, his hand on the knob, and stared at her.

"Good-bye, Adam," she said.

"At least you've dropped the Mr. Gase."

"Good-bye," she repeated.

His eyes trailed from her braided hair down to the tips of her bare toes and back again to her face. "I rather like that gown, Catherine," he said with a smile. "Tonight it suits you."

Then he was gone, the door closing slowly behind him. The silence that lingered in the close, warm room was deafening. Adam always had the last word, she thought. And far too often, it was a word that surprised.

This time there had been no claims that they would make love again. Nothing had been said about his return or that they would ever see each other again.

She sat on the edge of the bed and stared at the basket, but all she could see was Adam's lean, weathered face and the streaks of gray that lightened his temples and gave him a devilish look. His eyes, dark blue beneath black brows, held a hint of the pain she had seen more than once. Now she knew the source of the pain—two years in a Louisiana prison. From what little she knew, the sentence had been unjust; without her testimony, history would have repeated itself today.

Cat rubbed at the sleeve of her gown. Just thinking of Adam made her dizzy. She felt as though she were treading on the edge of a high precipice; she needed only one gentle shove to fall into an abyss.

What was it exactly that she wanted from him? Why should she want anything at all? He had broken through her reserve, had brought her sleepless nights and bittersweet memories of his kisses. Did she want anything besides more of what they had already shared?

Impossible, because more would mean wanting to be together beyond all else, sharing each other's company, talking, laughing, riding side by side. More would mean caring for each other. More would mean love and marriage.

Cat could not love again; for a multitude of reasons, marriage was not for her. She'd left Belle Terre at the age of seventeen, heartbroken, disgraced, and betrayed. A fallen woman, her mother would have said. Even though few might know now, ten years later, what had happened to her, both at Belle Terre and in the year afterward, her ownership and appearances at La Chatte—and the false reputation she held concerning Emile—had placed her in the same position. She could never serve as the wife of a respectable man.

Why, she asked herself, would she ever want to do such a thing? Even if she could care for someone again, a possibility she refused to accept, love and marriage did not go together, not that she had ever seen. It was asking too much of a man to be true.

She thought of Gerard Constant and his invalid wife, Louise. Never once in all the years that she knew them had she witnessed so much as a shared laugh between them, let alone a moment of tenderness. Louise had spent most of her time either in her room or in the dark, oppressive parlor. Never on the gallery, where she might see her husband.

"The air, you know. I might catch a chill." Cat had heard those words each time her mother had suggested an outing.

For his part, Gerard was either riding in the fields playing the part of gentleman planter, drinking in the

251

study, or staying in town for visits to his quadroon mistress.

The Constant daughter, Arianne, had not fared much better than her mother when she wed Claude Reynault, a neighboring planter almost as old as Gerard. Cat had heard rumors at the casino about Reynault's having made his own arrangements in the city—a *placage* it was called, as if giving adultery a name made it respectable.

In all the years at Belle Terre, Arianne had never been a friend or companion to Cat. She'd ordered her about, making certain Cat remembered that though her mother was a distant cousin to Gerard, Marie and her child were in reality nothing more than servants. Worse, she'd scolded her younger brother Julien for the hours he spent with "that uncouth peasant."

Still, Cat felt sorry for Arianne. No woman deserved the betrayal of a man.

Cat's mother had talked rarely about her husband, Henri. "He was an aristocrat," she said when Cat would ask to hear stories about him. "A handsome man. A true *gentilhomme*."

"So why does Arianne call me a peasant?"

"Arianne does not know the meaning of the word." The dark look on her face warned against further questions.

Neither Henri's vaunted lineage nor the memories of their brief marriage had brought her mother joy. Gradually Marie grew more sullen and withdrawn; at her death, the twelve-year-old Catherine had vowed that when she wed, it would be to a man who could make her laugh. To her youthful mind it had seemed the primary requisite.

And then there were Gaston Ferrier and the devoted Madame Ferrier. He gambled and flirted with other women while she stayed home with his child. It was a situation Cat had seen time and time again in the society that so readily condemned her.

No, Cat had not one loving example to call upon when considering the institution of marriage. It most certainly could not be for her.

And she did not love Adam. She couldn't. Which left only one possible relationship for the two of them, if they were to have any relationship at all.

Slowly she removed the checkered cloth from the top of the basket and glanced inside at the napkin-wrapped bundles tucked around a bottle of amber sherry. Adam had gone to a great deal of effort to see that she was taken care of . . . in more ways than one.

Her gaze shifted to the door. How well she could remember the half smile on his face as he stood with his hand on the knob and studied her gown.

She twisted one of her braids.

Bon appétit, indeed. Fool that she was, she had an appetite, all right, but it wasn't for bread and cold shrimp.

Chapter Eighteen

Two nights later, Emile Laverton sat alone in his office in the Swamp, staring at the ribbon of smoke curling from his cigar and pondering the situation with the *Américain*. Bringing him here had been a mistake; it had served only to send him back to Cat.

Emile did not often make mistakes. When he did, someone paid.

He flicked an ash into the brass bowl at his elbow. Adam Gase was a tough one to break. He'd thrown demands back in Emile's face . . . sneered at them, even. No one did that and lived. He must have been wracked with pain from the ordeal he'd been through under Michael's practiced hand, yet he'd made his way across the room and out the door, his body erect, his stride purposeful, his arms loose at his sides—like a man leaving a bank or a café.

Emile could recognize courage even while he destroyed it. He would rather enjoy killing a righteous man. Especially one who had disturbed his *petite chatte*.

Cat swore to him that nothing was bothering her. Emile knew different. She wasn't sleeping well, hadn't been since Gase came along; the tiredness was stark in her eyes. And she did not seem to take much pleasure in the money she made, more often than not declining his suggestion that they go over the accounts after the gamblers had departed.

Her restlessness concerned him the most. The casino had never been in better condition, but in the two days since the trial—and since her hours with the *Américain* in the hotel—she had insisted on airing the draperies, polishing the chandeliers, scrubbing the floors and walls. Even Michael had been pressed into carrying the upstairs hall rug outside to be beaten. The Irishman hadn't liked it, but after a moment's discussion with Emile he had been made to see the full range of his duties.

Cat was obsessive, tended to brood. And she was far more vulnerable to being hurt again than she realized.

But Emile realized it; indeed, he knew her far better than she knew herself. It was Gase who hardly knew her at all. Gase didn't care about her vulnerability; he didn't care about her past. He wanted only to use her for his pleasure, as though she were nothing but a whore.

Beware of men, Emile had warned her more than once. It was a warning Cat had temporarily forgotten.

He crushed the cigar against the curved side of the brass bowl. He had to bring her back to the way things were before; the only way to do that was to kill the *Américain*.

But not right away. Gase had been filling Cat with stories about his arrest and conviction, stories she took to be lies. If he were to be murdered, she might begin to wonder if he had spoken the truth, to suspect that he had been silenced in order to stop the accusations. Cat was a troubled woman, but she was not a stupid one. Indeed, it was because of her cleverness that La Chatte de la Nuit had become such a success.

Doubts could edge into her mind, and she could possibly figure out the truth. Mourning the death of a man she would consider her sacrificed love, she could allow an estrangement to grow between them. Emile could not take the risk.

He never took risks.

His eyes strayed to the closed cabinets along the wall to his left. Most of the men with whom he dealt were convinced that behind those doors lay boxes of records, detailed accounts of his business dealings, of whorehouses and slave runnings, of bribes and thefts, of smuggling and rape, and, when the situation demanded, of murder.

He did, in truth, keep some of his files in the Swamp, but additional papers were stored elsewhere. Filled with the names of supposedly respectable men, public figures like Judge Lawrence Osborne, the documents were his insurance against harm. He had hinted at their existence; more than one man threatening to kill him had backed off, knowing certain exposure would follow Emile's death.

After years of accepting bribes and bedding youthful whores provided by Emile, oftentimes more than one at a time, Osborne had developed a belated conscience. Besotted by drink, he had not flinched at the threat of public exposure to his deeds. And he had died. It was unplanned but highly fortuitous that Adam Gase had come along and offered himself as the most likely suspect in the murder. Cat should have stayed away from the trial.

Emile would take great pleasure in killing Gase— once he knew that the death would not hurt Cat. Nothing must hurt her ever again.

He thought back almost nine years to a dark stretch of the river . . . to a sound of crying in the night . . . to a sudden splash . . . He was the one who had heard. He was the one who had run to the rescue.

A knock at the door ended his reverie.

"It is unlocked," he called.

A huge Negress, as wide as she was tall, waddled into the room, her right hand grasping the shoulder of a young girl. Dressed in a faded gown, torn at the hem, the girl twisted her hands nervously in front of her. With her head bent, golden hair obstructing her features, Emile could see only that she was plump, her breasts full and hips rounding from a modest waist.

He gave his attention to the Negress. In her red skirt and blouse and with black face and coiled black *tignon* rising above her broad shoulders, she looked like an enormous apple. Dark eyes were lost in folds of fat, but when she grinned, she flashed a row of even white teeth.

"Good evenin', M'sieur Emile," she said cheerfully. "This 'un I had to show you personal-like."

She shoved the girl forward. "Look 'er over and tell me, if you dare, that Miss Aurora can't provide what she knows the m'sieur wants."

Emile felt a stirring in his loins. "Look up," he ordered.

The girl slowly raised her head and stared at him with glazed blue eyes. An ugly bruise marred the ivory smoothness of her cheek.

"I like them unmarked," he said sharply. "And not drugged."

"Just a touch of laudanum. Won't last long. And don't worry none about that mark on her face. The other end's just fine. Like a little baby. I ain't touched it, and ain't no one else dared to, neither."

Emile's hand dropped to his lap, and he nodded for Aurora to continue.

"She came in with a shipment from the East; ain't been off the boat more'n a day. Prime flesh, all of 'em is, but this one's the primest of 'em all. They thought they was headed for some kind of adventure down here in New Orleans. Ready and willing to leave home." Aurora's big body shook with a laugh. "We got some adventures waiting for 'em right enough, ain't we, m'sieur?"

Emile thought of the room off the office—of the wide bed and of the whips and rope hung on the walls. Their use depended upon his mood and the company he kept. From time to time he used them all.

Right now he was in an ugly and lustful mood.

He looked at the girl. "What's your name?"

She hesitated, and he repeated the question.

"Lorelei," she whispered, her head once again lowered.

"She's a sweet thing, M'sieur Emile. You just take a look." Aurora worked at the back buttons of the girl's dress, slipped it from her white, rounded shoulders, let it fall to the floor.

Lorelei wore nothing underneath.

Emile leaned back in the chair, studying the pink tips of her high breasts and the pale hair between her thighs. She was a tempting morsel. He stroked his hardened manhood. Very tempting indeed. Maybe one quick . . .

But he liked to take his time, and he had someone waiting at his house in the Vieux Carré, someone who wanted to please him, who did whatever he bade. Someone who helped him avenge the wrongs to Cat, although the woman had no idea that retribution was part of the pleasure he took from her.

He shook his head with regret. "I've got other plans tonight, Aurora. Save her until her face has healed. And no more drugs."

Aurora planted her hands on her hips. "They'll be lots o' men wantin' this little baby."

Emile's eyes narrowed. "I don't doubt you can keep them away from her."

Aurora dropped her arms. "You be the boss," she said with a shrug. "Pull up your dress, child."

Lorelei did as she was told, her movements slow as though she moved under water. Aurora refastened the gown and with a brief "You just let Aurora know when you want her," led the girl from the room.

Emile stared at the closed door, a hint of a smile on his thin lips. Lorelei did indeed offer something to look forward to. The cut of a whip would show quite nicely across her tight, rounded buttocks.

Emile prided himself on his use of the whip. He knew exactly how much pressure to apply to a girl's body. He broke the skin only slightly, brought the thinnest of red lines to the surface. Sometimes he liked to taste the droplets of blood. Lorelei's blood would taste sweet. If she behaved, he would keep her for a while; there was time enough to send her back to Aurora for use in the whorehouse the black madame ran for him.

Lorelei would behave . . . or be taught to do so.

Women were creatures to serve under the whip. All women except his *petite chatte*. His relationship with her was different from any he had ever experienced. He would protect her until his dying breath, and in turn she would be loyal to him.

For other, more corporal pleasures, there was always someone like Lorelei. Images of her subjugation brought a glint to his pale eyes, and he stood, adjusting the uncomfortably tight crotch of his trousers to a better fit. Turning down the desk lamp, he locked the door securely after him and made his way along the crowded street of the Swamp.

For all his obsession with elegant dress, he felt at home here, far more than he did in the Vieux Carré. This den of pickpockets, robbers, and deserters was where he had grown up. His father had been a small-time thief and his mother a whore who had died when one of her customers decided she did not provide sufficient favors for his cash.

Or so his father had told him. Emile barely remembered her. But he remembered his father very well. A cruel man, he had trained his son to follow in his steps.

Emile quickened his gait. He was going to a woman who appreciated his cruelty.

He walked the mile and a half to his destination, the house he maintained on Bourbon Street. Few knew of its existence—Michael, the waiting woman, and Cat. Unfortunately, Adam Gase did, too—Cat had taken him there after the foolish duel—but Emile could not see how that knowledge would do him much good.

A servant admitted him at the front gate. The woman was waiting upstairs in bed, already naked, the scarlet satin cover resting just below her full breasts, red hair spilling across her white and rounded shoulders, her lips parted, a look of raw desire blazing in her green eyes. She looked the way a mistress ought to look.

In the flickering light from the bedside lamp, he could see the fine lines around those gleaming eyes and the wrinkles in her neck. She looked every one of her thirty-five years.

As he walked closer to the bed, she watched him with great concentration. One of her long nails stroked across a nipple, and the tip of her pink tongue licked her lower lip. She was supposed to be a lady, he thought with a derisive laugh. She was more whore than Lorelei would ever be.

His body, already heated by the fair young girl, throbbed with exquisite pain.

"I see you are ready," he said.

Arianne Constant Reynault, daughter of Gerard and sister to Julien, now the wife of the wealthy and unfaithful planter Claude Reynau¹*, lowered her eyes until they rested at the rise of his trousers. "I see that you are, too, Emile."

He slipped from his close-fitted coat and unfastened his cravat. "Come," he ordered, "and finish the undressing."

"Whatever you say." She flung back the scarlet cover. The sheets, too, were a brilliant red, and her thighs, separated by a thatch of black hair, were white and full-formed against them.

A half dozen feet from Emile, Arianne stood and gave time for him to study her. She took care of herself, he gave her credit for that. For all her roundness, her muscles were tight and her pale skin smooth and unsagging. Only her face gave evidence of her age.

But then, Emile wasn't interested in her face.

Slowly she closed the distance between them, hips undulating, bare feet silent against the carpet, not halting until her body almost touched him. She was tall for a woman, almost as tall as Emile. He covered a breast with his hand and squeezed. She cried out, but she did not pull away.

"I grow impatient," he said.

Her fingers gripped the waistband of his trousers and she pulled him closer to the bed. She worked at the buckle of his belt, then at the buttons of his trousers. They fell to his knees, freeing his manhood. She stroked him. He felt himself close to bursting.

Shoving her backward, he fell against her sprawled body on top of the scarlet sheets and took her quickly. Once, twice, a half dozen thrusts and he was done. The first time. Unsatisfied, she writhed beneath him. He would have her again. And again, in various ways. Most of them with pain, but then she liked the receiving of it as much as he did the delivery. For all of his fifty years, he had lost none of his virility; he was capable of performing much of the night, sleeping briefly between each session, growing more inventive as the night became the early morn.

He had yet to use any tools of torture other than his own body on the eager Arianne, but he knew that eventually he would. Each time he penetrated her, each time he slapped her buttocks or pinched her breasts, each time she cried out, he drew a special pleasure. The satisfaction he derived from sex with Arianne was as much for *la petite chatte* as it was for himself—more so, perhaps, for he did not really need the woman. He always had a Lorelei waiting for him back at the Swamp.

Emile was awakened from one of his middle-of-the-night naps by a soft knock at the door. He sat up, immediately alert. Beside him, Arianne slept, her hair a tangle against the sheets, her mouth lax to emit a low snore. All was dark around him; dawn was still hours away.

Again came the knock.

The servants knew not to disturb him. He slipped from the bed and walked to the door. It opened without a sound.

"What do you want?" he asked brusquely of the woman standing in the hallway.

She stared at her hands, avoiding the anger in his eyes and the sight of his spare, naked body. "I am sorry to disturb you, M'sieur Laverton—"

"Your apologies do not interest me. I assume something is wrong."

"A woman outside . . . she arrived alone in a carriage, driving herself." The servant swallowed nervously. "She says something about Mademoiselle Douchand. I—"

Emile did not wait for her to finish. "You should have told me immediately. Inform her I will be right down."

He threw on trousers and shirt, for once paying little mind to the neatness of his attire. Without bothering with stockings, he pulled on his shoes and moved quickly down the stairs to the open courtyard. Low lamplight revealed the hooded figure of a woman standing close to the fountain, her back to him.

"Who are you?" he said as he came to a halt beside the oleander bush a dozen feet away. "What do you know of Mademoiselle Douchand?"

She turned and dropped back the hood of her cape.

"Delilah!" he said, his alarm growing.

"I thought to find the m'sieur here."

"Where is Cat? Is she hurt?"

"If tonight is the same as all the other nights of the past few weeks, Mam'selle Cat is at this moment tossing and turning in her bed at the casino."

Emile's eyes narrowed. "You dare disturb me because she cannot sleep?"

Any other listener, man or woman, would have quailed beneath his icy tone, but Delilah's chin lifted defiantly.

"I could not come at any other time, not if I wished to keep my visit secret. The casino is closed, and the mam'selle is retired for the night. As always, Ben sleeps soundly. I hope to return before he wakes."

Emile waved his hand in impatience. "I care not how he passes the night."

"You care little for anyone, m'sieur. Except Mam'selle Cat. I dare disturb you at this hour and in this place because I fear you do not understand the source of her distress."

"Whatever bothers Mademoiselle Douchand is not your concern."

"Like you, I care for mam'selle."

"She pays you well."

"You insult me, m'sieur."

Emile felt an urge to slap the defiance from her face . . . or to remove it with more manly and ultimately satisfying means. He had approached her once and she had let him know she was not interested. At the time he'd not been inclined to take her, but circumstances changed. If he decided he wanted her, he would have his way.

"I see you will not leave until you speak your mind. I suggest you be brief and to the point."

"Mam'selle Cat grows more unhappy with the passing weeks. All day she works with a frenzy that worries those who know her well. All night she paces . . . by the tables when La Chatte is open, by her bed when the casino is closed. There is only one condition which could bring about such behavior. The mam'selle is in love."

"Impossible."

"I speak what I know to be true."

He laughed sharply at the conviction on her face. "I assume you mean with the *Américain*."

"She has admitted him to her heart as she has no one else in her life." The words were thrown at him, as though she dared him to dispute what she said.

"You are a romantic fool if you believe such a thing," Emile snapped.

"I speak of a woman's love. Not a child's dreams. I gave her a love charm the night the *Américain* came to La Chatte, but I believe the feelings would have grown without the gris-gris."

Emile fought an impulse to brush Delilah off as a superstitious charlatan. She was with Cat more than anyone, and his *petite chatte* was too important to him for mistakes to be made. In truth, the servant was echoing some of his own thoughts, except that she put a more permanent cast to Cat's preoccupation.

"Go on," he said, determined not to act hastily.

Delilah's large brown eyes stared up at him with suspicion. "Does M'sieur Laverton now believe what I say?"

"I wish to hear more. Surely you have not driven yourself here at this hour to say only that your mademoiselle is in love."

"I have interrupted more than sleep, *n'est-ce pas?* Do you not have a woman upstairs? I thought so. Mam'selle Cat believes that the m'sieur is not interested in such things. But I know different."

"You will keep such thoughts to yourself, Delilah."

"I am not afraid of the m'sieur."

"You are an ignorant quadroon. Good only when you lie on your back, your legs spread."

Her eyes flashed with anger. "Which I would not do for you." She waved her hand in disgust. "You call me ignorant? It is you who is stupid. I know that if you destroy Adam Gase, you destroy the mam'selle. If you keep them apart, she will have a long and lonely life,

265

worse than the years she has already known becaus[e] this life extends to the end of her days."

"She has told me nothing of such a feeling."

"She does not tell you everything."

"But she has told you of this attachment?"

"The mam'selle does not herself know of the powe[r] of this feeling. But I know. The French have a saying *L'amour et la fumée ne peuvent se cacher.*"

Love and smoke cannot be hidden.

"Tonight, M'sieur Laverton," she continued, "yo[u] call me many names. But you cannot convince me I a[m] wrong. Believe me or not, if you do not heed my word[s] you will see the truth of what I say. The mam'selle wi[ll] know unhappiness all of her life."

Emile stared past her to the whirling water in th[e] fountain. Delilah was an impudent *chienne*. But if sh[e] spoke the truth . . .

"You seem to think I would be at fault," he sai[d] directing his cold stare back to her.

"And so you would be . . . if, as I believe you wish t[o] arrange, great troubles befall the *Américain*. Mam'sel[le] Cat does not know that you plan such things. Sh[e] would not believe you could harm someone she car[es] for." She stared up at him in open scorn. "Mam'selle [is] the ignorant one."

Emile slapped her hard across the face. "You will n[ot] speak of her in such a way again."

Delilah's head snapped back, but she held h[er] ground, her tawny cheek reddening from the impact [of] his hand. "You may lash out at the bearer of bad truth[s,] but that does not mean what I say is wrong. Leave m[y] mam'selle and the *Américain* alone. Do nothing t[o] discourage what is growing between them."

"Do you think the bastard cares for her?"

"I do not know if his feelings are yet mature. Le[ft] alone, he will come to treasure her. I believe this in m[y] heart." Delilah pulled up the hood until it obscured h[er] face. "I stay too long. It is time for me to leave. Ta[ke]

266

heed of what I say. Do not interfere, or you will greatly regret having done so."

Emile watched as she hurried past him, through the gate and toward the carriage which awaited her on the street, her cape billowing after her. No one gave him orders. No one. He would yet have Delilah as his own, and soon . . . for a few hours.

But to the matter at hand. So he was never to harm Adam Gase? If Delilah spoke the truth, then he found himself in a predicament, wanting as he did nothing more than to crush the life from the bastard who had brought him so much annoyance.

There was only one thing he wanted more, and that was to protect Cat. He'd been doing it for years, and planned to do so always. But to turn her over to another man? Such a thing would be difficult indeed.

But not impossible, not if Cat truly wanted this man. Perhaps what he should do was give him to her and let her take her fill. The *petite chatte* that he had rescued, had nursed back to life, had watched over through the years—this Cat would not long suffer the pangs of a *grande passion*. Emile knew that in some ways she was very much like him. She knew the evil that existed in the world, and she knew how to protect herself against it. Adam Gase was only an unexpected—and temporary—distraction.

A plan began to formulate in his mind.

He turned toward the stairs. Perhaps, before Arianne had to leave for her plantation at the first light of dawn, another session with her would sharpen his mind. He thought better when he was satisfied.

Perhaps this time he would introduce her to the whip.

Chapter Nineteen

Adam stared at the long, tall row of sugarcane swaying in the afternoon wind. With September in its second week, he estimated harvest as less than two months away.

"It's a good crop," said Tom Jordan, who stood at his side in the field. "And don't say it's thanks to me. You're as much responsible for it as I am."

Adam held back a response. It was true that during his imprisonment he'd sent messages to his manager—through a cooperative trustee he saved by crushing the life from a cottonmouth about to strike the man in the neck. But it was what Tom had done with those messages—and the fact that he'd hung around at all when Adam's release was still unknown years away—that had saved Belle Terre's fields from withering to decay.

Tom was a loner, a gruff, hard-working man who did not solicit praise. He liked results from his labors, and the two of them were looking at those results now.

"Knowing what to do," Tom continued, "anyone could have brought this land around. Anyone who gave more than a passing interest to it." He shook his head, a look of disgust settling on his weathered face. "The good-for-nothing who owned it before neglected it badly. Played the gentleman planter too much. Never will I understand these Creoles, not in a thousand years."

"There are no finer planters in the world, Tom. If that is where their interests lie. Gerard Constant's problem was that he didn't want to sweat."

As he spoke, Adam glanced down at his bare chest, which was glazed with perspiration. In truth, he felt good after several hours under the sun, working the fields beside Tom and the freed man Bodeen, occasionally checking the progress of the other men scattered about the Belle Terre acreage. He didn't think so much when he strained by the hour clearing away dead cane and turning the soil row after row after row . . . didn't think about town and about when he'd be going back there . . . didn't wonder about what to do concerning Laverton . . . didn't see a pair of violet eyes staring mockingly at him as he departed from a New Orleans hotel room.

Or at least he didn't see those eyes more than once or twice an hour, which was far less often than he did when he was at ease. Catherine wasn't Laverton's mistress, so what exactly was their relationship? Did she figure at all in the trial two years ago? The questions were as puzzling as they had ever been. As soon as he put in a little more time here, he'd try once again to answer one or two—especially the one that had occurred to him regularly during the past two days: what was going on between Adam and Catherine?

He knelt and scooped up a handful of Louisiana dirt, let it sift through his fingers, marveled at its richness. God, how he loved this land.

And then he remembered Catherine's thick black hair and the cool, silky way it felt against his hand, against his chest. She might not appreciate the comparison, he thought, grinning to himself—her hair to Belle Terre dirt. Women were funny about things like that.

Bodeen's deep voice called out from somewhere at

the edge of the field. "Rider's coming, Massa Gase."

"Anyone you recognize?" Tom yelled back.

"Ain't no one been here before, not that I recollect."

Adam stood and brushed his hand against his trousers. He doubted it was one of his Creole neighbors. For one thing, he hadn't had the time or inclination to encourage their calling, and for another, he doubted they would consider a convicted felon as worthy company for themselves or their families. As far as he was concerned, a stranger could mean only trouble.

His long legs measured the row in quick strides, bringing him to the edge of the canebrake where he'd removed his shirt. He tugged it on, figuring his scarred back was not the business of any stranger riding by. The shirt remained opened to reveal the damp hair on his chest, and the tail brushed against his soiled trousers.

Squinting into the bright day, his hand raised to his brows, he saw a man riding toward him across the stretch of ground that lay between the house and the cane. His mount was a magnificent blood bay mare, and he was clad in jodhpurs and riding boots. Adam recognized him right away.

He glanced at Tom, who had just caught up with him. "Emile Laverton," he said brusquely.

"Been kinda interested in meeting him."

"That's not necessary."

"I'll hang around," insisted Tom just as Bodeen arrived to flank Adam on the other side.

"Count me in, too," said Bodeen, his brown eyes lit with a glint of determination. In his left hand was a shovel, which he stuck in the ground in front of him.

"I'd rather talk to him alone." Adam kept his eyes on the approaching rider. "You two go on back to the house."

"You're not wearing your gun," said Tom.

"I don't imagine that Laverton is, either. He hires his protection, and it looks like this time he left his

271

number-one gunman at home."

"He don't look so tough to me," said Bodeen. His hand cradled the handle of the shovel. "I could take him with one swat."

"You tempt me, friend. But Laverton is mine."

"We'll be watchin' from up there," vowed Bodeen.

"I can't stop you from that. Wouldn't want to."

Reluctantly Tom and Bodeen, the latter trailing with the shovel held tightly at his side, started toward the house on a route that took them directly into the mare's path. Laverton's horse did not swerve so much as an inch, and at the last minute the two were forced to jump out of the way to avoid a collision.

The bastard always had to prove he was in control.

Adam stood in the narrow band of shade provided by the cane and watched his visitor's approach.

Laverton reined his mount to a halt three feet from him. The mare's head bobbed proudly, and she eyed Adam with disdain before bending her neck to crop at the grass. Her rider was far more subtle in his appraisal as his eyes looked coolly down from beneath a narrow-brimmed hat, his gloved hands light on the reins.

"Good afternoon, M'sieur Gase," he said with a nod.

Laverton was a real dandy, Adam thought, which only proved how much ugliness fine wrappings could hide.

"I'd say I'm glad to see you again, Laverton, but I'm sure you wouldn't want me to lie."

"Be warned, m'sieur, that I did not ride out alone."

Adam's eyes searched the grounds behind the mare and shifted toward the row of trees to his right that marked the edge of the river road, then left to the oaks that lined the Bayou Rouge.

"Michael is here, I assure you. Knowing your determination to threaten me at every turn, I took the precaution of bringing him. Harm me and at best you would find yourself returned to the prison camp you have taken in such distaste."

272

"That's one way of putting it."

"At worst, and far more likely, you would not live to draw another breath."

Adam grew tired of staring up at the rider and shifted his gaze to the plantation house behind the mare. "Get to the point."

"As always between us, the only point that matters is Mademoiselle Douchand."

Adam stared back at Laverton. "Is something wrong with her? Is she ill? If you've harmed her in some way—"

"She suffers from an aberration."

"A what?"

"A lapse in her thinking—"

"I know what the word means," said Adam. "I just didn't expect you to use it. What kind of lapse? Has she decided she wants to get the hell away from you as fast as she can? That wouldn't be an aberration, just good sense."

"I do not have time for an exchange of insults. Let us get to the business of my call, which is to correct what was perhaps a misapprehension on your part concerning our last conversation."

"The night you dragged me to the Swamp."

A look of irritation passed across Laverton's sharp features. "At that time I warned you against harming the mademoiselle."

"You ordered me to stay away from her."

"A request that you immediately disobeyed."

"Is that why you've come all the way out here? To tell me I've been a bad boy?"

"You do not let up, m'sieur."

"Neither did Brother Red." Adam spat at the ground in disgust. "Look, Laverton, I've got work to do. If something's bothering you, get off the horse and say it."

Laverton's pale eyes studied Adam. At last he shrugged. "For once you make good sense." Dismounting, he ground-tethered the mare to a large rock lying at the edge of the field and turned to face Adam, a riding crop tapping against his calf-high boot. "I have been made to realize a situation which cannot be ignored. It would seem that Cat—Mademoiselle Douchand—has developed an attachment for you."

Adam looked at him in surprise. "That's the last thing I expected to hear."

"It is, I assure you, the last thing I wished to say. But it is the truth."

"I'm the aberration you referred to."

"I know that it is temporary. She will soon come to her senses. But in the meantime she suffers a discomfort I cannot allow."

"A discomfort." Adam thought that one over a minute but had no idea what conclusions to draw. "You're taking a great deal on yourself, coming out here to speak for her. What is she to you? Your daughter? A niece? A ward?"

Laverton's expression was unreadable. "She is my responsibility. You need know nothing more."

Adam raked a hand through his hair. "Has she told you herself how she feels?"

"She does not confide in anyone. But there are those who watch and who know. She has many who care for her."

Adam remembered the man and woman who came for her in town and expressed concern about her welfare. At the casino he had observed the deference shown to her by the servants passing out food and drink, and by the dealers and croupiers. He could well believe she was held in affection by her staff.

"And you think I'm the cause of this discomfort."

"I do."

"I'll be damned."

"So shall we all, m'sieur."

"What am I supposed to do about it?"

Laverton's pale eyes narrowed. "Make yourself

available to her."

"The sun must have gotten to me," said Adam with a shake of his head. "You sound as though you came out here to act as Catherine's pimp. Which is about—"

With a low cry Laverton raised his crop and brought it slashing toward Adam's face. Dodging, Adam grabbed the descending arm, twisted hard, and sank his fist into Laverton's midsection. As Laverton clutched at his stomach, another fist landed against his jaw and he sprawled backward into the grass, the crop lying at his side.

Adam felt an overwhelming urge to grab him by the lapels of his tailored coat and jerk him to his feet, to knock him senseless, to strike him again and again, to see the blood spurting from his face . . .

The click of a gun sounded at Adam's ear.

He held himself motionless. "O'Reilly," he said, his eyes pinned toward the ground, "you better ask the boss here whether he really wants you to shoot. When he can talk, that is."

The cold tip of a gun barrel pressed against his neck. "Maybe I'll ask his lordship"—the Irishman's voice was soft and menacing—"and maybe I'll just decide he wants me to do what I'm paid for doing. Which is removing bothersome pests like yourself."

"No, Michael," managed Laverton.

Adam looked past the fallen figure and saw Bodeen and Tom running toward them across the field. Tom held a shotgun in his hand.

Adam glanced at Laverton, then at Michael. He waved his men away. They halted halfway across the wide lawn, but they did not return to the house.

Rolling to his side, Laverton slowly brought himself to his feet. He brushed at the dust and grass that clung to his coat and jodhpurs and leaned down to pick up his hat, then raised cold, hate-filled eyes to his attacker. A red lump was already forming on his jaw, throwing the narrow lines of his fox face out of proportion.

"I will destroy you," he said, his pale eyes iced with hatred.

"After I make myself available, I assume." The gunpoint dug against Adam's neck. "Your boy didn't understand. You'll have to call him off again."

A nod from his boss, and O'Reilly backed away.

"Listen to me carefully," said Laverton. All the venom in his eyes was echoed in his voice. "If you do not do what I say, I will destroy not only you but also this land. Houses burn. Crops are cut down during the night."

"I'm listening, but you're not making sense. First you threaten me if I go near her; now I'm ruined if I stay away."

"You are not to question my motives, M'sieur Gase. Know only that I am a dangerous man."

"I never doubted it for a minute. Tell me, Laverton, does Catherine know you're here?"

"She is never to know."

"And if I tell her?"

"Everything you care about will be lost, and all for naught, as I will deny such an absurd story. She will believe me. Do not doubt it for a moment."

Adam wanted to argue, but too many times Catherine had told him he lied about Laverton. "This availability. How far is it supposed to go? Conversation? Bed? Marriage?"

Laverton smoothed his thinning brown hair and settled the hat squarely on his head, the narrow brim tilted downward against his high forehead. Only the swelling and slight discoloration of his jaw gave evidence he'd been in a fight.

Freeing the mare, he mounted and stared down at Adam. "You will go as far as the mademoiselle chooses. And for only as long as she wants."

He gestured to O'Reilly that it was time to leave. "Do not disappoint me, m'sieur," he said to Adam. "I mean what I say."

Adam watched as his visitor reined the mare away toward the river road. In the canebrake behind him he heard the sound of another horse, Michael joining his master.

Adam found himself caught in a mixture of anger, disbelief, and puzzlement. The hate in Laverton's eyes had been impossible to mistake, but then so had the mocking pride on Catherine's face when he left her in the hotel room. If she cared for him in ways beyond what they had shared in bed, she had a strange way of showing it.

He headed for the cistern and a splash of cool water on his face and body, his thoughts growing more confused with each step. What would she say if she found out about today's conversation? Did she really feel an attachment for him that left her in discomfort? Laverton believed it enough to threaten him with ruin . . . as if anything Laverton threatened could frighten him into action.

But what if the bastard was right?

Adam admitted to a feeling of pleasure at the thought. True or not, what in hell was he supposed to do next?

An hour later, dressed in clean shirt and trousers, Adam sat in the parlor of his home, sipped at a glass of brandy, and decided he was no closer to an answer to his questions than he had been back at the cistern.

"Mister Adam."

He glanced toward the open door and saw the shy face of Tacey, the slender young woman that Bodeen wished to wed.

"Yes, Tacey, what is it?"

"Someone's riding up the front lane. A colored. Ain't never seen him in these parts before."

"It's a day for company, isn't it? Go on to the back. I'll see after him."

Setting down the glass, he walked through the central hallway and out the front door, stood on the shaded gallery and watched his second visitor of the day approach. A large black man, he sat astride a huge roan. When he reined the horse to a halt at the base of the steps and removed his hat, Adam recognized him as the man who had come for Catherine at Laverton's house on Bourbon Street.

"Good afternoon, Mr. Gase," the visitor said. "Name's Ben Washington. I work for Miss Cat."

Adam watched him dismount and, after a slight pause, walk up the steps, his eyes downcast. There was in his demeanor more than a trace of the deference usually shown by blacks to whites. When he stood on the gallery, Adam saw that he topped his own six-foot height by at least two inches and outweighed him by fifty pounds.

Ben was dressed in dark-blue work trousers and a coarse brown shirt and his boots were covered with Louisiana dust, but Adam found him far more welcome than his well-dressed visitor of an hour ago. Idly he wondered if the two men had passed each other on the road.

Adam held out his hand. Reluctantly, the black man took it for a brief, firm shake.

"We got to talk," said Ben. "I rode hard to get here before dark, and I've got to be heading out soon. I hope you've got the time to give me now."

"Would you like to go inside?"

Ben shook his head. "Out here's just fine."

"How about a drink?"

"Water for my horse. That's all."

Adam glanced back at the door and saw Tacey's wide eyes staring out. "See that someone takes care of the man's horse. And get us some lemonade. I can't believe he'll turn that down."

In a few minutes the bay had been led away by one of the plantation workers, and a pitcher and two glasses sat on the gallery's wicker table. The men settled into the chairs on either side. Ben's broad body seemed unsuited to the straight-backed chair, but he swore that he was comfortable enough.

Accepting the drink, he held it in his hands without taking a swallow. "What I came to say is hard to get out. I promised I wouldn't ever tell."

Adam saw the struggle Ben was going through and did not interrupt, directing his gaze instead to the tree-lined dirt road that led in a straight line from the river levee to the front of Belle Terre.

"It's about Miss Cat . . ." Again a pause. "Delilah—that's my woman—thinks it's time some shaking up was done around the casino. And I'm thinking this time maybe she's right."

"Could Delilah have spoken with Emile Laverton about her mistress?" Adam ventured.

Ben thought that one over. "Wouldn't put it past her." He glanced suspiciously at Adam. "Why do you ask?"

"Laverton seems to feel an extraordinary bond for Catherine. He's made it clear on one or two occasions recently when our paths have crossed."

"Miss Cat's a fine woman," said Ben. "Lots of us feel that way about her."

"I was just considering the kind of a man Laverton is. Surely you're not claiming he's like the rest of the people around her."

"Mister Emile is not like anyone else you'll ever meet. You've already paid with two years of your life for the way he is. Don't look surprised. I know what happened, but it's nothing I could swear to in court. I just know. Trouble is, things are getting even more complicated. Let me talk, Mister Gase. Hear me out."

Adam nodded in silence.

"I don't suppose you've been told Miss Cat had a child."

"A child?" Adam sat stunned.

"A boy."

Adam remembered how she'd gazed down at the Ferrier infant with love and then with pain.

"I didn't know," he said, feeling helpless to add more. But his mind worked. Catherine with a child of her own. There had been no evidence of her motherhood at La Chatte. What had happened to the boy? Something bad, he was sure. Only something bad would have put the despair in her eyes.

Ben looked around at the gallery and at the shade trees dotting the lawns on either side of the main house. "Got in the family way when she was living at Belle Terre."

"Catherine lived here?" It was another shock. "She said only that she knew the former owners."

"She knew 'em, all right. That was before Mister Emile and I found her . . . but I'm getting ahead of my story. It's a long one, Mister Gase. I hope you've got the time."

"I've got the time, Ben. Go as slow as you need."

Ben downed the lemonade and set the glass aside. "This first part all happened when she was just a child herself. Not above seventeen, she was. She and her mama were some kind of relatives to the man you bought the place from."

"Gerard Constant."

"That's the name. Her mama was long dead by the time she got herself messed up with Gerard's young son. He must have been no good at all, that boy, lying about love and how he was going to make her mistress of Belle Terre someday. She loved this place then the way she still does, and she believed every word he said. Trouble was, when Julien's daddy found out, he saw otherwise, said she had to leave. Made big promises about setting her up in town, but Miss Cat soon found herself on her own. And with a baby on the way." He looked at Adam. "She was a child having a child. But she didn't come back here crying for help. Not Miss

Cat. She didn't even let 'em know about her condition. Took herself to the Ursuline nuns and said she would do whatever work they needed if she could stay there until her baby was born."

"Surely they didn't turn her away."

"They're fine folks at the convent, Mister Gase. Through the years I've got to know 'em real well. They see my black skin, of course, but it doesn't seem to matter as much to them as it does to most whites. And they didn't turn away that poor child. She had her baby, all right. She named him Henri after her dead daddy."

"Where is he now? He must be eight or nine, isn't he?"

"Would be, Mister Gase, if he'd lived. The sad part's just beginning." Ben shook his head slowly. "That poor little boy got the yellow fever. It took lots of people that year, but it doesn't seem hardly fair that it took a six-month-old baby who didn't ever hurt anyone in the world. Miss Cat took it as a judgment from God."

Adam hurt for the young Catherine, picturing her losing everything she cared about in the world. He wanted nothing more at the moment than to hold her in his arms and tell her all would be right.

"It's along about here that Mister Emile and I come into the story." Ben sat in silence for a moment, his thoughts elsewhere, and Adam knew he was remembering a painful scene.

"I was working on the docks then. It was late, after midnight, and I'd had a drink or two, the way I did before Delilah came along and showed me the error of my ways. Decided I would walk the wharf as far as it stretched. I'd come to a part where the ships were all deserted, mostly barges, anyway, and flatboats, the ones the Kaintucks come down on. There wasn't anyone about, not that I could hear, and the night was so dark you couldn't see your hand in front of your face, white or black though it be. The first thing I noticed was the glow of a cigar directly up ahead.

"'Who's there?' someone asked. It was Mister Emile, only I didn't know it at the time. 'Who's asking?' I said back. I didn't hear an answer, but then I wasn't worried. I'm bigger than most, and I was carrying a knife.

"I kept on walking toward that cigar, too stubborn to change my path just because someone else was in it and too ignorant to know that I couldn't take on anybody I chose. I was right up against him before Mister Emile spoke again, and then all he said was, 'You're not the man I was waiting for.' I felt a little pressure against my stomach, and I knew right away he was holding a gun. 'Just passing by,' I said, stepping backward and deciding that maybe I ought to be heading the other way. I'm not a coward, but I'm not a simpleton, either."

Ben's broad hands rubbed at his thighs. "That's when we heard the splash and a cry maybe twenty, thirty feet on up ahead. Sounded more like an animal than a human being, but somehow both of us got the idea right away that someone had fallen in the river. I headed straight for the edge of the wharf, but I got to give Mister Emile credit, he was right behind, throwing off coat and shoes the way I should have done. He was the one who jumped in first, and I was close after. River was running seven, eight feet that night where we were, and the current was swift. With no moon or stars, all we had to go by was the sound we heard. It was a miracle we found her."

"Catherine," Adam whispered.

"It breaks my heart to remember the way she fought us. Said something about wanting to die. But that Mister Emile, he just wouldn't let her. I wasn't much help to him except to get her up on the wharf. He kept saying something in French. Later, I knew he was calling her *ma petite chatte*. Still does."

"Somehow I can't imagine his risking his life for

a stranger."

"I guess it was the way he felt that night, hearing tha splash, but he sat on the dock and held that poor half drowned girl in his arms, and he said things he's never talked about since. His daddy must have been a mean son of a bitch, 'cause Mister Emile mentioned something about having a kitten once. His daddy drowned that little animal while he was watching. 'But I've saved her,' he said. Over and over. 'She's mine she's mine.' It was the strangest thing I ever heard a man say, only he didn't sound like a man that night more like a little boy."

Laverton had called Catherine his "responsibility" to Adam. She must have been that during all the years since the night on the river. His kitten. His *petite chatte*. Adam remembered the way she had once said she didn't like the Mississippi. Everything that had puzzled him about her was falling into place, in ways he could never have imagined. He'd been thinking so much about his own troubles that he hadn't given enough time to considering hers.

"Mister Emile took her back to that office of his in the Swamp. He tended her better than any doctor I've ever seen. Paid me to quit my job and help. Swore me to secrecy about her even being there. She came down with a fever, and that man bathed her body over and over, then wrapped her in blankets when the chill came. Every time she went to sleep, he had me go outside to make sure nobody did anything loud like fighting or shooting, the way they sometimes do in the Swamp.

"It was a week before she came around, and another week before she would say who she was or where she lived. That's when she told us about the baby and the convent. Tears streamed down that poor girl's cheeks when she spoke, but I swear to you, Mister Gase, that's the last time I ever heard her cry. The rest—about Belle Terre and how she'd been treated there—we found out gradually.

"At last we took her back to the convent, but Mister Emile didn't really let her get away from him. He paid money to the church to make sure she was allowed to stay there and work, even though the nuns said he didn't have to. He hired me to hang around and make sure she was not mistreated. Mister Emile doesn't trust anybody in this world, not even those nuns.

"Miss Cat helped in the school with the older children, but she refused to get near the nursery, where there were some poor little orphan babies being raised. Helped out in the office, too, showing the nuns how to keep their books, which I figure is kinda what gave Mister Emile the idea he came up with.

"Through the years she talked about Belle Terre, about the way she would own it someday. It sounded like dream talk to me, but then four years ago she heard the place had fallen on hard times and was up for sale. Prideful woman though she is, she swallowed that pride and asked Mister Emile for a loan. He gave it right away, even while he told her she would never be happy trying to bring back the past. She went to Gerard Constant in person, but he turned her down. He was broke himself, his wife dead, his daughter married off, and his son away in Paris married to some rich woman, but he didn't want any amount she could offer.

"He accused her of seducing his son and sending him into exile. Imagine that, Mister Gase. Said no way would she ever become owner of the land he'd forced her to leave. When the place went to you—although we didn't know who the new owner was at the time, just that he was an American—Mister Emile lent her enough to set up the casino and maybe earn enough money to eventually get what she wanted so bad. I've never seen anyone work so hard at designing a place or seeing that it was a success."

"Of course," Adam said, another mystery clearing in his mind. "No wonder the casino looked familiar. It's

284

patterned after Belle Terre."

"She loves this plantation almost as much as she did that baby, Mister Gase. Even made another offer two years ago."

"About the time I went to prison."

"I swear to you that all she heard was the place was coming on hard times again. Mister Emile was the one who told her."

"Mister Emile was the one who arranged those hard times," said Adam, "for his rescued little kitten." At last he saw the hard-sought truth behind his arrest. In Laverton's mind, he had been nothing more than an impediment to his kitten's plans. And so he had been removed.

Adam should have been elated that his search was done, but all he felt was an emptiness inside.

"Miss Cat gave orders to her banker friend to keep trying from time to time to complete a deal. Getting back here has been about all she's able to think about."

Ben hesitated, then settled his eyes firmly on Adam. "Not once did she let anyone close. Just Mister Emile and me and then Delilah. No other man or woman. Especially no other man. 'I don't need anyone,' she's told Delilah more than once. 'I don't plan to be hurt ever again.' She had plenty of temptations around those gambling tables, but never once did she give anyone more than a smile."

"Until I came along."

"Until you came along. You were just another American to her, at least at first."

An American seeking revenge, Adam thought bitterly. An American who didn't care who he hurt, as long as he got his satisfaction. At that moment, Adam did not like himself very much.

A hard thought struck him. What if he had done the same as the young Constant? What if she was going to bear his child? He sure as hell hadn't bothered to take any precautions.

285

"I guess it's too early to tell if she's—"

"Worried about another child? Put your mind to rest. Miss Cat has learned to take care of herself—in some ways, at least. Delilah makes up these potions. Gris-gris, she calls 'em. I caught her fixing one a few weeks ago and she confessed what she was up to. Miss Cat asked for something to protect herself from having a baby. She didn't want the same thing happening all over again."

Adam wondered when she'd gone to Delilah. Before the afternoon in the woods? Before the hotel bed? Whenever, Cat had known they would make love, just as he had known.

Ben sat forward in the chair. "The thing you've got to believe is, Miss Cat didn't have any notion about what happened to you two years ago. Maybe it's best she never learns. It would almost kill her to find out what Mister Emile has done, trusting him the way she does and ignoring all the stories she hears about him."

"I tried to tell her about him a time or two. She wouldn't listen."

"I'm surprised she bothered to see you again. But don't you get to thinking it was because of who you are. Until you got arrested at the judge's house and Mister Emile told her how things were, she didn't know who owned the plantation, told Delilah she didn't want to since she might start picturing people enjoying the things she wanted to be hers."

Ben paused to take a deep breath. "I guess the most important thing for you to keep in mind is that she didn't have any intention—ever—of getting close to a man again. That's why I rode out here, in case you haven't figured it out. She forgot all those intentions. She's getting close again."

The two men sat in silence for several minutes and stared into the twilight of the day. Fireflies glowed randomly in the semidark, and a chorus of crickets hummed unseen among the moss-draped trees.

"What we have here is a dilemma," said Adam at last.

"I'd say we do."

Adam tried to untangle the web in which he and Catherine found themselves. What had his wrath led him to do? When he made love to her on the grounds of Belle Terre, he had been after his own pleasure, but the lovemaking must have been devastating to her. Still, a week later she had come to his trial.

Adam felt a stirring of feelings he had never experienced before . . . a tenderness mixed with pain that was like a fist clutching his heart.

From out of the dark a pair of wounded eyes stared at him. "She's not to know you've told me all this," he said.

"I don't plan to tell," returned Ben with a nod of his head. "I'm trusting you won't hurt her."

"Not any more than I already have." He stood and extended his hand. This time Ben took it quickly. "Thanks," added Adam. "I'll do everything I can to see you're never sorry you came out here."

"I took a chance, that's for sure, but I figured Miss Cat hadn't made a mistake when she settled her attentions on you. It's for sure that woman of mine thinks she hasn't. Makes me almost jealous, the way she talks of you sometimes."

Adam summoned Tacey from inside and asked that the roan be brought around to the front of the house. The two men waited in silence, each lost in his own thoughts, until the horse was led to the porch, this time by Bodeen. The two men eyed each other for a moment, each seeming to like what he saw.

Ben thanked Bodeen and mounted. Adam, watching in silence as the roan headed back down the lane, thought about what he should do.

"It's getting kinda crowded here in the country," said

Bodeen, "what with all these town folks riding out."

"It's been an interesting day, Bodeen. An interesting day."

He thought about Belle Terre . . . about how much the place had come to mean to him. He could understand Catherine's obsession to possess it. More than anyone else in the world, far more than Emile Laverton, he had the power to see she got what she wanted at long last. Belle Terre was his, but there was one way she could rightfully return.

And not, he added emphatically, in pants and shirt riding astride a black mare through the back woods. She ought to be dressed in finery and seated in a well-appointed carriage, her route from town along the river road and up the front lane. She ought to stride up on the gallery, her magnificent head held high, her eyes flashing with satisfaction, to walk through the front door, and to know she was home.

He saw his course. Turning toward the door, he glanced at Bodeen. "I'll be needing Keystone saddled in about an hour or so. With so many people calling on us, it seems only fair that I return the gesture, wouldn't you say?"

"You're riding into town tonight, Massa Gase?"

Adam nodded. "It's a curious thing, Bodeen, but I've decided that for once Emile Laverton ought to get what he wants."

Chapter Twenty

"*Bonne nuit, messieurs,*" Cat said with a nod as two of her patrons headed toward the foyer and the door that opened to the front of La Chatte.

"*À bientôt,*" they returned jointly, matching smiles in their warm brown Creole eyes.

Cat turned from them, her eyes drifting around the casino's smoky, half-filled main salon. Her loosely worn hair felt hot and heavy against her neck, and her white silk gown clung to her body. Two hours until closing time. Would the night ever end?

Strolling amongst the gamblers, smiling determinedly as she walked, stopping to listen to inane flirtations and meaningless anecdotes, all she could think of was that her feet hurt and her face ached.

Worse, she didn't care if on this warm and busy evening every man in the place broke the bank. What was she supposed to do with the money now? She certainly couldn't spend it on her original cause.

Adam would never sell Belle Terre. Thinking that he would if she made the offer tempting enough had been no more than a part of the weakness that had overtaken her in the New Orleans hotel.

She broke off that line of contemplation, just as she had done each time during the past several days whenever it returned to ruin her peace. It did her no good to dwell on the obvious; she couldn't change the truth just by willing it to change, any more than she could alter the past.

A late arrival in the doorway caught her eye. As she had done a hundred times in the past few days, she glanced at the dark-suited man, hoping to see a tall, lean American with a challenge in his dark-blue eyes. As had happened a hundred times before, she saw someone else and cursed herself for being a fool.

"The mademoiselle frowns. Could it be she does not approve of her guests tonight?"

Cat found herself looking into the concerned face of one of La Chatte's regulars, Alfred Colbert, a sixty-year-old Creole widower who owned the Vieux Carré's finest boutique.

"M'sieur Colbert," she said, forcing another smile. "You have caught me doing the inexcusable."

The widower's gray eyes twinkled. "And, pray, what is that, *ma belle amie?*"

"Thinking. I absolutely forbid it anywhere on the premises, but for myself I forgot."

"I know just the punishment. You must stroll by my side for the little tête-à-tête."

"M'sieur, that is no punishment."

"I have not yet mentioned the subject for our talk. You must visit my little shop and allow me to dress you in the colors that will serve as proper accompaniment to your beauty." He glanced at the high neck and long sleeves of her gown. "The white is lovely, of course. But the black . . . *bah!"*

"M'sieur—"

"Do not look surprised, mademoiselle. I have seen you in the city. Few would recognize the famous La Chatte in such a gown, but clothing is my business. I know how well it can disguise. For most of the mademoiselles and mesdames, rarely is it used to—how is it the Americans say it?—to turn the silk purse into the sow's ear. Always La Chatte must do

290

the unexpected."

Cat linked her arm in his. "I will stroll with you as you request. But you must promise not to speak of anything more serious than the latest fashions from Paris."

"For me this topic is a very serious one indeed. I will attempt to convince you of its importance."

For a half hour the two strolled arm in arm, and Cat gave her attention to the topic which was above all others essential to his happiness. Shortly before midnight he excused himself—"I am not the young man that I once was, my friend, and while my heart is considering options that would shock even the famous La Chatte, my mind tells me such activities must remain only memories"—and Cat bid him *adieu,* again taking up her wandering from room to room.

How warm the casino seemed, she thought, wishing a breeze would waft through the open windows. In truth, she wished for many things, chief among them a chance to change her behavior of the past few weeks. As though M'sieur Colbert had never appeared, she returned to the worries he had interrupted.

How had she allowed a man—a plain-spoken, bitter, stubborn, selfish man—to disrupt her life? He had her seeing him when he wasn't there, dreaming about him when she was able to sleep at night, and worst of all, doubting the word of her dearest friend in all the world.

She nodded to a pair of young men settling down to a game of *écarte,* then moved on.

Emile had done nothing. Nothing close to the accusations that Adam had made, accusations too horrible to contemplate, much less accept.

Wending her way from the main salon into the side room, she walked past the tables of food and drink, making certain that the supply was adequate for the remainder of the evening, and remembered a basket of food resting on a hotel bed.

Adam had been considerate that day of the trial—

among other characteristics she would not bring to mind—but for all that consideration, he still believed the world was rotten, and therefore Emile was rotten. For a while—perhaps still—he believed she shared Emile's guilt. He had originally come to La Chatte seeking revenge against imagined wrongs, and what had the unapproachable Cat done?

After years of celibacy, she had allowed him to make love to her. Knowing he would only hurt her the way she had been hurt before, she had let him have his way with her again. Even now, she could not get him from her mind.

The reason was clear and undeniable. She'd realized it in the middle of a sleepless night. She loved him with a completeness that was beyond any emotion she had ever felt before. She loved the wry way he had of smiling, the bluntness of his approach to life, the strength and courage he had shown in court when he faced another unjust trial. She loved the sun-bronzed texture of his skin, the dark hairs curling on his forearms, the way his brows almost met over his dark-blue eyes.

She loved the way her spirit soared when he pulled her into his arms. She loved the firm touch of his hands on her body. She loved the salty taste of his skin.

Accepting all these things about him, she must never see him again. Not if she were to have any sort of life after he was gone.

The decision was one she'd made in the hotel bed, hours after she set aside the untouched basket. She could not live her life waiting for a man who showed up only at his own whim. With all the determination that was in her being, she'd reached the conclusion that her happiness must never depend upon him.

If he ever again showed up at the casino, she would call upon several of her helpers—Michael O'Reilly, for one, if he were present—to toss him out. If he accosted her on the street, she would turn from him. If he persisted in his approach, she would scream for help. Of course, she would never seek him out at Belle Terre.

The resolutions pushed her to the edge of despair, making impossible for the moment her feeble attempts to smile.

She looked around to see Ben walking toward her through the late-night assemblage, his huge frame neatly clad in the formal wear that was the uniform of the La Chatte staff.

"Where have you been?" she asked, exhibiting more agitation than was her wont. "You said you were going to check on one of the suppliers, but surely it could not have taken you this long."

"Sorry, Miss Cat. I ran into complications, but maybe they're settled now. Things going all right here?"

"Things are just wonderful. Why shouldn't they be?" Without waiting for an answer, she wheeled to continue her perambulatios through the casino that was a replica of the plantation which had once been her home. Now it seemed that it could not even be her dream.

No Belle Terre. No Adam. The conditions under which she must live her life hit her anew; they winnowed into the most hurtful stricture of all. No Adam.

Another hour crept by, another hour that did nothing to ease her aching feet or her aching face or, least of all, her aching heart. Once when she went to check on supplies, she caught sight of Delilah and Ben in the small storeroom behind the main salon. They were in heated conversation, and for the first time that night Cat felt an interest in something around her. She edged near the door. The pair fell silent and with hurried nods moved past her into the casino.

Something was going on.

As she turned to follow them, she was aware of whisperings in the salon, low confidences that she had not heard before. She walked toward the roulette table, where a trio of determined gamblers were still trying their luck.

"*L'Américain,*" one of them said.

It could not be . . . Her eyes darted toward the door leading into the front hall, and she caught her breath, at the same time cursing herself for the surge of lightness in her heart.

Adam, clad in the frock coat and trousers he had worn the first night they met, was striding toward her, his silver-shot black hair unruly, a determined look in his eye. The crowd, thinned by the lateness of the hour, parted to give him room.

Just when she'd vowed never to see him again, he appeared, looking as distinctively handsome as she remembered, at once both powerfully masculine and graceful as he made his way across the room. The salon that had seemed warm to her earlier became an inferno, and she fought a rising panic.

Her eyes flew to the croupier standing across the table, his back to the latecomer. "Isn't it almost time to close down?"

The croupier shrugged. "Another half hour, mademoiselle."

Unable to do otherwise, she looked back at Adam, watching as he circled the table and stopped close at her side. Had it been only three nights ago that he had made love to her and later brought her the basket of food? Three long days and nights? It had seemed an eternity. How she longed to throw her arms around his neck and hold him tight. Equally, she wanted to scream for him to go away and leave her to whatever peace she could find.

"Hello, Catherine." His voice was mellow and deep.

She forgot her resolve to call for help. Heart pounding, she gave him the brief, false smile she'd been practicing all evening. "Hello, Adam. I'm surprised to see you here." *Especially when I have just vowed never to see you again.*

"I should have been here long ago."

"Nonsense." *At least I will not see you alone.*

"We need to talk." He leaned close, and she caught a whiff of the sunlight he carried with him, even in the middle of the night. "In private."

Could he read her mind?

"As you can see, I am busy," she said, waving to the dozen or so onlookers who still remained in the salon.

His eyes glittered into hers. "As you so eloquently put it, Catherine, nonsense."

She smiled nervously.

"Messieurs, faites vos jeux!" ordered the croupier.

Several coins fell onto the marked table as the roulette wheel began its spin.

"I'm not leaving until we talk."

"You cannot come in here and order me—"

He tossed a coin onto the table. It rolled in a narrow circle, then came to a stop on the seven. Once before he had gambled on that same number; too well she remembered the results.

"I win," he said, "and we talk. You win and I leave."

"You seem very confident of yourself."

"There are some things which are meant to be, Catherine. Don't you know that by now?"

He really was speaking nonsense, but with so many watchers within earshot she declined to tell him so, remembering as she did that he was always quick with a retort.

"Rien ne va plus," said the croupier from across the table.

Cat held her breath. The wheel stopped.

"Sept."

Cat was not surprised. Gesturing toward the back door, she said, "We can talk in the storeroom."

He shook his head. "I have another place in mind. Shall we?" he asked, nodding toward the front hallway.

Did he mean to take her outside?

She caught the eye of Ben, who stood by the end of the table. "I'll be right back. See that all is secured," she said, then walked ahead of Adam into the foyer. As she neared the front door, she felt a guiding hand at her back. He was directing her toward the stairs!

"No!" she said, coming to a halt.

"I said in private, Catherine, and I meant it. Do you wish to be carried?"

Her eyes darted to his; she read determination in their depths. Abominable man, she thought, even as she considered the attraction of snuggling in his arms as he bore her to the second floor.

"The study, then," she said, aware that the remaining gamblers had drifted into the foyer to watch and to listen. Lifting her long skirt, she hurried up the winding stairs. When they reached the middle of the upstairs hallway, out of sight and hearing of the curiosity seekers, she whirled on him. "I don't know what this is about, Adam, but you can be sure it won't be a repeat of the hotel room."

Adam looked at her with such seriousness that she caught her breath. "Not exactly a repeat, but not entirely different, either. What I have to say to you is not best said in your study." His hand caught hers and he brought it to his lips, kissing first the back and turning it to kiss her palm.

Cat shivered.

"I would like to see your room," he said.

She tried in vain to pull free. "What more do you want of me, Adam?" she asked in a small voice. "Haven't you taken enough?"

His answer was a look of such intensity that she felt her knees weaken. "Very well," she said, covering his effect on her with a sigh of impatience. She opened the door and glanced at him. "Remember, however, that one call from me and a half dozen men will be up those stairs in a second."

"I'll remember," he said as he followed her through the door.

She moved quickly to turn up the lamp on the

nightstand. Adam's eyes roamed the sparsely furnished room, picking out the chest of drawers, the wardrobe, the rocking chair, and at last the feather bed. Closing the door behind him, he slipped the bolt into its moorings. "So that we won't be disturbed."

She walked around him and shoved the bolt back into its unlocked position. "In case I have to call for help, I would not like the hinges pulled from the frame."

With her back against the door, her hands tight around the knob, she stared at him. "You wanted to talk. So talk."

"Marry me."

"I beg your pardon?"

"Marry me," he repeated.

"Are you drunk?"

"No."

"Then you've been out in the sun too long. It's baked your mind."

He stepped close. "Don't you want to marry me, Catherine?"

She could look no longer than a second at the dark glint in his eyes, and the set of his lips was impossible to contemplate. Hurrying around him, she scooped up a small bundle of fur that had crawled from beneath the bed. With her back to Adam, she rubbed her chin against Balzac's head. In response, the kitten purred.

"I could propose in French, but it would be an abomination," said Adam. "Would you like me to try?"

Cat's mind reeled. She could not think . . . could not respond.

His hands gripped her shoulders and he turned her to face him. His fingers played in her hair. She continued to stroke her chin against the kitten's soft head. "This is Balzac," she said foolishly, then added with even greater foolishness, "I named him after a young French writer. He's the rage of Paris now."

A smile tugged at Adam's lips. "I've heard of him."

He took the kitten gently from her; instead of complaining at leaving his mistress's familiar hands, the traitor purred all the louder. Adam set Balzac in the center of the bed, then once again rested his hands on her shoulders. This time his thumbs stroked her throat. Too well, Cat knew he could feel her racing pulse.

"Look at me," he ordered.

Against her will, she did as he instructed. Their eyes held for a long moment.

"Just as I thought," he said softly, but did not explain. "I'm going to kiss you, Catherine. Again and again until I get the answer I want."

She took his words as a threat and whirled away from him. Moving quickly across the room, she came to a halt beside the open window. From outside came the sound of departing carriages as the casino closed for the night. Within minutes the street would be deserted as the Creoles returned to their wives and mistresses. A short time later everyone would be gone from the downstairs rooms. Unless Ben stayed around to make sure she was all right. Remembering his whispered conversation with Delilah, she wondered if perhaps they hadn't expected Adam to arrive.

She forced herself to turn and face him, glad of the space that separated them. "I can't imagine why you would think to suggest such a thing as marriage. As though I would agree to it . . . as though my happiness depended upon . . ." She fell silent, fearful that her protestations too easily revealed what was really in her heart.

"Maybe I'm thinking of my happiness."

Catherine laughed sharply. "And I thought you were getting all you wanted from me. Anytime you wanted it. Are you telling me I'm wrong?"

"We're good together. You know it as well as I. And we've both suffered—"

"How do you know about me?"

Adam stared at her, and even from across the room

she could sense the solemnity of his mood. "It's in your eyes and in the expressions on your face. Do you know I've never seen a genuine smile play on those lovely lips? A grin, a twist of bitter humor, but never a real smile. I had hoped that the thought of living with me at Belle Terre could change that."

"Belle Terre," she whispered. So shocked had she been by Adam's proposal that she had not considered its full implications. He was offering her a lifetime at Belle Terre.

"Whatever has happened in your past," he went on, "should not keep you from having a future. It's not at the casino. Not forever. You like the plantation, you said so yourself. Between the two of us, I imagine we've already weathered more tribulations than most couples who have been married a dozen years."

He began to close the distance between them. "And I repeat, we're good together. Maybe you need a reminder of just how good."

When he stood close to her, his mouth descending to hers, Cat could not think . . . could not reason . . . could do no more than feel the warmth of his lips, the probing of his tongue. Marry Adam . . . She had been determined never to wed, and she had no ready answer for him. Except, of course, to say yes.

As his arms stole around her, she felt herself swept into the same insanity that must have overtaken him. Her lips parted, and her tongue danced against his. Desire, hot and thick, pulsed through her veins.

The palms of his broad hands rubbed at her back, and she sucked at his tongue.

Her own hands flattened against his shirt; his heart, too, raced.

Just when she thought she would drown in the sweetness of his kiss, he pulled away and pressed his lips against her cheek. Holding her close with one arm, he stroked her hair. "I've done little but think about you during the past few days. About your lovely eyes and soft skin, about the way your hair curls against your face, about the way your body fits against mine. Tell me the truth, Catherine." Her name was a warm whisper against her cheek. "Have you thought about me?"

He kissed her again, this time softly, and spoke huskily into her parted mouth. "Have you thought about me?"

"I've thought about you," she managed.

His hands massaged her shoulders, her back, and the length of her spine, palms moving in circles against the fullness of her buttocks and anchoring her tightly against his swelling manhood.

"God, how I've missed you," he said.

His hips shifted and she felt the hardness of his shaft against her throbbing body.

"Did you think of this?" he whispered.

He circled her ear with his tongue. "Did you, Catherine? Did you?"

"I thought of . . . everything." She scarcely recognized her voice.

"Good."

Something in his voice brought her to her senses. She *had* thought of everything, including the way he had taken over since the first time they had met. He seemed to be offering her everything she had ever wanted, and yet she confessed to a bitter disappointment that he had not told her what was in his heart.

She pushed against him; catching him by surprise, she escaped his embrace and moved around him to stand by the foot of the bed.

He stared at her from a distance of three feet, and she forced her ragged breathing to slow. "You can't just walk in here, Adam, and take over my life."

"That's not—"

"Oh, yes it is what you're trying to do." Her throat tightened, and she knew she was dangerously close to tears. Anger held them back. "I don't understand

300

anything about you. First you come in here swearing to get revenge. You follow me, taunt me, hurl terrible accusations, and then you—"

"Then I ask you to marry me and try, with damned little success, to make love to you." His eyes darkened with a matching distress. "What's wrong with that?"

She twisted her hands in front of her. "I don't understand, that's what is wrong. Nothing you have said or done before has led me to expect such a declaration."

"Nothing?"

"Do not take me for a fool," she said bitterly. "A man can make love to a woman and not want her forever."

"Don't you want to be my wife?"

"Of course I do," she blurted out, then stood horrified at the admission. What she had planned to tell him was that she did not want to be hurt. He had offered her marriage . . . had offered her Belle Terre . . . but he had not offered his heart.

"If you want to marry me, then what in the hell is going on here?" he demanded.

"What about Emile?" she asked, falling back on their first and constant argument.

"Forget him."

Cat stared at him in disbelief. "Is this the avenging Adam Gase I see before me? You're the one who brought up his name time and time again. And now you say to forget him? What am I to believe?"

"Believe that I have pushed him from my mind. What is happening now is between me and you."

"What about the rest of the world? Don't you remember what you thought of me? Others believe the same."

He closed the distance between them so quickly that she had no chance to defend herself. With his arms encircling her, his eyes burning into hers, he growled, "To hell with the rest of the world. Above all women, I want you to be mine."

301

His words were what she needed to hear, and her doubts melted like ice beneath a noonday sun. This time when his lips covered hers, she matched his ardor with a fiery need of her own. Forgetting the vows she'd made during the past few days, forgetting the wise decisions she had reached, she clung to him and let desire dissolve her will.

She loved Adam with her whole heart; if he hadn't exactly declared his love for her, he was showing it in the way he caressed her; in the press of his lips, soft and then firm, parting and teasing, moist and sweet; and in the inexpressibly satisfying fervor of his proposal.

Cat slipped her arms under his coat and her hands moved to his back—his precious, scarred back. She held him tight against her and let the sensations of lovemaking envelop her. When his fingers fumbled at the front buttons of her gown, she helped him. When her own fingers worked in frustration at his shirt and at the buckle of his belt, he in turn helped her.

They pulled the clothes from each other's bodies, laughed at the disgusted look on Balzac's face as he jumped to the floor and hurried back to his den under the bed, fell into each other's arms on top of the counterpane. Adam's hand caressed a thousand places; each touch brought her a thousand trembling delights.

Cat had never known such abandon as her own eager hands returned his caress, her eagerness fed by a need that was beyond thought, beyond reason. Adam was hers forever, and she was his. The last barriers between them had fallen, she knew not how or when, but fallen they had. She had Adam's words as proof of the fact.

Marry me. In her heart, she had done so the moment he walked into the casino, although it had taken her weeks to accept the truth and strength of their bond.

No longer was the future bleak; her happiness soared along with her passion. As his hand cupped the fullness of her breast, she arched herself toward him, letting her whispered name burn time after time into her ear until she became *Catherine*. Not Cat, not anymore.

Tonight she became a new woman, forged in the heat of his love.

Her fingers stroked low on his abdomen, trailed through the thick, wiry hair, and held his shaft as she knew he wanted her to do. He bent his head to suckle at her breast, and his own fingers drifted lower, lower, stroked the inside of her parted thighs and settled against the throbbing center of her need. Unable to hold still beneath his expert assault, she shifted beneath the long, hard length of his body, her back cool against the slippery bed covering, her skin as damp as his where they touched.

So absorbed was she by him that she did not know which throat emitted the moans of pleasure or whose ragged breath stirred the night air. They were one, truly and forever, as they had never been before. When her legs parted and he filled her body, it was an act of joining that extended the joining of their hearts and of their will.

They moved together steadily toward completion, his thrusts matching hers, their explosions coming simultaneously and with equal force. She held him tightly, her head bent into the crook of his shoulder, and rejoiced in the savage delight he brought her.

He stroked her hair, her arm, her back, cradling her gently against his sweat-slick body.

"*Mon chéri,*" she whispered against his neck, resorting to the French of her upbringing. He lifted her chin. Abandoning the last vestige of her defense against hurt, the carefully guarded secret that she held in her heart, Catherine declared herself for all time. "*Je t'aime.*"

His response was a gentle kiss.

Chapter Twenty-One

A panther screamed somewhere in the dark of the swamp, driving Adam deeper into the thick underbrush. Naked and alone, he gasped for breath, thrust aside the curtains of moss that blocked his path, and stumbled onto the plant-choked bank of a wide and murky bayou, mist swirling around his ankles.

Again he heard the scream, closer than before. In the high screech lurked all the terrors of past and present that lingered in his heart.

Blind panic overtook him. He surged forward through the tall grass and prickly shrubs, desperate to distance himself from the blood-chilling sound. One foot caught in a thick mat of Virginia creeper and he fell, his body striking the gnarled root of a cypress tree. Twisting to his back, he looked up to see directly overhead the extended body of a seven-foot cat, blacker than the night, descending fast, jaws open and claws bared.

"Adam!"

The ground under him shook.

"Adam, wake up."

He jerked into consciousness and stared into a pair of dark and worried eyes.

"It's me," a soft voice said. "Catherine." She brushed damp hair from his forehead with a cool and gentle hand. "You were dreaming."

Adam cursed the dream and willed his breathing to slow. Slowly he brought himself back to reality, images of the swamp cat receding with each deep breath. He was lying in a feather bed, a black-haired beauty stretched beside him, her head bent to whisper words of comfort in his ear. From a nearby table a lamp sent out light that filtered with ghostlike dimness through the mosquito netting surrounding the bed.

The only thing that was similar to his dream was his nakedness, which seemed appropriate enough since his companion shared his state of undress.

His companion . . . the woman he had asked to be his wife. He came to full wakefulness as he stared up at her lovely, worried face. She had found out soon enough what kind of bargain she had got for herself, a man who hadn't made it through their first full night together without sweating in fright.

He scowled in disgust of himself. "Didn't mean to give you a bad turn," he managed. "Sorry I woke you."

She continued to stroke his face. "Don't apologize. Would you like to tell me about the dream?"

What was there to tell that she could understand, especially since he didn't completely understand the nightmares himself, unpatterned as they were in time and content? Only one characteristic was consistent: they always held a threat that was beyond his control—sometimes Brother Red, sometimes an animal like the panther. Who would have thought one would assault him tonight with Catherine lying in his arms?

It would be stupid and selfish of him to share his torment. She had torments enough of her own.

"It was nothing. Everyone has them."

She didn't look convinced. "But I want to know . . . to help if I can."

"Put it out of your mind. It won't happen again tonight."

"If you're sure."

"I'm sure."

She pulled away until no part of her touched him. "Of course I will honor your wishes."

He'd hurt her, and he hadn't meant to.

"I sincerely hope you mean that," he said, smiling across the pillow at her. "It's not often I'm made such a promise by a beautiful woman."

She studied him thoughtfully. At last her solemn countenance relaxed. "I am giving in rather easily. Don't expect it all the time."

Adam let his eyes move lazily across her features— the high cheekbones and straight nose, almond eyes the color of wild violets, parted lips, graceful neck, and all of it surrounded by a mass of tangled black curls. He did not neglect the tempting roundness of her breasts above the covering sheet. Shifting to his side, he stroked that roundness and was rewarded by her swift intake of breath.

More than ever, he was certain that he was doing the right thing in taking her as his bride. He'd told her the truth. They were good together . . . two damaged souls who gave each other strength. He hadn't expected to feel such tenderness for another human being ever again. She made him feel whole again, or at least more whole than he had ever expected to feel. If that wasn't love, it was close enough.

She held still while he continued to stroke her breast. He could see the hardened peaks of her nipples beneath the sheet. His own body was hardening in turn, and he continued the teasing torture. Her skin was warm even through the cover, her fullness firm and yielding at the same time.

Adam tried to remember exactly what had been said between them last night. His eyes locked with hers, and he moved his hand to caress her neck beneath the thick curls of hair. "I'm not sure you gave me a straight answer to my proposal."

"Not an outright yes." Her eyes took on a challeng-

307

ing glint. "Are you trying to withdraw the offer?"

"I just want to make sure you know what you'd be getting."

"If last night was a typical example . . ." Her shrug did interesting things with the edge of the sheet resting precariously across her breasts.

"I'd like to think so."

"Then you might do."

Knowing she watched him, he let his eyes slide across her face and lips and body so spectacularly outlined beneath the soft sheet. Sex was good for them, he thought. The best. But was he what she wanted for a lifetime? She'd said she loved him, a declaration he'd pretended not to catch, but in truth, caught up in the rapid changes in her life, she was probably confusing that elusive emotion with gratitude and passion.

And he offered her Belle Terre. He'd seen the unguarded look in her eyes when he reminded her of his home—the home that would be hers. She wasn't conniving for it, but after years of loneliness, years during which she had worked hard to save money for its purchase, she wouldn't be able to reject it, either.

Adam didn't regret asking her to be his wife. She could only improve his life. But he wanted to be certain that he could improve hers.

"You need to look at the complete package, Catherine. Nightmares, an obsession with hard, un-gentlemanly work, a prison record. And I'm certainly not given to socializing in town."

"Don't ever attempt an occupation that requires salesmanship. You'd starve trying to make a living."

"Why, am I too honest?"

"You tell me, Adam. Is that what you are?"

He caught a familiar hardness in her voice and wondered if she might ever lose it.

"Do me a favor," he said.

"What?"

"Before you answer once and for all time, ride out to

Belle Terre."

Her surprise was evident. "I've been there before."

"But not since I've been owner. Not really. Looking at it from the bayou is one thing, but from inside you might find it different." He wanted to add that she hadn't walked the floors of Belle Terre since Gerard Constant threw her out. As used to pain as she was, the shock of returning could be more distressful than she imagined.

He settled for a milder "You've admitted to hating the river. You might find that you feel the same about the house."

She looked past him for a moment, her gaze settling on the mosquito netting at his back.

"I don't think so." Her voice was soft, barely above a whisper.

"It hadn't been well cared for before I bought it, and the truth is, I've done little to improve on anything. The fields and equipment, yes, and even the slave quarters; the house itself has gotten little more than a regular cleaning."

"Repairing is my specialty."

"So ride out today and see how much repairing you'll have to do."

She hesitated. "Not today," she said at last. "Sunday."

"But that's four days away."

"The casino is closed then; I won't feel the necessity of hurrying back. You can have a dinner waiting for me. It will"—her voice caught for a minute—"it will be like old times. Sunday dinner at Belle Terre."

Adam leaned close to kiss the dark pensiveness from her face. "Sunday it is," he said, his hand returning to her breast. "But it seems a damned long time to wait."

Catherine slipped closer to him, her long bare leg against his. Bending her knee, she ran her foot up and down the back of his calf. "Then I suggest we make the most of the hour left to us. Dawn will be here soon, and unless you plan to hang around and see what keeps a casino running smoothly, you'll probably be leaving."

Her suggestion seemed an eminently sensible one.

"An hour, did you say?" He brushed his lips against hers. "That's not very long. We'll have to make the most of it."

She nodded solemnly, a glint in her eye, and he forgot the nightmares, the right-or-wrong of their being together, the reasons they were good for each other, and thought only how Catherine helped him hold back the night.

Under a late-morning sun, the one-horse carriage moved swiftly down the river road, Ben at the reins, Cat and Delilah silent on the two-passenger seat behind the driver's perch.

Cat's hands twisted nervously in her lap. So many things to think about . . . so many memories . . . so many changes. She hadn't been down this road in ten years. Thank goodness for the levee that blocked her view of the river and let her forget its brown, swirling depths. Thank goodness for Ben and Delilah with their solid, quiet strength.

She tried to picture Adam awaiting her on the gallery to Belle Terre, tall and physically powerful and comforting in that unsettling way he had about him.

But Adam was waiting to welcome her as his wife-to-be and as the future mistress of his home; this morning, beset by doubts, Cat felt unworthy of either title. Worldly La Chatte. Untouchable La Chatte. What a laugh. Adam knew she was neither.

And still he wanted her—at least he had four nights ago. Was he, too, having second thoughts?

Cat had a hundred worries on her mind; high on the list was the traveling gown Delilah had helped her select the day before at Alfred Colbert's New Orleans boutique. Lemon-yellow, tight at the waist and belling out with undergarments, its neck was rounded and edged with a touch of white lace, and the sleeves were full and short.

Alfred had insisted the color brought out the tawniness of her skin and the luster of her black hair, which she wore pulled high and away from her face, a mass of curls falling at the back from beneath a ridiculous feathered bonnet Alfred had sworn was *très chic*.

Long used to white or black, she felt like a piece of fruit ready to be picked.

Would Adam find her disappointing? Too plain? Too garish? Silly considerations, she knew, but worrying about her clothing kept her from dwelling entirely on her ultimate destination and on the reception she would receive from Adam. Adam with his nightmares and his moments of despair and bitterness. There were memories he would not share with her; there were memories she could not share with him. But when he held her, she felt that perhaps there was happiness for her in this life. Did he share her feelings of love? He must, she told herself, but the doubts would not go away.

If nothing else, he offered her Belle Terre. There had been moments during the past ten years when she feared this ride would never take place.

Many times through the years she'd tried to tell herself she was unwise to covet the place where she had known disgrace. But Belle Terre was also the only home she had ever known. Not once in all the years since she left had she pictured herself there along with any of the Constants.

"Not far to go," Ben announced over his shoulder.

Cat felt a sudden dread.

Delilah took her hand. "Nice to get out of the city, Mam'selle Cat. If we were back at the casino, you'd probably have the two of us sewing curtains for the study."

Cat looked gratefully at her. "Now that's something

311

I hadn't considered. Maybe next Sunday we could begin."

Delilah shook her head. "I should never have mentioned it. Ben tells me I talk too much." She continued with a list of the things that Ben considered she needed to change, ignoring the occasional look he threw at her over his shoulder, but Cat, appreciating her efforts at distraction, could not concentrate. She knew this stretch of the road, knew that around the next bend she would be able to see the double row of oaks that lined the lane leading to the main house of Belle Terre.

The sight of them was not the shock she expected; that particular reaction came when Ben turned the carriage into the lane and she got her first full look at the front of the house. It sat a quarter of a mile back from the main road in the center of a wide lawn, moss-draped oaks dotting the landscape on either side, a larger version of the casino.

Four columns supported an open gallery that fronted the upstairs; below was another gallery where her mother had sometimes sat in the evenings, when she'd had the time after supervising the running of the plantation house and the care of its invalid mistress.

Underneath the oaks a young Catherine had played. Later, after Marie's death, she'd been too busy supervising the house and grounds . . . seeing to the vegetable garden near the slave quarters, and the dairy and smokehouse . . . keeping the household books . . . ordering supplies. There were a million tasks essential to the smooth running of such a plantation, and she remembered them all.

Cat's palms grew damp. If this was the place she considered home, why was there a cold knot in her stomach?

Adam stood at the base of the front steps and moved forward to assist her when she stepped from the carriage, her dress and petticoats swishing as she moved. He placed a chaste kiss on her cheek, but there was nothing chaste in the appreciative glance he gave her. "You look lovely, Catherine. Welcome to Belle Terre."

She glanced at the brown jacket and tie, at the starched shirt and fitted trousers, then back to his lean and handsome face. "You look lovely yourself."

For a moment she felt a ripple of pride. She *did* look nice, and, more important, she was being welcomed by a handsome, exciting man who had asked her to be his wife. That he was also the owner of Belle Terre added an especially sweet *lagniappe* to the occasion.

If Gerard Constant could have the least inkling of what was going on at this instant, he would be turning over in his grave. He'd thrown her out . . . and out, she should have stayed.

The thought of her nemesis ended her pride, but Adam, seeming to sense her changing mood, took her hand to guide her up the stairs and into the front hallway—before she could protest . . . before she could tell him of her doubts.

"Let me show you around," he said, holding tight to her arm, and Cat nodded silently.

The walls of the long hall were papered in a faded rose, at the top, a six-inch band of cypress molding painted to resemble marble. She glanced into the parlor which, in Louise Constant's day, had been kept dark. Adam had the draperies opened to let sunlight shine onto the mahogany settee and rocker and an overstuffed leather chair that she had never seen before.

Straw matting covered the floor, just as it had during the summer months when she was growing up. She wondered if Adam bothered to replace it with the velvet Brussels carpet that Louise directed to be laid during the winter.

Next to the parlor was the study where Gerard and Julien had decided her fate. "I'll look at it later,"

313

she said.

Across the hallway was the dining room, down the center of which stretched the long table which could seat twenty at one time. Mahogany horsehair chairs lined the walls; hanging from the open-beamed ceiling was a matching pair of oil-burning chandeliers. Cat had always thought it the most elegant room in the house; somehow it seemed smaller than she remembered and, with its frayed draperies and worn chair covers, definitely shabbier.

But then Adam had warned her the place needed her touch.

"Would you like to see upstairs?" he asked.

She shook her head. "I'd like to stay here a moment," she said as the memories rushed in. In this dining room she had sat across frm Julien and Arianne for countless numbers of meals. When he was at home, Gerard took his imperious place at the head; Louise rarely appeared at the foot of the table, instead asking that her meals be served in an upstairs room. Until her death, Marie had always sat by her daughter's side; afterward, from age twelve until that disastrous day when she left, Cat always sat on her side of the long table alone.

The talk—about the latest gossip in town, the price of cane, the inadequacies of the American governor— was always in French, guided by the patriarch of the family with Arianne adding her caustic comments from time to time. Julien's eyes often caught Cat's, and they shared an unspoken communication that said how foolish the other two were to be absorbed in such mundane manners when outside there were woods to explore and someday worlds to conquer.

Later when Cat took over her mother's duties, she would have liked to join in, but she never felt welcome.

So many ghosts lingered in that one room, and Cat forced herself to the present. "Could we walk outside?" she asked.

"Of course."

He led her to the hallway, through a combination sitting and storage room that stretched across the back width of the house, and out the door. To her right was the brick kitchen and smokehouse and on beyond, the vegetable garden, the slave quarters, the dairy, and the stable. Farther on were the buildings where the cane was processed into syrup and then into raw sugar. Straight ahead she could see the gazebo and the cistern; on beyond was the line of trees that marked the Bayou Rouge. Far to her left stretched the life blood of Belle Terre. The fields of sugarcane.

Seeing it from this view, she thought it all looked different somehow, unfamiliar even, but that was absurd. Belle Terre was home. So why could she not lose this feeling of dread? It seemed as though Gerard Constant had put some kind of curse on her that left her unable to feel the peace she had so longed for . . . a curse that no gris-gris of Delilah's could dispel.

"You don't look pleased," Adam, at her side, said. "I told you it wasn't in good condition."

She forced a smile. "I was just thinking about getting some whitewash and spending a day or two out here."

"You're supposed to spend longer than that. Or have you changed your mind?" He gave her no chance to respond. "Let's walk out to the gazebo. Dinner isn't quite ready yet, and I'd like to talk."

"Not the gazebo," she said, suddenly unable to stand with Adam in the same spot where she'd bid Julien *adieu*.

He studied her. "Just a walk then. Wherever you say."

She nodded, and they began to stroll slowly toward the shade to the right of the house where the trees were thickest. Adam removed his coat and tossed it over the low branch of a nearby oak, then loosened his tie. She took pleasure in the way the white shirt fit across his broad shoulders.

He caught her staring at him. "So much for being the

315

gentleman host," he said with a grin. The grin died. "Have I told you how beautiful you are today?"

Again came the comforting pride, and she felt herself begin to relax. "You're just glad I didn't wear one of my widow's weeds."

"I would have had to take it off if you had."

"You shock me, sir."

"I doubt that."

Cat felt a warmth spread inside her. "You asked me out here for dinner, remember?"

"I asked you out here for an answer, Catherine."

She stared up into his dark and probing eyes; never had she loved him with greater intensity than at that moment. There was nothing more satisfying, she thought, than being with the man who wanted her to be his. If only he came to her untroubled; if only she came to him the same.

"I lived here before," she said softly.

"I know."

"How?" she asked, alarmed. "Who told you?"

"One of the slaves who remembered you as a young girl. She said you used to help her in the kitchen."

"Tante Amie," said Cat, caught in the pleasant memories of a kindly face and unfailingly gentle words.

"She's still called that."

"I had no idea she would still be alive. She was an old woman when I left."

"Claims to be sixty, but there are those who say she's shaving a decade or two off the number. She's been working mostly in the slave quarters, caring for the children and nursing the sick. When she heard you might be returning, she let me know soon enough she expects to work again in the house."

"That sounds like her."

"She's not the only one who remembers you, Catherine. I asked them to stay away for a while, but I can call them now."

316

Tears formed at the back of her eyes. "Later. It's all a bit more emotional than I had expected. Did anyone" —she had to force herself to continue—"tell you why I left?"

"No particulars. Just that you'd quarreled with Gerard Constant and decided to move to town."

"I was a poor relation," she said. "He didn't approve of me."

"He must have been more of a fool than I thought when we were negotiating over Belle Terre."

An uncomfortable silence settled between them. Her thoughts were in a tumble as Cat unpinned her bonnet and held it in her hand, then hung it from a twig of the oak under which they stood. The yellow feather trembled in the breeze. She took a deep breath and concentrated on the beardlike moss suspended from a tree behind Adam. At the casino, caught by the yearning he aroused in her, she had told him she wanted to be his wife. After days of consideration, she knew that the final answer he awaited could not be so simple.

"I may not be the woman you want, Adam." She held up her hand to still his protest. "Not if you expect children. I . . . can't have a child."

"Until I met you, I had decided not to take a wife. You are what I want."

She met his steady gaze. "Are you sure? Most men—"

"I'm not like most men."

She let her fingers touch his face, as they had been longing to do ever since the walk was begun. His skin was warm from the noonday sun. He took her hand and kissed each of the fingers in turn and then the palm.

"No," she said in a whisper, "you're not like most men." She pulled her hand free. "But there's something else. There's Emile."

"I told you to hell with Emile Laverton. We're

317

discussing me and you."

"I promise not to bring him up again, Adam. But in return I'll need a promise from you."

"I'll not have him at our wedding."

"He wouldn't come."

"Then what?"

"If you truly . . ." Cat paused, swallowing the words *loved me.* "If you truly want me to be your wife, then you must promise not to hurt him in any way."

"I haven't noticed he's had any unusual health problems since I rode into town."

"I'm serious, Adam. I know there's still hatred in your heart, and I have no right nor power to ask that you put it aside. But I can ask that you not harm him. You said you're not like most men, and I have agreed. You have a strength within you that can be frightening."

"Do I frighten you?"

"Sometimes," she admitted. "You make me change the way I think about myself, and that can be upsetting to a woman who believes she knows the pattern of her life. But Emile has been special to me, too. I cannot see him harmed."

"If I find proof that he killed Judge Osborne or in any way had anything to do with my imprisonment, I'll see him in prison."

"And I'm trusting no such proof exists. I just don't want you to grow frustrated thinking he's getting away with something and decide to take the law into your own hands."

"Is this request your own idea?"

"Of course," she said, hurt. "I haven't seen Emile in days. He would be most distressed to know I was trying to protect him."

"I promise not to shoot him in the back."

"Adam—"

"I promise not to shoot him at all. Is that what

318

you want?"

Cat twisted her hands in front of her. "I don't want my two favorite men to destroy one another. That's not asking very much."

She felt Adam's dark gaze on her for a long while. At last he said, "You have my promise that I will not kill him. But in turn, I want a promise from you. Sell the casino."

"What?"

"You heard me, Catherine. Sell the casino. Break your ties with town."

She shook her head in protest. "I don't know if I can."

"There should be many potential buyers for such a profitable place."

He was right. She'd had offers enough for La Chatte since its beginnings. But it was her refuge, her source of comfort and of strength beyond just the income it provided. She had conceived it and built it into a success. Even if her plans to buy Belle Terre had gone through to completion, she never meant to let it go.

"I'm not after the proceeds," said Adam, "if that's what is worrying you. After the harvest, Belle Terre should be heading back toward solid financial grounds. Any money you've accumulated will remain yours."

"I'm not worrying about the money."

"So what does worry you?"

Whether I'm doing the right thing in being here . . . whether you ask too much too soon . . . whether you will be true and faithful for the rest of our lives . . .

She stared up at him, wanting to tell everything that was in her heart and mind, but she could not bring herself to speak of her remaining doubts.

"Silly things worry me, Adam," she said. "If you're sure I ought to sell the casino, then of course that is what I should do." Not exactly a promise, she told herself, but she knew that he took it for such. She felt terrible for deceiving him. If only he could understand, but he looked so uncompromisingly confident, standing there and saying what she needed to do. She had no other choice but to lie.

She *would* sell La Chatte. She would . . . in time . . . as soon as she knew in her heart that the marriage would work.

"Listen to us, Catherine," he said, "extracting promises from one another. It almost sounds as though we ought to draw up a contract," he said.

"A marriage contract? With terms set out for both sides? That doesn't sound very romantic."

His hands caressed her shoulders. "No, it doesn't. Then how about this? I want you to be my wife, Catherine Douchand. I want you to spend each night in my bed. I want to see you each morning when I awaken. I want to work in the fields and know that when I walk back in the house you will be there. I want to look up from my work sometimes and see you watching me."

He pulled her against him and kissed the corners of her mouth. "I want you to want me as much as I want you."

A tingle of excitement shot through her. Adam loved her. Cat could believe nothing less. With his sweet words sending out such warmth, she had only one response. "I'll marry you, Adam, as soon as you want."

His lips covered hers and let her know with passionate thoroughness that he approved of what she said.

When at last he broke the kiss, she stared up at him. "Tell me one thing, Adam. The other night when you played at roulette . . . Incredible odds were against your winning again. What would you have done if you lost?"

"Waited until the casino closed. Somehow I would have got up those stairs."

"But that would have been claiming winnings you

didn't deserve."

"Don't I deserve them, Catherine?" Again he kissed her. "Don't I?"

"Yes," she managed when she was able to speak. She wrapped her arms around his neck and, knowing that everyone on the plantation must be looking, returned his kiss with all the ardor that was in her heart.

Chapter Twenty-Two

Two weeks after Adam's proposal, Cat stood in the portal of a small chapel in the Vieux Carré, the sun bright in the late morning sky, the street and walkway sparsely occupied. Officially it was the first day of autumn, but the southern Louisiana weather was still warm and sweet with the green-grass smells of summer, even on this side street in the city.

All in all, it was a beautiful day to be married, a fact she had told herself more than once, but another consideration kept intruding, the idea that she was making a terrible mistake.

Cat directed her attention to a restless pigeon shifting back and forth on a ledge high against the brick church wall.

"You can fly, fat bird," she whispered, "far, far away, while I . . ."

She sighed. Trapped, that's what she was. By her own words and, more, by her own wants. Until today she'd been convinced that she wanted Adam as her husband. If all went according to plan, in less than an hour she would be his. Forever and ever. He could love her, ignore her, betray her—all accepted practices in the society she knew—and there was little she could do.

She stared up in envy at the bird. Maybe all brides had doubts just before the ceremony. In that case, she was most definitely a typical bride.

A second pigeon joined the first and set to cooing. A male, she figured, bent on seduction. With a flutter of wings, the pair took off but not before a splat of bird droppings landed on the banquette less than a foot from her satin-slippered foot.

Not a good sign, she thought, and turned toward the vestibule of the church. Waiting inside were the few invited guests: Odom and Wardwell from the bank, Joseph Devine, Alfred Colbert; standing close to the door were Ben and Delilah. Cat had insisted they be allowed to attend the wedding, even though it was against custom to allow black people at such ceremonies, and reluctantly the priest had agreed.

But they had not yet come completely into the church, instead placing themselves firmly beside the open doorway immediately after transporting the bride from the casino.

Everyone invited was close by to help in the celebration of the marriage. Everyone except the groom.

He must be having doubts, too, she thought as she stepped past her servants into the interior. He must be taking his time on the carriage ride from Belle Terre. It really wouldn't do to let him see her waiting on the street like some overeager spinster. But she'd felt panic setting in, and she'd needed a breath of fresh air.

Inside, a dozen wall sconces, each holding a pair of lighted candles, cast a soft and flickering light on the paneled walls and wooden floor of the vestibule. The air, stirred by a draft that wafted from the sanctuary itself, was cool and sweet with the scent of fresh-cut flowers someone—Adam?—had ordered placed at the altar.

Cat welcomed a moment of relaxation. The one thing that pleased her was the chapel where the ceremony would be held. "I'd like nothing so grand as the cathedral," she'd said, and Adam had agreed.

Accustomed as she was to the black dress and veil, she was not so certain of her appearance. Her silk gown, the color of honey, was rounded at the neck and tight at the waist, billowing to a fullness that swept the floor. In her hair was a single blossom from a late-blooming magnolia; it nestled in her upswept tresses like a velvet jewel.

"No veil," she'd told Alfred Colbert, who had insisted on providing the gown as a wedding gift. "I will don a lace cloth when the time comes."

"Je comprends," he'd responded with a twinkle in his eye. "I do recall the dreadful disguise you wear into town."

This morning Alfred stood with most of the guests across the entryway from her. He gave a nod of approval. He had understood her request about the veil, all right. For her wedding she had wanted no disguise.

Five minutes in the confines of the vestibule, five minutes during which she was the object of speculative glances from the wedding guests, Cat found herself desperate to stand in the open air once again. She contended herself with moving to the door close to Delilah and Ben.

In a tight collar and tie, Ben looked decidedly uncomfortable. "Think I'll take a walk," he said.

Cat understood his uneasiness.

"Mam'selle Cat grows nervous," said Delilah, who remained close by her side.

Cat shot her a sideways glance. "How can you tell?"

"The handkerchief."

Cat glanced down at the scrap of linen twisted in her gloved hands, then back at Delilah. "Just impatient." She shoved the telltale handkerchief into the pocket of her gown.

"The *Américain* is a man to drive one to impatience."

"I want to get the proceedings over with. You know I don't like to waste time."

"Certainement . . ." Delilah hesitated, then venturing softly so that only her mistress could hear, she added, "But there is something I have been waiting for the mam'selle to discuss."

"Not motherly advice," said Cat with a hint of surprise, her own voice equally soft. "You're not much older than I am."

Delilah shook her head. "I speak of the gris-gris."

"Oh."

"Surely now—"

"I still want it."

"But as a wife—"

"I will not be a mother again," Cat said with finality. "I've told Adam as much, and he has agreed."

Delilah stepped away, her black taffeta gown rustling in the quiet. "I did not mean to intrude. Of course I will provide what you wish."

Cat reached out and touched her arm. "You're not intruding, Delilah. I appreciate your concern."

"Then perhaps you will listen—"

"I've changed my mind," Cat said with a thin smile on her face. "Maybe you *are* intruding. No babies, Delilah. Not ever."

The two women stared at each other, and Cat saw that Delilah was ready to continue with her arguments.

A shadow at the open portal stopped her response. Cat turned toward the new arrival, her heart quickening despite all her doubts. She found she could even smile. The smile died as she watched Madame Ferrier enter, her son in her arms.

Joseph Devine was the first to reach her. "Madame Ferrier, good morning."

"Bonjour," she said, then turned toward Cat. "Forgive me, mademoiselle, for appearing where I have not been invited. But when I heard of the wedding, I could not stay away. Mine was such a happy occasion."

The woman did not look happy at all, observed Cat

as she studied the wide-set eyes looking up at her and the fine-boned face darkened with solemnity.

"Of course I forgive you. But I must admit you surprise me. The last time I saw you—"

"—was in court, *n'est-ce pas?*"

Cat nodded. "You testified to what you saw and remembered. Neither Adam nor I can have a quarrel with that."

The infant, grown several pounds heavier since Cat first saw him on the balcony of the Ferrier home, stirred restlessly, and his mother whispered cautions in his ear.

Joseph stepped closer. "Here," he said, taking the boy in his arms, "let me hold him."

"He has decided he does not like strangers," protested Madame Ferrier.

The baby proved her wrong, immediately smiling at the lawyer and exposing a row of tiny teeth behind his lower lip.

"He sees me as a friend, not a stranger, madame," said Joseph with more warmth than Cat deemed the occasion warranted.

The blush stealing onto Madame Ferrier's cheeks gave evidence she was not displeased.

"Mademoiselle," she said to Cat, "I have not come to stay. I want only to extend my wishes for your happiness . . . and to apologize."

"Apologize? Whatever for?"

"For my stupidity on the day we met. I was filled with pride and did not understand your gesture."

"There is no need—"

"Ah, but there is. No longer do I harbor such a foolish feeling." Her eyes moistened. "No longer do I have a reason. My husband . . ." Her voice broke.

"Madame," said Joseph, stepping close and placing a free hand on her shoulder.

She smiled tremulously at him. "I am a stupid woman, and you are being very kind." She looked back

327

at Cat. "My husband is gone. *Mort.*" The last was barely above a whisper.

"When? How?" asked Cat.

"In the village of Baton Rouge eighteen days ago. He had left us to earn money at the gaming tables he had heard about. The city was cruel, he said. There were opportunities elsewhere for a man of his talents. A fight over a game of cards . . . a knife." Her eyes were downcast and she spoke in a barely audible tone. "I know little more."

"I am sorry," said Cat.

"As am I, madame," agreed Joseph. "I had not heard. Please accept my condolences."

"Few people know." Madame Ferrier straightened. "I did not come seeking pity but to give you this." She pulled a small package from her pocket and handed it to Cat. "A small gift, but it is one I have made myself. I know you will accept it with more grace than I rejected your own generosity."

Cat opened the package and stared down at a linen handkerchief, delicate rows of pink and yellow flowers embroidered along its edge. "It is lovely, Madame Ferrier," she said.

"Monique, please."

"Monique," said Cat with a smile. "I am in need of such a gift. I will carry it to the altar."

If the chance ever comes.

Cat shook off the thought.

"Forgive my boldness, Madame Ferrier," said Joseph, "but how are you getting along? If you are in need of legal services, let me offer myself. Without fee, of course. The world can be a cruel place for widows and orphans."

Monique looked at him in surprise, her blush returning. "You are most generous."

"And you are far too lovely to wear such a look of sadness on your face. You must miss your husband very much."

"At the end Gaston was not the man he was when we were married. The games of chance, the drinking." She caught herself. "Please forgive me for speaking ill of my late husband. I must sound cruel and ungrateful."

"Never," said Joseph, shifting the youngest in his arms and taking the mother by the hand.

Cat regarded the pair. They made a handsome couple, Joseph with his fair hair and Monique with her brown tresses, each slender and short of stature, each fine of features.

A handsome couple, she thought again. Perhaps they could take her place today . . . in case Adam did not appear . . . in case she succumbed to everything her instincts told her and made her escape while she could. There was really no reason not to do just that. Her new wardrobe had been delivered by Ben and Delilah out to the plantation and into the waiting arms of Tante Amie, but Cat would gladly sacrifice each and every gown if she could lose the apprehension in her heart.

A sudden thought struck her. What if Adam was late because his path had crossed with Emile's?

It seemed unlikely. Only two days ago she had seen her old friend, and he had wished her well in her marriage. As usual, his countenance was unreadable, but she had taken him to be sincere. Both agreed that it would not be appropriate for him to attend the ceremony, considering the way the groom felt about him.

But if not Emile, then what had detained him? The possibility was strong that, like his bride-to-be, he was at this moment debating whether to change his mind.

"Damn!" Adam muttered to himself as he strode away from the city stable where he'd left horse and buggy, his long legs taking him down a deserted and sunless alley toward the chapel where Catherine waited.

If she hadn't already fled in disgust.

What a morning to break an axle, and on a lonely stretch of the river road. He'd left Belle Terre plenty early, planning to give the dray horse time to rest before the return ride out of town, but it had taken him an hour to locate a wheelwright and another before he was on the road again.

He wiped his hands against an already soiled handkerchief and thrust it into his pocket. What a sight he was for his bride to see, his trousers and suit coat dusty, his hands stained with grease from helping restore the carriage to working order. He had brought not so much as a comb to smooth his unruly hair.

It was damned certain he'd never make a dandy like most of the Creoles, but then Catherine already knew his flaws. He hoped she wasn't having regrets; he wasn't. He was restless away from her, aroused when she was near, and her satisfaction was as important to him as his own—a remarkable change for a man who only a month ago had believed the world was a place devoid of beauty and goodness.

Catherine was both beautiful and good. She made him forget his troubles, and he knew he did the same for her. It was very possible that their marriage just might work.

So lost in thought was he that he didn't see the stocky figure blocking his path.

"A good morning to you, Mr. Gase."

Adam brought himself to a halt, staring at the spread-legged man and at the pistol holstered against his thigh. He regretted that he'd left his own gun under the seat of the buggy. "Get out of my way, O'Reilly. I've no time to fool with you."

"Late for your wedding, are you? His lordship was worried you might have a change of heart and leave Miss Cat waiting at the chapel."

"And you're here to see that I don't."

The Irishman's broad, flat face broke into an ugly

grin. "Aye, that I am. Been on the lookout for the past hour or two."

Adam shook his head in disgust. "Miss Douchand is my concern now. Not yours, and not your boss's. Tell him that for me." He attempted to push past O'Reilly, but a powerful hand caught the lapel of his coat, crushing the wilted flower that the slave Tacey had pinned in place just before he left.

"My orders come from his lordship, not the likes of you."

Adam brought his forearm up hard against O'Reilly's wrist, breaking the grip. There was no mistaking the hate blazing in the Irishman's green eyes.

"If I hadn't been told—" growled O'Reilly.

"Told what, not to fight me? Hard orders for a brawler like you. Does Laverton tell you when to piss?"

The Irishman took him by surprise, a rock-firm fist coming up from what seemed the ground and catching him full in the eye. Adam staggered backward, caught himself, and shook his head to clear away the stars. He saw the next punch coming, threw up an arm to ward it off, and landed a blow hard against the Irishman's stomach, at the same time lifting the pistol from its holster and tossing it aside. He ignored the sound of rending cloth across his back.

O'Reilly hugged his middle and fought for breath, glaring at Adam with an ugly glint in his eyes, his battle-scarred face twisted in a snarl.

Anger burned in Adam. He'd promised Catherine not to touch Laverton, but nothing had been said about his messenger thug. And he was damned tired of being threatened every time he ventured on a city street. During the past years, he'd learned a thing or two about defense; it was time to put them to practice.

"Come on," he taunted, gesturing with both hands. "Let's see how tough you really are."

O'Reilly pushed forward, a feral snarl issuing from his throat. Adam stepped to the left, seized him by the wrist, yanked sharply until O'Reilly whipped around in place, and brought the arm up hard against the Irishman's back. O'Reilly fell backward, his weight coming down on his trapped arm, and the snap of bone was easily heard in the deserted alley.

Immediately Adam let go his hold, and with a groan O'Reilly fell to the ground, his legs twisted under him, the broken arm, his right, hanging limp and useless. Gingerly he used his good arm to cradle it against his chest.

"You're a dead man, Gase," he growled over his shoulder.

"Laverton's orders?" Adam said.

"Mine." O'Reilly brought himself to his feet and turned to face Adam, his eyes dark as the alley shadows, his upper lip marked by beads of moisture. "On the grave of my mother, I swear to see you dead."

"You need a doctor," said Adam, unimpressed.

"All you'll be needing is a hearse."

The Irishman wheeled and trudged toward the far street, his arm still held against his body. Picking up the discarded gun, Adam thrust it into an inside pocket, further throwing off the line of the already ruined coat. By the time he made it to the end of the alley, O'Reilly was out of sight. A man and woman, strolling by on the banquette in their Sunday finery, gave him a curious look, then hurried on as if to put distance between themselves and the disreputable-looking stranger.

Adam heaved a sigh of disgust. He'd been half expecting something like this to happen, but the broken axle had pushed it from his mind. Laverton couldn't quite let go. It was damned certain that now neither could O'Reilly.

He glanced at the sky and saw the sun was ominously close to being directly overhead. Would Catherine be surprised that he was late? Probably not. Like him, she'd learned to expect the worst.

He touched his swollen eye. It must be discolored by

now, a purplish red to go with his dirty suit. Flexing his shoulders, he heard the tear in his coat lengthen. He set out at a quick pace, figuring that waiting around wasn't making him any prettier.

It took him five minutes to reach the chapel; he sent up a prayer of thanks that Catherine had not chosen St. Louis Cathedral for the service; his walking inside that grand structure in such a condition would have humiliated her as much as his tardiness.

She must have heard his hurried footsteps on the banquette, for she stepped through the open portal and, three feet away from him, came to a sudden halt. The sunlight caught her wide-set, lovely eyes as she stared in dismay at him. Not in dismay, he amended, but, hell, in open horror.

"Hello," he said, grinning. "Sorry for the delay."

Her glance took in the complete picture. "Your face . . ." she said at last.

"Not much to look at, am I?" His appreciative eyes roamed over the finely hewn features she presented, the parted lips, the slender neck, the tall, gracefully shaped body. The honey-yellow silk of her gown rested easily against her tawny throat and bosom.

"You make up for me," he added, his voice grown husky.

"I thought—"

"Haven't I told you that you think too much?"

She stepped close and touched his face, her fingers cool and comforting against his skin. "What happened?"

"I'll tell you later," he said, knowing that he would not reveal the complete truth. Whatever quarrel he had with Michael O'Reilly would remain his own. "Haven't we got a wedding to attend?"

He caught the doubt in her eyes and waited for her to respond.

She studied his face, his bruises, and his mouth before moving back to his eye. Her expression lightened. "If you think, Adam Gase, that you're going to get out of this by brawling just before the ceremony, then just think again." She linked her arm in his. "You've got guests to greet and, as you pointed out, there's a wedding to see to. And later, if you're up to it, a wife to welcome to her new home."

Chapter Twenty-Three

I've married a stranger.

The thought had first struck her after she'd said, "I do," and watched as a gold band was slipped on her finger.

Throughout the wedding luncheon, the swift good-byes, and the long buggy ride out to Belle Terre, Cat couldn't get the idea out of her mind. Who was this dark-haired, lean-faced man sitting close to her, reins in his expert grip, his thigh brushing against her skirt and reminding her of the intimacies they would soon share once again?

He'd taken off his tie and torn coat, and she was very much aware of the way his shirt fit his muscled arms and body, and the way dark hairs curled at his throat.

She knew the touch of his lips and his hands as well as she knew anything; she knew he had a troubled spirit, knew he loved Belle Terre—and yet it seemed she hardly knew the man. Except for a long-ago seen aunt and uncle in Pennsylvania, his family was all gone, but that wasn't a point of conflict. She, too, had no one—except now, a husband.

What kind of little boy had he been? Had he played games, climbed trees, read books by the light of a late-night, forbidden lantern the way she had done? Had he always been so serious . . . so commanding?

She didn't even know what he liked for breakfast. Whatever kind of a husband he would make, she wondered if she'd be much of a wife.

He spoke little on the journey, only to say a thug had assaulted him in an alley on his way to the chapel. She had known that as usual he was holding something back from her, but then she was holding something back from him—the realization that she might have made a terrible mistake, one they would both regret.

Why hadn't she listened to her doubts before he arrived at the chapel? She'd been able to think of a dozen reasons why they should not wed. But when he showed up with his hair mussed, his eye blackened, and his clothes stained and ripped—and most of all with a rueful grin on his face—she'd been unable to remember anything except how much she loved him.

Shadows were lengthening into dusk by the time she first spotted the rows of oaks that led to the plantation's main house. Her hands tightened convulsively in her lap, gripping the wilted magnolia she'd removed from her hair, and she fought a rising panic worse than her apprehension on her first visit two weeks ago. Then she'd known she would be leaving before the day was done. Now Belle Terre was home.

With a flick of the reins, Adam hurried the horse into a quick pace and they were soon turning into the long lane and heading for the house.

"Sorry I can't offer you a wedding trip for a while," said Adam, smiling at her. "After the harvest, maybe. How about Christmas? Or would you rather spend our first Christmas here?"

"I'll let you know."

He brought the carriage to a halt, and Cat stared at the line of people waiting to greet them—the house servant Tacey standing close to the field hand Bodeen; Tante Amie, her short, broad figure bent forward and her rheumy old eyes moistened with tears; Tom Jordan beaming in wholesome welcome even while he looked distinctly uncomfortable in coat and tie; and a half dozen others whose names she would have to learn.

All waited to greet her as their new mistress. Her panic grew. Surely they had heard she was the notorious La Chatte, casino owner and temptress to a thousand men. Not a respectable wife.

She must have been mad to think she could take control of the place she had left in disgrace. All those dreams for all those years—they were about to come true. They had been her sustaining force ever since she first heard Gerard Constant was giving up his land, but she suspected with sudden insight that in her heart she had never expected them to come true.

Tom was the first to step forward after Adam helped her to descend. The magnolia blossom, her lone accessory, fell unheeded to the ground.

The plantation manager extended his hand. "Good afternoon, Mrs. Gase. Welcome to Belle Terre."

Cat stiffened as she accepted the firm handshake. "Thank you, Tom."

He glanced at Adam's black eye. "Glad to see you've already shown him who's boss."

Behind him the servants laughed, ignoring Cat's denial. From a nearby oak a woodthrush added its distinctive song to the merriment, but Cat could not still the growing suspicion that, no matter how much she wanted to believe otherwise, she did not truly belong.

Adam shrugged. "Looks like I'm going to be outnumbered around here." He guided her past Tom and began the introductions. One by one, each accepted her extended hand—except for Tante Amie, who hugged her to her ample bosom, then held her at arm's length.

"Never thought I would see this day, child," she said. Snuffling, she let loose her hold and reached for a handkerchief in the folds of her skirt. "You'll make a fine mistress of this old place. And anyone doubts it will be hearing from me."

Cat felt her own eyes moisten. "I'll be needing all the help I can get."

Tante Amie shook her head. "And I'm thinking you probably know Belle Terre better than most anyone. Ain't changed much in ten years, only got older. Like the rest of us. Pardon me for saying so, Massa Gase, but we been needin' a lady around here. This is Miss Catherine's home."

Adam rested an arm around Cat's shoulders. "No need to apologize. I've been thinking the same thing."

His words served only to increase her doubts, and it was with more reluctance than pride that Cat let him guide her onto the gallery. Sweeping her into his arms, he carried her into the front hallway. Only the two of them entered, and Adam continued to hold her close, cradling her with sure strength against his chest. Cat's arm was wrapped around his shoulders, and she could feel his muscles tighten as he looked at her.

She took in the baskets of fall flowers that lined the entry. "They're lovely," she said softly, then glanced at him. How close his lips were, and how warm his breath on her cheek. "Did you have them sent to the chapel, too?"

"With Delilah's help."

At that moment Delilah and everyone else from the casino seemed a million miles away.

"Shouldn't you put me down?" she said, her eyes locking with his. "You've had a busy day."

"I plan on a busier night."

Cat's breath caught.

He kissed her lightly. "Welcome home, Mrs. Gase."

"Is it really?" she said, not bothering to hide the uncertainty in her voice. "Is Belle Terre really my home?"

"Of course it is." He set her down. "We have the rest of the day to ourselves. You didn't see much of the place before. Would you like to look around and see what you'll be responsible for? I expect you to do a better job than I've done."

Cat stared at his lips and found she wanted very much to be back in his arms. Maybe Belle Terre really would be home, but that was because Adam was here. She forgot her feelings of unworthiness and doubt, knew only that she was where she belonged, where she had yearned so desperately to be for so many years. Most important of all, she was beside Adam—beside her husband, not a stranger—knowing he desired her, feeling that desire like a blast of heat, reveling in her own burning need.

She'd have a lifetime to hear of his exploits as a child, a lifetime to learn what he liked at the breakfast table. Right now she needed to bond herself to him in a way that only a wife could—she needed to lie with him in his bed in his home. Then she would know she was truly his, and that Belle Terre was where she belonged.

"The house is ours?" she asked.

The glint in his eye told her he caught her meaning. "Until we call someone. They've all managed to find chores elsewhere."

"Then I want to go upstairs," she said, her voice strange and thick. Without waiting for a response, she turned and hurried up the stairs, ignoring the worn carpet and banister, wondering only which room he had chosen to be theirs. He quickly caught up with her and, hand at her waist, guided her to the room that had once belonged to Gerard Constant. Paneled in rose-wood, it was the largest of the plantation's four bedrooms and opened onto the upstairs gallery from which could be seen the Mississippi.

Gerard Constant's room. She couldn't think of the irony of the moment, not with Adam standing so close. The past, with all its bitterness and tragedy, must be forgotten. What better way to begin than in Adam's arms? She heard him close the door behind her. Her eyes took in the dimly remembered mahogany wardrobe and mirrored dresser, the matching chairs close to the window, the fresh-waxed cypress floor with its square wool rug in the center, and at last the large canopied bed; she'd never seen the bed before. Walking across the room, she ran her fingers across the ivory quilted comforter.

"I bought the bed for you," Adam said, as if he could read her mind. "As a wedding present."

With slow deliberation she turned back the comforter, revealing the matching ivory sheets, and turned to him with a smile. He was standing very close. "Thank you, Adam. It's a wonderful gift."

"I'm glad you think so."

Staring at the smoldering look in his eyes, the bruise only serving to highlight his hunger, she forgot her gratitude, forgot her worries, forgot her doubts.

"I want you now, Adam," she whispered. "Now."

"What's stopping you?"

"Oh, Adam." She threw herself into his arms and pressed her open mouth against his, her tongue licking his lips and demanding entrance, then exploring the sweet, moist interior that he offered.

All her anxieties exploded under the assault of her frantic need. Only his penetration of her body would ease the ache inside, and she pulled at his shirt, tearing the buttons from their moorings just as she had done that first time in the woods, impatient to feel his tight skin beneath her fingers, craving the pressure of his hard chest against her swollen breasts.

With frenzied thoroughness, she trailed kisses against his lips and cheeks, barely able to gentle her assault as she neared his injured eye, moving down his neck, settling for a delicious moment at the hollow of his throat to check his pulse with her tongue, all the while her hands searched out the contours of his chest.

Adam's magic fingers worked against the nape of her neck and tangled in her upswept hair. Tendrils fell under his manipulations, and he whispered her name over and over. The sound was sweeter to her ears than any song of a thrush.

In the valley between her thighs she felt a pulsing that was close to pain, her arousal taking on the edge of panic, as though if she did not have him now, hard and fast and quick, she would never know the pleasure of his body again. She lifted her skirt and tugged at her petticoats until they fell to the floor, kicked them aside, and hungrily thrust her silk-shielded body against the enlarged evidence that he, too, was ready.

"Catherine," he whispered huskily, "you go too fast."

"I can't wait," she moaned against his open mouth.

His answer was a low groan. He pulled at his trousers, freeing his manhood, then, kicking off his boots, set his expert hands to the last of her underwear and to her stockings and slippers, leaving her clothed in only her silk wedding gown. She helped him as best she could, but her hands shook with an arousal that was beyond her control.

Half dressed, she fell back on the feather mattress. Adam's body covered hers. Her breasts throbbed for his caress, but she knew more urgent demands and could not wait. Later, she promised herself as she thrust one hand between them and felt his hard shaft, stroked and guided it to its awaiting home.

His mouth covered hers, his tongue raking her teeth and tongue in a companion invasion of her eager body. Her hands found their way beneath his shirt and she rubbed against his back, barely aware of the raised scars that marked his splendid torso.

Convulsions of pleasure swept through her as he thrust again and again, deeper each time, his manhood massaging her at the point of her greatest need. She matched his thrusts with her own frantic writhing, behind her closed eyes a panorama of darkness with flashes of imagined light. Her satisfaction came in spasms, each sharper than the one before, until at last

341

she cried, "Adam!" and let pure rapture hold her in its velvet grip.

His own satisfaction followed almost immediately, adding a ripple of joy to what had seemed the perfect fraction of time. He held her close and she buried her face against the crook of his neck, willing the moment to last, giving her pulse time to slow. He seemed in no hurry to move, and they clung to each other in silence, only their breathing breaking the stillness.

At last he lifted his head and stared down at her. "You drive me crazy. Do you know that?"

"I don't know what happened to me," she said, embarrassed by her eagerness.

"Whatever it was, let's hope it happens again."

He rolled away from her, exposing the twisted skirt at her waist, her bare abdomen, the thick black triangle of pubic hair, and open thighs damp from his sweat and spilled seed. Embarrassment turned to shame at her lack of control and she hurriedly covered herself with the dress.

He shifted her higher on the bed where her head could rest against the pillow. Standing only long enough to undress himself, he lay beside her, his head propped against one hand. "I'm afraid your wedding gown is ruined."

"Not ruined," she said, ineffectually smoothing the wrinkles, then added with chagrin, "although I doubt I'll be making another appearance in it today."

"You're mistress here now. You can do anything you please."

She stared up at his bruised face and gray-streaked hair. Never had she loved him as much as she did at that moment. She wanted to tell him just how much, but somehow she found herself shy. He would sense she wanted to hear him say the same, but she knew the words of declaration must come unsolicited.

Besides, he already knew how she felt; she would not bore him with repetition. "Speaking of pleasing," she

342

said with a smile, "you managed that very nicely."

"Now that's the smile I've been waiting for. You really are happy, aren't you, Catherine? No doubts about our getting married? No doubts about Belle Terre?"

"None." She heard herself add, "Do you have doubts?"

"None."

She knew he was thinking of the pleasure they'd shared.

A moment of greediness swept over her. Adam found her desirable, which was wonderful, but she wanted him to think of her as respectable, too . . . despite the far-from-respectable way she had just behaved. Only then would he view her truly as his wife.

"There's one thing that worries me," she said. "Before, I didn't think about it so much, but now . . . The truth is, most Creoles believe a wife isn't supposed to take such joy in bed. Which is why they take mistresses."

"That's ridiculous."

"But it's what young girls are taught—and the men seem to accept it as truth. Could there be something wrong with me?"

He began to work at the buttons of her gown, his fingers brushing with accidental regularity against the hardened tips of her breasts. "I don't think so. But I'm willing to investigate further, if you want."

"So soon?"

He folded back the bodice of her gown and ran his hand over her silk chemise. Her breasts strained against the touch.

"I imagine there's food set out for us downstairs. If you'd rather—"

"I don't think so," she said. "We had a late wedding luncheon in town, remember?"

He leaned down and licked at a hard nipple thrust against the cool silk. "Whatever you say," he whispered

343

against the valley between her breasts. "I'll bring something up later."

She gave up on respectability. "It'll probably be much later," she said, shivering.

She proved to be right.

Cat did not leave the bedroom until the next morning, allowing Adam to wait on her with deliveries of food and brandy and a tub of hot water. She especially enjoyed the way he took his bathing chores so seriously, making sure no part of her body went untouched—some parts more than once.

She attempted to give him the same service, but he proved impatient, rising from the water after she had spent no more than five minutes stroking his inner thighs and teasing higher, holding his manparts in her hand to learn exactly how he was put together. She found herself back on the bed, a wet, demanding husband hovering over her. She'd not wanted to get out of bed again until the morning sunlight streamed through the open window on the east side of the room.

Adam was already gone when she awakened. She wondered if he was already at work in the fields, an idea she found disturbing on this, their first full day as man and wife. But the harvest could be as soon as one month away; if she knew nothing else about life on a sugar plantation, she knew that human considerations took second place to the crop.

She allowed herself only a few minutes of stretching, paying scant attention to the soreness of her body after hours of strenuous activities, and got up to find her clothes neatly hung in the wardrobe, each dress in a pastel color from the rainbow, since she'd promised Adam never to wear black or white again.

Delilah and Tante Amie had done an efficient job in caring for the garments. The thought of her servant sent her scurrying through her belongings for the all-important voodoo powder that she needed after last night. Stirring the gris-gris into a glass of water she poured from a bedside pitcher, she swallowed it down, then turned to the lesser of her morning ablutions.

She chose a green chambray, brushed her hair and let it hang loose about her shoulders, and at last made her reluctant way down the stairs, leaving behind a bedroom with rumpled and stained sheets, a tub of cold and dirty water, and a damp rug where the bathwater had splashed. Whoever took on the chore of straightening the mess would have no doubt about what had taken place.

But then she hadn't been very subtle, dragging Adam upstairs the way she had only minutes after they arrived. She couldn't picture Gerard and Louise Constant ever behaving with such abandonment; she'd sometimes wondered how they had managed to bring their two children into the world.

She found Adam sitting on the downstairs gallery. He stood and pulled her into his arms. "Good morning, Mrs. Gase," he said, greeting her with a warm kiss. "I trust you spent a restful night."

"Part of one," she said. "I expected to find you already hard at work."

"Tom's running things today. I thought we would have breakfast and take a more thorough tour of the place, let you ask questions, and see how you will want to change things."

"Now that's an offer no woman can refuse."

True to his word, he spent the day with her answering her questions, kissing and holding her close when they were alone, treating her with open admiration as she showed him she knew how a plantation should be run. He made her feel that she was truly at home.

He made her feel respectable. He made her feel loved.

Much later, when they had retired, he showed her

their wedding night had been only the forerunner to other nights of love. Once she asked him to turn his back to her, and in the dim glow from the bedside lamp she placed gentle kisses on each of his scars. When she was done, he shifted back to her, a wild light in his eyes, and made love with such rapturous intensity that thought she would go mad.

On her second day as mistress of Belle Terre, she rolled up her sleeves and got to the real work of bringing the house about to her expectations. Tacey, who for all her small size proved a hard worker, was joined by two other women, twin slaves named Polly and Prissy, and together the four of them began taking the dining room apart, lowering the pair of gas chandeliers, polishing the chairs and long table, taking down the dusty drapes and rolling up the rug, washing windows and scrubbing the floor, measuring for new draperies and covers for the twenty chairs.

She threw herself into the work with the same compulsion that had driven her at the casino—only this time she was not trying to forget Adam's effect on her; this time she welcomed it. And she wanted very much for him to know that in taking her as his wife he had made a wise choice.

While they worked, she shamelessly queried Tacey about life on Belle Terre.

"Massa Gase is a good man," Tacey avowed, her young, dark face set in a look of no-nonsense certainty. "Ain't his fault he can't set me free."

Cat questioned further and heard about how her man Bodeen had received his papers making him a free man of color. "He can go anywhere he wants," said Tacey, "but he don't go 'cause of me. I got eight long years to wait 'fore I'm thirty. Be old and shriveled then."

Thinking of her own twenty-seven years, Cat said, "Maybe not. There's always the chance you'll age well."

But the normally shy Tacey, caught in her private worries, would not be appeased. "Besides, no man gonna stay with a woman that long, not if he don't have to. You and Massa Gase got legal papers that keeps you together; we got only each other's word."

Tacey fell silent as though she regretted her forward pronouncement. Cat smiled at her reassuringly. "There's no paper strong enough to keep a man who wants to go," she said, touching the servant's hand. "Bodeen cares for you. Trust him."

Her words sounded strange to her ears, since she couldn't quite believe her own happiness would truly last, but Tacey didn't seem to notice as she thanked her for the reassurance and returned to dusting.

Cat thought over the news that Adam was trying to free his slaves. She felt a sharp disappointment that he had forgotten to tell her of his plans, at the same time she acknowledged a surge of pride that he would even consider such radical action. More than ever, she realized she'd married a complex man.

On the morning of her fourth day at Belle Terre she took it into her head to see him at work in the fields. A jug of lemonade in her hand, she made her way across the back lawn toward the canebrake. She found him halfway down one of the wide rows. He stood spread-legged as he surveyed the towering stalks. She looked at his open-throated shirt with its sleeves rolled up to the elbows, at the bronzed skin of his neck and forearms, at the tight pants tucked into the calf-high boots he wore to protect himself against the occasional snakes that made their way into the fields.

In the sweat-stained clothes that clung to his body, his hair damp against his forehead, he was like no other planter she could remember. Gerard never once shed so much as a drop of perspiration, and Julien only at play.

When Adam turned and grinned at her in welcoming

surprise, she forgot Gerard and Julien and hurried to offer him the lemonade.

A week after her arrival, she was visited by Ben and Delilah, who declared they had a special gift for her.

"And you're welcome to him," announced Delilah. "That animal's been howling and roaming ever since you left."

As she spoke, a golden streak jumped from the carriage and made a dash for Cat's skirt.

"Balzac," she said in delight as she cradled the growing animal to her face, his rough tongue licking her cheek.

Adam, who'd taken the Sunday morning off from his field work, joined her at the front of the house. Declining to step inside, the visitors agreed to a drink on the porch, the women taking a cup of tea and the men a glass of brandy. For his part, Balzac accepted a bowl of cool water and stayed close to his mistress, straying only to bat at an occasional fly that buzzed close.

The talk was mostly about the size of the crop. It was Adam who brought up the casino.

"Any buyers come by to look?" he asked Ben.

Ben glanced at Cat before answering. "I wouldn't know. Mr. Emile got a new man to run the place for Miss Cat, but he doesn't confide in me. Best to ask someone from the bank."

At the mention of Emile, Cat felt a tensing of the atmosphere and knew that Adam was watching her.

"We probably need to do that," he said.

She nodded and changed the subject back to the upcoming harvest, which was little more than three weeks away. Delilah and Ben soon left.

As she and Adam stood in the lane watching the dust of the departing carriage, he said, "You have put the casino up for sale, haven't you, Catherine?"

Not just yet, she wanted to say, *but soon . . . soon.* The words caught in her throat. As much as she loved him and wanted to be with him forever, like Tacey she couldn't quite believe that her man would really stay around forever.

She picked up the purring Balzac who was rubbing himself against her skirt. "I don't know why you have to ask such a question," she said, her heart pounding at the deception. "You told me to, didn't you?"

Unwilling to let him read her eyes, she turned and headed for the house. She knew her worries were foolish—didn't he prove every moment of each day and night that he was content?—but she couldn't put them from her mind.

If only he put his feelings into words, she would abandon the world for him.

Late that evening, as they sat on the downstairs gallery and watched the fireflies glow in the dark, he brought up the Constant family.

"You never talk about them, but you must have lived with them for years."

"There's nothing much to say. I was little more than a servant, after all. When I grew up, I left."

"And became the owner of La Chatte."

"That's right. I worked with the Ursuline nuns for a few years, then Emile loaned me the money to build the casino. It didn't take long to pay him back." She turned to him. "Why all these questions, Adam? Is something bothering you?"

In the dark she couldn't read the expression on his face, but then neither could he see the half-truths in her story that surely must be reflected in her eyes.

"I just think it would do you good to talk."

Cat felt a sudden, piercing fright. Adam must never know what had happened at Belle Terre to cause her to leave. He must never know the shame of her weakness

349

when she'd thrown herself in the river . . . must never know the cowardly reason she could never bear his child.

"I would," she said sharply, "if I had anything to say."

Hurrying inside, she made her way upstairs. Adam did not join her in bed until a long time later, and when he did, she pretended to be asleep. For the first time since they'd married, they spent the night without making love.

And for the first time since the wedding, he suffered a nightmare. When he jerked awake in the early-morning hour, his body bathed in sweat and Cat attempting to soothe him, he refused, as he had done in her casino bed, to tell the details of his dream.

The next night, after long hours of hard work, they made up for the previous evening in a frenzy of lovemaking that left them both exhausted. The nightmare did not return.

The pattern of their life was set as another week slipped by and then another, days of hard labor and nights of love. Neither sought the other out for the consolation of a few quiet minutes of talk together, except to mention their respective progress at their tasks over dinner and later in the privacy of their bedroom to whisper hot words of encouragement as they fell into each other's arms.

He didn't bring up the subject of her past again, neither did he mention Emile, but for all their physical familiarity, Cat could not feel as close to him as she had at first. True, she was holding back her innermost thoughts, but she knew that so was he.

And then the harvest was begun, long hours from dawn to dusk of cutting the cane, then bearing it by mule-drawn wagon to the shed where it was crushed in the large rollers Adam had bought, the resulting juice boiled down in vacuum kettles until it processed into sugar.

Adam had hired extra hands for the work from the neighboring plantation owned by Claude Renault. Too well Cat remembered Renault's wife from those years at Belle Terre. Surely Arianne had heard of the new mistress of her former home, but Cat's fears that the ill-remembered woman would make an appearance and bring up the past proved without foundation.

For her part in the complicated process of turning cane into crystals, Cat helped where she could, seeing that the hands were well fed, that records of their progress were accurately kept, that in general nothing distracted Adam from the work at hand. Balzac, who had taken to the country with all the intensity of his wild forebears, did his share by stalking any rodent or bird that came near the activities.

The crop was a good one, and she shared in Adam's pleasure. But they were too tired at night to do more than kiss, and she missed his lovemaking.

At last the raw sugar was stored in barrels awaiting shipment downriver. When the arrangements had been made for the pickup and sale, she and Adam treated all the workers to a feast at the side of the house—vats of jambalaya and beans and rice, whole hams and roasted chicken, hot breads and sweet potato pies. It was a feast she had spent days preparing with help from Tacey and Tante Amie and the other women slaves who were considered too old to work in the fields.

Later in bed she and Adam treated themselves to a different kind of celebration, one they both decided was long overdue. As she lay contentedly in his arms, feeling well and truly loved, Cat decided that her uneasiness around him must surely be a thing of the past.

She even allowed herself to consider discarding the gris-gris that she secretly took each morning. Adam deserved a child. Giving him a son or a daughter was the one thing she could do for him that no one else could do.

And to hold Adam's baby in her arms . . . She just might be able to manage it. Maybe, she thought. Maybe soon.

Early the next morning Tom left with the barrels on one of the steamboats that serviced the river plantations, and Adam, planter that he was, was explaining to Cat over breakfast the rotation of crops that he planned—stubble in the newly cut field next year and corn and peas the year after. Their peace was disturbed when they heard what sounded like a gunshot from the woods behind the house.

Adam set down his cup of coffee and listened for a moment. "I told some of the men they could hunt deer," he said. "Still, they shouldn't be so close."

"It was just one shot. Whoever's out there must have realized where he was and moved on."

"Maybe." Adam picked up his cup, then set it down. "Think I'll take a look around."

He was at the back door, Cat right behind him, when they heard a shout. It seemed to come from the row of trees and shrubs that lined the bayou on the far side of the cistern.

Cat ignored her husband's order to stay behind and followed him outside. She had to run to keep pace with his long stride as they headed in the direction of the bayou. A figure emerged from the trees. It was Bodeen running toward them, a woman cradled in his arms.

"Tacey!" she cried, and hurried after Adam.

They met Bodeen in the shadow cast by the tall cypress cistern.

"She been shot," Bodeen said in anguish as he held the still woman close to his chest. "I found her down close to the water. We got to do somethin', Massa Gase."

Blood stained the front of the slave's gown, so much

that it was hard to see just where the wound was located.

Adam pressed his fingers against her throat. "There's a pulse. Let's get her inside."

They laid her on a cot in the downstairs back room. Cat watched in heart-pounding silence as Adam ripped open her gown and inspected the torn flesh. "Shoulder wound," he said, relief in his voice. His fingers probed further. "Looks like the bullet went clean through."

By this time a crowd of black people had gathered at the front door. Cat ordered Tante Amie inside. "We'll need hot water," she said, "and some clean rags."

Tante Amie nodded once, barked orders to Polly who stood close to the door, then turned to Adam. "I knows what to do, Massa Gase. Treated a gunshot wound or two in my day. Now Bodeen . . . ," she said, taking over, "you just get outta here. Tacey's gonna be just fine, but it won't do no good to have you gettin' in the way."

"I'll help," said Cat, kneeling beside the unconscious young woman. She watched in apprehension as Adam disappeared into the main hallway. He returned in a minute, a pistol thrust into the waistband of his trousers and a shotgun in his hand.

"No," she cried, rising. "Whoever did this is probably long gone."

"Maybe," he said, but he continued moving toward the door. Cat trailed close behind, her heart in her throat.

Bodeen followed the two of them past the dozen men and women gathered outside. "I'm comin', too."

Adam paused to glance over his shoulder. "There are a couple more shotguns in a case in the study. Pass them out to the men who can use them, but wait for my signal before you come down. We wouldn't want to be shooting each other."

Cat gripped his arm, terrified of the danger he was

353

putting himself into.

He smiled grimly. "I'm trusting you to see that Tacey gets taken care of. And I'll probably be wanting some coffee and brandy when I get back."

He spoke with finality, and she knew by the look in his eye that there was nothing she could say to keep him from those woods.

"I'll have it waiting," she said. "Just be careful."

While Bodeen went inside for the guns, she watched as Adam strode across the sloping lawn past the cistern, past the ramshackle gazebo, and at last into the trees. Slowly she turned and went back to the house.

Chapter Twenty-Four

Adam set one foot cautiously after the other as he moved through the grove of oak trees close to the bayou, taking care to circle the clearing where he and Catherine had first made love.

Maybe Tacey had been hit by the stray bullet of a careless hunter . . . Maybe, he thought as he stood at the edge of the clearing, but he doubted it. More likely, whoever was stalking these woods was not after deer; more likely that person was Michael O'Reilly. Adam had been expecting him, figuring his arm had ample time to heal.

That was why he'd told Bodeen and the others to wait for his signal. The Irishman was his problem, not theirs, and he felt guilty enough about Tacey without adding any more injuries to the list.

He was certain he stalked O'Reilly, but he couldn't help hoping he was wrong.

The morning was cool with a hint of autumn; unseen birds set up a chorus in the trees. He recognized the clear, rolling call of a jenny wren and the more piercing song of a cardinal, ordinarily pleasant sounds, but this morning they served only to accent the stillness of the woods.

He took another step and another, his eyes watchful as the dead leaves crackled under his boots. A sudden movement to the right, in the direction of the bayou, sent him whirling, shotgun raised, in time to see the rump of a doe darting through the brush away from the trees.

As he lowered the gun, the skin at the base of his neck tingled. Something—or someone—was behind him. He shifted the weapon to his left hand and drew the pistol from his waist. He eased to his right toward the protection of a broad tree trunk and whirled, dropping the shotgun.

He caught O'Reilly by surprise. The Irishman was standing on the far side of the clearing, waiting to draw bead on his intended victim with a double-barreled pistol.

Forgetting the tree, Adam raised his gun and fired, at the same time throwing himself forward on the ground. O'Reilly's shot, fired a fraction of a second too late, zinged past him. The boom of the dual explosions echoed in the stillness.

The Irishman stared at him in disbelief, his gun slowly lowering. A dark stain spread at his middle as he dropped to his knees. He opened his mouth to speak, but only a gurgling sound came out. He swayed once . . . twice . . . then fell forward, face smashed against the ground. By the time Adam got to him and nudged the still body over with one boot, he was dead.

Gradually the noise of the gunshots stopped ringing in Adam's ears, but there was no bird song to take its place.

He stared down at the once-tough brawler who lay sprawled awkwardly on the carpet of clover and fallen leaves, his features lax, a trickle of blood streaming from the corner of his mouth, his eyes frozen wide with the shock of Adam's attack. Already the stench of death fouled the air.

Here was the man who had arranged the false testimony that sent him to the swamp prison, who had more than likely slain Judge Osborne and left him to pay the price.

He'd liked to taunt Adam, to threaten him. Today there had been no time for talk.

Adam felt no exultation, but neither did he feel regret. O'Reilly would have killed him or anyone else who angered him. He'd come damned close with the innocent and unarmed Tacey. Laverton probably didn't know that he was on the grounds of Belle Terre.

A crashing sounded in the trees lying between him and the house. Bodeen, the first to get to him, came to a halt at his side and stared down at the body.

"He the one, Massa Gase?"

"He's the one."

Bodeen lifted the shotgun he was carrying. "Gotta be sure he's dead."

Adam rested his hand on the gun barrel and lowered it. "He's dead, all right. No need to waste another shot."

Bodeen contented himself with spitting on the dead man's face.

A half dozen Belle Terre men arrived on the scene. Trailing close behind was a white-faced Catherine, who pushed past them and threw herself into Adam's arms.

"*Mon Dieu,*" she whispered, and clung to him, her arms wrapped tightly around his waist and her face pressed against his chest.

"It's over," he said over her head, his arms resting gently around her, the pistol still in his hand. "What are you doing down here, anyway? I told you to wait at the house."

She tightened her hold and spoke against his shirt. "Tacey's resting . . . I heard the shots—" Her voice broke.

"It's over, Catherine," he repeated. "There's no need to get upset now."

"Ain't that the man I seen out here once't before?" asked Bodeen.

"You may have," answered Adam.

Catherine stared up at him in puzzlement, then, easing free of his embrace, glanced down at the body. "Michael," she said. "What is Michael doing here?"

"Looking for me."

Catherine shook her head and shuddered. "Michael," she repeated, as if she expected him to respond. "I don't understand," she said, turning her attention back to Adam. "He takes orders from Emile—"

"Not this time."

He could read the questions in her eyes and knew he had a great deal to explain. He glanced at Bodeen. "See that he's brought back up to the house. We'll get him into town later." He took Catherine's hand. "Let's go back for that coffee and brandy you promised. We'll talk inside."

Arm in arm, they made their way through the woods and across the back lawn. Neither spoke until they had looked in on the resting Tacey, who had been settled in a makeshift bed in the parlor—"Didn't want her to be movin' too much," Tante Amie explained—and were settled with brandy-laced coffee on opposite sides of the dining-room table.

"She came to for a few minutes just after you left," said Catherine as she stared over his shoulder at the shifting curtains of an open window.

"Was she able to talk?"

"Too much. We had to stop her, order her to rest."

"Bodeen says she's a stubborn woman. But then I haven't found one who isn't."

Catherine ignored his comment. "She was at the cistern when she heard a cardinal singing somewhere down by the bayou. They're good luck, you know, and she wanted to spot it. She followed the sound into the woods. That's when her speech got a little incoherent—"

"Probably disturbed our visitor about his business."

Catherine shifted her gaze to him. "Which was?"

358

"Killing me."

Her knuckles whitened on the coffee cup. "How do you know?"

"Because he promised he would." Adam told her the details about the fight on the way to the chapel. "I know he had worked for you a long time, Catherine. I'm sorry if—"

"Don't be," she said sharply. "He shot Tacey. He wanted to kill you. He was not a man one could like."

Adam was tempted to compare him to Laverton, but said instead, "The sooner you separate yourself from everything in town, especially that damned casino, the better. When I take the body in, I'll stop by the bank to check on the sale."

Catherine shoved away from the table and stood. "Don't bother."

"Why not?"

"I haven't put La Chatte up for sale."

A sharp disappointment struck Adam. "You let me believe that you had."

"Because you insisted that I do so. I couldn't see that it was necessary."

She glanced away from him and then back, as though she had to force herself to look him in the eye.

Adam caught her distress, but he could not let up. Too often she evaded his questions, and now he saw that she lied.

"Again I ask, why not?" he said. "Didn't you expect to be out here long? Or maybe you just weren't sure."

"You have to understand that for four years La Chatte was my home . . . the only place I felt at ease. And to let it go so quickly . . ." Her voice broke. "I couldn't do it."

Adam's disappointment turned to anger. "Laverton's behind this, isn't he? Did he order you to disobey me?"

Catherine gripped the back of her chair. "You're not listening to me, are you?"

"I'm listening, all right. I just don't like what I hear."

"Adam, the decision was my own. I'm not a fool, nor a child to be ordered about."

He stood and rounded the table to stand in front of her. "No, you're not, but you should have known I wanted only what was best for you."

"Do you really, Adam? Do you really?"

"Of course. That's the role I play as your husband."

"I see. You tell me what to do, and I do it. Just like a Creole husband. It's not a very equal arrangement, is it?"

"You were too damned long on your own."

"It was a life that served me well."

She whirled from him, her shoulders straightening, her spine held ramrod stiff. His hands itched to grab hold of her and shake her until she saw some sense.

"You don't understand," she said.

"I understand, all right. You think I ask too much of you."

"You haven't *asked* anything."

"Would you have agreed if I had?"

His question stopped her. They both knew the answer.

With her slender back to him, her hair a mass of black curls against her shoulders, she looked stubborn and vulnerable at the same time, and, as always, imminently desirable. If he couldn't shake her to his point of view, maybe he could try a different kind of persuasion, one that would involve the upstairs bed.

Even as he considered it, he knew it was no solution—not for the long term if their marriage was to last.

"We're both angry and upset, Catherine . . ."

She shifted back to face him, her chin tilted at an angle of defiance. "Don't try to placate me, Adam. I'm not so angry and upset that I don't know what I'm saying."

Adam's hands clinched in frustration. He wanted to kiss the fury away or turn her over his knee for a well-deserved spanking, but he decided to give up, if only for the time being. "I'm going upstairs to pack a bag. Tell Bodeen to get a wagon ready. I'll deliver O'Reilly's body—"

"Not to Emile."

"No, I won't bother your friend. Don't lose any sleep worrying I might upset him." He liked the flash of anger in her eyes.

"When can I expect you back?"

"I'll get here when I can. A day or two . . . I can't say. Maybe longer. I'm not making any promises."

She nodded once and held herself stiff. "I wouldn't expect you to."

The distance between them, no more than a few feet, seemed vast and impassable. She gave no hint that she would welcome his embrace. He started to leave.

"Be careful," she said to his back.

He paused in the doorway to the hall. "I'm indestructible," he said, looking back at her. "Don't you know that by now?"

Indestructible, indeed!

Cat tossed in her lonely bed.

No one was indestructible. Especially Adam, whose luck away from the roulette table was frightening to contemplate. Half the times she'd seen him in town it was after he'd been assaulted. He drew trouble to him like the bayou drew bugs.

And she'd let him leave without making up. So what if he didn't understand her insecurity? So what if he didn't see how she needed to protect herself? Few men that she'd ever met would have.

All she could think of was that she'd let him leave angry . . . as if the casino was worth coming between them. It seemed very unimportant to her right now. What if, at this very moment, he was finding consolation in town? She'd compared him to a Creole

husband, and too many of them found that consolatio
at the gambling table, in a bottle of spirits, or in
woman's bed.

Adam wasn't a gambler and she'd seldom seen hir
drink.

That left the bed.

No, she told herself. Not Adam. He wouldn't do suc
a thing.

For a long while she continued to toss and turn, s
much so that even Balzac, whom she'd let in fc
company, took refuge under the bed. Somehow sh
managed to get a few hours' sleep out of the miserabl
night. She arose just after dawn and did what sh
always did when she was troubled—threw herself int
work. Tacey was awake, her temperature normal afte
a restful night, and Catherine offered a prayer c
thanks as she decided to give her attentions to th
neglected flower beds that stretched across the base c
the front gallery and down each side of the house.

When so many real needs called to her—mendin
and candlemaking and pickling, to name a few—sh
knew she'd chosen a frivolous task, but she wanted t
work at something that would make Belle Terr
special . . . something that would mark it as hers.

As she spaded and weeded the ground, declining th
occasional offers of help from several of the wome
slaves, she tried to concentrate on what kind of plant
to put out. Maybe some flowering shrubs—oleande
would be nice. Or what about roses? She'd heard abou
some of the river planters who were importing rose
from England just to make their places fancier.

Belle Terre could be as fancy as any of them.

But not without Adam. She was back to worrying,
condition evident to anyone who watched the fervo
with which she wielded the spade.

She stopped for lunch and worked half the afternoor
Why wasn't he back?

He'd left angry. Maybe he was angry still. If sh

362

hadn't insisted on a kiss at the wagon, she doubted he would have offered more than a spoken good-bye. And they hadn't been married much more than a month.

There was always a town woman.

She pushed the thought from her mind. She had enough worries without dreaming up any more.

As she knelt in the dirt, her once-yellow gown stained black despite the protective apron, she told herself the trouble was the casino. She should have put it up for sale. But she knew in her heart that whatever was wrong between them went far deeper. Adam ordered her to sever all connections with her past. He could not understand what a difficult thing that was for her to do.

Love wasn't trying to change a person. Love was accepting that person the way she was.

Adam didn't love her. The idea was heartbreaking and left her hollow inside. She couldn't accept it. Maybe he loved her in a different way. Maybe to him, love was the same as possession. Marriage—for the husband, at least—was ownership. Every Creole man she had ever met felt that way.

The more she tried to reason out the situation, the more confused she became. She tried to convince herself she was making too much of their first argument. She didn't quite succeed. One thing was certain: should he come home today, she must not let him find her looking as she did—face dirty, gown stained with soil and sweat, hair matted in a crude bun against the back of her neck.

Whether he sought them out or not, he was bound to see the fancy women who walked the New Orleans streets. If there was one thing Cat knew she could do, it was compare favorably to them. All men, Creoles or otherwise, liked a woman who looked good.

Tossing down the spade, she hurried around the house to wash hands and face in a bucket by the back door, then went inside, taking time to check on Tacey and ask one of the servants for a bath to be set up in her room.

An hour later, dressed in the green chambray that Adam admired, her hair brushed and loose about her shoulders the way he liked, she was back downstairs filled with determination to greet her husband with reserved warmth and not . . . definitely not . . . to throw herself at him and cover his face with kisses as she was inclined to do.

She returned to the parlor to find that Tacey and her bed were both gone.

Tante Amie came to the door. "She didn't feel right, Miss Catherine, staying in the main house."

"Nonsense."

"It was the way she felt, and it seemed to me that worrying the way she was, she'd get on her feet faster if she was in her own room. Bodeen saw to the moving. She's restin' just fine." Tante Amie gave her a studied look. "Seems to me she's restin' more than somebody else I could mention."

Cat pretended not to understand. "Do you think I could have a cup of tea?"

"Set yourself down. I'll be right back."

For an old woman, Cat thought, Tante Amie had as much energy as she. It was while she was waiting for the woman to return that she heard a vehicle coming up the front lane.

Forgetting her determination to be reserved, she made a dash for the front door. As she stood on the gallery, she was disappointed to see not the plain wagon that Adam had taken to town but a fancy covered carriage, one that was unfamiliar to her, and pulling it, a magnificently matched pair of black geldings.

Oh, no, she thought in dismay, surely it wasn't one of their neighbors deciding to make a belated visit. The inside of the carriage was in shadows, and she could detect only one occupant—a man.

364

Reluctantly, she moved toward the steps and stood, her hand resting against one of the gallery's columns, the late-afternoon sun illuminating the front of the house in golden light. The driver reined in the geldings and sat for a moment in the shadows of the carriage. She knew he was watching her, and for a moment she considered calling for help.

She needn't have worried. From the corner of her eye she caught sight of one of Belle Terre's workers standing at the side of the house.

The newcomer descended from the carriage. Whoever he was, he was finely dressed in swallowtail coat and silk cravat, his patent shoes shiny, a top hat pulled low on his head. He was short, only slightly taller than Cat, and slender, and he moved toward her with a grace and sureness that spoke of great confidence.

He stopped at the base of the stairs. She did not recognize him until he removed his hat.

"Julien," she said, not much above a whisper.

"Bonjour, Catherine," he said, and continued in French. "How right you look standing there. I have pictured you thus a thousand times. But not even in my imagination did I picture you so beautiful."

He walked up to take her hand. As he lifted it to his lips, he kissed the back softly, lingeringly, then looked up, his stare warm with more than mere friendliness. "Can you not greet your old friend?"

Cat could do no more than continue to stare. With his even features and deep-set brown eyes, he had turned into a handsome man, even more so than he'd been as a youth. His lips were fuller than she preferred, a sign of weakness in a man, but there was nothing weak about the glint in his eyes.

In all the years since they'd seen each other, she'd rarely considered what she would do if he returned, or how she would feel. She always assumed he would stay far away.

To her surprise, she felt nothing—no bitterness, no

tenderness, no anger . . . nothing. Gone was any trace of the young girl who had been ruined and abandoned. If she experienced any sensation at all, it was an irritation at his cloying greeting. Old friend, was he? She remembered things differently.

She pulled her hand free of his hold and stepped backward. "Please speak in English, Julien. It is my language now. What are you doing here?"

His eyes darkened with disappointment. "Not, perhaps, the greeting I would wish, but then I did not get the slap in the face I deserved."

"I do not want to talk over the past."

"Surely it is unavoidable. I am in New Orleans on business for my company—an import business that has, thank God, been most successful. I have taken time to visit my sister, and she tells me you are now mistress of Belle Terre. Always she has loved it more than I and does not sound pleased, but I tell myself what a wonderful thing this is. How appropriate."

"I believe you predicted it long ago."

"Ten years, was it not? Too long." He sounded wistful.

Cat heard a stirring behind her and turned to see Tante Amie watching from the open door. "The tea is ready, Miss Cat. Seein' you have a visitor, I put out an extra cup."

Julien looked past Cat. "Tante Amie, could it really be you?"

"Hello, Massa Julien. You look a mite surprised I'm still alive."

"I can't imagine Belle Terre existing without you," he said with Gallic charm.

Tante Amie simply looked at him. "There ain't nobody in the world can't be replaced, Massa Julien. I heard your papa tell that to many a man."

Julien stiffened. "I am not my father."

Cat decided it was time to intervene. "Come inside Julien," she said with scant enthusiasm, "before the tea

366

gets cold. In the parlor."

If Julien was insulted by her lack of warmth, he gave no sign. Finding his way ahead of her without being shown, he took a cool look at the overstuffed chair that Adam had placed by the window, and settled on the settee. Cat could tell from the way he smiled that he expected her to join him. She chose the rocker and proceeded to serve him.

They sat in awkward silence for a minute, each sipping at the tea. Cat set to rocking. The longer she rocked, the more irritated she became. How could Julien just ride right up and kiss her hand? He had no shame—but then, it was a characteristic he had never been known for.

She broke the silence. "You have an import business, isn't that what you said?"

"Actually it is mine only in part. A family business in truth."

"Your father wanted you to marry money."

"The joke was on him. The real money did not come until long after I was wed, but I doubt I could have sent him anything, not after . . ." He broke off and gave her a look of sad regret.

"I said I did not wish to discuss the past," said Cat.

He sighed in exasperation. "This is absurd, *n'est-ce pas?*" he asked, setting down the cup. "After all that we meant to each other. Please tell me you have forgiven me."

He sounded forlorn, and Cat resisted an urge to scold him for his whining. In the final analysis, all she had really meant to him was a few nights in the hay.

"I forgave you not long after you left, Julien. Other considerations held my attention."

"My father took care of you, did he not?"

Cat remembered the small sum of money with which Gerard had sent her out on her own. "He did as he saw best."

He accepted her words without question, just as he

had accepted his father's assessment of their affair ten years before.

Resting his cup on the table, he turned mournful eyes to her. "I have never forgotten you, *m'amie*. But you were more than that, were you not?"

"Don't you have a family now back in France?"

He shrugged. "A wife and two daughters."

And for a while there was a son. Cat found the words on her lips, but she could not say them. The infant had never been Julien's child, not really, not in any way that mattered.

"Return to your family with my best wishes," she said.

"My wife . . . she does not understand me. And"— he hesitated as if struggling for words—"she does not satisfy. Only you, Catherine, only you, my first love."

Cat knew she should feel insulted, should order him to leave, but she could not ignore the unhappiness that he made no attempt to hide. He offered no threat to her, only a vast regret for all that had gone before.

"You chose her," she said.

"It was a great mistake."

She thought he was close to tears. Julien, who had allowed her to be cast from her home . . . Julien, who had forgotten his promises to her at the first sign of difficulty. This same Julien now looked at her in the hope that she would forgive and forget.

Julien suffered two failings: he saw things as they affected him and only him, and he wasn't very smart.

Perhaps she should have been angry, but he made her only sad. For him she had once pined; later she had cursed his memory. But through her travails she had eventually grown strong. Julien, weak and unhappy, had not fared so well.

She looked at his handsome face and sad, spaniel eyes. How many years she had resisted thinking of him! Even his name had been banished from her thoughts. She'd been fearful of the pain such memories would bring, and now that she was with him again, the strongest emotion she could summon was pity.

"I've missed Belle Terre," he said. "France has never been home."

"So why not bring your family to Louisiana? You could buy property, settle down."

"My wife would not agree to such a move."

Cat got a clear picture of life with Madame Constant and the girls.

"My life has given me little happiness, Catherine, and so much regret."

"Don't—"

He hurried on. "I have never forgotten you, *ma chérie*. Never. You have remained in my heart."

He meant the words, as much as he was able to. For the moment. While she was near.

"Oh, Julien," she said, moving beside him on the settee. He needed comfort—not the kind a woman gave a man she loved, but the kind offered to a child.

How much pleasure they had shared during their younger years as they roamed about the surrounding wilderness—in those innocent days before they'd become lovers—but she must never have loved him, not even when she met him in the barn. He had represented safety and security; he had represented Belle Terre. If they had ever married, the union would have been an unhappy one. She would have ruled him just as his wife ruled him now.

And he would have sought consolation in town.

She brushed a lock of hair from his forehead. "Your father was right to separate us, Julien. His reasons were wrong, but we never would have suited."

"Non—"

The door to the parlor opened with a creak. As though they had been doing something wrong, Julien jumped to his feet. She stared at the grim-faced man standing in the doorway.

"Adam." She stood beside Julien. "I didn't hear

your wagon."

"Apparently not."

He remained where he was, tall and solid, his rumpled shirt open at the throat, his coat tossed over his shoulder, and directed his attention to the man at her side. "You must be Julien Constant. I heard in town that you were visiting your sister." He stepped into the room. "I hope I'm not interrupting anything. Or maybe I hope that I am."

His meaning was unmistakable. Catherine could hardly believe she heard right. "Adam—"

"Hello, Catherine." His voice was flat, his eyes cold.

"You're angry."

"Without reason?"

Julien cleared his throat. "Surely, m'sieur—"

"Perhaps you should leave," she said, turning to Julien. "My husband has just been on a long journey and he's obviously tired."

She prayed for Adam to speak and remove the awkwardness of the moment, to bid Julien good-bye, to ask about France, about his business . . . anything except stand there and watch her with those unsettling eyes. He remained silent.

At last Julien bowed slightly. "Another time, perhaps, we can continue our visit." He reached for his hat, nodded at Adam with a brief "M'sieur," and made a wide berth around him as he went out the door.

Catherine and Adam stared at each other and listened to the departing footsteps, to the creak of the carriage, and at last to the clop of horses' hooves slowly fading down the lane.

She shook her head. "I can't believe you're so upset."

"What would you have me do? Ask him if he was enjoying his stay?"

Catherine's defenses rose. "I knew Julien long ago. I wasn't doing anything wrong."

The coldness remained in his eyes. He didn't believe her. But why not? She had been sitting by an old friend . . . and that's all Julien was, as far as Adam was concerned.

Unless he had a guilty conscience of his own and was transferring his own infidelity to her.

But she'd already decided that was impossible.

"Tell me about him, Catherine." Adam's voice was as cold as his eyes. "Tell me about those early years when you lived at Belle Terre. You always close up when I mention them. Maybe it's finally time we had a long talk."

Chapter Twenty-Five

Adam saw the shuttered look in her eyes that he had seen so many times before. She was about to lie.

"There's nothing to say about those years. Julien lived here while I was growing up. He left soon after I moved in to town."

"And that's all."

She looked away. "That's all that is important. He's not been very happy. I was . . . comforting him."

Adam felt something inside him snap. The bastard that had abandoned her to bear his child—and it meant damned little whether he knew she was pregnant since he'd never done anything to make sure she was all right—that same bastard was accepting her consolation. Which was needed because, as she put it, he wasn't happy.

Neither was Adam at the moment.

"Comforting him?" he asked. "How far did you plan to carry it?"

"You think it was something else?"

He didn't know what to think. She'd lied to him about the casino. Lied about her relationship with Julien. Maybe she'd gotten so used to lying that she didn't know how to stop.

She'd shown tenderness as she stroked Julien's brow. He'd stood in the doorway long enough to see

373

that, regardless of what she claimed now. It had taken Adam a damned long time to get such tenderness from her.

He shook his head in disgust. He'd hurried home, his business in town taken care of, O'Reilly disposed of through the proper authorities, and everyone satisfied. He'd been ready to make up for their argument over the casino's sale.

So much for good intentions.

Right now, he knew only one thing for sure—with Catherine continuing her evasions the way she was, if he stayed much longer, he would tell her everything he already knew about Julien and, worse, about what had happened after she left Belle Terre. They would have a row that would be hard to forget. Already he had gone too far.

"I'm getting out of here for a while. I'll be back later and we can talk."

She looked as though he had struck her. "What do you mean, out of here? Where are you going?"

"Just out."

He turned his back on her and headed for the stairs, taking them two at a time, telling himself he needed a long, hard ride on Keystone, his destination anywhere just as long as he got away and cooled down. He had just entered the bedroom and tossed his coat on the bed when she caught up to him.

She slammed the door closed. "I've been waiting for hours for you to get back. Hours. Worrying. Thinking about what to say and how to make up."

He started toward her. "Catherine—"

"So where are you going? Back to town?"

"I said, just out. We both need some time to calm down."

"You are going back, aren't you? I didn't think you'd do it."

"Do what? What in hell are you talking about?"

The evening moonlight streamed through the window, lighting the room with an eerie glow, lighting Catherine's face.

Her eyes were dark with anger. "What men usually do." Her voice was high and scornful. "Look for someone else. Tell me that wasn't what you did last night."

He couldn't believe she meant what she said.

"You wouldn't believe me no matter what I answered."

"Not any more than you believed me about Julien. Admit the truth. You slept with someone else."

"I did *what?*"

"You heard me. That's why you thought I might do the same."

Adam had already been accused of too damned many things he hadn't done. And he'd paid dearly. This latest filled him with a rage that even his first arrest hadn't aroused.

"Stop it, Catherine," he ordered. Deliberately he let his eyes roam over her body so enticingly gowned in the green dress she knew he liked, lingering at her breasts, then moving to her lips. "If it's sex I want, I can get it right here. And you know it."

"What about variety? Isn't that what men like? One woman after another? I heard evidence enough at the casino. Bragging about conquests that I pretended not to understand. As if women were a prize to be sought and then discarded."

"Stop it."

But she was beyond reason. She drew back her hand to slap him. He caught her by the wrist and pulled her hard against him. "I thought you were different," she said, her eyes glaring up at him, her breath coming hard. "But you're like all the rest—"

"Shut up, Catherine."

He spoke harshly, disgusted with himself as well as with her. With her body pressed to him, the disgust and anger turned to another emotion—one more primal

375

and more difficult to control.

Whatever she read in his eyes caused her to cry out. He stopped her cry with his lips. The kiss was bruising, and she fought against his embrace, but he could not stop.

His tongue forced its way inside, raking her teeth and tongue, and he bit at her swelling lips. His hand kneaded one breast as he clutched her to him. He felt her struggle, and the fire in his loins flared.

He broke the kiss and stared down at her. She fought for breath, her eyes wide, and he read desire in their depths. The sight pushed him beyond reason. He'd been right with his taunt. He did not have to ride into town to get satisfaction. His wife offered it, even if it was against her will.

She made a dash for the door. His fingers caught at her skirt, and the chambray tore. His grip held, and he jerked her backward, twisting her until she was pressed against him. His arms held her in a steel vise as once again his lips claimed hers. He loosened one arm and sent his hand to roam roughly along her spine and cup her buttocks, pulling her against his groin. His body was hot and aching for her; he felt her quiver beneath his assault and knew she felt the same about him.

He broke the kiss and whispered her name raggedly into her open mouth.

She shoved away and fought for breath as she glared at him in blazing defiance. With the moonlight casting shifting shadows on the high-cheeked planes of her face, she looked like a creature from the wild.

"I'm getting out of here," she said.

He shook his head. "Too late."

"You'll have to take me by force."

"I doubt it."

"I'll fight you to my last breath."

"Tell the truth for once, Catherine. You want me as much as I want you."

His fingers clutched the rounded neck of her gown

376

and ripped downward, exposing her thin undergarment and the hard nipples clearly visible underneath.

"You're an animal." She spat out the words.

"As I recall, you've torn my shirt a time or two."

"No gentleman would say such a thing."

"Did you have a particular gentleman in mind? Julien Constant, perhaps?"

"Adam!"

"I told you I wasn't a gentleman when I proposed. Just a man. Comfort me, Catherine. I need comfort, too."

Again she ran for the door. He caught her and shoved her against the wall, his body imprisoning hers, and the battle was enjoined.

Again his hips ground against hers as his lips hungrily sought her throat, the swell of her bosom, the tips of her breasts. He laved the nipples through the chemise. He felt the arch of her back as she offered herself to him, even as she shoved against his shoulders, and he knew she was caught in a rising rapture as much as he.

His lips trailed to the damp curve of her shoulder and neck; she tasted sweet and warm; the sound of her heavy breathing drove him close to losing the last thin hold on his control.

"You want me, Catherine," he whispered against her skin. "Admit it."

Her answer was a whisper of his name.

He pulled the clothes from her body and carried her naked to the bed. Stripping, he joined her beneath the covers. She turned from him, as if she could not completely give in to his desire, but he gave her no time to think . . . no time to resist. As he pulled her firmly against him, her buttocks pressed against his swollen shaft, he let his hands exact a passionate toll from her as he explored the long, pulsing curve of her body, his fingers settling at last between her thighs. She was hot and moist, smooth and soft, her body incredibly complex and utterly desirable.

"Tell me you want this," he said into her hair.

Her cry was savage as she twisted to face him. "Adam," she whispered, then repeated his name over and over between the kisses she burned against his cheeks, his eyes, his mouth. The night exploded around them as his hands stroked, massaged, searched every part of her body. Desire was a demon that claimed his heart, his mind, his soul.

As much as she aroused his rapture, he was insatiable. No single pleasure could satisfy, not tonight; he wanted everything. He let her know, although neither spoke, low moans and heavy breath saying what words could not, his hands and lips speaking the language of love.

He did something he had never done before—trailed hot kisses against her pubic hair, her thighs, and inside her parted legs, finding the hard, raised nub that pounded in ecstatic need. Her hips rose to meet the seeking tongue and lips; it seemed to Adam that her body sang with the rhythm of his ministrations.

He brought her to fulfillment, felt the hot waves of rapture coursing through her as she cried out his name.

His body slid upward, his lips still working against her sensitive skin, lingering at her breasts, then hovering close to her lips as his hand parted her legs. She arched her body to meet him and he entered quickly, locked in her tight trip of arms and legs.

"You'll get there again," he whispered huskily, his words punctuated by the thrust of his manhood.

Her second climax came at the same time as his own explosion into ecstasy. Neither let go of the other; they seemed more completely one than they had ever seemed before, their ragged breaths mingling, their sweat-slick skin rubbing, all the rhythms of their bodies beating in the same time.

It was, Adam knew, a strange night of love, clashing as they had done in jealousy and hurt, lashing out at

378

each other as only two people who were so intimate with each other could.

It was a night he would never forget.

Even after her breathing had slowed, he continued to hold her close. She was his; tonight he had shown her that there could be no one else. She knew it, too.

Adam faced a realization of his own: after weeks of marriage, he wanted Catherine as his wife more than he had the night he proposed. Whatever troubles lay between them . . . whatever lies . . . they belonged together. Fate had dealt them ugly hands; they knew surcease from their troubles only with each other.

Somehow he must make her understand how things were between them.

"Catherine—"

She slipped from his arms, her tangled hair shadowing her face. "Please, no talk. Not now."

She turned her back to him and held still.

"I won't let you do this," he said. "Too many times you say later. But it's later now. You'll have to hear me out."

Adam tried to think of the words he should say, but he was not good at expressing his thoughts.

"I had some pretty ugly suspicions tonight . . ." he began. "I didn't trust you."

He waited for her response, but when none was forthcoming, he went on. "And you didn't trust me. Did you really think I would go into town and sleep with another woman?"

This time he was determined to wait as long as it took for her to speak. After a moment she shifted to face him. She brushed the hair from her face and said, "It's what men do."

"That's what you said before. You thought I was different, you said. And you no longer think so?"

"I . . . I guess I got a little carried away."

He grinned. "Which wasn't all bad."

"No," she said, a small smile on her lips, "it wasn't all

379

bad." The smile died. "I wasn't doing anything wrong with Julien. He looked so miserable that I really was trying to comfort him."

"And I'd rushed home to get a little comforting for myself. After spending a miserable and lonely night in a hotel bed by myself, I saw you touching him, and I blew up. We've got to learn to trust one another," he said.

"That's hard for me, Adam."

"I know."

He saw the struggle she was going through. She wanted to confess everything she had been holding back—he knew it beyond any doubt—but she couldn't quite bring herself to do so.

"You didn't have any supper," she said with a rueful smile.

It was such a wifely thing to say that he could have made love to her all over again.

But it wasn't what he wanted to hear.

"I'm not hungry," he said. "Are you?"

She shook her head. "Just tired."

He wrapped her in his arms. "Then let's get some sleep."

She nodded and snuggled against him.

Patience, he advised himself, that was what he needed. If she couldn't talk tonight, then maybe tomorrow. After his day's work he would give her another chance to explain about Julien and the past. He knew that nothing would be completely all right between them until she did.

For a long time he remained awake, thinking of the woman who lay beside him, retracing the events in both their lives that had led them to this point. He suspected that despite her avowed tiredness, she was doing the same.

When Cat awoke the next morning, Adam had already gone to the fields. She stretched and pulled the

380

cover close, snuggling down in satisfaction against the sheets that still bore the scent of their lovemaking. Dear Adam. He deserved a better wife than she.

She'd given herself a strong lecture during the night—all in silence, of course, but nevertheless she'd not spared herself any reproach. Adam was right. They needed to trust each other. She would confess everything. Today. And she would promise never, ever to hold anything back from him again.

She got up, gathered the remnants of her clothing, and set about dressing. She hesitated before taking the dose of Delilah's gris-gris. Maybe now was the time to think about starting a family.

And she would, just as soon as she talked to Adam and told him why she had feared having another child. If anyone could banish those fears, it was her husband. She had too many fears. He could banish them all. For once she had complete faith in him.

She was sitting in Adam's leather chair in the parlor planning on what she would say when she heard another carriage at the front of the house. She caught her breath. Surely Julien hadn't returned.

This time she let Tante Amie answer the knock at the door. She heard the rustle of silk. Tante Amie stood in the parlor doorway and said with less than total graciousness, "Those Constants sure are ones for visiting. This time it's the sister."

She stepped aside, and Arianne Constant Renault, more voluptuous than Cat remembered her, entered the parlor, full red skirt brushing across the carpet, a folded matching parasol in her hand. Her auburn hair was piled high beneath a black feathered bonnet. Cat was certain she had rouged her cheeks and mouth.

"Tea, please," Cat said to Tante Amie as she stood, then turned to her guest. "It's been a long time, Arianne. Are you alone?"

"Julien seemed unwilling to return. I assume he was treated rudely by you and your barbarian husband."

381

Cat looked at her in astonishment. "My husband is not a barbarian."

"He's an *Américain, n'est-ce pas?*"

So Arianne had not changed. She was still the outspokenly rude person she had always been. But Cat was different. No longer would she take Arianne's insults without a response.

"Is that why you've come? To teach me manners as you tried to do when we were young?"

Unabashed, Arianne studied Cat coldly, then took the settee, which was placed at a right angle to the leather chair, and spread her full skirt to either side.

Cat saw three choices open to her: she could jerk the woman to her feet and wrestle her from the room, she could summon someone else to perform the task, or she could listen to what Arianne had to say.

She chose the least violent approach and settled back in the soft cushions where she had been sitting, her hands gripped on the armrests.

"My visit has several purposes." Arianne's green eyes took in the room. "The place has deteriorated. I remember it as looking much grander. And to think," she said sharply, "you are its mistress."

"My husband and I like our home just fine."

"Ah, yes, your husband. I should have known what kind of reception Julien would receive. Emile has mentioned him in detail."

"Emile?"

"A friend from town." Her slight smile revealed small, white teeth. "I believe you know him."

Cat's disbelief was impossible to hide. "I didn't know he knew you."

"He most certainly does. Intimately."

There was no mistaking the implication of her words, and impossible images of the two together arose in Cat's mind. Emile didn't even like women . . . or so he had led her to believe.

Arianne hurried on. "He is inordinately fond of you,

Catherine, so much so that I'm afraid the dear man has done things you might not like."

Cat knew as well as she knew her name that she did not want this conversation to take place, but having chosen the course that she had, she could not pull herself from the chair.

Polly brought in the tea, and both women kept silent until they were once again alone.

"I can't believe that Emile has confided in you, Arianne. No matter how intimately you know him."

Arianne stirred her tea, then set it down untouched. "Perhaps confide is the wrong word, but I have overheard conversations which he assumed I could not hear. One with a Negress from that casino of yours—"

"Delilah?"

"Possibly. It was something Biblical. At any rate, she took it upon herself to tell him how impossibly wild you were about your husband. Of course this was long before he proposed."

A cold fist clutched at Cat's heart and she had to force herself to breathe.

"Go on," she said, knowing that nothing short of a fire would stop Arianne now.

"Perhaps you would like some brandy, dear. You always were emotional. It's in your blood."

Cat refused to respond.

"The darling—Emile, of course, not your husband. I hardly know M'sieur Gase. Yet. There is something about a barbarian that arouses one, but then I don't have to tell you that." The look in her eyes was that of a predator. "Anyway, Emile took it upon himself to visit Belle Terre. It was after he left, I believe, that your American decided to marry you."

"How do you know all this?"

"That Irishman. Emile really shouldn't trust him. It took only a small bribe to find out exactly what took place out here. The man has a remarkable memory."

Cat knew that she shouldn't ask . . . knew that she

was playing into Arianne's hands, but she felt very alone at that moment. She had to know.

"What did Michael say?"

"Emile threatened to destroy Belle Terre if the American did not take care of you. The implication, of course, was that marriage was not necessary, but it would be very nice."

"And I'm sure you learned how Adam responded."

"He knocked Emile to the ground. An impetuous sort, it would seem. But of course he married you. Perhaps he realized the wisdom of Emile's suggestion. Sooner or later, one usually does."

Cat trusted Adam. "I don't believe you," she said.

"Of course you do. You just don't *want* to."

"I'll call my husband in from the field and ask him in front of you."

"Husbands have been known to lie. Believe me, I know."

"But why tell me now? Just because Julien felt he was insulted—"

Arianne's eyes flashed angrily. "My brother was made to feel unwelcome by that brute you married, and you did nothing to stop him. Getting airs, aren't you, Catherine? Far above your class. I've been planning a visit for some time, and after Julien returned last night, I decided I had waited too long."

With all her heart, Catherine wanted to believe that she was listening to nothing but lies, told by a woman shattered by her own unhappy marriage and jealous that her former home had been taken over by someone else, but she could not. Arianne might hate the new mistress of Belle Terre, but she could not be too upset by her husband's infidelity with a mulatto, not since she had taken Emile as her own lover.

Adam said she must trust him. Oh, how she had tried.

She saw now what she hadn't understood before, the real reason Adam had shown up at the casino with a ready proposal on his lips. He'd been buffeted about by hard times, and he was protecting his land.

Never—not that night nor afterward, when he repeated his proposal at Belle Terre, nor on any of the nights since—had he lied with words of love. But neither had he told her the truth about why he took her as his bride.

Like a fool, she'd confessed what was in her heart, thinking she told him something he did not already know. But Delilah had told Emile . . . and Emile had ridden to Belle Terre.

Arianne's brittle laugh shattered her thoughts. "And here you are living in my home. Who would have ever thought one with your background would arrive at a position equal to my mother's?"

Cat forced her thoughts away from Adam and on to Arianne's ugliness. "You used to call me a peasant. I never knew why. My father was an aristocrat."

"Surely you don't still believe that, do you? Your father was—or rather, *is* unless he's died—one of those Cajuns who lives in the swamps. I understand they're more like animals than men, and their women run naked in the woods. It's no wonder your mother left him and brought you here. We were never supposed to tell, of course. It was your mother's request, and my father gave his word."

Cat's mind reeled. Henri Douchand alive? But her mother had always said—

Marie had said only that he was a French nobleman who had died in poverty, but she'd been stingy with any facts. It was more than possible that Arianne, curse her black heart, was continuing to tell her the truth.

"Does Emile know about my father?"

"Of course. He talked to Papa and learned all the details just before that dear man's death. That was when we met."

Emile had known for four years. It was another betrayal, heaped on all the others, and Cat edged dangerously close to hysteria. Sitting straight in the leather chair, her hands pressed against the padded arms, she forced herself into the worldly role that had served so well at La Chatte. "Is there anything else you wish to tell me, Arianne? I'd rather you let me know it all now, since you won't be welcome here again."

"I thought not. I must say, Catherine, you're taking all this very well."

Cat had heard enough. "I'm sure you want to get back to your own home. Please pardon me if I don't show you out."

She stood, praying her knees would hold out, while Arianne studied her.

At last Arianne pulled herself to her feet and reached for her parasol, which rested against the settee beside her. "If you tell Emile that I've been here, I'll say you sent for me . . . that you wanted to apologize for the insult to Julien. In the course of our visit, I told you about your father—just because I thought you ought to know. It was your husband who told you about the threats against Belle Terre. As a matter of fact, I might tell him anyway. I'll be seeing him tonight."

"He won't believe you."

Arianne's thick, painted lips curled into a sly smile. "Emile and I have a special relationship, my dear. He believes anything I tell him in bed."

Cat would accept that as fact right after she accepted the world was flat.

As Arianne rustled her way to the door, Balzac entered and, taking an immediate dislike to her red silk gown, lashed out with extended claws.

"Scat!" cried Arianne, her vicious kick too poorly aimed to prevent a rent in her skirt. She glared at Catherine. "I might have known you would have an undisciplined cat."

In his mistress's eyes, Balzac had earned a double serving of fish tonight.

Cat waited until she heard the front door slam before

sinking back in the chair. Balzac jumped into her lap and curled into a ball. She stroked the golden fur.

So much to contemplate . . . so much to comprehend. Adam . . . her father . . . Emile. Cat could barely breathe, and her heart pounded heavily in her breast as her thoughts skittered from one of Arianne's unthinkable revelations to another.

The easiest thing to accept was Arianne's eagerness to reveal what she knew. She had never been very bright, but she was more stupid than Cat had ever realized if she thought no one would know of her visit.

For the most part, she had told the truth. Of course Emile, learning how she felt about Adam, would react as he had. Delilah, too, had been doing her a favor to tell what she knew. Everyone was doing her favors. Cat stifled a sob. If she had one more thing done for her, she would die from the pain.

An hour passed, and then another. She knew there were a thousand chores awaiting her, but she had not the strength even to stand. Sometime in the middle of the day, she waved away Tante Amie's offer of food. She was barely aware of Balzac's desertion of her when Tante Amie left.

Adam, dressed in soiled work clothes, came in from the fields for a midafternoon dinner and found her still sitting in his chair. She could not look at him in the face.

"Are you all right?" he asked. "I've been thinking about you all day . . . looking forward to our talk."

She could barely consider last night, nor the way she had thrown herself willingly into all of her husband's demands; despite its moments of glory, it now brought her everlasting shame. "Sit down, Adam. I need to ask you something."

He chose the settee, his long, muscular frame looking out of place on the delicate furniture. "Ask anything you want."

Cat stared into nothingness. "Emile talked to you

here, didn't he? Before you proposed."

A pause and then a quiet, "Yes."

"And threatened to ruin Belle Terre if you didn't satisfy my unrequited affections."

"How in hell did you hear that?"

"Don't bother to deny it, Adam. I know."

"Whatever he said had nothing to do with my asking you to marry me."

"Don't lie, Adam. Not now."

"I'm not." Sitting at the edge of the settee, he reached for her hand lying on the armrest, but she moved it to her lap.

"Then why *did* you propose?" Her voice rose to a dangerously high pitch. "What else do you know about me? Delilah's been intruding into my business, why not someone else? How about Ben? He's in on a few of my secrets."

She'd been speaking in anguish, but the answering silence struck her like a blow.

"Surely he didn't . . ." She could not go on. Forcing her eyes to Adam's, she saw the truth.

"He told you about the baby," she whispered. The stricken look on Adam's face told her she was right.

And about her attempt to kill herself. She could not say the words, but she knew. She knew.

"I want to take care of you, Catherine. To hold out the hurt. That's all you need to think about right now. Last night we promised to trust one another. You have to trust me now."

But Catherine was engulfed in more pain than any mortal—even Adam—could assuage. She felt humiliated, debased. And just when she'd let down her defenses, just when she'd known for certain all would be well.

Trust him? How could she? Adam had known everything from her willing ruination in the hayloft to her years at the convent. She didn't need to hear him describe the details. He knew. And he had kept that nowledge to himself.

No wonder he'd been so quick to think the worst hen he caught her with Julien. He'd assumed she was eakening beneath the overtures of her first love.

Unlike Arianne, Adam was no fool. The two years in rison had left him bitter and facing a life alone, but in er he'd found the perfect wife—someone whose life ad been worse than his.

He viewed her as an object of pity, not a woman to be oved as his equal. She was reminded of how she felt bout Julien.

Adam had married her not just because he needed a ife. He'd married her at least in part for more noble easons—she believed him about holding out the hurt nore than she had ever believed him before—but his obility sickened her.

Such feelings did not last. Eventually he would tire f her and turn to someone else, whether he realized it et or not. A mistress in town, a *placage,* not just an ccasional night with a whore. Even Emile had made uch an arrangement, although as usual Emile did hings in reverse, seeking his pleasure with a plantation ife. She could well imagine why he had chosen the vell-endowed Arianne, above her obvious charms. ach time he took her, he was getting back at the harm he Constants had done Cat.

In its own libidinous way, it was another noble esture.

She wanted to scream.

Instead, she lifted her chin and stared at Adam. "I'm ure that these are things I can eventually accept, but ou must pay me the courtesy of allowing me time."

"Damn it, Catherine—"

"Are you going to order me to smile and be happy?"

He raked his hand through his hair. "I tried to get ou to talk to me. You refused. But somebody has alked to *you.* If you won't tell me who, then I'll have to ind out elsewhere."

389

"You'll find out soon enough I had a visitor, an old acquaintance. Arianne Renault. Julien's sister. Emile's mistress."

If she could get any satisfaction out of the moment, it came from the look of surprise on Adam's face.

"At last, it seems, I have something to tell you that you don't already know."

"You're too calm," said Adam, his eyes boring into her. "Why aren't you pacing? Why aren't you screaming and throwing things?" He sat so close that his knee brushed against her skirt, and if she looked closely enough, she could count the bristles on his face.

But she could not do such a thing without bursting into tears, and she shifted her attention to the hands clutching in her lap. "I'm not going to give way to hysterics. I came close to doing that last night. But not today."

"The smartest thing I ever did was ask you to marry me."

Why? she wanted to scream.

Instead, she said simply, "Please leave me. You need to eat and get back to work. Aren't you starting a new cane field?"

"Catherine—"

"Respect my wishes, please. It doesn't seem like too much to ask."

He sighed in exasperation. "All right. We'll talk later."

She could not watch as he stood and made his way toward the door, but she could imagine every movement that he made. She wanted to look at the play of muscles under his shirt, at the way his hair fell against his collar, at his long, graceful stride. She wanted to touch him one last time.

She must not. She'd touched him last night, and she'd forgotten her resolve.

But that was then, and this was now. Her mind worked fast. Upstairs were the boy's clothes she had

390

vorn for her country rides. In the stable was the
Arabian mare Raven. Despite what Adam believed
bout her, she was not helpless. She must continue to
ake such care in everything she did. She must get
way. She knew how to do so . . . and she knew where
he must go.

Adam found the note on his pillow when he came in
rom work and began a frantic search through the
ouse for his wife:

"My dearest,
   I know you have tried to help me, even as you
helped yourself. But as much as I love you, I find I
cannot live at Belle Terre without being loved in
return. Pay me one last respect by not trying to
find me. You will only fail.

                                                Catherine"

Chapter Twenty-Six

Cat arrived at the casino long after dark and reined he mare toward the stable at the back of the property. She gave scant attention to the row of carriages lining he Carrollton street. The fact that business at La Chatte appeared healthy was of no importance; after ittle more than a month at Belle Terre, she seemed hardly a part of the place anymore.

"Miss Cat," the stablehand said with a broad smile as she led Raven inside his domain, "ain't nobody tole me o expect you."

"Nobody knew I was coming. And I trust you won't ell anyone who might ask."

"No, Miss Cat, ain't gonna say one word."

She left Raven in his expert care and made her silent way across the lawn, through the back door, and up the back stairs. Luck was with her; no one else saw her arrive.

She stopped outside the study door, both hoping and dreading she would find Emile behind it. Her heart might lie dead inside her, but the ride had given her ime to think—too much time—and at last she had let herself really consider Adam's accusations against her old friend.

She accepted now that he had tried to get Belle Terre or her by arranging Adam's imprisonment. She would

393

not let herself think of other atrocities he had committed, crimes that could undoubtedly include Judge Osborne's murder.

She shared in Emile's guilt. Belle Terre had been her dream, and she hadn't let Emile know that she was not willing to do anything to get it. Unknowing though she had been, she was the ultimate cause of her husband's grief.

Their fight last night would forever burn in her memory. From what Adam knew of her, he had every right to view her with mistrust. And she could never completely trust him.

The sex had been magnificent. She knew it had been the same for him, too. But eventually sex wouldn't be enough.

Even if it were, she had so much more to offer—a lifetime's store of devotion. But love was the one thing he had never asked from her. She had been faced with no other choice but to leave Belle Terre, to leave Adam. The distance she'd put between them still wasn't enough. She needed to keep traveling.

Not, however, until she did something about Emile.

She could not postpone their confrontation. Opening the door, she stepped inside and found him sitting behind the desk, impeccably tailored as usual, a lit cigar resting on the brass bowl at his elbow.

He glanced up as she closed the door behind her. She caught him in a rare, quick look of surprise.

"Cat, what are you doing here?"

She stood rigid, hands clinched against her trousers, and used all of her self-possession to say what must be said in a voice that would not humiliate her.

"I've left Adam."

"I see." His gray eyes trailed over her dusty clothes. "You rode in at night. That was foolish."

"It was necessary."

He crushed the cigar in the bowl and regarded her over the diffused smoke. "Has he mistreated you?"

394

She shook her head.

His foxlike features softened into an expression of satisfaction. "Then you've come to your senses. I knew that eventually you would. Perhaps the marriage can be annulled—"

Cat broke in. "I know about your visit to Belle Terre, Emile. And your talk with Adam. I know . . . everything." She cursed the break in her voice.

Emile arose and hurried around the desk to offer her a chair. "Let me get you some brandy."

"Coffee and some food would be better. If you can arrange it without anyone knowing I'm here."

"M'sieur Gase doesn't know you're at the casino?"

"No, but it doesn't matter. I'm not staying, and anyway I'm not certain if he'll try to find me."

"The man is a fool." He left, but was back in a few minutes. "Now," he said, settling against the desk in front of her, "tell me what this is about."

"I will not talk about Adam. I've come to ask about Henri."

This time Emile was better able to hide his surprise. "I know several people by that name, *ma petite chatte.*"

"Don't lie to me. Not now. I mean my father, Henri Douchand, and you know it. Where is he? Is he still alive?"

"You seem certain that I have this knowledge."

"I know that you do. Your mistress told me."

A look of such rage passed over his face that Cat regretted having told him, but it was gone in an instant.

"Then," he said coolly, "it would do me no good to deny it. I did learn of this man's existence. But he seemed no more than a source of distress, especially since he had made no effort to locate you."

"I'm not questioning your reason, Emile. But I should have been told."

"You must trust me to know what is best for you."

"I can't do that any longer. I can only trust myself."

A knock at the door brought her to her feet.

395

"The food, nothing more," said Emile.

He took the tray at the partially opened door while Cat stood at the side of the room. Resting it on the desk, he gestured to her.

"Eat, and then we will continue."

Cat faced him from across the room. "Not yet. What must be said is best not postponed. I don't know that I have ever adequately thanked you for all you have done."

"You have paid me with your loyalty, Cat. I treasure it."

"If you hadn't pulled me from the water—"

"This is not necessary."

"Oh, but it is. Too long I have refused to talk about it. I could barely let myself remember. When you found me, I was frightened and desperate, and until today could not imagine a greater misery than that which had befallen me. You would not let me die. I owe you my life."

She spoke the words with all the sincerity of which she was capable, but they did not fill her with the warmth that she had hoped. Whether Emile felt it or not, there was an estrangement between them now that could never be bridged.

"As I have said, *ma petite chatte,* you paid me with loyalty. No one else has done such a thing. Men and women can be bought. All, I believed, all of them. But not you. Above all others, you deserve to live."

"Living is not enough."

"You have La Chatte and money, much money."

"Money has never interested me, not as an end in itself. It cannot buy a husband, and it cannot buy a family. I thought it could buy a home, but as in so many other things, I was wrong. You must understand, Emile. You must tell me about Henri."

"It is not in your best interest."

"My best interest?" Cat burst out, unable to keep silent any longer about the cause of her current anguish. "Is that why you sent Adam to jail?"

His eyes narrowed. "Again, you seem certain of my guilt."

"I am."

"I thought you did not want to discuss M'sieur Gase."

"He's the center of everything I do and always will be. It matters not that I am no longer with him. I know that you did what you did to help me, but you were terribly wrong. I owe you my life, Emile, but Adam did not owe you his."

She stared hard at the man who had been her salvation. In that sickening moment she knew she could never regard him in such a way again.

"And what do you plan to do about this knowledge?"

"I plan to leave and never return."

"It would seem that we come to an end," he said without expression.

Cat felt numb, as though after all that had happened she no longer held the ability to suffer. "So it would seem. My father, Emile. I must know."

A tense silence settled between them. She thought for a dreadful moment that he would refuse to tell her and she would have to go into the swamps where the Cajuns dwelled knowing only her father's name.

"Henry Douchand lives near the Bayou Lafourche."

Cat sighed in relief.

"He made his living as a trapper, but three years ago," Emile continued, "he was forced to leave his home because of the *Américains* who buy up the land for plantations. He and his family have resettled farther down the bayou close to the Gulf."

"His family?"

"A large one, I believe."

She let the news sink in. Since the death of her mother fifteen years ago, she had believed herself an orphan. Now she had not only a father, but also brothers and sisters. And a stepmother, it would seem.

397

Had Henri and Marie divorced? Her mother had bee
a Catholic and would never have consented to such
thing.

"What kind of man is he?" she asked.

"I am not a judge of people. To me they are a
weak."

Not all, Cat wanted to say.

"I will go to him."

"I cannot allow you to go alone. Ben knows the wa
He will take you. But only after you have rested."

Ben knows the way. Cat wasn't at all surprised. Sh
was beginning to feel that she'd been living a dream life
one in which she performed all the necessary tasks d
getting through each day without knowing in the lea
what others were about.

"There's a possibility that Adam will come after m
for his pride's sake if nothing else, and I don't want hir
to find me. We must leave soon. I will have a lifetime t
rest."

At last Emile shrugged. "Very well. Now sit and eat.
will arrange for the journey."

Cat did as he instructed, finding herself ravenou
after the long day and the desperate ride.

Later she talked to Ben and Delilah, assuring ther
she understood why they had acted behind he
back, and with Emile she discussed the detai
concerning Michael O'Reilly's death. It was a con
versation between two people who barely knew eac
other.

She and Ben left by carriage shortly after ter
heading for a boat that would take them down th
Bayou Lafourche. The early November night was coc
and damp and the sky was cloudy, but she was barel
aware of her surroundings. It took all of her strengt
not to burst into the tears that she had not yet been abl
to shed.

*   *   *

Adam rode all the way from Belle Terre into the heart of the Vieux Carré with an icy fear clutching at him, the same fear that had taken hold of him when he read Catherine's note—the fear that he had lost her.

He loved her. It had taken him a damned long time to realize it—maybe too damned long. Her leaving had made him realize the truth. Trapped by his own bitterness, he'd been unwilling to listen to his heart, unable to believe her declarations. Or her denial of offering Julien Constant more than kindness. He believed her now.

I cannot live at Belle Terre without being loved.

She wouldn't have to—if she could forgive him for being a blind fool.

When she talked to him in the parlor, he'd been stupid not to see what she would do. If only she had screamed at him, had thrown a vase, had slapped him, he could have argued with equal force that she was looking at things all wrong, that together they could work things out between them.

But her stillness had stopped him. How could he argue when she sat there so passively and waited for him to leave? It was the only thing she had wanted, and he'd had to comply.

And then had come the note.

He'd get her back. By God, he'd woo her if that was what she wanted, and treat her with the respect she didn't think she deserved. Wooing his own wife—the idea gave him a strange satisfaction. But he didn't have the vaguest idea how a Creole woman was courted. In Pennsylvania he would have several private meetings with her, where they could talk and kiss if they so desired—even bundle on the cold nights.

He doubted if Creoles bundled.

And if respect didn't work? He had a few other tactics in mind that he might try.

He arrived in New Orleans at midnight and decided to look first at Emile Laverton's house on Bourbon

Street. There were few riders or carriages about at the witching hour, and no pedestrians. All this part of the city seemed asleep—except for the man and woman he surprised in the upstairs bedroom after he'd climbed over the outside gate and broken the lock to the courtyard door.

Having made his way stealthily up to the gallery, he stood in the bedroom doorway, pistol in hand, and took in the scene. A woman was sprawled naked on top of the covers, her body white and full against the red satin, her wrists bound to the headboard, her ankles to the posts at the foot. Red hair lay in a tangle against the pillow beneath her head, and her green eyes were wide with fear. Hovering over her, whip in hand, was Laverton. For the night's activities, he'd removed only his coat.

"Madame Arianne Renault, I presume," said Adam. "I don't believe we've met."

Laverton whirled. "What are you doing here? How did you get in?"

"I didn't want to bother your servant, but you've got a door to repair."

"Help me," whimpered the woman.

Laverton stared at the gun. "If you're looking for Cat, you have invaded the wrong house. She isn't here."

"But of course you've seen her."

"He's insane," cried Arianne, tugging helplessly at her bonds.

"How did you know where to find me?" asked Laverton as he lifted his stare to Adam's face.

"Arianne could not resist bragging to my wife that she would see you tonight. One of my servants overheard."

A feral growl sounded in Laverton's throat.

"Help," sobbed Arianne. "He'll kill me."

"I've come to find Catherine." Adam aimed the

pistol at Laverton's head. "Tell me where she has gone."

"She no longer wishes to be your wife. Surely you will not force your attentions on her."

"Where is she?" He cocked the gun.

"Shoot me if you must, just as you gunned down Michael. I will not talk."

Arianne screamed.

"Shut up, you fool," ordered Laverton.

"Do you think I would hesitate to pull the trigger? I shot O'Reilly, remember?"

"Of course you will hesitate. You will be arrested for my murder and returned to prison."

"Prison has no horrors for me now. Without Catherine I have no life."

Laverton glared at him with cold and open scorn. "Rather late in coming to that conclusion, are you not? But that is not my concern. You will not shoot. I alone can give you the information that you seek."

"There are others. Ben and Delilah, to name two."

"Ben is gone, and Delilah does not know, not exactly. Besides, they both realize what a mistake it was to trust you would provide adequate care for their mistress. Like Cat, they will not make that mistake again."

Adam felt a surge of the rage and panicky fear threatening his control, and his finger itched to pull the trigger.

"Shoot him!" Arianne cried out.

Laverton's long fingers kneaded the handle of the whip. "For that, *chienne,*" he said in her direction, "you will pay."

"Catherine's not at the casino," said Adam. "It would be too easy to find here there, and right now she thinks she doesn't want to be found. And since she's obviously not here, I've only one place else to look— her father's. Oh, yes, Tante Amie overheard that bit of

401

news, too."

"Shoot him!" Arianne screamed again. "I know where Henri Douchand lives."

Laverton was the first to lose control. "Damn you, woman!" he yelled, raising the whip over the supine body of his mistress. Adam fired, and Laverton dropped the leather grip to clutch at a bloodied hand.

The gunshot echoed in the room, and Arianne broke into hysterical crying.

Tossing the gun aside, Adam threw himself at Laverton, grabbing the front of his shirt, shaking him until his head rolled back and forth like the head of a doll. His thin brown hair, normally so carefully combed, swung like moss in a breeze.

Laverton attempted to resist, swinging at him with the wounded hand, but the efforts were useless against Adam's rage.

He gripped his enemy by the throat and squeezed, watched the pallid skin turn red, saw the gray eyes bulge. And yet he detected a look of triumph in those eyes and knew the cause. If he killed Laverton, he could not be sure that Catherine would ever forgive him. And he had made a promise to her.

"You're pathetic," he said as he loosened his hold. He could not resist smashing his fist into the hated man's face. Laverton fell to the carpet, and, after a slight moan, did not move.

Rubbing at his bruised knuckle, Adam stared down at the unconscious figure. All desire to kill him died. Just as he had regarded Michael O'Reilly, he felt no elation, no regret. Revenge tasted like ashes in his mouth. Nothing could bring back the years he had lost. Catherine had tried to tell him so.

Catherine, who was wise and wonderful. He'd made her a damned poor husband. He had to find her and spend the rest of his life making up for their disastrous beginning. If she would allow him to do so. After that last night when he forced himself on her, she probably never wanted him to touch her again.

But by damn, she'd have to tell him to his face.

A whimper from the bed brought him back to the present. He unbound Arianne, who wrapped herself in the crimson sheets and, sitting at the edge of the mattress, stared down at her lover.

"Why didn't you shoot him?" she asked. She kicked the unconscious body.

Ignoring her, Adam used the ropes from her wrists and ankles to bind Laverton.

From downstairs came a rattling of the gate leading into the porte cochère. "Police," a gruff voice shouted. "Open up."

The last thing Adam wanted was to be delayed by an investigation of a gunshot.

"Quick," he said, "tell me where I can find Douchand."

Arianne, once again in control, smiled, and she had the presence of mind to smooth her hair. "I can tell you much more than that. Emile has papers. Records of everything. The police will be far more interested in them than in anything else."

A woman scorned, Adam thought, could have her uses. "Where?"

The policeman shouted again.

"Packed away in a cupboard downstairs. It is locked, but long ago I learned how to get into my husband's locked papers. Emile"—she did not bother to give him so much as a glance—"must have thought I was a fool, but I will have the last laugh."

"Get dressed," said Adam. "I'll go let our visitor in. And then, Madame Renault," he said formally as though she hadn't been lying naked with legs spread only moments before, "you can tell me about this Henri. I have a tingling at the back of my neck that tells me my wife can be found with him."

403

Chapter Twenty-Seven

Cat sat in the front of the pirogue as it cut through the still, small bayou branching off the larger Bayou Lafourche. The air was cool and damp but not uncomfortable. Cypress trees rose on either side of her, their fallen branches reaching out like skeletal arms from the reeds along the flat banks, and the surface of the water was carpeted with duckweed. Heavy moss curtained off anything else that might be seen in the morning fog.

Behind her sat Ben, and behind him stood the Acadian Pierre who had been hired to guide them. Pole in hand, moving with a grace that she might have called poetic if she'd had presence enough to do so, he took them across water which was at times no more than two feet wide.

The craft, a hollowed-out cypress log, was his pride. "She'll ride on mist if we can't find nothin' else," he had proclaimed when Cat expressed doubt it would take the three of them where they needed to go. At the time, they'd been negotiating on a dock of the Bayou Lafourche deep in the Louisiana swampland where the schooner had brought Ben and her from New Orleans.

Smoothing the black gown she'd changed into at La Chatte, Cat admitted that Pierre had known exactly what he was talking about.

She was startled by the sudden appearance of an egret standing on one of the fallen branches, its slender white elegance above a pair of spindly legs stark against the shrouded bank. Her heart pounded as the bird lifted his pointed beak in scorn and took to the air, the five-foot span of his wings barely clearing the cypress-crowded swamp.

Silently she chastised herself for being so skittish.

She glanced to her left and gasped, "Snake," at the same time pointing to the curved head poking out of the water close to the pirogue.

Pierre laughed. "Snakebird. Dives for fish and comes up looking like that."

Cat felt foolish. She'd seen snakebirds, and egrets, too, for that matter, in the Bayou Rouge behind Belle Terre. If she was going to stay in the swamp for any length of time, she'd best get over her edginess.

"Miss Cat," said Ben, "you just relax. We'll be there soon."

When they were aboard the schooner he'd told her that Henri lived in a house close to this particular bayou, using the waterway to take to market the furs of the otter, muskrat, and raccoon that he trapped.

"Your papa has him a nice piece of land where he can do a little farming, too."

"How many times have you been there?"

"Now Miss Cat, don't get angry. Mister Emile made me promise not to tell, and I could see his point. No use in stirring up more than you could handle."

"How many times?"

Ben had shrugged. "Just once. Your papa didn't know who I was. He thought I was coming back in the swamp to catch some crawfish."

"What did he sound like?" she had asked in a rush. "Was he brusque or friendly, or what? What did he look like? Did you see his children?"

"You'll see for yourself how things are with him."

Reluctantly Cat had tried to be patient, but picturing

406

her father and the new family awaiting her, unsettling as it was, came easier than thinking about what she had left behind.

Gradually the bayou widened, and the swamp became less oppressive as they caught glimpses of a blue sky through the lifting fog and of the sun almost directly overhead. They occasionally spotted small docks on the right bank; tied to them were empty pirogues much like the one in which they rode. Except for one man who was walking along the bank with a fishing pole resting on his shoulder, they saw none of the swampland's human inhabitants.

Cat thought of Arianne's description of the Acadians: barbarians whose women ran around naked in the swamps. She'd never seen her solemn and dignified mother in anything more scandalous than a high-necked, long-sleeved nightgown. To think of Marie cavorting like a bare-skinned savage in the open air was impossible.

All Cat knew about the Acadians was that they were French settlers who originally came from a land far to the northeast and, outcast, had settled in Louisiana. Surely they could not be as Arianne described.

"The Douchand place is just up ahead," said Pierre, and Cat pulled herself upright. She straightened her bonnet, fiddled with the hair that was poked carelessly underneath, then gripped the side of the pirogue as he poled them faster through the deepening water. They rounded a bend, and she got her first glimpse of her father's home.

Someone had done a great deal of work, clearing the land a hundred yards back from the water, erecting a house, plowing the fields to each side.

While Pierre secured the pirogue to the dock beside another craft much like his own, she studied the scene. The wooden house sat back twenty yards from the water. The shingle roof, high-peaked with a gable at each end, extended over the front gallery to provide shelter. An additional room with lower roof had been added to each side of the original rectangle, as if in afterthought, and Cat wondered just how large a family she would find. The kitchen had been built close to the back, and behind the field on the far side was a barn, beside which she could see two cows grazing in the wild grass. A dirt lane extended across the back of the land.

Both yard and fields were surrounded by a post fence. A smaller fence protected the vegetable garden next to the kitchen.

As Ben helped her onto the dock, she stared in apprehension at the closed front door, waiting for someone to emerge and greet them. Just then a pair of barefooted boys, both brown-haired and suntanned and wearing homespun shirt and trousers, came around the house on the run, each yelling out warlike whoops. Cat estimated them to be six, at most seven, years of age.

They spotted the trio on the dock and came to an immediate halt, their wide brown eyes staring at the strangers from dirt-smudged faces. A silent communication passed between them, and simultaneously they darted toward the front door as fast as their short legs would take them, disappearing inside and letting the door slam closed behind them.

A moment later a man emerged onto the roof-shaded gallery. Cat saw that he was tall and broad, that like the boys he wore a homespun shirt and trousers, that his muscled arms were held loose at his sides. She could not see his face.

Ben and Pierre stayed behind as she made her way to the gate opening onto the front yard. The man walked down the front steps and along the dirt path that led from the house to the fence. She saw that he was bearded and bushy-haired, that both black beard and hair were streaked with gray, that his face was weathered, that underneath thick brows his eyes were a dark color and oval in shape, like hers.

She removed her bonnet, let her hair fall loose around her shoulders, and waited, barely aware of the people who had gathered on the gallery, unable to draw a steady breath, incapable of doing so simple a thing as open the gate. He came to a halt on the opposite side of the fence, a scant three feet away. Just as she'd suspected, his eyes were a violet hue. The creases around them looked like laugh lines, as though he smiled a great deal.

He was not smiling now.

The silence became unbearable. "Hello," she said, then added tentatively, "Henri," not knowing what else to call him.

"You know me?" His voice was rich and deep, with a touch of roughness that fit his bearlike countenance.

"In a way . . . if you are Henri Douchand."

He hesitated, staring at her. *"Mon Dieu,"* he whispered, "it cannot be."

"I . . ." She could not go on, could not hold back the spill of tears.

"Is it Catherine?"

She nodded.

"Ma fille!" he said, throwing open the gate and pulling her into his arms. He crushed her against his broad chest, not caring whether she wished such a show of affection. "Catherine," he said softly. He squeezed hard, threatening her ribs, then pushed her from him. "I have prayed for this day."

He stared down with eyes as moist as her own. "My daughter," he said. "My firstborn. I feared you were lost to me."

"And I only learned yesterday that you lived."

"It is a miracle," he said.

Cat agreed. "We have much to tell each other."

"But of course." He shook his head in disbelief, then repeated, "It is a miracle."

He turned toward the house. "Rose! Boys! Look

409

who has come at last. My daughter Catherine."

The woman who walked toward her wore her brown hair pinned at her neck in a bun; her homespun dress was plain and did not hide the roundness of her hips. Like Henri's, her eyes were marked by laugh lines, and her face was nut-brown from the sun. She was a pretty woman who looked as though she worked hard but did not mind.

Cat could read the puzzlement in the brown eyes.

"This is Rose," said Henri, not adding any other identification, then named off the others as they came down the path: a twenty-year-old slender young man named Robert, and in descending order by size, the teenagers Roger and Jacques and the twins Jean and Paul. They were all brown-haired and tanned and bore a distinct resemblance to their mother.

"There is an infant inside the house. Alas, another boy. Louis."

Cat took ungracious pleasure in being his only daughter as she stared at her sudden family. They stared back at her in open curiosity, not unfriendly but not openly welcoming, either. She did not blame them. For her, six brothers, counting the baby; for them, a grown sister. It was quite a change.

"Call me Papa," said Henri, squeezing her hand. "You left so young . . . before you could speak."

"Papa," she said, but the name sounded awkward on her lips. To cover her discomfort, she hurriedly introduced Ben and Pierre. Henri regarded Ben with great care, as though he were trying to remember where he had seen him before, but at last gave up.

"Come," he said to the assembly, "we were about to sit down to the meal. We will celebrate. There is food enough for all."

Rose heartily agreed, and Catherine was grateful for the opportunity to help set out a repast of boiled crayfish, sausages, and beans and rice on the long plank table which filled the main room of the house.

Henri started to ask her questions—she could see the eager curiosity in his eyes—but he caught the slight shake of her head and steered the tabletalk to himself and his family. They spoke about life on the bayou, about trapping, about the nearest village five miles upstream. Cat saw the love that bound them, felt its warmth extended to her.

Such familial love had long been denied her; she and Marie had never teased the way these Acadians did, had never laughed openly. Happy as the scene made her, she felt an infinite sadness for all that she and her mother had missed.

After the table had been cleared—Cat helping despite Rose's protests—the two-month-old Louis was brought in for his introduction. Rose held him high in her arms; plump and fair-skinned, he focused his brown eyes on Cat.

He was beautiful. She and Adam might have had such a child.

She forced the thought from her mind. Aware of an instinctive longing to hold the baby, fearing that if she did so she would at last break down, she stepped away. Henri watched her carefully, but he asked no questions. If Rose noticed her unease, she gave no sign.

It was only after Ben and Pierre had departed for the return ride to the Bayou Lafourche, after Rose had gone to one of the side rooms to nurse the baby, after Robert and Roger had gone to work the fields and the twins, under the grudging supervision of Jacques, had left to check the crayfish traps that she had a chance to talk to her father in private.

He was saddened by the death of Marie.

"I did not know whether or not she lived. She was so young, only seventeen, when we fell in love and married. She was just off the boat from Marseilles, sent by her family with no more than a handbag of belongings, to live with the nuns and find a husband. It was a common thing in those days. The Casket Girls they were called for the shape of their handbags. I was all of twenty-five, a man of experience I thought, in the city to sell my furs. I saw her on the street and my young blood flowed hot."

From the side room came the cry of the infant Louis.

Henri shrugged his broad shoulders, and his eyes twinkled. "Occasionally, Catherine, an old man's blood can flow the same."

"You're not old," she protested.

"Fifty-two . . . fifty-four . . . who counts?" he answered, grinning. "As long as the blood still flows hot."

He grew solemn. "Marie was not made for the hard, lonely life in the swamps. I did not understand. After you were born, she left, saying that she must take you back to Marseilles."

"She never made it to France." Cat could only guess at those first years her mother struggled as a seamstress in New Orleans, trying to care for her infant daughter while she supported them both. She told in greater detail about the years at Belle Terre, omitting only how those years had come to a tragic end.

"She had a hard, lonely life there," said Cat, remembering her mother's sad eyes.

"Ah, *my fille,* but she had you."

"And I had her. But I always missed the father I had never met. She told me little about you." Cat could find no purpose in revealing what her mother had actually said. As far as she could see, Henri had a woman and children who loved him, and whom he loved in return. He was a happy man. That made him as aristocratic as a man needed to be.

"When I was grown," she continued, "I moved into town and eventually went into business for myself." She ignored his questioning look. "Tell me about your wife."

Henri looked sheepish. "We have not stood before the priest. I hope this does not shock you, Catherine."

"I do not shock easily," she said, wondering what he

would say when she felt strong enough to tell him more details of her past.

"I did not know about what happened to Marie. In truth, I did not seek another woman for five long years. You must understand that for a man of appetite . . ." He grinned. "Again, I must shock you."

"Not at all."

His face saddened. "Now tell me, why the clothes of a widow? Has your husband passed from you? Is that what has sent you in search of your old papa?"

The ring, she thought, of course he saw the ring. And the black dress. His assumptions had been natural.

The weariness of her unhappiness—still heavy in her heart despite her newfound family—overcame her. "Please, Papa, I will tell you later."

"And of how you learned that I live?"

"I have much to say. Later."

"I am a stupid country fellow. You are tired. Come, we will find a place for you to rest."

He put her in one of the side rooms, the other serving as the bedroom for Henri and Rose and the baby. Upstairs in the attic, Henri had told her, were the beds for the boys. The bed he gave to her was ordinarily used by the oldest son, Robert. "He can sleep in the attic," Henri had said over Cat's protests, and she'd been too exhausted to give him much of an argument.

Each time she closed her eyes, she pictured Adam staring down at her as he had done in the parlor yesterday morning. *Mon Dieu,* she thought, could it have been only then? It seemed a lifetime since she had seen him.

And there were so many more days to get through, so many more years. Despair struck her, the same hopeless sense of loss that had nearly destroyed her when her baby had been taken by the fever.

She gave up on sleep and went outside to find her father down by the bayou. The time was late afternoon. He took her for a walk along a narrow path beside the

413

water, and with the dragonflies skimming across th
surface, she began to talk about herself . . . about how
she had learned to manage the chores at Belle Terr
until an argument with the owner sent her to the city
She was vague as to the source of the trouble, and he
father did not push for details other than to mentio
that of course Gerard Constant had had a son.

"I worked for the Ursuline nuns for a few years," sh
said.

"Just as your mother had planned to do."

Cat nodded. "And then I borrowed money to open
business of my own." She hesitated. "A gamblin
casino. I hope I do not shock you."

Henri threw back his head and let out a gusty laugh
"In truth, you are my daughter. I like a game of card
myself, especially *bourre.*"

She saw in an instant that she need have no worry h
would be ashamed. Her father accepted her as she ha
come to him—without judgment . . . without questior

"I've left my husband." The words slipped out.

Henri nodded and touched her hand.

"We quarreled," she said.

"It is not necessary to speak of painful memories, *m
fille.* I see that you love him very much."

"Is it so obvious?"

"To a father, *oui.*"

How much more understanding was Henri tha
Emile. Love for her father filled her heart.

"I am glad I have found you," she said.

His dark eyes watered. She hugged him and the
held on to each other in silence for a long while. At las
they made their way back to the house.

Supper was a more relaxed meal than the one serve
after she arrived. The twins, no longer shy around thei
new sister, argued over their haul of crayfish, an
Robert, teased about a village girl named Odile
claimed he would get his brothers later when they wer
alone. For her benefit the family swapped stories abou

ife on the bayou and they all went to bed late, even the
wins, but Cat was not much more successful at finding
leep than she had been in the afternoon.

The next morning Rose provided her with one of her
Iresses, and Cat took needle and thread to fit it more
omfortably to her figure. Clad in homespun, she
nsisted on helping with the morning baking and with
he wash.

"I am used to hard work, and in all honesty, you
lon't know how long I will be here. Let me be a true
art of the family if you can."

Rose grinned, a cheerful show of acceptance as
varm as the smiles she received from her father. "If it
akes hard work to make you feel at home, I'll do what I
an."

As Cat stirred the clothes in the washtub at the back
f the house, she found herself listening for a splash on
he bayou that meant a pirogue had arrived. When she
ung the garments on the rope strung behind the
itchen, she strained to hear the clop of a horse's
ooves on the lane behind the farm.

By suppertime of her second day, she knew that
Adam was not coming. She had laid a difficult trail, but
omehow deep in her heart, she had thought he would
ind her. It would do him no good. Her mind was made
p. Better a quick end to their marriage than a slow and
ainful death.

But still she listened.

She was unprepared for the knock at the door that
ame with the first light of day. It brought her to instant
vakefulness, and she struggled into the main room of
he house.

Henri emerged from his bedroom grumbling, and
ulling his trousers over long underwear as he
taggered, still half asleep.

Pulling close a borrowed gown much like the one she
sed to wear at La Chatte, Cat stood well behind him.
Vhen he opened the door, she could not make out who

415

stood on the gallery. But she recognized the voice.

"Mr. Douchand, please forgive me for the early arrival, but my directions were less than perfect. It's taken me two days and nights to get here."

"I'll forgive you, man," Henri growled, "if you tell me who you are."

"Adam Gase."

"The name means nothing."

"She hasn't told you about me?"

Henri shook his bearlike head. "I must be half asleep still. Who are you talking about?"

"Why, your daughter Catherine. Don't bother to deny her existence. I know she is here. I've come to pay her court."

Chapter Twenty=Eight

Catherine stood like a statue in the dim morning light. Was she still asleep? She must be. She thought Adam was here asking to court her. But that could not be. If he came at all, he would be furious, demanding, stubborn. Not quietly polite . . . not apologetic. Not the Adam she knew.

Henri gestured for him to enter. Cat clutched at the neck of her nightgown, her heart in her throat.

Adam stepped inside and saw her.

As Henri lit a candle and set it in the center of the table, she stared at her husband. He looked as weary as the ages, his eyes dark and sunken, his face shadowed with stubble and thinly drawn as though he hadn't eaten in a month.

Neither moved; neither spoke. His eyes called to her where his lips did not. Every instinct screamed for her to rush to him. If she touched him, felt his warmth beneath her fingers, she would know that this was not just a dream.

"Sit down, M'sieur Gase," said Henri, "before you collapse."

The moment for rash deeds passed, and for the first time since he'd entered, she drew a full breath.

"We do not often have visitors this far from the bayou Lafourche," her father continued, "but they are always welcome."

Adam dropped onto the bench. He looked awa[y] from Cat's face only once, and that was to stare at th[e] wedding ring she had been unwilling to take off. H[er] lips quirked, and she hurriedly dropped her hand fro[m] the neck of her gown.

Rose entered from the side bedroom. She wa[s] already dressed for the day. "Henri," she scolded gent[ly] as she twisted her hair into place at her neck, "put o[n] some coffee for our guest. He will think we do n[ot] know our manners."

Adam stood to apologize. "I am the one withou[t] manners."

Henri introduced him, giving only his name.

"Forgive me, Mrs. Douchand," said Adam. "Th[e] hour is too early—"

"But you could not wait," she finished for him. Sh[e] sent a knowing glance to Cat, then back to Adar[n] "There is no need for explanation."

Henri raked his fingers through his shaggy hair. "[I] should have been up before the sun anyway. We we[re] awake late. So much excitement with Catherine at la[st] returned—"

"Henri," said Rose, a warning in her voice.

"I'll start the fire."

Cat was aware of everything said, of each moveme[nt] in the room as Henri worked at the hearth and Ros[e] returned to the bedroom to fetch a crying Louis, b[ut] she saw and heard as if she were an onlooker and not [a] part of the scene. Nothing seemed real to her, not th[e] early light drifting in through the window, nor the du[st] motes it revealed in the air, not even the scrape of th[e] bench on the wooden floor as Adam again sat dow[n].

A scrambling in the attic at last broke the spell, an[d] she retreated to the safety of her room, closing the do[or] behind her, closing out the vision of Adam's fa[ce] turned to her, of his dark and watchful eyes that cou[ld] see into her soul. She dressed in one of Rose['s]

418

homespuns, trembling fingers working at the fastenings, brushed her hair, and slipped into her stockings and shoes. Each act was made with precision, each thought directed to her ablutions; it was only her fingers that would not stay entirely under control.

And her heart continued to beat erratically.

She could not hold out the tortured thoughts forever. Adam had come for her. It should have been a moment of glory . . . if she could accept the reasons that had brought him here. She could not. He had married her under threat of ruin, thinking that she was an object of pity. She served as mistress for both himself and Belle Terre, not truly as his wife.

Her calm of the past few days had been so surface-thin. One look at him and all the tensions and heartfelt worries, the sense of irretrievable loss—all had rushed back. She knew they would never be far away.

She forced herself to leave the bedroom. The four older sons were gathered around the table and introductions were being made. They accepted Adam without question as a guest; surely they must know who he was—surely Henri had talked to them out of her hearing—but they gave no sign that anything out of the ordinary was taking place this morning. In the land of the Acadians, company was always welcome.

For all the talk around the table, she and her husband said not a single word to each other. She was as tight as a spring, unable to eat, fearful that if she once opened her mouth, she would let out a cry of such anguish that shame would be added to her already miserable state.

When she hurried through the room and out the back door to join Rose in preparing breakfast in the kitchen, she expected Adam to follow her, but he did not.

She worked without thinking, scarcely aware of what she did, deciding only that when at last their confrontation took place, it would be explosive. Adam would demand she return, she would refuse, and there would be nothing but heartbreak between them.

Still, he had sought her out. For all her certainty that they could never be reconciled, she could not still a tingle of happiness that the realization brought. To court her, he had said. What could he have meant? If he thought she would be the first to ask for a private moment between them, he was very much wrong. She had told him all she needed to in her note.

After a quick and noisy breakfast, for which she was grateful, she began to see a pattern to his behavior. Throughout the day, as she went about the chores Rose reluctantly had assigned her, he was polite to the point of being absurd, never addressing her directly but always being there when she needed to lift a heavy bucket of washwater or secure the clothes to the line. He never regarded her directly, but when she wasn't looking at him, she could feel his eyes on her.

He talked to Rose, however, and to Henri and to the boys when their paths crossed. He must have been close to collapse—the tiredness had not left his face even though he'd washed and shaved and changed to a clean shirt he brought with him in a small valise—but he seemed inexhaustible, as if drawing reserves of energy from an endless source. Late in the afternoon she caught him cradling Louis to his chest, and she jerked her eyes away, hurrying outside to bring in the day's wash.

This was the man who had berated her for an innocent familiarity with Julien? This was the man who had used kisses to subdue her? Impossible. Throughout the day he had not once touched her hand.

Shortly before sundown she spied him talking to the twins Jean and Paul by the water. All right, she thought as she strode down to join them, if this was a war of nerves, he had won. "Adam," she said without prelude when she reached his side, "this is ridiculous. We need to talk."

Jean and Paul, exchanging a quick look, sidled away and darted down the grassy bank, their target a driftwood cypress log that extended into the water. Straddling it, one behind the other, they scooted to the end, their feet kicking furiously until they were each thoroughly soaked.

Adam shifted his dark and unreadable eyes lazily from their antics to his impatient wife. "It seems to me, Catherine, that's what I asked back at Belle Terre."

She swallowed hard, her arms stiff at her side, her nails digging into her palms.

"You've come a long way to find me. So speak your mind."

His eyes rested on her lips as she talked, and she found saying any more impossible.

"And then leave? I think not. Besides, it's not proper for us to be alone like this without a chaperone."

"A chaperone?"

"Louisiana men do not pay court without the presence of a third party. At least that's what I've been told. Pierre was most instructive. He hasn't always lived in the swamps."

He had her confounded. "I'm already your wife."

"Are you really, Catherine? Are you really mine?"

The questions, spoken softly, came from somewhere deep inside him, and she had no response. They stood staring into each other's eyes. She was the first to look away. He walked past her to join her father and brothers, who were coming in from the fields.

That night Adam insisted on sleeping in the barn. "I've slept in far worse places," he said to a protesting Rose, who at last took out bedclothing and made him a bed in the hayloft near a boarded-up window where there would be no draft. Cat did not know how much he slept, but she got little rest.

The next morning he went with Henri in the pirogue downstream to set otter traps. When they returned late in the afternoon, Henri caught her alone as she furiously spaded ground within the fence surrounding the vegetable garden.

"Marie left me for a better life, *ma fille,*" he said solemnly. "You have said she did not find happiness."

"Am I to find some kind of message in what happened to my mother? My circumstance is not the same as hers." She turned the dirt with a vengeance.

"Perhaps not, but is the result any different?"

"You told me that she had reasons to leave . . . that she was not entirely in the wrong. Did Adam fill your ears with his side of the story and tell you nothing of mine?"

"Your husband is a gentleman. He has not spoken of private matters."

Cat had a hard time believing him. It seemed to her the men were ganging up—and not just the men. It was Rose who suggested they take the rest of the day off and ride to a neighboring farm where a *fais dodo,* a country dance, was planned. The women and three younger boys took the mule wagon, and the others walked the three miles to the farm.

The house and farmland were similar in layout to Henri's. The dance was held in a cleared field by the barn. A crowd had already gathered by the time they arrived, three dozen people, Cat estimated, dressed in simple country garments, all laughing and talking as though they hadn't a care in the world. She was introduced as Henri's long-lost daughter, not as Adam's wife. Several of the young girls made certain they stayed in the handsome American's presence; Cat pretended not to notice.

Food was laid out on a long table that extended from a window of the kitchen. The babies were taken inside to a large pallet that had been laid on the floor. The mothers took turns holding watch.

A fiddle, an accordion, and a triangle provided the fast-paced music. Whirling about the hard-packed ground, Henri and Rose set a pace the younger couples had difficulty matching. Cat stood at the side pretending not to know that Adam was close by. The music never stopped, the tempo never changed, but her husband did not ask her to dance. Not that she would have accepted . . .

Robert danced with the young girl Odile, a wide-eyed beauty who as far as Cat could tell never said a word, instead staring up at her partner with rapt adoration. Cat felt a shiver of jealousy at such open and uncomplicated love.

Several tables were set up away from the dancers, and a few of the men sat to play cards. Above the wild fiddle and the stomping feet she could hear their laughter. They enjoyed the time and the company and the games—more so, she thought, than the gamblers who crowded La Chatte de la Nuit away from their children and wives.

She turned back to the music as the tempo slowed and found herself in Adam's arms. "I decided that this was one I could handle," he said with a smile, and her heart pounded so furiously in her breast that she wondered whether he could hear it over the fiddle. "I'm not much of a dancer," he explained.

He whirled her around the other couples, his eyes locked with hers. Her hand trembled in his, but if he noticed, he gave no sign. Where he touched the back of her waist, she burned. He kept a respectable distance between them, but she grew dizzy from his presence.

For someone who couldn't dance, he was performing with remarkable skill.

Surely he could read her rising agitation, and she concentrated on the open collar of his shirt . . . and at the bronzed skin it revealed. When she began to count the chest hairs that were visible, she decided she'd made a mistake, but there was nowhere to look that would not take her breath away.

A roll of thunder sounded in the distance, and a gust of cold air swept across the dancers just as the

423

music ended.

"We better get on home," Henri said as he joined them. "Storm's coming."

Adam let go of her, and she felt set adrift. She pulled herself together. "I'll get the twins," she said.

They made the return trip home fast and settled into their separate quarters. Cat lay in her narrow bed in the small room and listened to the thunder and to the wind howling around the farm.

She thought about Adam out in the barn.

He must be cold, she decided. The hayloft would not be nearly so secure as the house.

He probably didn't have enough cover, she concluded. The least she could do was to see that he got all he needed. One last wifely duty . . . nothing more.

She thrust her feet into the shoes by the bed, not bothering with stockings, and gathered the bedcover into her arms. Taking care not to make a sound, she let herself out the back door. Icy wind—winter's first blast—flailed at her and took her breath away. Her hair whipped wildly, and the thin nightgown clung to her body as she made her way from the house to the barn.

It took surprising effort to open the barn door and slam it closed once again. She made a dreadful amount of noise. Standing in the dark, she waited to get her bearings and listened for Adam to shout something from the loft. Maybe he was so deeply asleep that he hadn't heard her enter. Maybe he'd slept that way last night, too, untroubled by how close and how far away lay his tormented wife.

He probably didn't even see how tormented she was . . . how his presence ate at her and destroyed the rationality she'd spent the past few days trying to strengthen.

"It took you long enough."

He spoke softly at her side, and she jumped.

"Oh," she said, catching her breath, "you scared me

424

"You scared me, too, Catherine."

She knew he did not mean tonight.

"What are you getting at, Adam, about my taking long enough?"

"I expected you last night."

This was the Adam she knew. "What happened to being proper? What happened to needing a chaperone?"

"For all my resolutions, I've had a hard time keeping such considerations in mind."

Cat pictured the play of his lips as he spoke. She cleared her throat. "I only came out here to bring you more blankets."

"I see." He didn't sound convinced.

She heard him move away in the dark, saw the spark of a flint, and a lantern flared. He was dressed as he had been at the dance—in open-throated shirt and fitted trousers. In the flickering light his face was lean and solemn and his eyes watchful.

A clap of thunder sounded outside the door, and she started. Rain began to pound against the barn.

"Catherine," he said. His eyes glittered, and she read the unmistakable meaning in their depths.

The air between them was heavy with tension, and she could scarcely breathe. Wanting consumed all resolution. She was trapped, she could tell him . . . caught by the storm. She had to stay until the skies cleared.

She met his stare and gave up all pretense. "Take me to bed, Adam."

He did not argue but took the bedcover from her arms and guided her to the ladder, then followed close as she climbed to the loft. He held the lantern high so he could see her way, then hung it on a nail and stood aside, watching her and waiting, for what she did not know.

His own blanket was spread on the hay away from the covered window, in a corner that was surprisingly warm. She could hear the wind and rain, but the storm sounded no more turbulent than the conflicting emotions raging in her heart. She had left Adam for right and good reasons that seemed overpowering, but no reason on earth was strong enough to keep her permanently out of his arms. Not if he wanted her there.

The loneliness of her single bed seemed starker now that she was gone from it. She gave a moment's thought to the irony of making love to Adam in the hay, just as she had given herself to the young and lustful Julien.

But this was not the same. Before, she had confused true love with a need for a family and a home. She had thought her youthful lover could give her both.

Adam was Adam; that was all that mattered. With him, she was alive; away, she simply went through the motions of life.

She turned to tell him so, but the look of desire on his face stopped her.

"I had planned to ask you to marry me again," he said huskily as he dropped her bedcover. "Before we made love. I'll have to change my plans."

He gave her no time to wonder at his words. His arms went around her, and as a clap of thunder shook the barn, his lips claimed hers. The kiss was long and gentle; when at last his tongue touched hers, they each shuddered. She ran her hands up his sleeves, across his shoulders, against the back of his neck, letting her fingers relearn the contours of his muscles that she knew so well in her mind.

He broke the kiss to undress her and then himself. When they lay on the blanket, his hands and eyes explored the secret places of her body that she liked him to touch.

That night they became one. Love and primal need mixed within Catherine, each kiss given, filled with inexpressible longing, each touch received, an answer to her heartfelt desire.

His gentleness gradually heated to fiery demand

426

Here was the Adam who had brought her to ecstasy so many times, the thorough lover who knew where to stroke, knew where to linger. His lips moved across her burning flesh, his tongue licked the valley between her breasts, his hands aroused with inexorable skill the passions of the body and the hungers of the heart.

It was as though in the midst of a stormy night she was bathed in the hot light of day. Adam was her sun. He gave her life.

She showed him with torrid responses that she truly belonged to him, her hands and lips as thorough as his in the silent communications of love. They came together quickly, explosively, and embraced tightly long after the tremors had passed.

He moved away from her long enough to pull over them the covers she had brought, then quickly took her back in his arms. She rested her head against his chest and listened to his heartbeat.

She fell asleep, the first deep rest she'd had since leaving Belle Terre. She awoke to find him watching her. Outside, the storm had abated, but it was not yet light. From its position on the nearby post, the dim lantern gave out a soft glow.

Everything felt right, being with Adam as she held within her the lingering sensations of their lovemaking. But contentment was an illusion. For her, it never lasted very long. Nothing had changed, except that he had shown her for once and all time she belonged to him, no matter how far she ran. She marveled that it was possible to feel happy and miserable at the same time.

One question sprang to her lips, but she swallowed it, unable to ask him outright how he felt. She wanted him to volunteer what was truly in his heart without being asked. Anyway, he might not tell her what she wanted to hear. And if he did, how would she know he did not lie? Cat admitted the truth. She was a coward. She did not understand her husband or know what to expect

427

from him, but she was learning unexpected things about herself every day.

She remembered Adam's words just before he'd pulled her into his arms. "You took me by surprise, Adam, with all that talk of courtship." She felt dizzy with worry and wonder, but she could not keep entirely quiet. "Were you really going to propose again?"

"It's the natural ending to courtship. Before, I caught you by surprise. This time I wanted to do things right."

Before, you were thinking of Belle Terre—and maybe of saving me from my pitiful life.

"We do things backward," she said.

"Not everything . . . although we might give it a try. We've still got a few things to try in bed." He picked a piece of hay from her tangled hair. "Once we get in a bed."

She let his sweet, seductive talk soothe her troubled mind, and for a moment she forgot her cowardice. "Why?"

He shifted. "Because, for all its romantic appeal, a barn isn't really the ideal place for all the things I want to do to you."

Cat wanted to grin at his tender teasing . . . but so much still separated them. "I don't mean why you want a bed. Why propose to your wife?"

"Because I wanted us to start over. To do that, I had to give you a chance to say no."

"Would you have accepted no as an answer?"

"I'm not sure. I never let myself consider the possibility."

"You're awfully sure of yourself."

"If you think that, Catherine, then you don't know me very well."

Silently, she agreed, then questioned him. "How did you find me?"

She caught his hesitation, and knew that there were still many differences between them, many things that had not been said.

"Arianne Renault told me where I could find Henri," he said. "I figured you would be here."

She stared at him in surprise. "You asked her?"

"Not exactly. I asked her lover."

Cat let out a long sigh. "Emile."

Adam nodded. She listened as he described the scene.

"You're sorry I had him arrested," he said at the end.

"You told me that you would if you ever got proof against him." She thought about a wharf by the river, a dark night, cold water rushing in on her, insistent hands pulling her to air.

"You did what was right. But Adam, I owed him so much."

She could sense his drawing away.

"And think you owe him even now." He sat up. You've had a lot to take in over the past few days, Catherine. Too much for me to make an offer now."

Cat was grateful, for she was not sure exactly what he would say. If he loved her . . . ah, then she would have a ready answer. If he did not . . .

Her answer depended very much on how the offer was phrased.

She managed to keep her composure just as he did. The rain's stopped and it will be light soon. I'd prefer to get back to the house before anyone is awake."

They dressed hurriedly, and with her cover wrapped round her flimsy gown, she left the barn and made her barefoot way across the wet ground. A thought struck her, one as chilling as the air. She did not have with her Delilah's protective gris-gris. And she was not certain that she cared.

After breakfast Henri asked Adam to go with him and check on the storm damage to the otter traps.

Adam told her good-bye at the door. "We'll talk when I get back. That's all the time you'll be getting, Catherine."

Henri returned in the pirogue alone long after the

429

shadows of night had fallen, and Cat, unheedful o
Rose's assurances, was almost out of her mind.

The two women heard his footsteps on the gallery
Throwing open the door, Cat saw from the spill o
inside light that his head was bloodied. While Ros
went for a bucket of water and a rag, Cat helped hir
to the bench. His sons, who had been at the back of th
house, rushed through the back door, but Rose re
turned to shoo them outside. Only Robert, the eldes
was allowed to remain.

Henri took a minute to catch his breath, and Ca
knew he must have lost a great deal of blood. "Bastar
caught us from behind. Hit me. When I came to, Adar
was gone."

"What do you mean, Adam's gone?" cried Cat as sh
watched Rose work gingerly at the open wound abov
his right ear.

He looked at Cat with dark regret. *"Ma fille,* that
all I know. We went deeper in the woods than
planned, looking for new places to trap. We talked by
small stream away from the bayou. It was close to th
prison camp. I told Adam, and he nodded, as thoug
he knew the place. And then—"

He winced as Rose probed the cut. "It is not serious
she said. "You have a hard head, old man."

"And then what?" Cat edged close to hysterics.

"A thin-faced man. Like the foxes of the swamp. F
came from the brush. Adam yelled out a name, ar
then the blow was struck."

A dread chill settled over Cat, and her voice fell to
whisper. "Laverton."

"You know this man?" Henri asked in surprise.

"I know him How far away is this camp?"

"Two hours by pirogue."

"Please, Papa, you must take me to the place whe
you last saw my husband. And pray that we get there
time. If we do not . . ." She could not go on.

"I can get a dozen Acadian men to join me. But it

best we wait until the first morning light."

"I'll go, too, Papa," said Robert, standing tall and angry.

Henri nodded. "Not you, Catherine."

"You must take me." Her voice strengthened. She knew what had to be done. "I am the only one who can talk to this man. I am the only one who can save my husband's life."

Chapter Twenty-Nine

Morning found Adam sprawled in a small clearing in the middle of a swamp wilderness, his legs stretched in front of him, his arms bound behind the small wooden stake against which he was slumped.

As he came out of unconsciousness, his head shot with pain where he had been struck the evening before, and he struggled to sit up. Waves of agony and nausea swept over him, and he held himself very still. When at last he could focus and turn his head without fear of passing out again, he ran his eyes over the wall of wild vegetation and trees that grew around the clearing. An overcast sky held out the sun. From behind him came the sound of someone thrashing in the brush.

The scene was straight out of his nightmares of the prison camp. But it was all too real. And for all the closeness of the camp, it wasn't Brother Red whom he heard. Yesterday he'd had just a fractured second to glimpse who crept up on him and Henri. The last thing he'd seen before darkness closed in on him was the sharp, mad face of Emile Laverton.

He prayed Henri had escaped without injury. He should have shot Laverton when he had the chance back in New Orleans. But fool that he was, he'd been certain that this time the police could take care of their business. He'd seen the papers himself after Arianne opened the secret cabinet where they were stored. Hard evidence of Laverton's nefarious deeds, from the looks of the top layer. Evidence to put him away forever, if he didn't dangle at the end of a rope.

There were a lot of things he should have done in his life—like telling Catherine he loved her whether or not she could see the truth about her supposed friend. He should have done it before they made love, not waited so damned long afterward. And then the moment was gone, and they were once again talking about Laverton.

There was only one thing he could do—escape and make up for the omission.

Suddenly Laverton was beside him, kicking his ribs once, hard, to make sure he was awake. The usually immaculate Creole was in shirtsleeves, his clothes torn and stained with mud. His cadaverous face was covered with a heavy stubble, and his thin brown hair was as wild as the look in his eye.

He rambled on in French too fast and furiously for Adam to understand what he said. *Mort* was one word that stood out. Dead.

He pulled a knife from his waist and ran the flat side of the blade across Adam's throat. His eyes were devoid of reason, and Adam felt cold fear settle in his gut.

Laverton switched to English. "I set the trap well, do I not, M'sieur Gase? You will make a fine bait."

"For what?" asked Adam, forcing himself to forget the pain.

"For my *petite chatte,* of course. I came looking for her. I found you instead."

Adam tensed and flexed his leg, ready to kick out if Laverton moved just right.

Laverton pressed the blade harder against his neck. "I can kill you before you lift a foot, m'sieur. Just a quick turn of the knife, and then *mort.* She will come for dead bait as surely as if you still lived."

"What do you want with her?" asked Adam.

"What does anyone want with his possessions? To keep her. To have her with me always. I pulled her from the water. She is mine. Not yours. Mine."

"She'll never find us." If only he wasn't so damned weak. He strained at the bonds, desperate to smash Emile until he could no longer hurt Catherine ever again. But he hadn't the strength.

"I left a wide trail," said Laverton.

"Even if she does come, she will bring others."

"Not if she thinks you will be harmed. And with the knife held thus, she can think no other thing."

Adam wanted to believe Laverton was as wrong as he was insane. But Catherine had a stubbornness of her own that led her to do remarkable things. She'd come from poverty and despair to be the talk of New Orleans; she'd left the casino to take up a life with him; and when she felt betrayed, she had somehow found her way to the swamps and Henri Douchand.

Preposterous as it seemed, he didn't have much doubt she would find him now. Somehow he had to break free before that happened.

"The prison camp's near here, isn't it?" he asked, stalling for time.

Laverton's face moved close. "I trust you remember it well." His breath was sour.

"I remember Brother Red."

"Michael told me he was killed by one of the prisoners. A shame. From what Michael said, he was a man well suited to his job."

"There wasn't much Michael did not know about the ugliness of Louisiana, was there?" Still stalling, still flexing his leg, hoping Laverton would be distracted so that . . .

Suddenly Laverton stood and stepped too far away for Adam's foot to do any damage.

"Enough. Michael is dead. Catherine is gone. And that *chienne* Arianne had the nerve to spit at me . . .

spit at me as the police took me away. Ah, but the policeman who threw me into jail was one not named in the records that were seized. There is another place, I said . . . a private office where other records are hidden. I would tell. He had to let me free . . . let me destroy these papers or else he would have been thrown into one of his own cells. The prisoners would not have let him live."

Laverton paced as he walked, his voice thick with the pride of his escape, his eyes roaming the edges of the surrounding wilderness.

"Did you destroy them?" Adam managed to sit upright.

"I did not take the time. I am free. And Cat will soon be where she belongs. With me where I can take care of her once again." His eyes took on a glazed stare as if he looked at another scene no one else could see. "I lost another kitten once. My father made sure that I had nothing of my own." He laughed once, sharply. "But I outsmarted him. I saved the *petite chatte*. She did not drown. With my own hands I saved her."

Adam saw he had gone completely mad. He slowly bent his legs, trying to get the leverage to stand.

Laverton knelt beside him, using the knife handle to bludgeon his knees. Adam swallowed a cry of pain. This time it was the sharp edge of the blade that touched his throat. "Do not try that again, M'sieur Gase. Do not move or you are *mort."*

And then she was there, stepping into the clearing where both Adam and Laverton could see her. The brush behind her was still, and from overhead came the cry of a mockingbird. For a moment there was no other sound.

She did not look at Adam. "Emile," she said softly. "You sent for me."

Laverton smiled up at her from his crouched position, but his eyes retained their madness. The knife did not move. "I knew you would understand. I knew

436

you would come."

She stepped forward. "Of course I did. Haven't I always been loyal? Haven't I always trusted you?"

She was dressed in an oversized shirt and trousers. One arm hung loosely at her side; the other was held so that her hand was out of sight. With her hair hanging against her shoulders and her eyes staring out from a thin, wan face, she looked frighteningly young and vulnerable.

"Come, Emile," she said coaxingly, "I have a pirogue. The bayou is not far. We must leave before they find us."

"They?" asked Laverton.

"People always intrude, do they not? Men. You have always warned me against them. I should have listened." She held out one hand.

Laverton hesitated. "What about him?"

"Leave him," she said. "Come."

Adam could be quiet no longer. "Catherine, be careful."

She ignored him. "Put the knife down, Emile. Come with me."

"No," said Adam.

"The knife, Emile," said Catherine.

"But he hurt you, my kitten." Laverton spoke as a young boy might speak. "For that he must pay."

Adam felt the slice of the knife and a trickle of blood at his throat, and then a gunshot roared in the clearing.

The knife fell, and Laverton stared wide-eyed at Catherine. "*Petite* . . ." His words became an unintelligible garble. He swayed once before slumping forward in the grass.

Adam stared across the body at his wife, who stood with a smoking pistol at her side. Tears ran down her cheeks.

"He would have killed you," she said.

The gunshot brought a half dozen men toward the clearing, Henri first, followed closely by his oldest son,

Robert. They took one look at the body, and Henri pulled his daughter into his arms.

"We heard you, but were afraid to move in," he said gruffly.

"I am all right," she said, pushing away. "We must free Adam."

Robert used the fallen knife to cut Adam's bonds, and he stood shakily, his head reeling, his knees weak and pained from the pounding Laverton had given them with the knife handle. When Catherine threw herself at him, he almost went down again.

"I was so scared," she whispered against his chest. "So scared."

He held her tight, unable to speak for a moment, letting the dizziness pass away, rejoicing in the safety of his wife. He loosened his embrace and brushed a thumb against her damp cheek.

"I'm sorry you had to do it. But he is not worth your tears."

She stared up at him. "I'm not crying for Emile," she said, and stifled a sob. "The man I saw today was not the man who had been my friend. That man, if he ever did exist, died for me when he threatened you."

"Then why?"

"For you, Adam. Everything I do is for you."

He could not speak for a moment. "You're quite a woman, Catherine," he whispered, and then with a shaky grin added, "I didn't know you could fire a gun."

"Papa taught me while we were in the pirogue this morning."

"This morning?" Adam swallowed.

"Don't worry." She managed a brave, encouraging smile. "I wouldn't have pulled the trigger if I hadn't been certain of who would get shot."

Adam was relieved he hadn't known the particulars at the time. "You're quite a woman," he repeated, and let it go at that.

He pulled her aside while the Acadians took care of the body. They ignored the embracing couple as they went about their grisly business of carrying the remains of the once-powerful and feared Emile Laverton to one of the pirogues banked at the nearby slough.

Henri gave them a quick grin. "I will be waiting to take you back. It seems, my daughter, that you are giving me another son." He nodded toward the departing men. "One older than Robert. This is good. He needs a man from the world to explain the way of things. Not a simple farmer like me." He winked and was gone.

She insisted on inspecting the knot at the back of Adam's head, winced when he winced, then pulled the tail of her shirt free and used it to blot the blood from his throat. "It will not make much of a scar," she said.

Adam could not take his eyes from her face. She looked more beautiful to him now than ever before, and he was filled with his love for her. "It wouldn't be the first, would it?" he asked.

She brushed her lips against the cut. "I now have one more place to kiss," she said. "But you've got to start taking better of yourself. Regardless of what you think, you are not indestructible."

"Je t'aime."

Her widened. "What did you say?"

"Je t'aime," he repeated. "Is there something wrong with my pronunciation? I practiced it while Pierre guided me through the swamp."

Again, tears welled in her eyes. She smiled through them. *"Très bon, mon cher."*

"Don't get fancy on me, Catherine. It's going to take me a while to get the hang of the language."

"Very good, my darling. Very good. But why didn't you tell me you loved me in the barn? I had already told you how I felt a long time ago."

"Because I was a fool. You know how Americans can

439

be. I was going to, but then when Laverton's name came up and you seemed so upset, I was afraid that he would always come between us. I guess I was afraid you would turn me down. Or maybe later change your mind."

"You? Afraid? You've always been ready to take on the whole rotten world."

"Don't remind me," he said, crushing her to him. "How can a world be rotten when you're in it?"

"What happened to the bitterness?" she asked, pushing away and staring up into his eyes.

"All gone." Adam meant what he said. "It had already died before I read that note. I stood there in the bedroom and knew what I had let slip away from me."

"I thought you pitied me."

"A man does not vow to live with a woman forever because he pities her."

"And Emile's threats . . . ?"

"I would have burned Belle Terre to the ground myself rather than give Laverton any satisfaction."

"Then why? Why did you ask me to be your wife?"

"I told myself at the time it was because we had led the same kind of life. That we suited one another. That we needed one another. There were a lot of reasons that were part of the real truth. I had fallen in love with you only I was too blind to see it. There's a lot I've got to make up for."

He smiled. "Be my wife, Catherine Douchand, and live with me forever."

She kissed the corner of his mouth. "Wherever you say . . . at Belle Terre," another kiss, "in town," another, "in the middle of the swamp, if you want." She kissed him full on the lips.

"I assume that means yes."

"*Oui.*" She gave him an impish grin.

He kissed her long and hard, then held her close. "Belle Terre it is. I don't care whether you ever sell that blasted casino, my darling. You'll just have to run i

440

from the country."

"Whatever you say, Adam. Whatever you say."

Later that night, after Henri reported back that Laverton's body had been taken to the sheriff in the nearest town, after the younger boys were given a brief version of the events by Robert, after they had retired to bed, Catherine went with Adam to the hayloft. Rose started to protest, but one look from her husband and she hushed.

Holding his wife in his arms, Adam felt the need to talk before they made love. This time he was the one with things to say.

He started out slowly, describing the half life, half death of the prison camp, the maniacal cruelty of Brother Red, the grueling work and debasement to which he was continually subjected. "We hunted alligators during the spring and summer for their hides and meat. When they went into hibernation, we became lumbermen. Ever cut down a big cypress with your hands shackled? It's not easy. If we didn't work to suit the guards, out came the whip."

She shuddered.

"Maybe I shouldn't . . ." said Adam.

"No. Go on."

"I spent two years planning on what I would do when I got out. The thought of revenge kept me going. That's why it was so hard to put aside."

"It made you strong, Adam."

"It made me mean."

"Never. Don't ever say that again." Her voice was anguished. He kissed her hair.

"And the nightmares—" she said.

"—are a thing of the past. I'm sure of it. Thanks to you I have buried my ghosts."

A quiet settled on them. At last Catherine spoke.

"The baby's name was Henri."

441

Her words came out so softly that Adam could barely hear them.

"He was so beautiful," she said, stronger, "and he used to smile when I would hold him and talk to him about how I would take care of him forever."

Her voice broke, and Adam held her in a gentle embrace while she gained control.

"When the illness came, I vowed that if my son lived through his ordeal, I would devote my life to God forever. When . . . the end came, I thought that even God had deserted me."

"There is no protection from yellow fever, Catherine. It was not your fault."

"The nuns tried to tell me the same thing, but I couldn't believe them. I know now. But it took me a long time. Not until I met you did I find it possible to forget my own worries." She smiled up at him and he was relieved to see that she had held back her tears. Catherine was strong, and he loved her all the more.

"You were the first person I had ever met with troubles as bad as my own," she said.

"The same thought occurred to me."

"I held Louis this afternoon," she said. "While you were out back. I wanted to try my skills. I hadn't forgotten a thing."

Adam decided that called for another kiss. "Any particular reason you were seeing if you still could?"

Her eyes glinted. "You never know."

"Are you—"

"Probably not. But I would imagine there will be other opportunities for you to take care of that little chore."

"Beginning right now?"

She pulled aside his shirt and kissed his chest. "Beginning right now. If we don't get started, we'll never catch up to Rose and Henri."

Chapter Thirty

They renewed their vows in a small chapel in the village near the Douchand farm, and at the same time, Henri and Rose were wed. They made quite a picture, the newly married couple with their six sons, and the already married couple planning on having a few of their own.

After a wild *fais dodo* to which everyone came from miles around, Catherine said she and Adam needed to get back to Belle Terre.

"You're a farmer, Papa. You know the work is never done."

"You return to work? Where is the honeymoon? Rose and I plan a little trip."

"When?"

He shrugged. "Before the new baby arrives."

"Papa!"

"I did such a fine job with my first daughter, I would like to try for another."

Adam rested his arm around her. "Cat and I will take a trip when we can. I'd like to take her back to Pennsylvania to my home. There's at least an aunt I can introduce her to."

She stared at him. "You've never called me Cat before."

"I thought you preferred it."

She shook her head. "I have been Catherine to the

443

people who love me the most . . . and, of course, one or two who didn't, but I don't worry about them anymore."

"Catherine, it is," he agreed.

The next day, after an active night in the hay and a morning of good-byes, they rode in the pirogue to the dock at the Bayou Lafourche, where they could catch a schooner back to New Orleans.

Robert was their guide.

"Take care of Papa," Catherine instructed. "And take care of Odile."

He grinned, and she could see her father in the smile. "I will do my best."

In a warm and tearful meeting with Ben and Delilah at La Chatte, Catherine gave a brief version of what happened in the swamp.

Delilah got to the heart of the matter. "You shot M'sieur Laverton?"

"I'm not proud of it."

"You should be."

"Delilah," said Ben, "you talk too much."

The next morning they rode to the law office of Joseph Devine, who readily reported that Madame Ferrier and her son were managing just fine and he hoped to have news to report to them soon. Catherine saw right away that the news would concern another marriage.

"You'll need to look at Laverton's office in the Swamp. There are papers stored in the cabinets that should put a few of our citizens behind bars."

"I thought they were retrieved at his place on Bourbon Street."

"Not all."

Joseph brought them up to date on the latest gossip. Papers found in Judge Osborne's home indicated he had accepted bribes from Laverton to make sure Adam went straight to prison without a fair and open trial.

"The judge's sister said he had been mumbling something about telling all," said Joseph. "That's probably why he was killed."

"And the papers," added Adam, "were the reason for his home being torn up. Not the Spanish coins."

On another front, the lawyer reported Arianne Renault was being sued for divorce by her husband. He didn't appreciate that she was friendly with Laverton."

"What about his *placage?*" asked Catherine.

When Joseph shrugged, he looked almost Gallic. You know how these Creoles are. She's going back to France with her brother. They'll be leaving within the week."

He also said that Laverton's whorehouse had been closed down. "A curious thing," he said, shaking his head. "There was a young girl that the madame insisted was still an innocent. Lorelei was her name. 'Been savin' her for M'sieur Emile. Been waitin' for her rash to clear up.' She kept going on and on about it. Apparently she's the only person who ever remained pure in the place."

"Her rash?" asked Catherine and Adam together.

"It seems he liked his young innocents unmarked. But each time he came for her, she broke out in red welts. Monique—Madame Ferrier has taken her under her wing. Believe me, she really is an innocent, but she must have picked up a bit of knowledge at the brothel. She's young and fair and I predict she'll be a real beauty. Kind of feel sorry for her, though. She claims to have family back East, but won't give any names. Claims she's ruined forever and will somehow have to get by."

"So she's all alone?" asked Catherine.

"Apparently so."

"And desperate."

Joseph nodded. "She won't admit it, though. She's

445

a stubborn young woman."

Catherine understood. "Delilah," she said. "A Ben."

"Your servants? What have they got to do wi Lorelei?"

"Nothing yet. But they will be more than happy take care of her. See that she follows a straight pat Trust me, Joseph. Maybe Lorelei could stay at I Chatte . . . at least until it's sold."

"Sold?" asked Joseph.

"Is that what you really want?" asked Adam.

"You want me to sell."

"I've changed my mind."

She glanced at Joseph, then back at her husband. I would never cease to surprise her, not in a thousa years. "We'll discuss this later."

Adam gave one last instruction to the lawye "When Tacey was shot, she gave warning that someo was back in the woods. If she hadn't, chances are would have been killed. In a direct way, she saved n life."

Joseph grinned. "I see what you're getting at. A sla who saves his or her master's life can be given papers freedom. And it doesn't matter about the slave's ag

"Think you can manage it?"

"I'll get to work on it right away."

"Thanks," said Adam. "You've made Bodeen happy man. He's sworn that he won't leave Be Terre, but at least he'll have the option. And so will I woman. Everyone, black or white, needs the opti of being free."

Catherine poked him. "We'll discuss what you me: by that later."

Promising Joseph that they would give attention the problems of Lorelei, she and Adam left. Since bo Raven and Keystone were stabled within accessit distance and the November day was warm and sunn they rode by horseback to Belle Terre, choosing t

446

cross-country route that would bring them in to the back.

They made a brief stop in the woods where they had first made love.

"Tell me the truth," said Catherine as the horses drank from the Bayou Rouge, "how do you really feel about the casino?"

"I'd like to change the name. And hire someone to run it, someone we can trust. And don't get that gleam in your eye. This Lorelei won't do."

"I was just thinking . . . Of course we haven't met her, but if she's the way Joseph described, she could help out. There won't be many opportunities for her among polite society. Believe me, I know. It won't matter what happened to her, or what didn't. It's what people believe that's important. But at the casino—"

"Enough," said Adam, raising his hands in surrender. "I imagine we can work something out."

"There's one other thing," said Catherine. "About a man and woman needing the option to be free."

"I meant from ownership, wife. I don't own you and you don't own me. But we belong to each other. It's not the same thing at all." He kissed her as his hands stroked her shoulders and the nape of her neck.

"No," Catherine agreed, "it's not the same thing."

"There's always the clover," he said.

Catherine shook her head. "I want a soft mattress under me, Adam. For a change. As a matter of fact, I've been thinking of having the one from the casino brought out to our room."

"Do we have to wait?"

She laughed. "Heavens, no."

They bound the reins of both mounts to the saddles, and Adam slapped Keystone on the rump. "He'll make it to the stable."

"So will she," said Catherine, giving a similar slap to the mare.

They walked side by side past the gazebo. No longer

447

did it hold any dark memories for her. "That thing needs fixing," she said. "I'll get to it right after the new year."

She stopped. "Look, Adam. Look who's first to welcome us home."

He glanced in the direction she indicated. Bounding through the grass toward them, tail held high like a scepter, was the golden ball of fur known by the curious name of Balzac.